Praise for

The Magic of Lemon Drop Pie

"Heartfelt, heartwarming, joyful, and uplifting. You can't go wrong with a Rachel Linden book."
—Debbie Macomber, *New York Times* bestselling author of *The Best Is Yet to Come*

"A poignant, hopeful must read for anyone who has ever wondered about a different path. Rachel Linden creates unforgettable characters that will work their way into your heart and a compulsively readable story that will keep the pages turning late into the night. Five huge stars!"
—Kristy Woodson Harvey, *New York Times* bestselling author of *The Wedding Veil*

"A magical novel about second chances! Warm, witty, and wise, I loved it! Linden is a master at creating loveable characters! *The Magic of Lemon Drop Pie* is escapist reading at its best!"
—Jill Shalvis, *New York Times* bestselling author of *The Summer Deal*

"An enchanting tale about the one thing we've all imagined: a magical second chance. Rachel Linden expertly mixes romance, mystery, and family-drama into a delicious recipe of a story. With her trademark warmth, Linden delivers a captivating story with a magical heartbeat at its center."
—Patti Callahan, *New York Times* bestselling author of *Surviving Savannah*

"A triumphant story about chasing down a destiny, cleverly told and beautifully delivered. Rachel Linden reminds us on every page how wonderful and essential it is to believe in the magic of second chances."
—Susan Meissner, *USA Today* bestselling author of *The Nature of Fragile Things*

"Rachel Linden whips up an irresistible family drama oozing with charm and magic! *The Magic of Lemon Drop Pie* is a must read for anyone who longs for second chances. A gem of a novel that charmed me from get-go, perfect for fans of Sarah Addison Allen and Alice Hoffman."
—Lori Nelson Spielman, *New York Times* bestselling author of *The Star-Crossed Sisters of Tuscany*

"A delicious read, down to the very last lemon drop! Rachel Linden delivers a delightful escape, wonderful characters, and a magical experience that will leave readers hungry for her next book."

—Julie Cantrell, *New York Times* and *USA Today* bestselling author of *Perennials*

"With a skillful hand, Linden has filled *The Magic of Lemon Drop Pie* with well-drawn characters, lush descriptions of both food and locales, and an intriguing touch of magic. Lolly is a refreshing and plucky protagonist, and you'll be rooting for her to find the happily-ever-after of her own choosing!"

—Lauren K. Denton, *USA Today* bestselling author of *The One You're With*

"A charming, heartwarming story about 'what ifs' and second chances. Readers will fall in love with the cast of delightful characters, and I defy anyone to read this book and not want to immediately eat lemon meringue pie. A beautiful, life-affirming read."

—Freya Sampson, author of *The Last Chance Library*

"Simply delicious! A delightful, page-turning story of first love, second chances, family ties, and mouthwatering pies! With a little magic, engaging characters, and complications we could almost call our own, *The Magic of Lemon Drop Pie* invites us to consider our own lost or forgotten dreams, and gives us the essential ingredients of hope and courage to pursue them."

—Katherine Reay, bestselling author of *The Printed Letter Bookshop* and *The London House*

"A deliciously sweet tale about refusing to give up on your dreams and finding your bliss against all odds. Linden gives readers so much to enjoy— romance, family drama, and bittersweet second chances—all served up with the perfect dash of magic."

—Kate Bromley, author of *Here for the Drama* and *Talk Bookish to Me*

The Magic of Lemon Drop Pie

RACHEL LINDEN

BERKLEY
NEW YORK

BERKLEY
An imprint of Penguin Random House LLC
penguinrandomhouse.com

Copyright © 2022 by Rachel Linden
"Readers Guide" copyright © 2022 by Rachel Linden
Penguin Random House supports copyright. Copyright fuels creativity, encourages diverse voices,
promotes free speech, and creates a vibrant culture. Thank you for buying an authorized edition of
this book and for complying with copyright laws by not reproducing, scanning, or distributing any
part of it in any form without permission. You are supporting writers and allowing Penguin
Random House to continue to publish books for every reader.

BERKLEY and the BERKLEY & B colophon are registered trademarks of
Penguin Random House LLC.

Library of Congress Cataloging-in-Publication Data

Names: Linden, Rachel, author.
Title: The magic of lemon drop pie / Rachel Linden.
Description: First Edition. | New York: Berkley, 2022.
Identifiers: LCCN 2021061893 (print) | LCCN 2021061894 (ebook) |
ISBN 9780593440193 (trade paperback) | ISBN 9780593440209 (ebook)
Classification: LCC PS3612.I5327426 M34 2022 (print) | LCC PS3612.I5327426
(ebook) | DDC 813/.6—dc23
LC record available at https://lccn.loc.gov/2021061893
LC ebook record available at https://lccn.loc.gov/2021061894

First Edition: August 2022

Printed in the United States of America
1   3   5   7   9   10   8   6   4   2

Interior art: Lemon and flowers © helenpyzhova / Shutterstock
Book design by Alison Cnockaert

This is a work of fiction. Names, characters, places, and incidents either are the product
of the author's imagination or are used fictitiously, and any resemblance to actual persons,
living or dead, business establishments, events, or locales is entirely coincidental.

PUBLISHER'S NOTE: The recipes contained in this book are to be followed exactly as written.
The publisher is not responsible for your specific health or allergy needs that may require medical
supervision. The publisher is not responsible for any adverse reactions to the
recipes contained in this book.

To Dr. Kathryn A. Smith, my real-life Aunt Gert.
While you didn't give me lemon drops, you certainly
opened the world to me. I am so grateful.

The Magic of Lemon Drop Pie

1

My Life is a Lemon.

I faced the truth afresh, bent over a cold stainless-steel mixing bowl, whipping egg whites and sugar into stiff French meringue peaks.

"'Lolly's life goal number two,'" my sister, Daphne, read aloud, perched on a stool across the gleaming stainless-steel prep counter of the diner's kitchen. She paused and eyed the list of adolescent ambitions a far younger me had optimistically scribbled in sparkly purple gel pen in my middle school diary.

"'Own my own restaurant somewhere amazing.'" She glanced over at me skeptically. "Does managing our family diner in Magnolia count?"

I shot her a wry look. "I don't think Danish comfort food in a fifty-year-old diner was quite what I was imagining when I wrote that." So much of my life was not what I'd imagined when I wrote that. I leaned over the hand mixer with renewed vigor.

Outside the huge French-paned windows, the winter darkness was beginning to lighten with a touch of pearl as morning broke. More than likely the clouds would settle into a daylong light drizzle. Late winter in Seattle was often wet, chilly, and unremittingly gray. I usually loved this time of the morning—pie-making time, alone in the kitchen with a serene sense of purpose and Tanya Tucker warbling plaintively on the radio—but not today. Today the weather matched my mood.

"'Number three. Fall in love.'" She paused and squinted at the page. "You scribbled a note in the margin that says 'I'd like him to look like Freddie Prinze Jr. or Brad Pitt.'" Daphne shot me a curious look and wrinkled her nose. "Who's Freddie Prinze Jr.?"

"Did you ever see *She's All That*? No, I guess you were too young." I brushed a wisp of hair back into my bouncy ponytail. "It was the nineties. Freddie was dreamy, a total heartthrob." I redoubled my efforts on the meringue, which was now stiff enough to stand by itself in frothy white peaks.

Daphne studied the page. "What was this list for anyway?"

Closing my eyes, I was instantly catapulted back to my seventh-grade classroom, the buzz of hormones and invincibility, the smells of old linoleum, adolescent boys wearing too little deodorant, and girls wearing too much fruity body spray.

"Ms. Beeson's English class. We were supposed to write out a life goals list, a plan for the next twenty years. Which is sort of crazy given that most of us couldn't plan our way out of a paper bag when we were thirteen. She was big on plans. Pencil skirts and plans."

"That's ambitious," Daphne said, looking again at the list.

"It's kind of sad to read it now," I commented lightly.

"Sad how?"

I turned off the mixer. "Next month I'll turn thirty-three. It's been almost exactly twenty years since I wrote that list, and I haven't done a single thing on it." My tone was matter-of-fact but the realization stung, sharp and true. I had not thought about the list in years, but the reality that I hadn't managed to accomplish even one goal was disappointing.

Daphne closed the diary and tossed it on the counter, then

stretched, young and lissome in her yoga gear. Her sleek chestnut hair swung over her shoulders. Hair color was the only thing we shared in terms of appearance. Daphne took after our dad, small and leanly muscled, a dancer's build. I favored our mother's Danish side of the family—taller with rounded curves and high, broad cheekbones. She slid off the stool and surveyed me. "Do you still want all those things?"

"Freddie Prinze Jr. has aged really well. I like the whole silver fox look." I grinned, spooning meringue onto the deep-yellow fillings of six lemon pies, dodging her question. I wasn't even sure I knew the answer or could risk thinking too hard about it. I'd stopped dreaming about what I wanted roughly a decade ago. It was a luxury I simply could not afford.

Daphne glanced at her phone and gave a yip of alarm. "I've got to teach a vinyasa session in fifteen minutes." She yanked open the huge industrial refrigerator and grabbed an apple. "I've got class till four thirty, and then I'll come help with the dinner rush. Damien will give me a ride."

She was in her junior year studying for a dance degree at Cornish College of the Arts in downtown Seattle and was teaching yoga on the side to help pay for the outrageous cost of tuition. Her boyfriend, Damien, was a student at Cornish as well. I sighed and wiped my hands on my fifties-style green-and-white-polka-dot frilled apron, the standard uniform at the diner ever since I could remember.

"Help with dinner would be great. It's tough going when it's only Aunt Gert and me handling all the tables."

We exchanged a knowing look at the mention of our feisty great-aunt.

"Okay, see you tonight." Daphne threw open the back door and blew me an air kiss. "Love you much."

I caught it against my cheek. "Love you more." It was a childhood exchange Mom had taught us and one we still copied.

Daphne traipsed out the door, then poked her head back inside, looking thoughtful. "You know, it's not too late for you to do those things if you still want to."

I waved away her words. "Who would keep everything together around here? Who would be the glue?"

"I knew you would say that." Daphne pulled a face. "That's what they're going to put on your gravestone when they find you old and gray and collapsed face-first into one of your lemon meringue pies. 'I was the glue.'"

It was a horrifying thought. And sadly probably not untrue. I stuck my tongue out at her.

"Aren't you late for something?"

She shrieked and darted out the door. I watched her go with a mixture of maternal fondness and sisterly exasperation. Twelve years younger than me, Daphne had been only ten when Mom died. I'd stepped in to fill the hole in her life as best I could. Some days I thought it was almost enough.

In the sudden quiet of the kitchen, I made decorative peaks in the meringue with the back of a large kitchen spoon, then checked each of the six pies. Good, they had meringue all the way to the edges. It helped keep them from weeping, a peculiar pitfall of meringue. I'd been making six lemon meringue pies almost every day for the past ten years. My dad, Marty, the diner's chief cook, handled everything else food related with the help of his assistant cook, Julio, but I made our famous pies, the best in Seattle. Only I knew my mom's secret recipe. She'd made me memorize it the night before she passed away.

Popping the pies into the industrial oven, I set the timer and glanced at the clock. Still an hour until the doors opened at eight. Soon Dad and Julio would be in to start prepping for the day. My diary lay on the counter, a blast from the past with neon unicorns jumping over a bright rainbow spangled with stars. At thirteen I had loved that Lisa

Frank diary with its luridly cheerful cover, its crisp lined pages just waiting to be filled with the dreams and aspirations of my young, idealistic heart. Daphne had unearthed it a few days ago in a box of our childhood memorabilia.

I touched the cover with my fingers, lightly, wistfully, torn between wanting to toss it away and crack it open to eagerly devour every line. If I did, could I relive, if only for a moment, the confidence of endless possibilities, the naive presumption that just because I wished for something it was bound to happen? How brash that seemed now. And yet, still, how alluring.

I sniffed. Beneath the citrus scent of the pies beginning to bake I caught a whiff of regret, pungent and bitter as rosemary. I clicked on the old-school combination radio/CD player sitting under the window, tuning it to a classic country station, and opened the back door to get some fresh air, but in gusted a cool, wet wind that smelled like sorrow, sharp and briny as the sea. On second thought, I shut the door again and turned up the radio. Nostalgia was no match for Shania Twain's rockabilly girl power.

Scooping up the diary, I crossed the kitchen and tossed it onto my desk in the converted walk-in pantry I used as an office, then shut the door firmly. I had a family to care for and a struggling diner to keep afloat. I had no time for nostalgia or regret.

2

"Is that fresh pot of coffee ready?" Aunt Gert barked, bursting through the swinging kitchen door an hour after we opened for breakfast. "Norman is asking for another refill already." She clucked her tongue in disapproval.

"New pot should be ready by now. I started it." Dad looked up from a cutting board piled high with potatoes. Both he and Julio were up to their elbows in prep for the day. I stuck my head out the door of my little office, where I'd been crunching depressing financial figures.

"I'll get it."

Our breakfast offerings were simple—pastries from Petit Pierre, the French bakery down the street, and endless refills of mediocre diner-quality coffee. It was easy to handle the morning rush, although in the past few years, *rush* was too generous a word for the skimpy trickle of customers who darkened our doorway before lunch. Now, in the doldrums of winter, it was even slower than usual.

Aunt Gert gave me a regal nod. "Much obliged."

This morning she was wearing an orange-patterned caftan heavily bedecked with wooden beads that clacked as she moved. A matching turban perched over her wispy white hair. Beneath it, her hawk nose and icy blue eyes gave her the visage of a highly ornamented bird of prey, a falcon perhaps.

Dr. Gertrude Lund, my great-aunt on my mother's side, was an eighty-year-old esteemed professor emeritus of religion and mythology who had relocated from New England to live in the tiny cottage in our backyard almost two years ago. She was an opinionated, stubborn character with outrageous fashion sense and a razor-sharp intellect. Although her acerbic personality wasn't particularly suited to waitressing, she insisted on helping out at the diner, pulling her weight, as she put it. Regular customers had learned to fear the heavy tread of her orthopedic shoes.

I grabbed the pot of coffee from its place by the door, and Aunt Gert followed me into the dining room. "That old coot's just cheap if you ask me. Coming in here every morning and taking up a booth for hours and only ordering a cup of coffee." She pursed her lips and scowled in the direction of Norman, one of our morning regulars, who was occupying his usual table by the big plate-glass front window.

"I think he's just lonely. It hasn't even been a year since Mabel died," I reminded her. I had a soft spot for Norman and regularly slipped him day-old pieces of coffee cake if we had any left over. I understood grief, and while a piece of coffee cake couldn't soothe the pain of his wife's passing, I knew from experience that little acts of kindness were often a balm for hurting hearts.

Behind me Aunt Gert harrumphed. "You, my dear, are entirely too tenderhearted," she said. Then, pitching her voice loudly enough so Norman could hear across the room, she added, "You know what the Bhagavad Gita says about greedy people? Lust, anger, and greed are the three doors to hell. Not my words. Lord Krishna's."

"What a cheerful thought." I passed a middle-aged couple in hiking gear who were sitting in one of the booths, watching our exchange quizzically. Aunt Gert stumped behind me in her incongruously sensible black oxfords.

In the pale morning light, the diner looked quaint but a little down-at-the-heels.

The original warm, golden fir floor was scuffed and worn from more than sixty years of foot traffic. Some of the mint-green piping at the edges of the white vinyl booths was flaking at the edges, but the diner still retained much of its nostalgic charm.

The Eatery had been in our family since my maternal grandparents opened it as newlyweds in the 1950s, using their honeymoon money as a down payment on this little spot. It was located on the main street of the charming village of Magnolia, a quiet neighborhood nestled on the far west side of Seattle, swathed by Puget Sound on three sides. Magnolia was the kind of place where neighbors would pop by to drop off a pound of Manila littlenecks after an afternoon of clamming on Hood Canal, where you always recognized friends and neighbors standing in line at Petit Pierre for chocolate croissants on Saturday morning, and where the local bookshop, Magnolia's Bookstore, was ready with the perfect recommendation as soon as you came through the door.

I loved Magnolia and the Eatery. I'd grown up here in this diner, learning to walk by tottering from the vinyl booths to the round barstools tucked below the long white Formica counter. This was home. I inhaled sharply, taking in the decades-old scent of strong, bitter coffee and cracked vinyl overlaid with just a whiff of tangy lemon meringue pie. The scent of my childhood.

"Good morning, Norman." I topped up his coffee.

"Morning, Lolly," Norman greeted me. He was struggling to open a paper packet of sugar.

"Can I help? Those can be tricky." I tore the paper off the top of the packet and handed it to him.

Norman took the sugar and patted my hand. "You're a good girl, Lolly. And pretty as a picture. Why hasn't some fella scooped you up by now?"

"She's not lentils in a dry-goods bin. 'Scooped her up' indeed." Aunt Gert snorted from behind me. She had never married and had strong opinions on the subject of women's rights. She'd once shared a podium with Gloria Steinem at a women's liberation rally.

Swallowing a smile, I replied as neutrally as I could, "I don't have time for love right now, Norman. I've got my family and the diner. I'm very busy."

Norman blinked up at me with rheumy eyes, then looked thoughtfully past my shoulder for a moment as if trying to recall something. "Whatever happened to that boy, the one who was so sweet on you? He used to work here all those years ago, bussing tables as I recall. Such a nice young man, so polite. Had hair like a shiny new penny. What was his name?"

For a moment my mouth went dry. I had not uttered that name aloud in years. "Rory. Rory Shaw."

Norman's face brightened. "That's it. He seemed so smitten with you. Mabel always said he reminded her of a sunflower and you the sun. Whenever you'd come in the room, she said, he turned toward you like he was following the light."

I pushed my vintage cat-eye glasses up the bridge of my nose, careful to keep my face pleasantly blank. I could feel Gert eyeing me curiously, and Norman too. The truth was, Rory had had the same effect on me. We'd been each other's flowers. We'd been each other's suns. On the lists of regrets in my life, Rory Shaw easily topped them all.

"I guess some things just aren't meant to be," I said finally, giving Norman a small smile, trying to brush off his comment even though Rory's name sent a needle-fine dart of remorse straight through my heart.

"Well, I hope you meet another nice fella soon. Mabel and I were married for almost sixty years. We were so happy together. You deserve your own happiness, Lolly."

I nodded, wondering with a touch of chagrin just what it was about today that was bringing up so many reminders of my unfulfilled aspirations. "Someday maybe I'll be so lucky," I told him.

I glanced up and met Aunt Gert's shrewd gaze. She was watching me closely beneath the puckered folds of her turban, eyes narrowed as though trying to crack some cryptic code.

"Maybe you will," Aunt Gert said mysteriously. "Or maybe you'll choose another path altogether."

I glanced at her, surprised. Her tone seemed laden with significance. She couldn't possibly know about the life goals list sitting in my office. I looked away from her discerning gaze, afraid of what she might see. The disappointment, the longing. I felt laid bare today. I needed to pull myself together.

"Say, Lolly, you have any leftover pie?" Norman asked hopefully. "This morning I think I'd like a nice slice with my coffee."

"Sure, Norman. Let me check and see." I walked over to the glass-fronted refrigerated pie case that faced the front door, positioned to lure customers in as soon as they set foot inside. It was a strategy that had been working pretty well for more than sixty years. We rarely had pie left over at the end of the day. There was one lone slice of yesterday's lemon meringue pie sitting on a dessert plate inside. I pulled it out for Norman and then stopped, struck by a memory so vivid it rooted me to the spot. I'd been standing in this exact spot when I'd first laid eyes on Rory Shaw.

3

NINETEEN YEARS AGO
JULY

"Lolly, this is Rory, the new neighbors' boy I was telling you about." My mother stood in front of the pie case, her hand on the shoulder of a boy about my age. "He's just turned fourteen, so I'm sure you'll be friends."

I stopped squirting vinegar cleaner on the glass front of the pie case and surveyed the newcomer. He was tall and gangly, with pants that were a little too short, as though he'd shot up in the night and surprised everyone. His hair was a bright coppery auburn, like a new penny that still had some shine to it, and cut close to his head so that it tufted up a bit at the back. He had freckles and warm brown eyes. I couldn't decide if he looked geeky or cool. Maybe a little of both.

When I glanced at him my stomach did a funny little flip. I wasn't interested in boys like my best friend, Ashley, who had sported a parade of boyfriends since the fifth grade. But there was something about Rory's face I was drawn to instantly. Looking at him felt familiar, like walking into a warm room from the chill of a rainy afternoon. It wasn't love at first sight with Rory Shaw. But it was certainly a strong like. I backed up a little, feeling suddenly self-conscious. I was thirteen, all

ponytail and flat training bra and pointy elbows. Boys were foreign
territory.

"Want some help?" he asked, gesturing to the bottle of cleaner in
my hand. I met his eyes, the color of root beer, I noticed, and just as
lively.

"Okay." I showed him how to crumple pages of newspaper, and
together we wiped down the plate-glass window at the front of the
dining room while our mothers sat in a booth and had coffee. My mom
gave us each a quarter, and we took turns choosing songs on the jukebox. The jukebox had been a splurge for my parents when they took
over the diner the first year they were married. My mother adored old
country and western music, and they'd found it cheap when a western-
themed bar had gone out of business in Tacoma. It seemed incongru-
ous in a diner that served Danish food, but my mother hadn't cared a
bit. She always kept quarters in her pocket just so she could hear track
C9, Tanya Tucker crooning "What's Your Mama's Name." I'd grown up
on Johnny Cash and Hank Williams and Loretta Lynn singing about
love and heartbreak and feeling so true and so blue while my mom
served customers the flaeskesteg daily special.

I chose track F4 on the jukebox menu, Dolly Parton's song "I Will
Always Love You," which I thought was the most tragic and romantic
song in the universe. Then Rory picked a Johnny Cash song. Over the
music I eavesdropped on the adults' conversation as my mother cheerfully interrogated Rory's mom, Nancy. In the first week of July the
Shaws had moved from the Bay Area into the 1950s rambler across the
street, and my mom, a self-appointed welcome wagon for any new
neighbors, had promptly taken them a lemon pound cake and invited
them to stop in at the Eatery. Which they'd done this afternoon. By
the end of their conversation my mother was already planning to hire
Rory as a busboy at the diner when he was old enough and had invited

the Shaws over for a cookout that weekend. My mother had a plan for everyone's life.

While our mothers talked, Rory and I worked together silently. He was lanky but not awkward. He seemed remarkably easy in his own skin. It made me breathe easier just to be around him. I could smell him—the laundry scent of his soccer jersey and, beneath that, a hint of boyish clean sweat. There was something else too, something that reminded me a little of oak leaves and the sweet sun tea my mother brewed on our back deck in the summer. I kept sneaking glances at him as we worked. When our elbows bumped little sparklers of electricity shot down my arm, straight to my stomach. All we were doing was cleaning fingerprints off a window, but I would have cleaned that glass forever if it meant standing next to him.

That was the beginning.

4

Three a.m. and I was back in the diner's kitchen, rolling out six piecrusts in staccato bursts of agitated energy. I'd tossed and turned for hours in my little gabled bedroom before giving up on sleep, quietly slipping past our snoring basset hound, Bertha, and walking the half mile to the Eatery through the silent, chilly streets of Magnolia. Now I was making the daily pies and listening to Johnny Cash's greatest hits turned down low, trying to calm the tumult of my heart. I couldn't get that life goals list out of my mind.

I eyed the diary sitting on the stainless-steel countertop next to a slab of French butter, the frolicking happy unicorns oblivious to my inner turmoil. Wiping my hands on my apron, I flipped it open to the place where Daphne had stopped reading. In glittering purple letters the list read:

<u>Lolly's Life Goals</u>

    1. Live in another country

    2. Own my own restaurant somewhere amazing

3. Fall in love

4. Help my family be happy together 4 ever

5. Get my own horse

I smiled ruefully at number five. *Get my own horse.* The desire to have a horse had faded away about the time I got my driver's license, but in those early teenage years I'd dreamed of being an equestrian champion.

Number four . . . *Help my family be happy together 4 ever.* I winced at the blithe optimism of that goal.

"Turns out we don't get to decide whether the people we love the most are safe or happy," I murmured to my younger self. Ten years after I'd written this list, our happy little family was shattered as we lost the linchpin of our lives.

But the other three items . . . I traced the loopy script on numbers one and two. *Live in another country. Own my own restaurant somewhere amazing.* I'd always dreamed of living in another country. My junior year at Portland State University I'd done a semester studying abroad in London and fallen head over heels in love with England. For a while I'd planned on moving there and opening my own restaurant.

"Toast." I hadn't said the name aloud in years. It was my ideal café—eclectic and quirky (a little like me) and focused on sustainable, local, organic food. I could still conjure it up in my mind, the bright airy space with a vintage twist. I dreamed of creating a place for people to gather, a space with unhurried rhythms. I wanted it to foster an appreciation for simple, good food to invite meandering conversations, folks lingering over local wine, discussing great books and films. My dream for Toast was not just about serving a good meal, it was about creating an experience that invited people into a stronger connection with the Earth and with each other, into gratitude and thoughtfulness. I wanted to bring simple joy and goodness with every bite.

"Gather. Savor. Toast." I murmured the slogan I'd painstakingly created in a marketing class in college. I still dreamed about England and Toast sometimes, wistfully, with a touch of longing. It had never happened. Life got in the way. After Mom's sudden death, I came home and never left. I couldn't leave my dad and ten-year-old Daphne to cope alone, so I had stayed and taken on Mom's role at the diner and in our family as best I could.

I looked around the kitchen. I'd done all I could, but so many days it seemed like it wasn't enough. The truth was, I disliked many of the things about my role at the Eatery—crunching numbers, keeping up with ever-changing regulations, making the day-to-day operations run as smoothly as possible. I was responsible and organized, but I was not particularly keen on the logistics of running a struggling diner. It was a far cry from how I'd pictured my life running Toast. Yet I was the only choice after Mom died. Dad struggled with severe dyslexia; he could jerry-rig a burst pipe with some duct tape and a plastic bag and make a tasty karbonader, but the business side of things was alphabet soup to him. And Daphne had been so young when we'd lost Mom, too young to shoulder any of the responsibilities Mom had left behind. There had really been no one else but me to take her place. So I did.

I put down the diary abruptly and went back to the piecrusts. Life lists were tricky. Pie I could do. Sliding the circles of dough into the battered aluminum pans, I crimped the edges with quick pinches, then covered them with parchment paper and added pie weights. Setting the timer, I popped the pans into the oven to partially blind-bake the crusts. Cracking five large eggs, I separated the yolks and the whites, setting aside the whites for the meringue top. On the radio Johnny was singing "I Walk the Line" in his signature gravelly voice.

I whisked water, granulated sugar, cornstarch, salt, lemon juice, and lemon zest together over medium heat. Mom's secret recipe used Meyer lemons for a sweeter, richer flavor. That was one of her tricks.

That and European butter. With its higher fat content than American butter, it made a flakier crust.

"Lolly, what are the three secret ingredients that make this the best lemon meringue pie in the world?" She'd drilled me that last night before she died, demanding I recite every ingredient, every step, until she was satisfied I had it down pat.

"The three ingredients are Meyer lemons, European butter, and a leaf of lemon balm boiled into the syrup every time," I'd dutifully recited in her hospital room, feeling the weight of grief, of responsibility rest heavier on my shoulders with every word.

Lemon balm was an unorthodox choice for pie, but Mom had loved cooking with edible flowers and herbs. She'd taught me everything I knew about them. I reached for the little lemon balm potted plant growing on the windowsill over the sink and carefully pinched off a leaf.

"In the language of flowers, lemon balm means sympathy or good cheer," she'd explained once. "So every bite of this pie can help brighten someone's day."

I crushed the leaf of lemon balm between my fingers and inhaled the scent, hoping it would work on me. No such luck. I dropped the leaf into the pot and stirred. Every time I made these pies I felt her presence. She had loved lemons—their sharp, fresh scent and cheerful hue. She would slice a lemon in half and sniff deeply, happily.

"See, Lolly," she'd say. "Lemons brighten every day. They are a touch of kitchen magic, and we all need a little magic in our lives." She'd rub the peels beneath her fingernails so her hands always smelled like the brightest summer sunshine. But since her sudden death and everything that had come after, I had not been able to see lemons in such a positive light. They represented duty and loss more than anything else to me now.

I stirred the contents of the pot, thin and cloudy, about as appealing as dirty dishwater. In a few minutes it would begin to thicken and bubble happily. The scent rising from the pot was enticing, the sharp tang of lemon juice and the sweetness of dissolving sugar with just a kiss of the lemon balm beneath. I leaned against the counter and shivered in the cold kitchen, all tile and steel. I'd thrown an apron on over my joggers and sweatshirt when I came in, but I still felt the chill. While I waited for the filling to boil, I glanced over at the list still open on the counter, my eyes skittering away from number three. I knew what it said. *Fall in love*. Technically, I had accomplished that goal.

In an instant, a series of images flashed through my mind, bright and fleeting as sparklers on the Fourth of July. Tawny eyes crinkling at the corners with laughter. The cinnamon-colored stubble along his jawline that he'd rub across the tender skin of my neck just to hear me squeal. A constellation of freckles along the smooth planes of his shoulder blades. His strong arms wrapped around me, us fitting together so perfectly, my cheek nestled against the nubby wool shoulder of his fisherman's sweater, his mouth pressed against my hair. The way he said my name, like it was the answer to a prayer, so husky and tender it made me melt inside like a pat of French butter.

Rory Shaw. No question that I had fallen for him. Our path to love had not been smooth, but I'd fallen slow and hard, so thoroughly it took me years to recover. I wasn't actually sure I *had* recovered. For a moment I could have sworn I caught a whiff of sun-warmed skin and the honeyed oak scent of bourbon and sweet tea. For a moment the sorrow was so strong I couldn't catch my breath. He was the first and only boy I'd ever loved. The boy whose heart I broke. The boy who'd smashed my own heart into a thousand pieces.

I leaned over the pot to check the filling, then stepped back from the stove and dabbed at my welling eyes behind my glasses, afraid to dapple the lemon mixture with briny tears. A quiet agony, to still love a man who was so thoroughly out of reach, so terribly gone. Did it count if you did indeed fall in love but then it ended disastrously, entirely by your own hand?

"Pretty sure the answer to that is no," I whispered, trying to swallow the knot of grief clogging my throat.

So this was it, the truth about my lemon of a life. I was on the cusp of turning thirty-three, and that sparkly purple list of life goals spoke loudly about all I had not done. In the loneliness of the kitchen I felt the sharp slice of despair. How had it come to this? How had I not managed to accomplish even one thing on the list?

Across the room, over the door to the dining room, hung my mother's favorite sign. Painted on thin metal whitewashed to look vintage, it read: WHEN LIFE GIVES YOU LEMONS, MAKE LEMONADE. A saying so common it bordered on trite, but one my mother had firmly embraced nonetheless. She was a lemonade sort of woman, approaching every hurdle with a brisk, efficient optimism. If she were here now, I knew what she'd say.

"Stop crying over your lemon of a life, Lolly, and start figuring out how to make lemonade."

But she wasn't here, and her absence was a huge part of the reason my life was now quite lemony. I reread the sign and felt something stir in my chest, a flicker of determination. When I wrote that list, I'd had every intention of following through on every point. And indeed up until ten years ago I'd been well on my way to accomplishing each one, and then life had gotten in the way. It wasn't my fault that circumstances had derailed me. It wasn't fair either. But it had happened.

I'd been telling myself for years that I'd get back on track with my own dreams, just a little later on, when Daphne was older, when the Eatery was on firmer financial footing, when, when, when. Yet somehow that time never seemed to come.

It's not too late. My mother's voice, a loud whisper in my mind.

"How would I even start?" I whispered back.

But if I didn't do something now, when would I? I gave the list a sideways glance and made a snap decision. I simply could *not* reach my thirty-third birthday with all my goals still unmet.

"I've got a month," I said aloud, setting my chin firmly. And there in that cold kitchen, surrounded by the scent of bubbling lemon filling and Johnny crooning a strangely plaintive rendition of "You Are My Sunshine," I made myself a promise. "I will check at least one thing off that list before I blow out my birthday candles if it's the last thing I do."

Then I picked up the spoon and stirred the lemon filling vigorously, trying hard to focus on the future and all the possibilities that lay ahead, not looking back to the shattered past and all I'd left behind.

5

EIGHTEEN YEARS AGO
NEW YEAR'S EVE

New Year's Eve and I was alone in my room, halfway through *To Kill a Mockingbird* for freshman honors English. I glanced out the window and across the street. The light in Rory's room was on. That was odd. I thought he was at a party at Jessica Sharma's house. Jessica was the most popular girl of Rory's sophomore class, and rumor had it she was throwing a New Year's Eve party for fifty people. Invitations were highly coveted. I hadn't been one of the lucky fifty, but even if I had been invited, I wouldn't have been able to go. Tonight I had to stay home because my parents had gone with Mr. and Mrs. Shaw to a New Year's Eve party in Green Lake, and my parents had paid me to babysit Daphne. She was now sound asleep in her room across the hall, and I was regretting agreeing to watch her tonight.

I'd invited Ashley over to watch the ball drop, but she'd called this morning to tell me she had the stomach flu. So here I was, on track to have the most boring New Year's Eve on record. I squinted through the window, trying to see if I could spot Rory across the street. No movement. Maybe he'd just left the light on by accident.

I sighed in disappointment and turned back to my chapter, keeping one eye on Rory's window. After the Shaws had moved in across the street the previous year, our mothers quickly became great friends, and Rory and I found ourselves together pretty often. Most Mondays, the only day the diner was closed, the Shaws came over for a game night. While the adults played poker in the dining room and drank beer and dirty martinis, Rory and I would watch a movie in the den. Rory loved our old basset hound, Myrtle, and he was good with Daphne, who was still a toddler. She would crawl all over him, poking her fingers into his ears and nostrils, and he'd carry her around on his back like a horse.

We were not best friends. I had Ashley for that, and Rory had a couple of good guy pals from the high school soccer team, but we were friendly. Rory was a year ahead of me in school, but he always made a point to greet me if he saw me in the hall between classes. We didn't hang out together outside the Monday-evening game nights, but I felt happier knowing he was across the street. I never felt on edge with Rory. He made me feel at ease in my own skin. When he was around, the world was just right somehow.

I sighed again and checked the clock. After eleven. My stomach rumbled and I hopped out of bed. Time for a little night snack. Maybe I would turn the TV on and watch the ball drop, although it would feel sad to do it alone. I padded softly down the stairs, careful not to rouse Daphne. Myrtle snuffled hopefully at my heels. She was a consummate beggar.

Flipping on the light in the kitchen, I grabbed a plate and shook a handful of Triscuits out of the box. I dropped a Triscuit for Myrtle, who looked dolefully at me and wagged her tail. She was hoping for cheese.

"No cheese tonight, girl," I told her, grabbing an apple from the fruit bowl. I started to slice it, using the good paring knife my dad sharpened every month. Chop. Chop. Cut out the core. I hummed as I worked, a peppy rendition of "Auld Lang Syne." Just as I cored the last apple segment, Myrtle bumped my leg with her low-slung, tubby body. The knife slid through the center of the apple and sliced hard across the pad of my thumb.

I gave a low, strangled gasp and dropped the apple and the knife, clutching my hand. Blood welled up instantly from the wound, glistening deep red, running down my wrist onto the counter. Oh, this was bad. Feeling a little faint, I tried to think. My heart was pounding and my head felt light. The pain was sharp. Myrtle, sensing something was amiss, woofed, staring up at me in puzzled concern.

"Oh no-no-no. Oh, girl, what are we going to do?" I grabbed a dish towel and wrapped it around my injured hand, then clumsily picked up the phone and called the Stewarts' house, where my parents were at the party. No one picked up. Ashley's whole family was down with the stomach flu and couldn't come help me. I chewed my lip, panicking just a little. I didn't think it was bad enough to call 911, but even if I did need a doctor's care, I couldn't leave Daphne here alone. Nor could I imagine taking her in an ambulance. She'd be terrified. I hesitated for only a minute and then called the Shaws' house, praying that Rory really was home. My heart was racing and I felt a little dizzy.

He picked up after two rings. "Hello?"

The relief was instantaneous at the sound of his voice. "Rory, it's Lolly. I just cut my hand and it's bleeding a lot." Suddenly I started to cry. "Can you come over?"

He came immediately. His hair was wet from the shower, dark copper strands curling damply over his ears, and he was in a soccer T-shirt and a faded pair of sweatpants with a hole in one knee. I met him at the door, holding my injured hand above my head. I thought I'd heard you should do that when you were bleeding. Myrtle wagged her tail when she saw Rory, then whined softly, unsure what was happening.

"How bad is it?" he asked in concern, kicking off his running shoes and eyeing my hand. Spots of blood were seeping through the dish towel. It looked gruesome.

I grimaced. "I don't know. I didn't really see the cut. I was sort of in shock."

Rory frowned. "Do you want me to drive you to the ER? I'm supposed to have an adult with me, but since it's an emergency . . ." He watched me earnestly. He was fifteen now and had his learner's permit.

I hesitated, then shook my head, holding my injured hand high in the air as if raising my hand to answer a question in class, trying to keep calm and think clearly. "I'm not sure it's that bad. I hope not. I already tried to call my parents. They didn't answer. Daphne's asleep upstairs and I just don't know what to do." I teared up a little again. My thumb was hurting a lot.

"Let's take a look at it and see how bad it is," Rory suggested calmly.

I nodded and sniffled. "Okay."

He took me by the elbow and carefully led me to the sink in the kitchen, gingerly unwrapping the dish towel. I squeezed my eyes shut as he assessed the wound.

"Oh, ouch," he murmured. I opened one eye a crack. I'd sliced a segment the size of a dime out of the pad of my thumb. It was just an open wound and still bleeding profusely.

"How bad is it?" I whispered. "Do I need stitches?"

Rory surveyed the wound. He'd taken a first aid course that fall, and I knew he was interested in becoming a doctor of some sort. "It's bleeding a lot, but I don't think stitches are going to help. There's nothing to stitch. The skin is gone. We need to clean it and apply pressure and see if we can stop the bleeding."

"Okay," I said faintly, relieved that he so capably seemed to know what to do.

"Here, sit down." He grabbed a chair and helped me sit, my arm still over the sink, dripping blood into the drain. "Where's your first aid kit?" He spoke in the same measured, calm tone, which in turn made me feel calmer.

"Upstairs bathroom," I mumbled. I was feeling a little faint all of a sudden and sick to my stomach, my vision going dark around the edges. I leaned my head against the edge of the sink while he went to get the kit and closed my eyes.

"Lolly, are you okay?" Rory was suddenly there at my side, leaning over me, peering intently into my face. He had his hand on my shoulder, steadying me.

I nodded. "I think so. It just hurts a lot."

"I'm going to bandage the wound, okay?" Rory instructed. "Just lean against me if you need to."

I nodded and rested against his side, grateful for the comfort. His T-shirt was worn and soft. He smelled like tea tree shampoo and himself, that hint of oak leaves and sweet tea that made me want to inhale deeply every time I was around him. We'd never touched like this before. I was super aware of every one of his breaths, of the taut muscles of his torso against my cheek. I felt both reassured and a little flustered to be so close to him. I liked it quite a bit actually. I leaned in a little closer.

"This is going to sting a little," he murmured. "Just for a minute."

I gave a strangled shriek as he poured hydrogen peroxide solution over the wound. It fizzed and bubbled. He leaned down and blew on it. "My mom always did this," he explained, smiling sheepishly. "I don't know if it helps, but it always made me feel better."

And strangely I did feel better. He grinned at me and I managed a small smile back.

"Just a couple more steps," Rory said soothingly. He blotted the wound with a clean square of gauze, then bound it snugly with more gauze and taped it. I could feel his hands shaking a little as he worked, and he was breathing fast. I realized he was nervous and trying not to show it. He was trying to be strong and take care of me. I gritted my teeth and squeezed my eyes closed, concentrating on not crying. I wanted to seem strong and brave too.

"Okay, we're done."

I opened my eyes. Rory was sweeping all the detritus into the trash can, even the blood-soaked kitchen towel. The flower pattern was probably beyond saving. He packed up the first aid kit too. When he was done it looked like nothing had happened.

"Thank you." I looked at my bandaged thumb. It was the size and shape of a chicken drumstick. "Do you want to stay and watch the ball drop?" It was only a few minutes until midnight.

"Sure. I should probably make sure the bleeding has stopped before I go." Rory guided me into the living room and switched on the TV, turning it to the Times Square New Year's Eve celebration on NBC. He tucked an afghan around my legs and propped my injured hand above the level of my heart with a stack of pillows. Other than my mom, I'd never had someone care for me like this. It was unexpectedly sweet.

We sat together on the couch, not touching but not far apart. Myrtle lay at our feet, content now that things seemed normal again. She drifted off to sleep and started snoring softly. On TV, Times Square looked frigid and festive, teeming with people celebrating the New Year. I snuck a look at Rory. He was watching the TV.

"I thought you were at Jessica Sharma's party tonight."

He shrugged. "Yeah, I was. It was okay, really loud. I just wasn't feeling it. I left early."

"I'm glad." I sniffed, still feeling a little shaky. "Thank you for coming over. I didn't know what to do."

He gave me a steady look. "I'll always be here for you, Lolly," he assured me, and I believed him. At that moment it was the most comforting thought in the world.

The countdown began in Times Square. "Ten . . . nine . . . eight . . . seven . . ."

I looked at him again. He'd poured us the sparkling cranberry juice my mom had left for Ashley and me in the fridge since we weren't old enough to drink champagne. I took a sip and watched his profile. I felt light and effervescent with relief, almost as though I were floating a few inches above the couch. I was profoundly grateful that he was beside me, that he had come to my aid tonight. Sitting next to him, I felt happy and content.

"Four . . . three . . . two . . . one. Happy New Year!" Times Square erupted in celebration. Rory quirked an eyebrow at me and raised his glass in a toast. I leaned over awkwardly and we clinked glasses.

"Happy New Year, Lolly."

"Happy New Year." We drank.

On the TV screen flashed a montage of celebrations from around the United States. People in party hats and sparkling sequined evening attire in Atlanta, people gathered around a bonfire toasting with beer in Wyoming. In Maryland a group of senior citizen ladies in swimsuits stood at the edge of the Chesapeake Bay and on the count of three jumped in together.

"I've always wanted to do that," Rory commented, watching the ladies splash and shriek in the water. "I think it's called a polar plunge."

I considered for a moment. "We could do one tomorrow." It was a crazy notion, but I was having such a good time with Rory I didn't want it to end. The thought of doing something a little adventurous with him was exciting.

His eyes lit up. "Really?"

I didn't think about my injured hand or how we would convince our parents to let us go. I just promised.

"Sure." I shrugged. "Meet me here at ten tomorrow morning. I know just the place."

"Wow. Just wow."

Late the next morning Rory stood with me on the long, lonely swath of rocky shoreline at South Beach in Magnolia. He looked around him, taking in the panorama—the steely, restless waters of the sound stretching away to the green mound of Bainbridge Island, and beyond the island, the snowcapped Olympic Mountains rising majestically against a cloudy sky. He gave a low whistle. "Lolly, this is amazing."

I smiled, shivering in the chill air. I couldn't agree more. It was a cold, clear New Year's Day, and my mom had dropped us off at Discovery Park, a vast area of evergreen forest and fields and bluffs that ran along Puget Sound just a mile from our house. With its acres of walking trails, lighthouse, and beautiful, remote South Beach, the park had always been one of my favorite places. My parents had been taking me to South Beach for as long as I could remember, and today I wanted to share it with Rory. It would be the perfect spot for our polar plunge.

Bundled in jackets and scarves against the January wind and wearing swimsuits underneath our coats, we stood on the remote northern part of the beach, past the lighthouse and the small parking lot. A cold breeze ruffled Rory's wavy copper hair and made the freckles stand out on the planes of his cheekbones.

"Ready?" I asked a little nervously. It was so cold and the water would be freezing as well. I was rethinking my rash promise of the night before. I'd told my mom we wanted to take a hike. I was pretty sure she would not have let us come if she'd known what we were planning. I also hadn't fully considered the cut on my finger the night before. I'd brought a quart Ziploc baggie and a rubber band and was planning to wrap my hand in the baggie to keep it dry. Now, in the cold light of day, it seemed like a dumb idea.

He nodded. "Sure, let's do it."

"Come on." I gestured for him to follow me as I headed down to the water. It was so clear I could see the strands of seaweed drifting above the bed of sand and smooth colored stones at the bottom. Farther out in the water a seal popped his head above the surface and looked at us curiously. Waves lapped gently against the shoreline. I shrugged out of my jacket and sweatshirt, unlaced my tennis shoes, and peeled off my leggings; and stood shivering and covered in goose pimples in my one-piece bathing suit on the cold, wet sand. Rory did the same. He came to stand beside me and wrapped his arms around his bare chest. I carefully stuffed my hand in the baggie, and Rory helped me secure the rubber band around my wrist. Hopefully my bandage would stay dry inside the bag.

"Okay," he said, seeming to brace himself. I'd never seen him shirtless before, and I could feel my cheeks warming at the sight of all that exposed freckly skin. My cheeks were the only part of me that was warm, however. My thighs felt frozen already. And once we jumped in, we'd have a long, cold, wet walk home. I hesitated. I could feel Rory beside me, looking at me. Trying to be brave, I dipped a toe in the water and gasped. It was so cold it physically hurt.

"Ready?" Rory reached out and took my uninjured hand. His palm was warm against mine. I nodded and took a deep breath. This was a terrible idea.

"One . . . two . . ." he counted slowly, his eyes on me. I could feel him tensed to spring forward into the water.

"Stop!" I shrieked at the last second. "It's just too cold and I'm chicken."

Rory let out a huge exhalation. "Me too," he said, grinning wide. "I was kind of worried we'd get hypothermia before we made it home, but I didn't want to back out. We can be chicken together."

"Sounds perfect," I said, grinning back at him. I clumsily worked my leggings and sweatshirt back on using my one good hand, laughing although my teeth were chattering. We dressed as fast as we could, a little giddy with relief.

"Want to hang out a little bit here or go straight home?" I asked, zipping myself into the warmth of my puffy coat. Pure bliss.

Rory looked around. "Let's stay. If I go home, I have to help my dad take the Christmas lights down. This is way more fun."

"Come on then," I led the way to a huge bleached-white driftwood log that had been lying on the beach for as long as I could remember. In the lower part of the trunk, near the base of twisted, gnarled roots, was a sheltered spot in the sand, perfect for two people to sit in. I sank down in the sand, careful of my injured hand, and gestured for him to join me. He slid down next to me.

"Do you know where you are right now?" I asked him.

He gave me an amused look. "Is this a trick question, like for head injury victims? Date, time, current president?"

I laughed. "It's not a trick question. This is my favorite spot in the world."

He sobered and looked around him. "I can see why."

It was breathtaking from this vantage point. Snowcapped mountains, the choppy gray glint of the water, the rocky beach empty of people. It was majestic and serene and a little wild. I loved it.

"Sometimes you can see baby seals resting on the shore over there." I pointed. "And usually there's no one on this part of the beach."

Rory rested his forearms on his knees, leaning back against the trunk, looking relaxed and at peace. "This is so much better than spending the day taking down Christmas lights," he said. "My dad always uses up all his swear words for the year in like an hour. Thanks for rescuing me."

"You rescued me first," I said lightly.

My parents had come home at one a.m. and found me on the couch, hand bandaged and elevated, and my head on Rory's shoulder. Both of us were asleep, and the TV was still on. I think they felt guilty that I hadn't been able to reach them and that Rory and I had been forced to handle my medical emergency by ourselves. My mom was so grateful to Rory for taking care of my injury that she talked Mrs. Shaw into letting Rory come with me for part of the day today. I'd convinced her to just drop us off and let us walk home. Now we had half the day to spend how we chose.

"I've never brought anyone here before," I confessed.

Rory looked at me curiously. "Why me?"

I shrugged. "I wanted to share it with you."

And that was the truth. I'd never even shared this place with Ashley. But looking at Rory next to me on the sand, I knew it was the right decision. He belonged here, sitting next to me.

I don't know how long we stayed there that day. It must have been hours. At first we were silent, just enjoying the wild beauty. But then, gradually, we started talking, sharing back and forth. We talked about everything. Rory told me all about his dream of becoming a sports medicine doctor and working with a professional sports team. I told him about my dream of opening my own restaurant. When we got hungry, he pulled out a slightly smashed Snickers bar, and we shared it, keeping an eye out for harbor seals and watching the mammoth container ships steaming south toward the Port of Seattle.

Sitting there together, with our backs against the smooth driftwood log, alone with the water and sky and the cry of the gulls, it felt like we were the only people in the world. We chatted about music, AP English, Rory's last soccer season. We discovered we both loved Keith Urban and *To Kill a Mockingbird*. I told him that if I ever had a daughter I wanted to name her Scout after the protagonist. Rory did an impression of the nasally tone of our AP English teacher, Mrs. Keen, and I laughed so hard that I tipped over in the sand, which made him laugh until he couldn't breathe. Lying in the sand, ribs aching from laughing, I felt a bloom of happiness. I could be silly around him or serious. Either way, he looked at me like I was the most special person on Earth. Under the warmth of his gaze, I felt bright and funny and favored. When we finally rose to hike back up the trail and make the mile walk back home, I did so with a pang of regret.

"Hey, thanks for bringing me along today." Rory shoved his hands in the pockets of his jacket. He hesitated. "Can we come back again sometime?" His expression was hopeful and a little vulnerable.

"Sure." I shivered and tried to wiggle the circulation back into my frozen toes. "This was fun." That was an understatement. The afternoon had been one of the happiest I could remember. Not even Ashley and I had so much fun.

Rory held out his hand, little finger crooked. "Pinkie promise?" He said it in Mrs. Keen's twang.

I grinned and hooked my pinkie with his, and we shook on it. "Promise," I replied in my best impression of a robot voice.

Rory reached out and tugged the end of my ponytail. "You're something else, Lolly Blanchard."

I looked down, feeling bashful. "Come on, we've got a long walk home."

I didn't know it then, but those few hours on the beach were a turning point of sorts. That was the day we truly became friends. And that was the day, without even realizing it, I started to fall for Rory Shaw.

6

"Rise and shine, morning glory."

Blinking in the pale morning light filtering in through the window above my pantry-office desk, I lifted my head from the stack of invoices and bills where I'd accidentally fallen asleep. I'd been dozing, half dreaming about Rory and that long-ago New Year's Day on the beach. Aunt Gert was standing over me with her hands on her hips. I squinted at her. She was wearing a khaki ensemble that I was pretty sure I'd last seen on Jane Goodall in a National Geographic documentary. She looked like she was ready to venture into the wilds of equatorial Africa in search of a family of chimps. The only thing missing was the pith helmet.

"Greetings and salutations," she said, eyeing me suspiciously. "Did you sleep here all night? Terrible for your spine."

I sat up, scrambling for coherence and searching for my glasses. I found them and slipped them on. "I came in early to make the pies and must have drifted off."

The pies were now sitting in two perfectly gleaming rows on the counter, cooling. My life might be a slow-burning bushfire, but my pies were perfectly composed.

"Humph." Aunt Gert pursed her lips. "I fed Bertha and let her out to have a wee before I came over. By the way, you left this on the prep table." She held out my diary, open to my life goals page. I snatched it from her, embarrassed. Had she read it? We didn't have a close relationship. The thought of her scalpel eye dissecting my life goals made me shrink a little inside. She, who had accomplished so much.

Besides being a professor at a prestigious women's college in New England, Aunt Gert had worked for the United Nations on a special council on world religions during the Cold War. She'd hiked the Atlas Mountains and lived with Bedouins and studied the religious practices of remote tribes along the Amazon. Compared to her, my accomplishments looked paltry.

Aunt Gert was eyeing me in a way that made me uncomfortable. She was generally a pull-yourself-up-by-the-bootstraps sort of woman, not high on empathy or displays of affection, but occasionally I caught glimpses of a tenderheartedness and compassion that surprised me. She was looking at me now with an expression that hovered somewhere between disapproval and sympathy. It made me squirm.

I turned away and tucked the diary in my top drawer. "Daphne found my old middle school diary when she was looking through some boxes for a school project." I shook out my hopelessly rumpled kitchen apron, which was smeared with lemon filling. "It's funny to look back on the things we wanted when we were young, isn't it?" I tried to brush off the life goals list as inconsequential, a childish fancy.

"On the contrary, I think we're the most honest when we're young," she replied brusquely. "It's later in life we get good at lying to ourselves."

I took a moment to let that sink in. "Do you have any regrets about your life?" I asked suddenly. "Would you change anything if you could?"

I knew only the broad strokes of Aunt Gert's life. Her hardscrabble upbringing on a berry farm in southern Ohio. How she'd gotten herself a full ride to Columbia University through sheer perseverance and a brilliant intellect. She'd had an illustrious career, but I didn't know how she felt about her life. What, if anything, did she think of longingly when lying in her narrow twin bed at night?

She paused for a moment, then shook her head decisively.

"Life is too short for second-guesses." She sniffed. "You make the best choice you can, and then you stick with it. I don't look back." She gave me a shrewd look. "What about you? Are you regretting your life choices at so tender an age?"

"I don't know if I'd call them regrets," I hedged, tucking a stray strand of hair back into my ponytail and smoothing my bangs. I could feel them swooping wildly to the left across my forehead. "Maybe just thinking about what-ifs. I had to make a lot of hard decisions; a lot of things happened that I didn't have control over."

She made a small grunt of agreement. "Your mother's death."

I nodded. "Sometimes I wonder what my life would look like if she were still alive." I pictured Rory, and my voice faltered. "I know it can't be changed, but I do wonder what if. What would my life look like now?"

Aunt Gert eyed me speculatively. "If you were given the chance to find out, would you take it?" she asked.

It was obviously a theoretical question, but she was staring at me intently, as though my answer really mattered.

"Of course," I stammered. "Why wouldn't I? But it's impossible."

She cocked her head at me. "Is it? Often we say 'impossible' when what we really mean is 'unknown.' So many things are possible; far fewer are known to us. You will discover this soon enough."

I just sat looking at her, unsure how to respond.

"Well, you're young." Aunt Gert clapped her hands together briskly. "You still have time. You have so much opportunity still laid out before you despite your present circumstances. You must try, as my dear colleague the esteemed mythology professor Joseph Campbell used to say, to 'follow your bliss.'"

"Follow my bliss?" It sounded like a slogan in a yogurt commercial.

Aunt Gert nodded again. "You must follow your bliss no matter the circumstances life thrusts upon you."

"But what does that mean? I have responsibilities. I can't just up and leave everything to pursue my own happiness," I protested.

Aunt Gert snorted. "Who said anything about happiness? Don't be a ninny. You are mistakenly equating bliss with happiness. They're not the same thing."

"They're not?" I asked in bewilderment, wondering briefly if anyone in my life had ever called me a ninny before. "What's the difference?"

"Happiness is fleeting, fickle, often based on our circumstances." Aunt Gert waved a hand dismissively. "If you chase happiness, you will more often than not end up disappointed by the very nature of life. Life is hard, brutal at times, and often unfair. But following your bliss, that's entirely different. It means facing your present reality with honesty and courage and, in the midst of it all, continuing to pursue each spark of joy, even if it is a tiny pinpoint in the darkness of your life. Do not give up. Continue to look for the light in your life—it is always present somewhere, some small thing to be grateful for, something to celebrate, a way to give joy to others, a new way to grow. Move toward the light in life; seek it out no matter what. This is the essence of what it means to follow your bliss. You must be honest. Pay attention. Seek joy."

"'Be honest. Pay attention. Seek joy,'" I repeated. "Is that Joseph Campbell too?"

"No, that's Gertrude Lund." She paused to let the self-reference sink in. "By the way, the toilet in the women's washroom is clogged." And she turned on her heel and marched out.

7

"Okay, so you've got a month to accomplish one goal on the list, right?" Eve, my best friend of more than a decade, handed a waiting customer two bars of her homemade orange blossom goat milk soap and tucked the payment into her metal cash box. It had been half a day since my very-early-morning conversation with Aunt Gert, and now I was perched on a stool under the awning of Eve's stand at the Ballard Sunday Farmers Market, brainstorming ways to complete at least one thing on my life goals list.

"Right. One month. One goal." I shivered and rubbed the arms of my cashmere, pearl-button cardigan. It was only early afternoon, but it felt like dusk, with dark gray clouds piling up in a threatening sky. Despite the looming gloom, the farmers market was doing a brisk business, and the street between the rows of stalls was bustling with shoppers.

"And if you don't?" Eve asked.

"I will have failed at everything I wanted to accomplish in my life," I said lightly, my tone belying the bleak truth of my words. In the cold light of day, the stakes felt even higher than when I'd made my vow in the kitchen in the early dark of the morning.

Eve raised her eyebrows at me. "Read the list again," she commanded.

I drew my diary from the pocket of my vintage cherry-red poodle skirt and complied. Taking advantage of a momentary lull in customers, Eve leaned back against the table stacked with wares, listening intently. Today she was wearing a long, plain white apron, like a butcher's apron, with jeans and a tank top that showed the arboreal tattoos snaking around her slender, toned right bicep. Even though it was drizzly and February, hovering somewhere in the low fifties, she seemed impervious to the cold.

With her pixie cut, shaved up the sides and dyed a cotton-candy-pink hue, she radiated a distinct wholesome back-to-nature aura combined with a razor-sharp punk edge. Indeed, she personified her entire brand of organic handmade goat milk products, Gritty Girl Soap Co. No one would guess that five years ago she'd been the youngest hotshot marketing executive at a high-powered New York City firm with the accompanying panic attacks and developing baby ulcer to prove it. We'd met during a junior year semester study abroad in England and bonded over trips to the British Museum, the Borough Market, and Notting Hill, two fresh-faced American girls with the world as our oyster. Life had turned out quite differently than what we'd imagined all those years ago in London, but we'd been best friends ever since.

"Get a horse. It's the easiest thing on the list to accomplish," Eve said when I finished reading. "You can keep it at my farm." She dusted her hands, problem sorted.

"Yes, but unfortunately I don't really want a horse anymore." I'd actually crossed out number five in red pen. "And I think for it to really count, the goal has to be something I still want now."

That left just four items. Three, actually.

Eve seemed to read my mind. "Number four?" she asked quietly.

"Is already impossible," I responded quickly. My family would never *be happy together 4 ever*. That goal had slipped through my fingers ten years ago.

I worried my lower lip, ping-ponging between the remaining three in my mind. Which one had the best chance of success?

Eve crossed her arms and considered the remaining options. "Number one and number two are problematic. If you live in another country or own your own restaurant, you're probably not going to be able to manage the Eatery at the same time. Are you willing to give that up?"

I paused, considering. "I don't know how that would work," I admitted finally. "Dad and Daphne can't survive without me."

Eve gave me a sideways look. I knew she disagreed with me on this point. On a lot of points, actually. She paused to offer a sample of basil cuticle balm to a woman pushing two Boston terriers in a doggy stroller. The woman took the sample, then moved across the street to the organic bakery stand to examine their sourdough boules.

"So that leaves"—Eve counted back on her fingers—"number three. Fall in love."

"Yeah, fall in love," I affirmed. It made me feel a little panicky just thinking about it, but I had to admit it was the most likely one on the list.

Eve snapped her fingers. "A Russian mail-order husband off the Internet," she suggested. "I'm always getting spam ads promising that love is just a click away." She grinned at me.

"I don't think ordering a husband off the Internet actually qualifies as falling in love," I protested, laughing. "Plus, I'm pretty sure it's illegal."

She shrugged. "Technicalities."

I gazed down the street of the Ballard Avenue Historic District at the couple of blocks of white awnings fluttering in the breeze. Unlike our local Magnolia Farmers Market, which ran only in the warmer months, Ballard, the Seattle neighborhood to the north of us, ran their market all year round, and Eve was there each week manning her stand. Often I'd slip away from the diner for an hour or two on Sunday afternoons, ostensibly to help Eve handle the customers, but really I just hung around behind the counter and chatted with Eve.

Eve drummed her fingers on the table. "What about dating apps? I've heard Bumble's not bad. Women get to make the first move." She tilted her head and considered me thoughtfully.

"I think I'm just not cut out for online dating." I shook my head, thinking back to my last venture with dating apps a couple of years before. It had been a wasteland of men trying too hard to impress me, of overpriced cocktails in swanky, hip bars in Capitol Hill. Walking into each bar and restaurant feeling awkward and uncomfortable in high heels, aware even before I sat down that it wasn't going to work. Some of the men were full of themselves. Some were nice enough. None worked out. I gave up after six months and felt such a sense of relief when I deleted all the apps that I never tried again. "Maybe I'm just undatable." I opened a sample tub of chapped-hand salve with calendula and rubbed a dollop into my palms.

"Oh, right." Eve rolled her eyes at me. "Because men don't like cute hipster women with perky breasts who run successful businesses and bake pies every day. You're like Seattle's June Cleaver. What's not to like?"

"Marginally successful business," I corrected, for the sake of honesty. "Well, sort-of-slowly-declining business."

"Fine." Eve conceded. "Struggling business. But, Lolly, you're smart and kind. You're responsible. You're the most loyal person I've ever met. And you've got this whole adorable vintage vibe going on." She gestured to my cardigan, poodle skirt, cat-eye glasses ensemble. "You're totally datable. That's not the problem." Eve leveled a knowing look at me.

"Oh? So what is?" I hopped off the stool, feeling self-conscious at her matter-of-fact assessment of my attributes. I needlessly straightened a stack of charcoal facial cleansing bars.

"You can't fall in love again because you're already in love." She gave me a pointed look. "You're still stuck on Rory."

I didn't answer. A couple approached, carrying take-out Starbucks cups and a cloth bag brimming with kale and long spears of brussels sprouts. "Do you have any beard balm?" the man inquired, and Eve gave him a sample of her Cedar Beard Balm for Dapper Gents. It smelled like pine sap, peculiarly pleasing and bracing at the same time.

Eve turned back to me after the man had paid for a tin of beard balm. "You can't get over him. You broke his heart and broke your own heart, and even though you made him leave, you've never actually let him go."

She wasn't wrong.

"I don't know how to let him go," I admitted honestly.

"Don't know how to or don't want to? Those are two very different things." Eve crossed her arms and fixed me with a surprisingly sympathetic look. "Lolly, I love you like a sister. You're my best friend. You've rescued me from some very dark places. And I wouldn't be a good friend if I didn't tell you the truth. Rory is *gone*. He is married and a father. He isn't stuck on you. He's living in Florida with his wife and child, I'm sure enjoying his dream job as team physician for whatever sports team hired him down there."

"The Tampa Bay Rowdies," I volunteered. "Soccer."

Eve shook her head. "The fact that you even know that is just sad."

"I know it is." I turned away to hide my flushed face. I was embarrassed by Eve's assessment. In truth I felt a little caught out. I knew that Eve loved me, that she had my best interests at heart, but I couldn't help feeling like my tender heart was standing stripped and naked in front of her. I felt exposed, criticized. The problem was, she was right.

"If you're actually going to check off something on that list, you're going to have to get unstuck," Eve said gently but firmly. She tapped the cover of the diary, sitting next to a stack of oatmeal-and-honey solid lotion bars wrapped in burlap and tied with twine.

"How?" I asked, snatching up the diary and tucking it back into the wide pocket of my skirt.

"No idea." Eve shrugged. "You're going to have to figure that out for yourself. But I do know one thing. You can't stay where you are and expect a change. It's Newton's first law of motion. Objects at rest stay at rest. Objects in motion remain in motion. I'm paraphrasing." She cocked an eyebrow at me and waited.

I always forgot that while Eve had majored in marketing at the insistence of her high-powered CEO father, she'd minored in physics simply because it intrigued her.

"Am I the object in this illustration?" I asked dryly.

"Yep." Eve hauled a small wooden crate from under the table and grabbed a handful of lip balms. Blackberry–sweet corn, rosemary-mint, and coriander-lime. She eyed me and said matter-of-factly, "Lolly, you are an object at rest. You have to start the ball rolling; move forward or you're never going to get where you want to be."

She was right. I knew she was right. But deep in my heart, if I was perfectly honest with myself, I couldn't imagine a future that was better than the things I had lost. I was held back by the dual pull of responsibility and regret. I could not countenance leaving my family or leaving my responsibilities at the diner. And I could not imagine falling in love again. Eve had pegged it correctly. I was terribly stuck. I was aching to move forward, determined to move forward, but I had no idea how to do so. I was an object at rest, and I desperately needed someone or something to give me a shove in the right direction.

8

The morning after my chat with Eve, I woke to find a note propped against the French press on the kitchen counter.

Come see me when you're up. —G

It was early and still pitch-dark outside. On Mondays the diner was closed, but I woke before dawn anyway, just from force of habit. From the kitchen I saw the light shining in the guest cottage across the yard. Aunt Gert was awake. Bertha, the basset hound we'd gotten after Myrtle passed, whined, standing by the door, wagging her tail with a doleful yet expectant look on her jowly face.

"Here you go, girl." I scratched her head for a moment, then let her out into the backyard and measured out her food in her bowl by the kitchen counter. A moment later I heard her scratch at the door to be let in. She knew breakfast was waiting for her and didn't care to be outside in the damp cold any longer than she had to. I let her in, and she headed straight for her food bowl, her improbably low-slung body almost touching the tile floor. I pressed the lever on the electric kettle to start my essential morning coffee process, then quickly ground fresh beans and measured four heaping spoonfuls of Stumptown Coffee into my French press. While I waited for the water to boil I went to see Aunt Gert.

Still in my joggers, eyes gritty with sleep, I wandered across the backyard to the guest cottage my parents had built years ago. A cute little box nestled beneath the arms of a giant sequoia, it had a huge picture window and an arched front door—a tiny house before tiny houses were cool. I stood at the front door, yawning as a steady light mist fell softly on my head, and knocked once.

Two years ago, Aunt Gert had written to my father and asked if she could come stay with us. She had no one else, she explained, promising to not be a nuisance and offering her services in the diner. In truth none of us was thrilled. My mother had always been her favorite relative and had insisted we maintain contact with her while I was growing up. We had even visited her in New England twice when I was in elementary and middle school. Although my mother and Aunt Gert had enjoyed a close relationship, Aunt Gert was not a warm person, and her prickly demeanor had been both fascinating and intimidating to me as a child. However, my mother had been almost like a daughter to her, which is why, when we got her letter, Dad had written back and agreed, even though Mom had been gone almost eight years by that point. She was family, he explained to Daphne and me, and you don't turn away family, even if that family happens to be a brilliantly eccentric religion and mythology professor with a penchant for wildly patterned caftans.

At my knock, Aunt Gert opened the door. She was wearing a bright pink silk robe embroidered with turquoise cranes against a lush backdrop.

"Cool robe." I admired it.

"A gift from an enamored Chinese diplomat when I visited Shanghai years ago," she said, waving her hand dismissively and standing back so I could enter. As I brushed past her I caught a whiff of a musty, exotic odor—black pepper and incense and star anise, hinting at foreign adventures long past.

The space was small and brightly lit, a little cluttered with heavy books and an entire wall of shelves displaying mementos from her travels. She was steeping green tea at the tiny table for two, a sudoku puzzle book open before her.

"Tea?" she asked.

"No thanks. I'm making coffee over at the house."

She gestured to the other chair. "Sit, please." It was more a command than a request.

I sat.

"You're probably wondering why I summoned you." She gazed at me a little imperiously.

"A little." I shifted in the hard chair, eager to get back to the kitchen. The coffee was calling my name. Aunt Gert went over to the shelves and rummaged in a small, ornately carved silver box, then came back to me and held out her hand. She was wearing several large, exotic rings. A heavy gold one with a cabochon ruby and one in the shape of a peacock with jeweled feathers caught my eye. "Here, a gift for you. Call it an early birthday present."

Surprised, I held out my hand. Her fingers were cold and bony and strong. She dropped several small objects the size of marbles into my open palm and stepped back. I stared at the gift. In my hand sat three dime-store lemon drops—the bright yellow candy shaped like lemons and sanded on the outside with sugar. The kind of candy grandmas keep in jars for years because no one ever eats them.

"Oh . . . thank you." I glanced up at her, trying to hide my surprise. What a strange gift.

"They're not what you think." Aunt Gert sat down in the opposite chair. She met my eyes, her own gaze intent. "These are special. They can show you the life you could have had. They can show you your true path."

I blinked. My *true path*? What was she talking about? As she studied me I had the unnerving suspicion that she could read my thoughts. I wouldn't put it past her. There had always been an edge of the transcendent about her, a whiff of something slightly mystical, and it wasn't just the sandalwood incense she burned in a little tray in her bathroom.

Aunt Gert leaned across the table and gripped my hand so hard it hurt, but, by contrast, her expression was unexpectedly soft. "These were a gift to me when I was a young woman feeling stuck in my life. They can change everything."

I looked down at the little candies in my palm. I knew the taste and texture of them, had sneaked them from my own grandmother's dusty candy jar when I was a child. "I don't understand," I said. "Change everything how?"

Was Aunt Gert struggling with the early stages of dementia and it was just manifesting now? The thought was frightening.

"You think I'm crazy," she said, smiling enigmatically, then sat back and bobbed her tea ball in her teacup, the liquid a pale green. The scent was gorgeous, jasmine and green tea. "My dear, life is not defined by the limits of your own experience. The reality of the universe far transcends the paltry boundaries of your own understanding. As the great Saint Augustine once said, 'Miracles are not contrary to nature, but only contrary to what we know about nature.' He was right. Miracle, magic, whatever you want to call these." She nodded at the lemon drops. "I am giving you a chance to glimpse your life more fully, to perhaps change your path and arrive at a better end. I am giving you a chance to *follow your bliss*."

I was completely bewildered. *Miracles. Magic. Follow your bliss.* How did all that relate to the three lemon drop candies she'd given me?

"Try it," she urged me. "See what happens." The steam from her tea wafted up, lazy and fragrant. I felt like I was sitting with a fortune-teller or fairy godmother, if the fairy godmother was just a little bug-eyed and more than a little intimidating. "Suck on one of the lemon drops before bed and say aloud a thing you wish you could change, a regret from your life. Then go to bed, and when you wake up, you will live one day of your life as it might have been if you'd made a different choice. Don't be alarmed. The effects are only temporary. The following morning, you'll return to your normal existence as if nothing has changed." She paused and took a sip of scalding tea. "But, of course, in one day, everything can change."

"Okay, um." I scooted the chair back and stood, concerned by Aunt Gert's statements. She was a genius and eccentric, but this all sounded downright crazy. If she really was starting to suffer from dementia (and frankly, what else could this be?), how were we possibly going to cope? We were barely handling things as it was. I shrank at the thought.

"Thank you for the gift," I said, eager to make my escape. I needed coffee and a few minutes alone to collect my thoughts.

"You don't believe me, but it doesn't matter. Just promise me," she said, her tone commanding. "Promise me you will try one tonight. Do exactly as I told you. Humor an old woman." There was a peculiar glint in her eye that made me uneasy. She gestured toward the door, shooing me out. "Tell me all about it tomorrow."

I nodded. "All right, I promise." I tucked the lemon drops in the pocket of my joggers and made a mental note to try to remember to suck on one tonight just so I could assure her I'd done it when she asked tomorrow.

She followed me to the door to usher me out, but paused with her hand on the knob. "Be careful. Make wise choices." Her eyebrows, so pale they were almost translucent, furrowed into a deep, portentous V. "You never know what will happen, what you could gain or lose when you alter your own life story." And then she opened the door and stepped back without another word.

9

I forgot all about the lemon drops until the next evening, after a particularly frustrating conversation with Dad at our weekly state-of-the-diner meeting.

"So we're making it, still keeping afloat." Dad eyed the financial papers splayed out between us on the stainless-steel prep table with a touch of weary relief. He stood across from me in the kitchen, the sleeves of his white T-shirt rolled up, a chef's apron tied around his middle. As I watched, he dumped two pounds each of ground veal and pork into a giant bowl and started mixing them by hand. On his bicep his navy tattoo, an anchor with the initials *USN* woven in rope, flexed with his movements. He was making frikadeller, Danish meatballs, for the dinner special while Aunt Gert presided over the last of the lunch customers. In front of the deep stainless-steel sink, Julio was peeling potatoes. Angel, Julio's younger brother, was prepping the dish cart, getting ready to start bussing tables. The Eagles, Dad's favorite band of all time, wailed faintly from the radio/CD player, a crackly rendition of "Tequila Sunrise."

"Barely," I corrected, tapping red-circled figures on the papers with my pen. Bending over the figures, I pushed my vintage cat-eye glasses up higher on my nose. They were my favorite pair, sassy aluminum frames set with fake rhinestones at the swoopy corners. They had the annoying tendency to slip whenever I looked down, but I loved them anyway. "We're just barely keeping our heads above water. We have fewer customers than last year, and expenses are higher. Dad, the next thing, big or small, could sink us."

I sifted through the papers, bills, and spreadsheets splayed out between us, feeling discouraged. The news was bleaker than usual. The Hobart dishwasher had broken down last week, and the repair had been essential but costly, eating into our already-meager profit. It had been touch-and-go every week for the last few years, and the trend was not looking promising.

Dad blew out a breath and nodded, pushing back a strand of thinning black hair with the rolled-up sleeve of his shirt. "Okay, we'll just have to figure something out." He dumped a cup of grated onions and a cup of whole milk into the ground meat mixture and stirred. My eyes stung at the acrid onion scent, and I blinked back tears. In the bright light of the kitchen Dad looked tired, with bags under his dark deep-set eyes. Frankly, I couldn't remember a time when he hadn't looked tired.

At sixty-five, Marty Blanchard was the hardest-working man I knew. Small and whipcord lean, he'd grown up roping cattle on a ranch in Wyoming and then served a ten-year stint in the navy. After he married Mom, he'd worked ceaselessly at the diner, acting as the head cook, janitor, and general handyman. Although I was the first one at the diner in the mornings, he was the last one to turn out the lights at night. I couldn't remember the last time he'd had a vacation or even gone to see a movie. Not since my mother died and our finances and the Eatery had begun a slow downward slide. He was a man of few words, but of deep loyalty and care. He'd been devoted to my mom and her death had gutted him, yet he had persevered, tirelessly working for Daphne and me.

"Dad, we really need to think about making some major changes around here if we're going to keep our doors open," I pressed gently. It was a sore subject, one we did not see eye to eye on. "Did you read any of those articles I printed out for you on the success of the local and organic food movement along the West Coast?"

"No." Dad shook his head, cracking an egg into the bowl with one hand. "I didn't need to. Lolly, we can't make big changes to this place. Your mother had a vision, just like her parents before her, and it's up to us to carry out that vision. It's your legacy." He cracked three more eggs with swift, economical motions.

"But if we don't make some big changes, we could lose it all," I blurted out, frustrated by his blind loyalty to an ideal that was growing staler with every passing day. "Dad, the restaurant business in Seattle is getting tougher. Lots of places are going under. Most people don't want to spend money at a place like the Eatery. Nostalgia just isn't cutting it anymore. Almost nobody eats this heavy Danish comfort food now." I pointed to the heaping bowl of ground meat waiting to be formed into egg-size meatballs and then fried in butter. "They want farm-to-table, organic, sustainably sourced food. It's just the reality of the current restaurant scene."

I gripped the edge of the table, leaning toward him in my urgency to be heard. We had all poured our lives into this diner, my grandparents and parents and now me. We couldn't lose it all just because we failed to adapt to changing times. This diner symbolized so much of our lives and history. It was our heartbeat, more home than any house we'd ever lived in. It was place and family and legacy all rolled into one. Behind me, Glenn Frey softly wailed "Peaceful Easy Feeling," which felt ironic considering I was so agitated I was practically vibrating. "We have to make some changes before it's too late," I urged him.

"This diner has a reputation, a legacy. You don't mess with legacy," Dad said firmly, with finality. He sprinkled a cup of bread crumbs and a cup of flour across the ground meat and stirred.

I closed my eyes and took several deep breaths through my nose, trying to tamp down my panic and frustration. I'd been fighting this same losing battle about the restaurant for the last few years, but Dad refused to listen to reason. "We have to do something," I pressed. "This isn't working anymore."

"Okay, let's bring the fiskefrikadeller special back on Sundays." Dad twisted the cap off a plastic bottle of seltzer water and emptied half the contents into the bowl with the ground meat. "That's always a crowd-pleaser," he said in a compromising tone. "That should help get the numbers up."

I sighed hopelessly and stepped back. He just didn't get it. He didn't understand the precarious nature of our situation. We could lose everything, and his solution was to bring back cod fish cakes? He'd learned to cook in the navy and then polished those skills with my own maternal grandmother, learning how to make all the meals at the diner before my parents took it over, but he was an old-fashioned cook, with a limited repertoire and a resistance to change. I suspected the idea of change scared him.

I opened my mouth to press my point, then took another look at his exhausted face—the stubborn, stricken set of his jaw as he methodically mixed the seltzer into the ground meat—and swallowed my words. He had never recovered from my mother's death, but had soldiered on to take care of Daphne and me. It had cost him everything—any semblance of a life of his own—but he had not once complained. It wasn't his way. He had simply served us with a quiet, steady devotion, with no thought for his own happiness or comfort. I looked at the tendons straining in his scrappy arms as he mixed, then at the top of his head, the white of his scalp peeking through his thinning hair, and my heart softened. He was doing his best. We were all doing our best. I hoped with everything in me that it was good enough. I suspected one day soon it would not be.

"Okay, Dad, I'll put the cod cakes back on the menu," I said finally, acquiescing once again. It didn't matter what I wanted the diner to be, what I dreamed of and knew it could be. I had a pile of sketches in a drawer in my office, a whole notebook of ideas that, with a few dollars and a little elbow grease, could turn the Eatery from comfortable and a little shabby to the kind of hipster cool that Seattle was famous for.

I could see it in my mind's eye so easily—a Mason jar of succulents at every table, old travel posters from the fifties in simple white frames, a record player in the corner with a collection of big-band-era hits by Glenn Miller and Duke Ellington, and a menu that focused on fresh and local offerings. We could make the shabby into retro cool, but Dad could not seem to imagine letting it change even that much. I'd had to wheedle hard just to get us to switch to paper straws and compostable take-out containers last year.

Dad carried the bowl of frikadeller over to the fridge and set it on a shelf to chill. "Julio, hombre, how are those potatoes coming?"

Apparently, our meeting was over. Dad paused next to me. "Don't worry, Lolly girl. We'll figure it out," he said, chucking me under the chin and giving me a tired smile. "We always do."

I nodded and gathered up my papers, frustration churning like an eggbeater in my gut. I was so tired of standing here week after week and having the exact same argument. It was grinding me down. I didn't want this to be the sum total of my life: struggling to keep a floundering diner afloat, barely scraping by week after week, utterly stuck in a life that seemed smaller with each passing day. Something had to change.

Late that night, already tucked into bed wearing my most comfortable pair of flannel pajama pants and an old, faded green-and-white Portland State University sweatshirt, I remembered the lemon drops. The clock read one a.m. I was bone-tired, but the thought of facing Aunt Gert tomorrow morning and admitting I had not kept my promise was enough to propel me out of bed again. She'd already asked me first thing this morning if I'd taken one, and I'd sworn that I would remember tonight. She had a gimlet eye that could shrivel you with just one look. And, to be honest, I was just the teeniest, tiniest bit curious. Of course, I didn't believe dime-store candies could magically change my life. It was absurd, unthinkable, something found only in fairy tales. But that didn't mean I didn't wish it were true.

A small part of me, the childlike part, wished there really were some magic in the world. What if I could actually turn back the days and months and years and make a different choice, taste a different life? How remarkable would that be? What a gift—to start afresh. To follow my bliss, whatever that turned out to be.

My joggers were slung over the back of a chair, and I fished one of the lemon drops from the pocket. In the dim glow coming from my bedside light, I examined it, turning it over in my palm, licking it tentatively. It tasted different from the candies of my youth, not the standard fake lemon flavor but a brighter, more . . . puckery flavor. Like real lemonade. It reminded me of my mom, of how her hands always smelled. Perhaps these drops really did contain a little bit of kitchen magic. The thought made me smile.

I popped the candy in my mouth and got back into bed, then lay there staring up at the ceiling of my tiny dormer room, sucking on the hard ball, waiting for it to dissolve so I could go to sleep. It was the best lemon drop I'd ever had, the flavor just straddling sour and sweet. It tasted of bright July afternoons, of lemonade stands and paper cups and crunching ice cubes, of wading in the frigid water of Puget Sound, of laughter and a fizzle of joy in my chest for no reason at all.

I lay there sucking it as the minutes ticked by. Finally, it was just a sharp little sliver on my tongue. As I reached over to turn off the bed-side light, I paused. What had Aunt Gert told me? I had to say aloud one of my regrets in life, a decision I wanted to change. I glanced at the unicorn diary sitting on my bedside table. I thought of the frustrating conversation I'd had with Dad that morning and how hopelessly stuck I felt at the Eatery. I thought about the first two life goals on the list that felt so impossibly out of reach now. I thought of being an object at rest.

1. *Live in another country*

2. *Own my own restaurant somewhere amazing*

Two for one, inextricably linked in my mind. As I turned off the light there was only one word sitting on my tongue, fondness and re-gret as sharp as that sliver of lemon candy.

"Toast."

10

A harsh beeping roused me from a deep sleep. I sat up with a muffled groan, blinking in the pale gray light of early morning, and scrambled for the source of the horrible sound, nothing like my usual alarm, which played the June Carter Cash version of "Keep on the Sunny Side" every morning at five a.m. And then I froze, looking around in blurry confusion. This wasn't my bedroom.

I was sitting in a double bed with an old-fashioned carved wooden bed frame, wearing a pair of beige silk pajamas that were certainly not what I had been wearing when I'd fallen asleep. Heart pounding, I fumbled for the cell phone on the bedside table next to me and silenced the incessant beeping, then glanced around for my glasses, panic fluttering in my throat. Where was I? I found a pair of frames next to the cell phone, sleek round tortoiseshell ones with gold accents, not really my usual style. I tried them on hesitantly. The room sprang into focus. They were my prescription.

It was a small gabled room, outfitted with a comfortable-looking overstuffed armchair, a ponderous antique wardrobe, and a worn Persian rug. Curiouser and curiouser. I crawled on hands and knees to the foot of the bed and peered out a small French-paned window to the street below. It was a picturesque narrow lane flanked by small, brightly painted buildings crammed together cheek by jowl. A striped awning advertised CREAM TEA AND HOMEMADE SCONES from across the street. The name of the tea shop looked familiar. And suddenly I knew.

"Brighton." I sat back down on the bed with a thump, stunned. "I'm in England."

I'd always intended Toast to be located in Brighton, a charmingly quirky seaside resort town on England's south coast. Brighton had captivated me from my first visit, with its jaunty holiday air, shingle beach, and ornate Victorian pier. I'd even located the perfect building to house the café, an old converted factory in the North Laine area that was abandoned and for sale. But then my mother's death had put an end to all those aspirations. I'd never returned to Brighton and Toast had faded into a long-dormant desire. Until this morning.

I shook my head. Surely this was a dream. I'd fallen asleep thinking about Toast and my time in England, and now I was dreaming it. But somehow, in my gut, I knew that explanation, tidy as it was, wasn't entirely true. This felt all too real, vivid and solid, not fantastical like a dream. I felt down to my cold bare toes that I was actually in Brighton. How was it possible?

Suck on one of the lemon drops before bed and say aloud a thing you wish you could change, a regret from your life. Aunt's Gert's instructions came back to me. *Then go to bed, and when you wake up, you will live one day of your life as it might have been . . .*

Surely not. It was ridiculous to even entertain the notion. Impossible. And yet . . . I gazed out the window at the familiar street, hope fluttering in my stomach. I had been here before. Eleven years ago I'd indulged in a cream tea, sitting in the front window of that little shop across the street, smearing warm scones with clotted cream and rasp-berry jam.

Could it be true? Was I actually, amazingly, against all common sense, somehow living a different version of my life, one where Toast was a reality? It was a terrifying thought but oddly exciting. What did this mean? How long would it last? What had Aunt Gert said when she gave me the lemon drops? I closed my eyes and tried to remember, feeling a little panicky.

Don't be alarmed. The effects are only temporary. The following morn-ing, you'll return to your normal existence as if nothing has changed.

I remembered her saying those words, sipping tea like it was the most ordinary sentence in the world. Okay. I blew out a breath. Just a day then. Even if this wasn't a dream, if I was, indeed, somehow mi-raculously in Brighton, England, this was only temporary. I gave a little sigh of relief.

Picking up the cell phone, I glanced at the time and date. It was later than I normally slept, already past seven. The date read Wednes-day, February 23. I'd gone to sleep sucking on that lemon drop on Tuesday night, the twenty-second. Okay, so no weird juju with the space-time continuum. That was a relief. It was the day it was supposed to be. I was just not where I thought I would wake up. I looked around the room, then over at the tea shop again, my apprehension melting into something else, a growing sense of anticipation.

What if I had one beautiful, extraordinary day to revisit England, to actually see what my life would have been like had I chosen to open Toast? What a strange, improbable, amazing gift.

I shifted, realizing I was sitting on a hot water bottle, and extricated it. It was still lukewarm. I looked around the room cautiously, then was struck with another thought. What did I look like? Was I still me, or was this some weird *Quantum Leap* scenario where I'd switched bodies? My mom had loved *Quantum Leap* when I was a kid. She had a little crush on Scott Bakula and his chin dimple. I hopped up and peered at the oval mirror hanging next to the wardrobe. The reflection staring back was decidedly me, albeit with a few changes.

"A bob? Bold choice." My hair was smooth and sleekly bobbed and highlighted with caramel notes that didn't quite match my pale complexion. It washed me out a little, to be honest. I put my hands on my hips, noting to my surprise how bony they felt. I lifted my shirt and turned sideways in amazement. I was skinny, skinnier than I had been since I'd hit puberty. Chic skinny, with pronounced clavicles and wrist bones. In real life I wasn't overweight, but I had a few softer curves. Not in England, though. No wonder I felt chilled to the bone. No padding against that brisk seaside air.

I stared at sleek, skinny me in morbid fascination. My face looked older, a bit wan. Maybe it was the lighting. Or maybe chic skinny didn't really agree with me.

Just then the phone rang from the bedside table. I hesitated, then picked it up. The facial recognition feature unlocked the phone immediately.

"Hello?" Did my voice sound a little British? I could have sworn my accent had an English tinge. How posh.

"Well, this really does take the biscuit. He's gone and done it again, the bloody wanker." The woman on the other end had a strong northern English accent and sounded shrilly outraged. "While your lover boy's faffing about, we've got a regular dog's dinner of a delivery order over here. No sprouts, no swede. Just iceberg for the salads. It's not like we're over-egging the pudding to ask him to follow a simple list and just once, for the love of all that is holy, *deliver what we ordered*!"

Wincing, I held the phone away from my ear but could still hear her clearly, though her sentences were just as indecipherable. I heard her words but was scrambling to understand what they meant.

I had to think fast. Whatever this woman's relationship to me, she was looking to me for some sort of intelligible response. The only problem was, I hadn't the faintest idea what was going on. I was all of a sudden in way over my head.

"Um, sorry. Who is this?" I tried to buy time.

A long pause. "What do you mean who is this? It's *Nicola*. Your head chef. Remember me? Are you mad? How many pints did you have at the pub last night?" She sounded indignant.

"Uh, yes, must have been one too many. So sorry," I stalled, frantically trying to recall all the UK idioms I'd learned in my brief stint in London. What had she said about a pudding, a swede, and something about . . . biscuits? And who was lover boy?

"Where are you right now?" I gritted my teeth, holding the phone away from my ear, already expecting the explosion.

"Where do you think I'd be? Where I always am. Where we both bloody *live*." Her voice, incredibly, went even higher in pitch. "I'm at Toast, and you'd better get over here, or we're going to have nothing to offer when we open for brunch except bog standard Tesco house salad!"

"Right, ah. On my way." But she'd already hung up. I looked around, the reality of my situation sinking in a bit more. I was myself but not myself, in England, in a life I knew nothing about, apparently running my own restaurant with a highly volatile British chef. How in the world was I going to navigate a day in a life I didn't have the first clue about?

And who was lover boy? Was I single? Married? I glanced down at my hand. No ring. That would have been complicated. I didn't know where my underwear or toothbrush was. I didn't even know if this was actually my house. I shook my head. Surely I was still tucked up in bed at home in Magnolia, sleeping peacefully and dreaming lemon-scented dreams. Surely I'd awaken to the scent of Dad frying bacon and Daphne belting out Ariana Grande tunes.

But I had no time to linger over the marvelous and deeply unsettling improbability of it all. Whether it was a dream or real or I'd gone stark raving mad, I was late for something. I hadn't the faintest idea where to find it or what to do about it once I got there, and I was still in my pajamas and really needed to pee. First things first. I took a deep breath, gathered my composure, and went in search of the toilet.

Thirty minutes later I emerged into the pale, pearly light of a crisp late-winter English morning. I was feeling a bit steadier on my feet, having located the bathroom, my clothes, and breakfast in that order.

I'd surmised that it was, indeed, my apartment after finding a photo of myself with a group of people gathered around a simple black-and-white sign that read: TOAST. I studied the faces. All of us wore an expression that was a mixture of exhaustion and euphoria. I flipped the photo over. The caption read *Opening day, May 15, 2016.* Almost six years ago. Brighton. Toast. I'd done it. I felt a wave of bittersweet pride. In some other life I'd followed my dream and opened Toast.

The rest of the apartment was decorated in my usual vintage style, but it felt plain, a little forlorn. Nothing in the refrigerator except expired milk and a few wrinkled pears. I had no pets, just one small African violet sitting on the tiny kitchen table. Even it looked dejected, with a few fuzzy leaves curling brown at the tips. There was only one chair. Strangely there were no family photos. That gave me pause. Where were photos of Daphne and Dad? I wondered what my life was like here in England. Was I happy? Did I have friends, a social life? Was I in love?

My closet was a major disappointment. I'd stared for five minutes at the neat line of hangers in the wardrobe, eyes roving over the prim and proper beige pencil skirts and fitted navy blazers and crisp white button-downs. Where were my vintage tea dresses? My bright jewel-toned fitted wool cardigans, my polka-dotted cigarette pants? Was this really my closet? It was . . . sensible to the point of being boring. The most color I could find was a blouse with a pussycat bow in a very subdued blush color, which I donned, pairing it with tan slacks and pearl earrings. I looked in the mirror. The woman staring back at me looked eminently respectable and professional but a bit severe. A grown-up version of me. I looked like someone who didn't have a lot of fun.

Fortified with coffee (instant, weak; oh, England, why the love affair with instant coffee?) and a half packet of Hobnobs tea biscuits, happily the delicious milk chocolate—coated kind, I set off in search of Toast. The GPS on my phone indicated that it was a brisk fifteen-minute walk away in the North Laine area of the city, so I set off, keeping one eye on the route as I soaked up the atmosphere of Brighton.

Although still baffled by the surprising situation I'd found myself in upon waking, I couldn't help feeling elated to be back in this city that I loved. Oh, how I'd missed it! I'd come often during my semester abroad, taking the train down from London. I was impressed by London but found its size and pace intimidating. Brighton, with its warren of charming alleys, its gray seaside jauntiness, felt perfect. It was by turns a little bohemian and just slightly tourist-tacky, with the merest hint of a seedy feel beneath its charming historical veneer. I found it delightful.

The city hadn't changed much in the past decade. I inhaled the familiar salt smell tinged with a touch of greasy fish and chips. Seagulls cried from the beach a few blocks away, wheeling above me in the cool morning air. My phone's GPS led me through the quaint narrow alleys of the Lanes, past boutiques and jewelers and high-end antiques shops housed in darling little storefronts with bright-colored facades and fancy signs. There were no cars allowed in this section of Brighton, and since most of the shops didn't open for another hour or two, it was quiet and fairly empty.

I wandered around a little, drinking in the atmosphere. It was as intoxicating as it had been when I was in college. I closed my eyes and breathed it in. Whiffs of pavement and gasoline, acrid cigarette smoke, and always the cold air of the sea. Oh, how I had missed it. Oh, how good it felt to be back. And right then and there, I determined to enjoy it, every last second, for as long as it lasted. I still didn't know the whys and hows of my current situation, but I'd dreamed of this very thing for so long. I vowed to relish it now.

My route took me past the Royal Pavilion, an enormous, lavish, domed seaside pleasure palace built for one of the British monarchs. It looked suspiciously like a rip-off of the Taj Mahal, with turrets and bulbous domes. Then across Church Street and up Jubilee Street into the North Laine district with its hippy, edgy, student-friendly vibe and myriad shops, cafés, and cool pubs. I turned down another, smaller street, and then I saw it. I stood for a moment, just staring in awe. TOAST it read in simple letters. It was housed in the exact old brick building I'd always thought would be perfect, formerly a factory of some sort, with a gleaming black-painted front and huge glass-panel windows that could be opened up when the weather was nice. It had a pale yellow-and-white-striped awning fluttering in the breeze and a profusion of stone planters that were now, this late in winter, housing a few forlorn ornamental purple cabbages. It was utterly charming. It was how I'd always pictured it.

A tall young woman with long black braids coiled around the crown of her head and cascading down her back opened the front door and waved to me as she set a sandwich board out on the pavement. I returned the wave, sure that I was supposed to know her but having absolutely no idea who she was. This was going to be a very tricky day to navigate. I took a deep breath and crossed the street, holding my head high. The advice of my high school best friend, Ashley, came back to me. *Fake it till you make it.*

"You've got this." I felt a flutter of nerves mixed with anticipation. I was about to see just what I had been missing all these years.

11

The interior of Toast was just as charming as the outside. White walls reflected the light streaming in through the huge picture windows, and the wooden floor was painted a pale jade green. A jumble of endearingly mismatched tables and chairs dotted the main room, each decorated with a vintage cut-glass vase of winter branches. The entire back wall of the restaurant had floor-to-ceiling shelves stocked with local edible goods. Jars of East Sussex honey. Bottles of cider. Bunches of lavender and sage. It was cozy and serene and tidy. For so many years I'd dreamed of this place, and to see it here in real life was overwhelming. I felt a swell of emotion as I took it all in, pride mixed with sorrow, bittersweet.

The woman who had waved at me greeted me warmly, rolling her eyes at the noise coming from what I presumed was the kitchen at the back.

"She's in rare form this morning," she murmured to me. Jamaican British, I guessed by her accent. She was wearing a name tag, thank goodness.

"Thanks for the warning . . . Chandice," I said rather belatedly.

"I'll get everything sorted in the front of house before we open for brunch," she said. "You'll have enough on your hands with Nicola today."

"Great. Thanks." I took another long look around. The interior was just the right mixture of Scandinavian serene and offbeat inviting. I loved it. I wanted to live right here forever.

"Is that you I hear mucking about out there, Lolly?" A strident call from the back roused me, and I hurried down a passageway into a bright and gleaming industrial space. There were several crates of lettuce standing forlornly in a corner. A huge pot of something savory steamed on the stove. A sous-chef or member of the kitchen prep team stood at a long table, dicing and chopping a mountain of vegetables. Another team member stood at the stove, stirring several pots alternately. They both murmured a greeting, but no one looked up, keeping their eyes on their work. And in the middle of the kitchen stood a woman I assumed was Nicola.

Dressed in chef's whites, her arms akimbo, spiky blond crew cut sticking straight up, she wore white clogs and a thunderous expression. She was probably in her early fifties, short and sturdily built, with a work-worn face.

"Good morning." I decided to stick to general pleasantries until I got a feel for what exactly was going on around here.

"This is the last straw," she informed me bluntly. "I know you're shagging Colin, but he's got to go." She gestured dramatically to the bins of lettuce.

Oh boy. Who was Colin? Did "shagging" mean what I thought I remembered it meaning?

"What happened?" It seemed like the safest question.

She grimaced. "Does Colin grow some of the best produce in East Sussex? Yes. Are his heirloom tomatoes sweet enough to make the angels weep? Absolutely. But he can't get our bloody order straight. This is the third time he's mucked up this month. We can't keep scrambling to change the menu at the last minute or serve subpar dishes. It's true that I lust after his root vegetables, and I know you're a goner for those dreamy bedroom eyes, but you've got to find a different supplier. It's a matter of professional conduct." Speech concluded, she folded her arms and waited, her expression stony.

I stood there, mind racing. What could I possibly say? Then inspiration hit. "Absolutely, and I want to talk about this more thoroughly. Could we have a meeting tomorrow to talk this through?" Because tomorrow, presumably, if what Aunt Gert said was accurate, I would be safely back in my normal life and whatever strange sort of magic was at work would have ironed itself out to normalcy. I decided to put off as much as I could today, push it all to tomorrow and let the universe sort it out somehow. It was, I thought, a fairly good plan under the circumstances.

Nicola nodded curtly. "Fine. Tomorrow before we start. So what do we do about the menu today?"

"What have we got to work with?"

For the next twenty minutes we took an inventory of on-hand ingredients, bandied about ideas, and finally settled on replacing the salad for the eggs Benedict with roasted potatoes, and the swede (which I finally identified as rutabaga by surreptitiously googling it on my phone) with roasted parsnips instead. Having to think on the fly was both hair-raisingly terrifying and sort of fun in an electrifying, adrenaline-fueled way.

"Are we all set?" I asked finally when we'd agreed on an alternate menu.

Nicola nodded. "It'll do." She wiped her sleeve across her brow. "I'm getting too old for this utter nonsense. I need a bloody holiday."

"You should take one," I answered neutrally.

"Ha." She snorted. "That's rich coming from the woman who hasn't taken a single day of holiday since we opened."

"Really?" That couldn't be right. Hadn't Toast been open for almost six years?

She sighed dramatically. "This business will suck your life away. But we're addicts, right?" She shook her head. "Look at us. What a pair. Working all the time, no vacations somewhere warm and tropical where they put umbrellas in your fruity drinks. Before you know it we'll blink and we'll be sixty—alone and wrinkled and eating a tinned pudding in front of the telly."

What a cheering thought. Really, I hadn't had a vacation in almost six years? What about seeing my family? Going home to Seattle?

"It can't have been six years?" I protested. "When was the last time I was back in the States?" I knew it was risky to ask a question that could seem odd to her, but I had to know.

She shrugged. "No idea. Not since I started working here."

I paused, taken aback. I hadn't been home in almost six years? What in the world did that mean? What about my dad and Daphne? There was a niggling sensation in my stomach, the premonition that something was amiss, stronger this time. I would never not see them for that long. It was unthinkable.

Leaving Nicola in capable command of the kitchen, I discreetly poked around until I located my office, thankfully identified by my name on the door. It was oddly similar to my office back at the Eatery, albeit slightly larger and with a window that opened. Definitely an upgrade.

I sank into the chair at my desk and took a deep, gasping breath. I'd done it. Navigated the first full hour of my alternate life. Once my pulse had slowed and I was feeling not quite so high on adrenaline, I began to spy on myself. The office was far more lived-in than my house had been. Tidy but cluttered. A mug of cold, bitter coffee balanced on a stack of ledgers, a laptop open to an accounts page that showed, at first glance, that Toast was in the black. That was a relief.

I opened the desk drawers. A toothbrush and deodorant and an extra set of clothes. A historical novel that still had the receipt tucked under the front cover. Apparently, I didn't have much time for reading. Still no family photos anywhere in sight. Just one of my mother as a young woman in Denmark. She was standing by the sea next to a large rock on which was perched the famous bronze *Little Mermaid* statue. They both wistfully gazed out across the water. I'd never seen the photo before, though her thick golden hair and the strong set of her shoulders were unmistakable.

I pulled out my phone and scrolled through the names, curious to see who was listed in there. So few I recognized. Most seemed like business associates. Thomas Drew—butcher. Kate Fowler—organic flower supplier. Eve wasn't listed in my phone, which gave me pause. Why was she not in my contacts? Surely we were still friends? It was a long but strangely impersonal list of contacts. I sat back and gazed around me, feeling a bit lonely, trying to get a handle on the shape of this life. Who was I? What kind of life had I built for myself? Was I happy? Was I living the dream?

A knock at the door pulled me from my questions. Chandice stuck her head in.

"Hugh just dropped off the cheese selection for the week. I thought you'd like to sample?"

I perked up immediately. Sampling cheese sounded fun. I was starving. The Hobnobs hadn't been particularly filling. The light, airy dining room was a beehive of activity. Four servers buzzed around, readying tables, wrapping silverware. Outside someone was watering the ornamental cabbages. I sat at a table with Chandice and tasted a half dozen local cheeses. A sharp English cheddar with a bite that lin-

gered just at the hinge of your jaw, a creamy goat cheese lavished with
a sweet onion chutney. Stuffing the last of a very toothsome local blue
cheese into my mouth, I looked around at the happy bustle with satisfaction. This is what I had always dreamed of, this bright hive of positive energy.

Chandice sampled the cheeses with me, then brought up a few
points of business. I muddled through the conversation by asking her
what she thought was best and agreeing with all of her suggestions.
Afterward we chatted for a few moments. There was a lovely sense of
calm about her. I could see why I'd hired her.

"How long have you been at Toast now?" I asked.

She calculated in her head. "It will be five years next month."

"And do you enjoy working here?"

"Absolutely," she said without hesitation. "I've been working at res-
taurants since I was sixteen, and this is by far my favorite. I like what
we create here, the experience we give people. It's a special thing we've
built."

I sensed a hesitation.

"Is there a but?" I prompted.

She smiled with a touch of self-deprecation. "My family always asks
why I chose this life. They don't understand. The long hours on the
floor. Difficult customers. Your feet aching so badly you can hardly
walk up the steps to your flat. Never a weekend off. You know it's hard
to make a living in this business. They want me to get married and give
them grandchildren or at least get a proper job with normal hours."

I nodded. I identified. She was describing every day for me at the
Eatery. And now here at Toast too. Sore feet and surly patrons happened regardless of location. It was the restaurant life.

We sat for a minute in silence. I wanted to ask her so many things
about myself. Was I happy? What sort of boss was I? But I didn't know
how to do it without seeming weird.

"Is now a good time to confirm the menu changes for today?" she asked.

Scanning the menu she brought me, I found myself nodding approvingly. Everything was local, sustainable, and ethically sourced. There were only a dozen or so dishes on the menu, but each was mouthwatering. Sussex cider pork belly served with homemade applesauce, roasted parsnips, and caramelized onions. A salmon eggs Benedict with house-made English muffins and fresh local free-range eggs. Several vegetarian and vegan options with a South Asian flair. It all sounded delicious.

As we finished up the menu changes and Chandice went off to print the new ones, my phone rang. It was the florist who was delivering new seasonal table greenery. Her van had broken down outside of Bolney, wherever that was. I assured her a late delivery would be no problem, then made a note to tell Chandice about it as soon as I could. No sooner had I hung up the phone than a wine supplier popped in the door, wanting to discuss our order for our Saturday champagne brunches. Apparently, they were very popular. I put him off by asking him to come back tomorrow.

At the same time, I was fielding questions from the servers and was summoned back to the kitchen twice more by Nicola to discuss various tweaks to the brunch specials. By the end of two hours my head was spinning. I escaped to my office with a warm cheese scone I'd nicked from a cooling tray. Munching the scone, I tapped the wine merchant's next visit into the calendar app on my phone.

My calendar was busy. Appointments and reminders from early morning to evening most days. Once or twice I saw the name Colin. Otherwise it all looked like work. I studied the calendar with a frown. I didn't seem to have much of a social life apart from this Colin character, he of the reported bedroom eyes. And where was Rory in this life? Why were we not together? I'd been keeping an eye out for any sign of his presence in my life, both in my apartment and here at Toast, but there had been nothing. He wasn't even listed as a contact in my phone. I frowned. I had no way of figuring out what had gone wrong, why we were still not together even here in this alternate life. That bothered me more than a little.

On impulse I googled his name, glancing around my office as I did so, feeling a little furtive and guilty. I had a strict no-googling-Rory policy in my real life. It kept me sane. In real life I knew he was married to Emily, and it did me no good to follow his life. But here, I wanted to know if things were different. Within a minute I found his social media profile. It listed him as working for the Tampa Bay Mutiny. That hadn't changed. His profile pic was taken at a soccer game. He and Emily in matching baseball caps and sunglasses, laughing into the camera, arms twined around each other. I stared at the photo in disappointment, then clicked out of it. Evidently some things had stayed the same.

Feeling oddly deflated, I navigated to the photo app on my phone, curious to see what it could tell me about my life. I felt a little like I was voyeuristically spying on someone else's life. Technically it was my own life, but it still felt illicit somehow. I scrolled through more than a hundred photos before I stopped. What the photos showed about my own life was just plain depressing.

Almost all of the photos were taken at Toast or with the Toast employees at what looked like various pubs. Lots of group shots of me holding a pint with people I recognized as kitchen and waitstaff. There were a couple photos of me and a tall, sweet-looking man whom I surmised was Colin. In all the shots we appeared to be hill walking or standing in a large garden, me holding a bunch of beets or an armful of zucchini. Nicola was right, Colin did have bedroom eyes. In the photos he looked tall and a little gangly, but adorable, wearing an English driving cap and a sheepish grin. He had a freckled complexion and ginger hair. He reminded me of Rory. Apparently I have a type.

I sighed and clicked off the phone. In some ways Toast was just as I imagined it, but in other ways this day was not quite what I'd envisioned. It wasn't just the question of Rory, although that weighed heavily on my mind. It was my apparent lack of a good work-life balance. Did I have friends, hobbies, interests outside the restaurant? The photos I'd just seen would seem to indicate that I did not. When I'd spent all those hours imagining Toast, I hadn't really considered the pace and the workload. I'd grown up in a restaurant. I should have known better, but somehow I'd imagined Toast as a little bubble of peace and prosperity. I'd imagined the customer's experience, not the hectic juggle behind the scenes to provide that memorable dining experience. I slipped my feet out of my kitten heels, already regretting the choice of footwear. Did British me have no common sense when it came to shoes? I longed for my clogs, the friend of servers everywhere.

A knock at the door. Chandice poked her head in. "Sorry to be a bother, but seems we've hit a snag with the reservation system. We've somehow overbooked several tables."

"Be right there." I stuffed the last of the scone into my mouth and slipped my pinchy shoes back on with a groan.

12

Three thirty pm. A few stragglers were sipping mimosas and picking at the remains of their meals, but the frantic pace of the last few hours had finally slowed. Thank goodness. I was starving and had a dull headache from racing around in a dozen different directions all morning while trying to figure out how to juggle a life and a staff and a restaurant that I really knew nothing about. I'd pulled it off, though, and it had been oddly satisfying to be a part of what I'd dreamed of building for so long. Tiring, but satisfying. The atmosphere at Toast all morning had reminded me of the energy I remembered from the Eatery growing up, when the tables had been full and the air had buzzed with conversation and laughter.

I stood back now and watched an older couple clink glasses and finish off their second mimosas, gazing deeply into each other's eyes. Next to them, a family party of six celebrating an engagement talked and argued and laughed, reaching across the table to snag the last bites of one another's meals and sneak crumbs from the cheese board. I smiled in satisfaction. It was what I loved, inviting people into deeper connection over good food served with care, fostering a simple kind of joy.

But now, after several full-on hours without a moment to catch my breath, I needed to clear my head and get some air.

"Can you manage if I slip out for a few minutes?" I asked Chandice, who waved me out the door with an assurance that she could handle things in my absence. The dinner rush wouldn't start for a couple of hours yet, so this slow time was the perfect opportunity to slip away. I grabbed my phone and headed out the door.

There were myriad things for me to work on. There was a substantial stack of bills waiting to be paid back in my office, and when I checked my phone I found voice mails from an electrician about a faulty wiring issue, a local charity asking for donations for their raffle, and a woman who had trained in Paris wondering if we were hiring a pastry chef. I ignored them all and headed to the beach.

It was a brisk walk, just long enough to clear my head. I wound my way through the North Laine district, past antiques shops, falafel joints, artists' studios, and secondhand clothing boutiques. The beach was nearly deserted at this time of day, cloudy and chilly in February. Shivering, I pulled my stylish but thin coat closer and wished for the angora sweater (also in blush) that I'd spied in my subdued new wardrobe earlier in the day.

The pebbles crunched under my feet as I picked my way down to the water. The cry of the gulls wheeling above was both raucous and lonely at the same time. I took a deep, steadying breath, but the briny air did not center me. It smelled different than at home. No sweet smell of decaying kelp, like seaweed salad sitting a little too long in the fridge. No fringe of hazy purple-blue mountains on the horizon. Here was just the whitecapped slate gray of the water stretching to meet the paler gray sky. I inhaled deeply again, this time catching the oily scent of frying fish and chips. From farther down the beach, near the ornate Victorian pier, there came the high jangle of carnival music.

I pulled out my phone and dialed a number. It was one of only a handful of names I'd recognized in my phone, and I'd been thinking about calling all day. Why had I not been home in over six years? I needed someone to tell me. One ring. Two. Three.

"Hello?"

I let out a breath I didn't know I'd been holding. "Hey, Daphne, it's me."

A long pause. "Lolly?" The cold, questioning tone in her voice took me aback.

"Sorry, I know it's early there. Just . . . calling to say hi."

"Oh," she sounded surprised, not necessarily in a good way. Did we not speak often? I was getting the uncomfortable feeling that something was very amiss between me and my family.

"It's fine. I was up anyway. I'm studying right now."

"Oh, what for?"

"I'm trying to get into nursing school. I've got my CNA license, but Aegis pays way better if you're a nurse than just an aide, and we could use the money." There was a hard edge to her voice, a flatness that I'd never heard before. I scrambled to connect the dots. Aegis was a group of senior-care communities in Seattle. CNA certification. Was she working as an aide there now? What had happened to Cornish and her dance aspirations? I'd never heard her talk about wanting to be a nurse.

"That's great." My voice sounded too cheerful in my own ears. "You'll be a great nurse."

"I should go," she said abruptly. "I only answered because I thought it was an emergency."

"Ah, no emergency. Just wanted to hear your voice."

Another beat. "Oh. Well, here it is." I could feel her impatience over the connection. She didn't want to talk to me, but I wasn't ready to let her go. I had to know what had happened, where we stood, what had gone wrong. Where were all our family photos? And why hadn't I been home in so long?

"Um, how's Dad these days?"

She sighed. "Okay, I guess. You know he never really recovered after you left for England and the diner closed. It gutted him." There was accusation in her tone. "He volunteers at Union Gospel Mission but other than that, he just watches baseball and cooks dinner for us when I come home after the day shift, and that's pretty much it."

"Oh." I was taken aback. "And how about you? How are you?" I knew I sounded like I was interviewing her, which I was. I was desperately trying to understand the contours of our family dynamics.

"What's this about, Lolly?" Daphne sounded suspicious. "Why are you all of a sudden interested in our lives?"

"Just . . . just wanted to catch up. I miss you," I stammered. A family of Brits with a chubby toddler in tow passed me, the child crying, trailing a bucket and sand shovel, his legs limp as overcooked noodles.

"Oh yeah, since when?" Her tone was a challenge. "You went off to England a decade ago. You haven't come home in years. You left us. And now you *miss* us? Well, thanks for that, but it's a little too late. We're doing just fine, so you can go back to your super-successful restaurant and cool English life. You don't need to worry about us."

"Daphne, that's not what I meant," I protested.

"I've got to go." Her tone was final. "I've got a lot of studying to do."

"Okay." My voice was small, subdued. My heart hurt. "Good luck on your test."

"Thanks." *Click.* She hung up.

I stared at the phone, my eyes welling with sudden tears. "Love you much," I whispered, but there was no one on the other end to complete the familiar farewell. Daphne was already gone. Shivering a little with cold and sadness, I tucked the phone back in my pocket and trudged up the pebble beach toward Toast, stunned by this hidden cost of my dream come true.

13

I woke with a start and a searing headache and sat bolt upright in bed, gazing wildly around me. I was once more in my own familiar bedroom, wearing my old green Portland State sweatshirt. What time was it? What day was it? I checked my phone. Five a.m. on Wednesday, February 23. The day I had just finished in Brighton, England.

I flopped back on the bed with a groan, both relieved and a touch disappointed to be home once more. So it *had* been a dream. Of course it had. There was no Toast. No too-thin Brighton version of me with unflattering caramel highlights and a subdued wardrobe. But if it was a dream, why did I have this wretched hangover?

After Toast had closed in the wee hours of the morning, the staff had all gone out to a nearby pub. Chandice had been there and Nicola and a few others, and then, just as I was about to call it a night, Colin showed up. I recognized him from the photos on my phone.

He leaned in to kiss me, and I pulled him onto the dance floor instead. We danced awkwardly, my shoes sticking to the ale-soaked floor as Abba blared from the speakers. Colin twined his arms around me when a slow song came on and pulled me close. He smelled like turned earth and grated ginger, lovely but entirely unfamiliar.

At eye level with his pillowy lips, seeing the way he smiled at me with genuine tenderness, I wondered if in this other life I really loved him. He was perfectly sweet, but I felt nothing for him. In fact, dancing with him made me miss Rory all the more. I pulled back, feeling guilty and uncomfortable. Colin was alone in his affections. I was the interloper, the cuckoo wrongly placed in this relationship. By the end of the night I'd managed to avoid kissing him, spilled tartar sauce down my blouse, and drunk too much beer. It all felt surreal, like another person in another life, which, in a way, it was.

I closed my eyes, exhausted. Downstairs I could hear Dad whistling, and the enticing scent of bacon was curling under the door. Why was Dad making bacon at five in the morning? I usually rose alone and was at the diner baking pies by the time the rest of the household got up. Speaking of which, I needed to get moving, hangover notwithstanding. There were pies to make.

"Girls, bacon's on," Dad called up the stairs, his voice smoker-husky and so familiar.

I licked my lips and grimaced. My mouth was fuzzy, breath sour with the taste of British ale. I sniffed my fingers, catching the faintest lingering reek of tartar sauce and shepherd's pie, the unmistakable odor of an old British pub. I could swear it had been real. Real and elating and disappointing all at once. I swallowed hard, trying to orient myself once more to this life, this reality.

A sharp rap at the door and Daphne stuck her head in. I scrambled up and fumbled for my glasses sitting on my bedside table, finding my familiar aluminum cat-eye frames. Daphne came into focus as I slipped them on. She was wearing her yoga pants and an athletic top, her hair pulled up in a messy bun on the top of her head, yoga mat rolled up and slung over her shoulder by its strap.

"You awake?" she asked. "I'm subbing for a six a.m. class this morning, and Dad wanted to get up and make us breakfast before we leave. I told him not to bother—bacon and yoga aren't a great mix first thing in the morning—but he was pretty set on it."

"I'll eat your bacon." I hopped out of bed and hugged her so hard I squeezed the breath from her.

She squealed and pulled back. "Hey, what was that for?"

I couldn't respond around the lump in my throat. I remembered her voice on the beach, the flat, unwelcoming tone that spoke of hurt and rejection. She'd been working as a nursing-home aide. She'd felt so cold. Her words had been so dismissive, this girl I'd sacrificed so much for. But that was the point, wasn't it? In my English Toast life, I'd sacrificed entirely different things. So maybe that was the reality, that we sacrifice no matter what path we choose.

Daphne gave me an assessing look. "Are you okay? You look pale . . . well, paler than normal anyway." She leaned forward and sniffed me. "And you smell gross. Like . . . old beer."

"Weird." I tried to give a nonchalant shrug. Inside I was melting with relief that she was standing here in my doorway, criticizing how I smelled, relaxed and secure in our sisterly bond. I didn't know what exactly had happened in Brighton. Was it real? A dream? A little of each? I only knew it had changed nothing and everything at the same time.

Downstairs the smoke alarm went off, and Dad started swearing, using a colorful string of expletives he'd learned in the navy. Bertha started barking at the smoke alarm noise, adding to the commotion. I looped my arm through Daphne's, and together we went down to breakfast, back to my normal life. I'd never felt such a bittersweet mixture of resignation and relief.

"What happened to me?" I demanded, facing Aunt Gert's ample backside. She was wedged under a booth in the Eatery's empty dining room, scrubbing gunk off the underside of the table, preparing for us to open. I'd just been taking the pies out of the oven when I saw her come through the kitchen with a bucket of water.

She crawled out from under the table and sat back on her heels, rag in hand. "I will never know how people manage to get mashed potatoes in the rivets of the screws." She shook her head, then surveyed me. "So you did as I said and took a lemon drop." It was not a question.

I looked around and leaned closer, even though we were alone in the diner. "I did."

"And?" She dipped her rag into a bucket of soapy water, then dried her hands on the coat of the boxy, drab blue Mao suit she was sporting today. She'd told me once that she'd picked it up in Beijing on a visit sometime after the Cultural Revolution. It was one of the most unflattering garments I'd ever seen a person actually wear in real life.

"I woke up in Brighton, England, the owner of my very own local farm-to-table restaurant."

"Sounds remarkable."

I hesitated. "Yes. It was. The restaurant was at least."

"And the other part?" She was watching me with those sharp blue eyes.

I sank down in a booth next to her and put my chin in my hands. "It was what I dreamed of for so long . . . but it was different than I imagined. Toast was fabulous, a dream come true, but there was another side to it." I hesitated. "I had no life outside the restaurant, no friends or hobbies. And there were . . . other consequences, ones I wasn't expecting." I thought of Daphne and Dad and winced.

"That's often the way," she said thoughtfully. She wrung out her rag and scrubbed vigorously at the mint-green piping on the bench seat across from me. "When we make a choice, we necessarily limit all the other choices. Every path narrows our options, every decision closes many other doors. Yet we make a choice hoping we're trading all the other options for the one that will be the best."

"I guess that makes sense," I agreed.

"If you could choose that version of your life, would you?" Aunt Gert asked it casually, but her hands stilled on the booth's worn vinyl seat, waiting for my answer.

I hesitated, considered long and hard. Was my life in England better? To be my own boss, own my own space, serve people the food I'd always dreamed of, create a beautiful experience for them. And to do it in Brighton, England. The dream of living abroad. It was a heady combination. But what of that wan face in the mirror? The six years without a vacation? Colin of the bedroom eyes whom I felt nothing for. And the relational cost—the hostility in Daphne's voice, the cold indifference. I would gain my dream but lose my family. It was why I had given up Toast in the first place, because I could not give up my family for my own ambitions, no matter how tempting. Was that still true?

"I don't know," I said finally. "The cost seems so high."

Aunt Gert pressed her lips together and resumed scrubbing. "So perhaps you have not yet found your bliss after all. Well, you have two lemon drops left. Use them wisely and see what you discover."

With a glance at the clock hanging over the door to the kitchen, I stood but lingered for a minute.

"Aunt Gert, what happened to me in Brighton . . . was it a dream? A hallucination? It couldn't be real, right?"

Aunt Gert sat back on her heels. Her hair was wisping up in a little tuft at the back of her head like a Kewpie doll. For a moment she looked every bit of her eighty years.

"Let's just say those little drops transcend our narrow notions of time and space," she replied.

I struggled to glean a definitive answer from her philosophical words. "Is this some quantum physics concept? Parallel universes? Is it a dream, like Scrooge in *A Christmas Carol*? How does it work?"

She shrugged. "To be honest, I don't know. The woman who gave them to me never explained the mechanics. I just know they do work. Somehow they transcend the confines of our singular choices, our little linear worlds, and they show us higher truths. How do they work? They are in the realm of mystery and revelation. Label it a miracle or magic or string theory, a touch of the Divine, Charles Dickens, or Stephen Hawking, or whatever you like, the important part is not the *how*, it's the *what*. What do those little drops uncover about your life? What truths do they speak to your heart? That is the question you should be asking."

I nodded, feeling strangely both chastened and inspired.

"I don't know what to choose for the other two drops," I told her. "Any tips?"

Aunt Gert tossed her rag into the bucket and straightened, groaning slightly as her joints popped. "That's not for me to know, Lolly. Choose the things you cannot seem to reconcile in your heart, the losses or regrets you hold so closely you cannot imagine letting them go. The wise Saint Augustine says that we must be emptied of that which fills us that we may be filled with those things which we are lacking. I'm paraphrasing of course. But the point is, what is your heart longing for? What is lacking in your life? Focus on those things. And remember, whatever you do, keep following your bliss. Be honest. Pay attention. Seek joy. That is the key to unlocking your destiny."

I put my hand into my pocket, feeling the two hard little drops. Two regrets. Two chances. What did my heart yearn for? What would I choose?

14

"Hey, Lolly." Rory rolled his busboy cart past where I was dishing up slices of pie and putting them in the refrigerated pie case, ready to be served. It was a raw November evening, and the dinner rush was finally tapering off after a hectic few hours. He tossed a few bills on the counter in front of me. "Those two salesmen at table five left this for you."

"Oh, thanks," I said. I smoothed out the bills and my eyes widened. "This is almost as much as their entire dinner bill." I gasped.

Rory grinned. "Looks like being cute is paying off for you again, huh?"

I flushed and picked up an old bread roll, tossing it at him. It landed on his cart. "Good thing they're not tipping you for your aim," he teased.

"Shut up." I tucked the money into my apron. I couldn't meet Rory's eyes. It had been happening more and more lately. I felt so self-conscious when I was around him, aware of his every movement, as though I had a Rory-seeking radar embedded in my brain. If he was in the vicinity, I knew exactly where he was.

It was my sophomore year of high school and Rory had been work-

ing as a busboy at the Eatery for the past few months since school
started. It was a hard and menial job that didn't pay well, certainly not
as well as his job at the golf course had over the summer. I wasn't really
sure why he'd taken my parents up on their offer of the busboy job, but
I was glad. It meant I got to be around him almost every day.

"Okay, back to the salt mines," Rory said over his shoulder, rolling
the cart toward a recently emptied table by the front window. I watched
him go.

"You got it bad, girl," Crystal, the only other waitress at the Eatery,
observed, coming up close to me at the pie case. I was holding the pie
server in one hand and a dessert plate in the other, doing absolutely
nothing except watch Rory walk away.

"What?" I startled at her sudden appearance.

"Don't blame you. He's a cutie. That tight ass." Crystal stood next
to me, arms folded, and watched Rory bus a four top. She smelled like
mint gum and nicotine because she was trying to quit smoking for the
umpteenth time. Thankfully Rory seemed unaware of Crystal's scru-
tiny.

"I don't know what you mean," I denied primly, though I could feel
myself flushing a telltale bright red. I opened the dessert case and slid
in a few slices of pie on plates, trying to cool my face down with the
refrigerated air. Was I that obvious? Did I light up like an incandescent
bulb the moment he walked in the room? I felt like I did. This was *Rory*
we were talking about. The sweet gangly boy across the street. The one
who had taken care of me and bandaged my thumb. My good friend.
Except I couldn't quite seem to see him like that anymore.

At fifteen my awareness of boys was burgeoning, and I had suddenly started to take notice of Rory in a new way. We'd been close
ever since our failed New Year's Day polar plunge. Once a month or so
we'd hike down to South Beach to hang out together at our secret
beach spot, and we still saw each other on Monday nights for our par-

ents' poker night—but this was something different. Okay, the truth was that I'd developed a massive crush on Rory, my first. He'd sprung up over the summer and was now standing a few inches taller than me. For a girl who'd hit five foot nine, a boy who was taller than me was impressive. He was a star player on the high school soccer team, the best striker they had. He played every game, and I was in the stands for each one. I called it school spirit, but I watched only one player on that field. The bright coppery sheen of his hair under the lights, his nimble movements as he quick-footed around the other team's defense to score, the way his Adam's apple bobbed as he drank deeply from a water bottle at the end of a game.

And then, after he started working at the Eatery, we were around each other almost every day after school. I'd take orders and keep one eye on him, noticing the lean, ropy muscles of his forearms as he stacked dirty dishes, the agile twist of his torso as he wiped down booths. He was a hard worker, and the customers liked him. He had an easy way with people no matter their age. He could crack jokes with white-haired grandpas, impress mothers with his polite "Yes, ma'am," and charm little boys and girls by pulling pennies from behind their ears, his one and only magic trick. I loved watching him interact with the customers, loved seeing their faces light up like mine did when they spoke to him.

I was proud of him, this boy I couldn't seem to get out of my thoughts. I wanted the world to see how special he was too. God help me, I'd written "Lolly Shaw" in my unicorn diary in precise cursive script at least a hundred times. It was embarrassing and thrilling all at the same time. I was utterly besotted.

"You're telling me you don't have the hots for that boy?" Crystal smirked, popping her gum. "Okay, you just keep telling yourself that, girlfriend." Blue eye shadow had gone out in the last decade, but Crystal had missed the memo.

"I don't think of him like that. He's like a brother to me," I protested, a little louder than I meant to. I glanced up to find Rory watching us, a stack of dirty plates balanced on his arm. He had a strange expression on his face, and when our eyes met he looked away quickly. I had a sinking feeling he'd heard me. "Truly." I lowered my voice, cheeks flaming. "We're just friends."

"Uh-huh," Crystal gave me a knowing look. "Whatever you say. By the way, you're red as a tomato."

I fled to the kitchen, mortified, and managed to avoid Rory and Crystal for the rest of the night. Of course, I had been lying to Crystal. Even if I wouldn't admit it, Rory filled my thoughts during the day and more than once I'd awakened in the night with an ache spooling low in my belly, flushed with longing from a heated Technicolor dream about him, about us.

On nights like tonight when he brought over my tip, I suspected Rory might be flirting with me. Sometimes I glanced up to find his eyes fixed on me from across the room, but really I had no idea if he felt the same way about me as I felt about him. And that was absolutely terrifying because as much as I denied it, I was hopelessly, completely, utterly falling head over heels for Rory Shaw.

15

After my single day at Toast and subsequent early-morning conversation with Aunt Gert, I lasted approximately two-thirds of the workday at the Eatery before I texted Eve.

> Something's happened. Can I come over?

She replied immediately.

> I've got gin.

I pled a headache with Dad and Aunt Gert and left work early. The headache was convenient, but it wasn't a lie. I still felt hungover from the late pub night in Brighton the night before. I swallowed two aspirin with a tall glass of water and headed out the door. Daphne was coming in to help with the dinner rush, so they would be fine without me for a few hours.

I hopped into Florence, my battered old Volvo station wagon, a relic

I'd inherited from my parents when I turned eighteen. I was unreasonably fond of her despite the fact that the passenger door was jammed shut, the electrical components were finicky, and she was an unfortunate color best described as banana pudding. I battled through rush hour traffic and waited in line for the ferry. Soon Florence and I were gliding across Puget Sound, away from the high-octane buzz of the tech city, toward the peaceful remoteness of Vashon Island. I needed to clear my head, and Eve's little farm was the best place I could think of to do it.

A scant few miles from Seattle, Vashon Island always seemed a world apart. Gray whales and seals cruised the calm waters, the beaches were almost empty and achingly picturesque, and the island had no less than ten farm stands selling everything from homemade strawberry jam to lettuce on the old-fashioned honor system. Vashon was both rurally charming and decidedly hippie, a Mayberry for the Woodstock crowd. No wonder Eve had found her place there.

I drove the ten minutes from the ferry dock to Eve's farm through rolling wooded hills, pushing the speed limit and racing past the few other cars on the road. My brain felt like a hive of bees, throbbing with the high-pitched buzzing of alarm or excitement, I couldn't quite tell which. I had to talk to Eve.

I found her in the tidy red barn, milking the goats and listening to the Eurythmics turned up loud. She was an ardent lover of eighties synth-pop dance-rock bands. Dressed in a plaid flannel shirt with the sleeves rolled up to the elbows, Carhartt jeans, and her old pair of green Hunter rain boots, she had a bandanna tied over her pink hair and was coaxing a goat toward a pair of wooden milking stands.

"Oh, good, you're just in time. Here, you milk Daisy," Eve said by way of greeting. "I'll handle Dot." Holding the goat firmly between her knees, she whipped out her iPhone and turned down the music to a conversational level, then led the brown-and-white animal over next to me and secured her in the milking stand. She fastened her own goat into the other milking stand, shooed me toward my milk crate and pail, and got to work.

I didn't really want to milk goats at the moment, not in the midst of an existential crisis when my most fundamental life choices had been thrown into question, but I obediently sat down on the upturned plastic milk crate and patted Daisy's side. She was chewing the contents of a tray of grain and didn't seem to mind. I was not really dressed for farm work. My pleated gray tartan wool skirt and sunny yellow fitted sweater were ill-suited for a milking stool. I'd been in such a hurry to get here I hadn't bothered to change. Oh well. I tucked my skirt under my knees and got to work.

"Sorry, girl." I took hold of the long, tear-shaped teat and pulled rhythmically. A second later there was the satisfying hiss and ping of milk hitting the metal bucket. I was not a newcomer to the world of milking goats. I had spent enough time on this farm to consider myself goat-competent. Although I didn't plan on taking up goat farming anytime soon, I loved the atmosphere of the farm and found the rhythms of life here soothing, especially the slower human pace. I also loved the soothing greens and blues of nature in the Pacific Northwest, the spicy scent of rain-washed evergreens, the bracing chill of salt-laced sea breezes.

"So what's up?" Eve asked me. She bent down and murmured sweet nothings to Dot as she milked her, then glanced up again. "Rough day?" In the background Annie Lennox wailed quietly about love being a stranger.

I took a deep breath, sniffing sweet hay and the dusty, earthy funk of the goats. "Something really weird happened to me." And then I told her all about the lemon drops and Aunt Gert and Toast and Brighton.

I relayed all the details I could remember, every little thing, even Colin and the tartar sauce at the pub and my painful conversation with Daphne, even waking up with sour ale breath this morning.

When I was done, I darted a cautious look at Eve. She had stopped milking Dot and was sitting on her milk crate, arms on her knees, hands hanging loose, looking dumbfounded. "It was a dream, right? You dreamed you were in England?"

I shrugged. "I don't honestly know. I don't think so. It felt so real. I think somehow I was really there. I think I actually lived a day of the life I could have had."

Eve gave me an assessing look, as though she were taking an internal step back and trying to determine the state of my mental health. She chewed her lip and said nothing. Slowly, she took her phone from her pocket and paused Annie Lennox belting out "Here Comes the Rain Again."

"Don't look at me like that. I'm not crazy."

"I don't think you're crazy. But I do think dear Aunt Gert gave you acid-trip candy for your birthday." She raised an eyebrow. "I don't know what's in those candies—LSD, some extra-potent cannabis, magic 'shrooms. Whatever it was, it's obviously strong stuff." She released Dot from the milking stand. The goat jumped friskily away to join the others in the barn.

I shook my head. "It wasn't an acid trip. It was too normal, just a normal day running Toast. No floating purple elephants or trippy stuff. Just normal me, in uncomfortable shoes, running a restaurant in England."

Eve opened her mouth, then shut it again. She seemed at a loss for words, a rarity for her. One of the goats, Susan B. Anthony I think it was, wandered over and nipped the cuff of her flannel shirt. She brushed the goat away and slipped off the shirt, revealing a black ribbed tank top underneath. It put the flower garden climbing up her arm and spreading across her shoulder on full display.

She'd gotten the tattoos one at a time, one or two a year, ever since her meltdown. Each one stood for something specific in the language of flowers. A white chrysanthemum bloomed on the inside of her wrist for truth. A fern frond arched across her inner arm for sincerity. Delicate yellow sprigs of rue traced their way up her bicep for grace and clarity. A pink rose for happiness peeked from her shoulder blade. Together they symbolized a woman who was discovering her true path in life, uncovering her authentic self on the journey. I was the one who had first introduced her to the language of flowers, the knowledge passed down from my mother to me. But Eve had made the language her own, a testament to finding her way.

"I know it sounds crazy," I said quietly. "And I can't explain what happened, not exactly. But after my day in England, I've realized something. I thought about it all the way over on the ferry. Aunt Gert asked me if I would choose Toast, England, that life if I could. And the answer is no. After seeing what it would really be like, what I would have to give up, I wouldn't change my life now to have that other version of it, not Toast and Brighton, not that distance from my family. And that's important to know. Disappointing, but important." I released Daisy from the wooden contraption that held her in place, and she daintily pranced off, little black hooves kicking up bits of straw. We were silent for a few minutes. I waited nervously. Eve was my best friend. What if she didn't believe me? What if she dismissed me as crazy? I wouldn't blame her a bit.

"No *is* a good answer. Sometimes it's better than a yes." Eve moved toward the spacious pen taking up one half of the barn, shooing Daisy and Dot in front of her. "A basic principle of physics: if you're moving in the right direction, you'll reach your destination eventually. This realization about Toast is a first step." She opened the gate and herded the goats inside, then latched the gate and tossed a few flakes of alfalfa hay into the feed trough. She often managed to combine her interests in physics and philosophy into pithy little nuggets of wisdom aimed at getting me to improve my life. So far I think she'd been disappointed with the results.

"You believe me?"

"I wouldn't go that far." Eve slanted a look in my direction. "Honestly, Lolly, I don't know what to believe, but you know what? I don't care it if was a miracle or a dream or a result of LSD-laced gumdrops."

"Lemon drops," I corrected her.

"Whatever. I'm in favor of anything that gets you unstuck in your life. If this lets you move on, I'm all for it. Far-fetched as it sounds."

I let out a breath I didn't know I'd been holding. "You don't think I'm crazy?"

"Oh, I think you're completely crazy." Eve slapped dust and bits of chaff from the knees of her Carhartts. "But that doesn't mean this isn't a good thing."

I was quiet for a minute. "Remember Perth? That phone call?"

She laughed low in her throat. "Yeah, I remember. The night I finally lost it. A 'complete emotional breakdown' I think is how my therapist later described it. What about it?"

"I think this is my Perth."

She crossed her arms and tilted her head, reminiscing. "Two in the morning and I was jet-lagged and up with stomach pains from that baby ulcer I was busy developing. I was so stressed out. I'd been sent to bag that huge Australian corporate account, and it was such a big responsibility and such a good opportunity for me. And yet all I could think, sitting there in that soulless hotel room, was that I couldn't do it anymore. Contemplating the next fifteen or twenty years of my life felt like looking down the barrel of a gun pointed straight at me. And I knew if I got up and left the hotel, if I went to that meeting, I was pulling the trigger on my own happiness."

"You FaceTimed me at the Eatery. You were hyperventilating. I'd never seen you lose it before."

She'd been wearing a plush white robe, her sleekly highlighted blond hair wrapped up in a bath towel. And she'd been crying. Barefaced and ugly sobbing. I'd never seen her such a wreck.

"Worst night of my life. And the best one. It was the beginning of the end of everything I'd been aiming for. I'd spent years striving to get somewhere only to realize I didn't want to be there after all."

"And it was the beginning of all of this." I swept my arm around—the cute barn and herd of goats, the modest A-frame wooden cottage with a riotous patch of wildflowers by the front door.

"Yep, I skipped that meeting and gave my notice the same day. I walked out of the hotel and just . . . left. It wasn't responsible or professional, but it saved my life," Eve murmured, looking past me, lost in the memory.

She hadn't gone home. She'd bummed around Australia for three months, chopped her hair off, got a wicked sunburn, drank a lot of Victoria Bitter, and figured out what she really wanted from her life.

"And you ended up here."

"As a single goat farmer with pink hair and a really skinny bank account." She laughed. "Living the dream."

"I want that," I said wistfully. "Not goats. But my own version of living the dream. And I know now it's not Toast and England, but I also know I can't keep on with things as they are now. I don't want my life to just be Dad and Daphne and the Eatery anymore. I need more. I just have to figure out what it is. Aunt Gert keeps telling me to follow my bliss and also to think about what my regrets are. I have no idea what my bliss is yet, but I have plenty of regrets."

Eve returned to my side of the barn. "You have two lemon drops left?"

I nodded, feeling for them instinctively in my pocket. Their hard grittiness was reassuring in my hand.

"Are you going to take another one?"

I nodded. "I think so."

"What are you going to choose?"

"I don't know yet." I dropped my gaze. "I've been thinking a lot about my mom. What it would be like to see her again, even if just for a day."

Eve's face softened in understanding. "That would be a gift. If you see her, give her a hug for me."

"I will."

A long pause.

"And the other one?" Eve asked. "The last drop?"

I cleared my throat. "I'll give you three guesses but you'll only need one." I said it lightly, jokingly, but Eve understood immediately.

"Rory."

I nodded. Eve's mouth tightened. "That could be a truly terrible idea," she warned.

"It might be," I agreed. "I haven't decided yet what I'll do." I thought of my mom and of Rory. She'd always adored him and had been hoping we'd end up together since the day the Shaws moved in across the street. She'd been elated when we finally got together and she had died before our love story imploded. I had a feeling she would be devastated if she knew how things had turned out.

A moment later the opening bounce of drum and keyboard chords jolted me from my thoughts. Eve was watching me carefully with a mischievous smile playing around the corners of her mouth as Annie Lennox's whiskey-hoarse voice belted out the first unmistakable chords of "Sweet Dreams (Are Made of This)." I rolled my eyes at her, and she laughed, then slung her arm around my shoulders and squeezed me tight. "Miracle lemon drops or not, I hope you find what you're looking for, Lolly," she said simply. "Now come on. This bottle of botanical gin isn't going to drink itself."

For a moment I leaned my head against her shoulder, right against the place where a lotus flower tattoo bloomed in vivid fuchsia against her pale skin. Lotus—a symbol of enlightenment, regeneration, rebirth.

Together we walked toward her cottage, gravel crunching under our feet and the light beginning to fade into the soft blue of early evening. For a moment I felt happier and more content than I had in a long while. I had no idea what lay ahead, but I knew that whatever it was, I was not alone. I had a best friend who loved and supported me. I still had almost a month to reach at least one of my goals. I had two lemon drops in my pocket to use as I chose. And for the first time in a long time, I was starting to believe that something good was waiting up ahead for me after all.

16

"Come on, come on, Rory. Where are you?" I whispered, my hands shaking with nerves as I hurriedly zipped myself into my decidedly not-parent-approved party dress. It was the night of Rory's high school graduation, and I was sneaking out to attend a party. Rory was giving me a ride. The party was being held on the other side of Magnolia at Jake Hollins's massive beachfront house on Puget Sound. Florence had a dead battery and wouldn't start, so Rory was bailing me out. I'd told my parents I was going to Ashley's house to sleep over, but that was a lie. Ashley had left with her family for vacation that morning.

It was so cliché I felt embarrassed even before the night began. But I had to go. It would be my last chance to see Rory. He'd just worked his last day bussing tables at the Eatery the week before. He was going to spend the summer staffing a camp for aspiring soccer stars in California. Then in the fall he would start college at Michigan State University, majoring in kinesiology, the first step on his path to becoming a doctor for a professional sports team. And I would stay in Magnolia and finish my senior year of high school. I was still hopelessly in love with him, and he had no idea.

I texted Rory.

Ready?

He texted back.

B there in 2.

I kept an eye out the window as I slipped a sweatshirt and jeans over my party dress. I couldn't walk through the house in my party clothes. My parents didn't know I owned the dress, and there was no way they'd let me out of the house if they saw it. All this sneakiness was uncharacteristic of me. I was a good girl who didn't get into trouble, but tonight might be my last shot to get Rory's attention and make him see the truth.

I blew out an impatient sigh and wondered what was keeping Rory. I was surprised when he offered me a ride. I figured he'd be going with Jessica. For the past six months Rory had been dating Jessica Sharma. She started dropping by the diner almost daily just after Thanksgiving, ordering a malted milkshake she never drank and flirting with Rory, asking for help with calculus even though she was already getting an A in the class. She was whip smart, and not just about academics.

"Rory, can you help me with this?" she'd ask, twirling a long caramel strand of hair between her fingers. "I understand everything better when you explain it."

I'd always sort of admired Jessica, although I never really knew her. We ran in different circles. I had a handful of close friends, was on the yearbook staff, and worked most evenings at the diner. Jessica was captain of the cheerleading squad and in the honor society. She was beautiful as well as smart—slender and coltish, brimming with confidence and enough canniness to know how to hold a man's attention, something I'd had no practice at yet. We hadn't been in each other's orbits until she set her sights on Rory. But my opinion of her changed quickly. I watched her watching him, and I worried. She wasn't a bad person, but she had a calculatedness to her I didn't entirely trust. I suspected she saw Rory as some sort of status symbol. I wasn't sure if she would have even glanced his way if he wasn't the captain of the soccer team. Now I found myself resenting her, equal parts protective of Rory and jealous of the attention he gave her. Seeing her with him made me feel like I was being eaten from the inside out by envy and longing.

I kept waiting for Rory to see the truth, but he seemed oblivious to both Jessica's ulterior motives and my raging crush on him. He treated me like he'd always treated me—with a warm fondness, like his sister or cousin. And he seemed amused by Jessica, flattered, drawn in by her flirting and attention.

I tried to play it cool, fervently hoping he wouldn't fall for Jessica, desperate for him to wake up and realize how perfect he and I were together. And yet he continued to be entranced by her charms. I felt stuck. How could I hope to compete with Jessica Sharma? I couldn't confess my feelings to him. If he didn't feel the same, I'd never be able to face him again. It would destroy our friendship. And I couldn't risk that. So I said nothing, but my heart physically hurt every time I saw them together.

In retrospect I should have been bolder. I should have told him how I felt, but I was insecure and frightened to lose him, this boy I loved down to the tips of my toes. I had no experience with boys and no idea if he felt more for me than friendship. So I watched miserably as Jessica gradually drew him in until they were officially a couple. It was agony.

Out my bedroom window I saw Rory come out the Shaws' front door and head toward his battered old Subaru. He was wearing his soccer jersey, presumably to match the other members of his team who would be at the party. The soccer guys liked to dress in uniform for parties sometimes for team solidarity. Somehow Rory made that combo of red jersey, athletic shorts, and knee socks look like dynamite. I felt my mouth go dry. Time to go. I ran downstairs and out the door, calling out a fleeting goodbye as I went.

"Hey," I said breathlessly, sliding into the front seat of Rory's car. "Quick, drive so my parents don't see you."

Rory gave me a bemused look but obligingly pulled away from the house. "They don't know you're going to this party?"

"No, they think I'm going to Ashley's house for a sleepover." I gave him a sideways look. "Don't look so disapproving. It's just a party."

"Okay, I'm just surprised," Rory shook his head, driving slowly down our street. "Lolly Blanchard being sneaky right before my eyes. I never thought I'd see the day."

I rolled my eyes at him and pulled the sweatshirt over my head, adjusting the deep sweetheart neckline of my dress. I'd secretly and specifically purchased the gorgeous cherry-red vintage cocktail dress for this party. I had found a pair of black cat-eye glasses at a retro clothing store near Pike Place Market to go with the dress, and the combination made me feel confident and sophisticated.

"Don't look for a minute," I instructed, shimmying out of my jeans and smoothing the hemline down. The dress nipped in at the waist and flared out in a high hemline that showed off my legs. "Okay, I'm good."

Rory gave me a sideways glance and did a double take. "Wow." He pulled up to a stop sign and turned, taking me in head to toe. "You look . . . wow." He shook his head, seemingly at a loss for words. I felt a flush of triumph. I'd never seen him look at me like that, admiration mixed with astonishment. He seemed genuinely stunned.

I slicked on some red lipstick and examined my reflection in the tiny square of Rory's passenger mirror, aware of his eyes on me. I looked glamorous, surprisingly sexy. Like a movie starlet from the 1950s, a bombshell ingenue. I sat back, feeling almost giddy with triumph. I'd worn the dress for only one person. And he had finally noticed me.

The Hollinses' house was gorgeous, separated from the sound by only a thin pebble-strewn beach. It was classic mid-1950s mod style, impeccably decorated. Jessica pounced on Rory as soon as we walked in the door. She gave me a hard glance, taking in my dress and how close I was standing to Rory, and her delicate nostrils flared as though she smelled something rotten. She took his arm possessively and steered him toward the kitchen. "I'm thirsty, babe. Can you get me a drink?"

Rory looked back over his shoulder and gave an apologetic shrug as they peeled off, leaving me alone. I wasn't the party type and had really only come to see Rory. Well, to see Rory while wearing this killer dress. If I didn't have the guts to tell him how I felt about him, at least I wanted his last memory of me to be in this dress, not my frilly Eatery waitress apron. Just for a moment I wanted him to see me as a woman, not just his good pal. I thought again of how he'd looked at me in the car. I knew he'd finally seen me as more than just a good friend. In that moment, in his astonished gaze, something had changed.

I wandered around for a few minutes, holding a beer and feeling like an outsider. It was a stereotypical high school party. Parents conveniently absent, music too loud, cheap beer, couples making out in all the rooms. I felt like I was on the set of a teen movie, a remake of *Say Anything* maybe. I ended up in the living room, wondering how long before someone passed out on the Eames chair or spilled beer on the cream wool carpet. My heels hurt in the too-high shoes, and I hobbled over to the vast wall of windows, wishing I were down on the beach and not here in a too-warm house that smelled like beer and sexual tension.

Part of the wall was a sliding door. I opened it and slipped out onto the empty deck, tucking myself to one side, away from the lights streaming out from the house. Alone in the chilly night air, I leaned over the railing, looking at the shimmer of distant lights from Elliott Bay and the Port of Seattle, replaying the look on Rory's face when he saw me and trying to recapture the brief flicker of joy I'd felt. I'd surprised him, and the knowledge felt amazing.

"I just think you two spend too much time together. It's weird."

I knew that voice, raised now in strident protest. My stomach tightened. It was Jessica. She and Rory were standing just inside the wall of windows in the living room, facing each other. They were arguing, not unusual for them. Her arms were crossed, and she looked like she was about to cry. They couldn't see me, I realized. I was in the shadows, and it was too brightly lit inside to see out onto this dark corner of the deck.

"That isn't true. C'mon, Jess. We're just friends. I don't see Lolly that way. She's like a . . . like a little sister to me. Honestly." Rory ran his hands through his wavy hair, his tone a touch defensive.

My stomach sank to my pointy black heels. A little sister. Suddenly I felt like a castoff in this dress, the unwanted girl playing at being a grown-up. What had I been thinking? It was humiliating.

Jessica looked slightly mollified. "Promise?" She gave him a half smile.

He pulled her close and kissed her on the mouth. "Scout's honor."

Inside I shriveled. They walked away, arms around each other. I suddenly realized how cold I was. I should go. There was nothing for me here. I leaned over the railing and tossed my untouched tepid beer in an arc down to the beach below, instantly regretting the action. No sea creature deserved a bath in Budweiser.

"Hey, that was a dollar's worth of really crappy beer."

I whirled. Jake Hollins, the host of the party and the star football quarterback of Ballard High, came out on the deck and slid the door shut behind him. He held out another red Solo cup of beer, and I took it reluctantly. He was the most popular guy in school, and I could understand why. Charming, rich, with tousled blond curls and a cocky air. He walked like a panther and, if word around school was correct, kissed like a revelation. I wondered, just for one brief moment, if it was true.

I was feeling reckless, humiliated and spurned, perhaps just a touch vengeful. I took a sip and coughed. It wasn't beer. It was vodka. A lot of straight vodka. Jake came to stand next to me and leaned his forearms on the railing. He was wearing a dress shirt and some expensive-smelling cologne, and beneath that he reeked of beer and confidence. He turned to me in the half light from the wall of windows behind us and smiled. His smile was always easy, but there was something hooded about his eyes. I could never quite figure him out. He made me a touch uneasy underneath that charm.

"So, Lolly Blanchard, what's your game?"

I blinked and took a big sip of vodka. It was like swallowing rubbing alcohol. I sputtered and coughed. "What do you mean?"

"Oh, come on. You're a puzzle. Beautiful. Untouchable. So quiet no one knows what you're thinking. You're an . . . enigma."

Uncharitably I wondered if that line really worked on girls. Were they impressed that he knew the word *enigma*? Had he learned it in SAT prep? Rumor had it he was headed for Yale; his dad was an alum.

"I didn't realize you even knew my name," I said as neutrally as possible.

He chuckled like I'd said something witty, and I realized he was drunk—very sociable and charming, but also drunk. "I know your name. I know more than you might think. For instance, I know you make the honor roll every quarter. And that you're really good at math. And I think there must be a lot more going on in that pretty head of yours than people think."

I was flattered despite myself. He was drunk, but still, Jake Hollins had noticed me and thought about me and seemed to be coming on to me. Unlike some other boy I was refusing to think about. I took another sip of vodka nervously. I didn't know how to feel about all of this. I didn't like or trust Jake Hollins, but it felt gratifying to have someone pursue me for a change.

"You know Rory Shaw told everyone to stay away from you, right?" Jake asked, eyeing me over the rim of his cup. "He warned all the guys—football, soccer, baseball—that you were off-limits. What's the deal with that?"

"Rory doesn't own me," I said quickly, still stinging from the conversation I'd overheard. I took another sip of vodka.

"Well, in that case, I just have one more question for you, Lolly Blanchard." Jake smiled lazily, his eyes never leaving mine.

"Oh, what's that?" The nipped-in waist of my dress was suddenly too tight. I couldn't quite catch my breath. Part of me wanted whatever was coming, but part of me, the more sensible part, was urging me to turn around and go back inside and leave this party for good.

"Do you taste as good as you look?" And then his big strong hand was against the back of my neck, pulling me toward him, and he was kissing me, hard and sloppy. My first kiss. He pulled me against him and maneuvered us so my back was against the railing and his body was pressed the length of mine. He was large, with a solid football build, immovable. His tongue was in my mouth, his grip insistent. For a moment I was caught by surprise, but my surprise melted into protest.

"Hey. No. Get off of me." I spat the words out, struggling to break free. "Stop." My cup was crushed against the railing, vodka splashing over my hand and dress. But he was either oblivious to my protestations or ignoring them.

"Come on, loosen up," he said, kissing me below my ear, ignoring my attempts to get out from under him. He pushed against me, rucking up the high hem of my dress with one hand. The railing was digging painfully into my back, and I could feel his groin against me, hard and unyielding. I felt a flash of pure panic. He was stronger than I was, and very drunk, and out here in the shadows no one could see us. There was no one to help me.

Flush with adrenaline, I screwed up my courage and kneed him as hard as I could in the balls. Jake grunted in surprise and pain, releasing his grip on me slightly. A second later I heard a strangled shriek of fury and caught a flash of red as Rory launched himself through the open sliding-glass door at Jake, throwing him sideways off of me. Jake collapsed on the deck like a deflated balloon, clutching his crotch and moaning.

Rory stood over him, legs akimbo, fists clenched. "She. Said. Stop," he spat out. He was the smaller of the two men. Jake was taller and heavier, but Rory was fighting mad. I'd never seen him so angry. He grabbed Jake by the collar of his dress shirt and punched him in the nose. Hard. His eyes flashed and his fist balled, ready to hit Jake again. A crowd was gathering on the other side of the windows, heads poking out the open sliding door, watching the showdown between the school's star quarterback and the star soccer player. And me standing there shaking, wanting to sink through the floor.

"You don't touch her, you hear me?" Rory said through gritted teeth. "You don't ever touch her again."

Jake swore loudly. "Get away from me. Get out of my house, man." His nose was spurting blood. Some speckled his dress shirt. I could see the pinpoint blotches. I was trembling all over, the crushed Solo cup in my hand, vodka soaking the front of my dress. Everything felt surreal.

"Lolly, are you okay?" Rory cut his eyes to me. He was panting.

Everything in him was on high alert, every muscle coiled. He was practically vibrating with anger.

I nodded. "Yes," I whispered. I had never felt so humiliated.

"Good." He released Jake's collar abruptly, and Jake fell backward on the deck, curled up in a fetal position, still holding his groin as blood dripped slowly down his chin. "Let's get out of here." Rory held his hand out to me. I took it.

Through the window I saw Jessica watching us, her mouth a thin line of displeasure. I'd wager she was going to have choice words for Rory later. He pulled me close to him and slung his arm around my shoulders, pressing me against his side, all lean muscle beneath the jersey. He shielded me as he guided me through the sliding-glass door. "Come on, I'll take you home."

In the living room the music was still pulsing, and the room was buzzing with speculation. By now everyone had congregated near the windows, and they parted for us as we came through. I kept my head down, cheeks burning with shame. Rory paused just long enough to whisper something in Jessica's ear and give her a quick peck on the cheek. She did not look pleased.

Rory kept his arm around my shoulders until we were at his Subaru. He opened the door for me and silently handed me his worn navy Columbia fleece, the one he kept in the car for hiking. It was fuzzy and smelled comfortingly of him. I pulled it on gratefully, then shut my eyes as he slid into the driver's seat and started the engine.

"Lolly, are you really okay?" he asked as we turned out onto the road, his tone concerned and protective.

I nodded. "I think so." Then, "Thank you for coming to my rescue." It came out hoarse. I was both mortified and incredibly relieved.

He glanced at me then with a flicker of something like admiration. "It looked like you were handling the situation pretty well yourself," he said lightly. "You've got quite a knee on you. He'll be sore tomorrow."

"Good." I blushed, crossing my arms defiantly. "Serves him right."

I didn't say anything more—about my horrible first kiss, or about the Solo cup of vodka, or about overhearing him and Jessica talking about me, or about Jake revealing that Rory had told all the guys I was off-limits. I was tired and overwhelmed and welcomed the silence that fell between us as he drove me back home. We pulled up in front of the house. The lights were still on in the living room. Chances were good Mom was in bed by now and Dad had probably fallen asleep watching a baseball game. If Dad woke I could say I'd come home because I wasn't feeling good, which was not a lie. The vodka was sloshing acidly in my stomach. I gathered my discarded jeans and sweatshirt from the floor by my feet.

Perhaps it was the alcohol talking, but something made me reckless. I had nothing to lose. Rory didn't care for me that way—he'd made that abundantly clear to Jessica—but I wanted him to know the truth before he left. I turned to Rory, just before I got out of the car, my hand on the door handle. "You know, it's funny," I confessed suddenly, meeting his eyes, trying to keep my voice from shaking. "I always thought my first kiss would be with you."

In the filtered golden light from the streetlamp overhead I couldn't read his expression. He went very still and didn't say anything for a long moment. Then he reached out and gently brushed his thumb across my lips. The calloused pad caught on my lower lip and pressed there for a second. I froze, heart pounding.

"I always thought so too," he said softly. Our eyes met, and I saw confusion in his gaze and something I couldn't quite name. It looked a little like longing and a lot like regret. Then he pulled his hand back and the moment was broken. I let myself out of the car and stumbled up the steps. He was still watching me, just a Rory-shaped shadow in the driver's seat of his car. He didn't drive across the street until I'd pulled on my sweatshirt and jeans over my vodka-soaked dress and opened the front door. Once inside I turned to watch his taillights wink out in the driveway of his house. I touched my fingers to my mouth, wishing he had been the one to kiss me, wishing I'd never gone to that stupid party at all, wishing once more, for the thousandth time, that I wasn't so desperately, heartbreakingly in love with Rory Shaw.

17

After the night of the party, I didn't hear from Rory all summer. We usually texted each other once or twice a week, sharing a funny anecdote from the diner or a bit of school news, but now there was only silence between us. I didn't know what Rory was thinking, and I was too self-conscious to reach out to him. However, when I thought of the warmth in his eyes, the way the pad of his thumb had traced across my lower lip, I felt a mixture of confusion and hope. Then, in late August, just before the start of my senior year, I found out Rory was back.

"Nancy says Rory's coming home from California tonight," Mom called as I swung through the kitchen door of the diner, arms laden with dessert plates. Rory had left the day after the party to staff the soccer camp in California. Throughout the summer I'd heard tidbits from Mom, that Rory was enjoying coaching fifth graders at camp, that he'd be home for a week before going out early to Michigan to get settled. That Nancy would be accompanying him. Jessica was not going with him, Mom told me. I was relieved to hear it.

"You should invite him here for supper. Our treat. Everyone wants to see him," Mom badgered good-naturedly when I came back into the kitchen to grab the coffeepots.

"Mom, Rory doesn't want to hang out where he used to work. I'm sure he's got better things to do."

Mom shrugged. "A free meal is a free meal. Besides, we're like family. Ask him."

I promised I would. Secretly I was thrilled and nervous that he was coming back. What would it be like to see him again? I was glad I'd said what I did in the car. It was true, and I didn't want him to leave for college clueless as to how I felt. But I had no idea what he'd thought of it, and he was still with Jessica.

The week passed quickly. I caught only glimpses of Rory from across the street. Jessica was often by his side. I felt a keen disappointment, but then what had I expected? He was making his feelings clear. Apparently, he really did view me as just a friend or little sister. I did text him, delivering my mom's promise of a free dinner if he stopped by, but I didn't hold out much hope.

The day before he left for college, however, Rory dropped by the diner without Jessica. My mom fussed over him, bringing him a huge plate of meatballs and roasted potatoes. All the staff came out to slap him on the back and catch up, talking about the summer and his future plans. I kept out of the way, busying myself with other chores. Only once did he glance my way, his eyes snagging on mine. He broke the glance, looking away. But I'd seen something in his eyes, an intensity that thrilled me. I didn't know what it meant, but I had an inkling it was something good.

Later that night I saw the light go on in his room across the street as I lay in bed with the shade up, keeping an eye out for him. Tomorrow that light would be out, his bedroom window dark. He would be far away in Michigan, starting a new college life. It was a lonely thought. I was just drifting off to sleep when something tapped against the glass of my bedroom window. I slipped out of bed and looked out. Rory was standing on the front lawn, arm notched back as he prepared to toss another pebble at my window. I lifted the sash and stuck my head out, heart pounding.

"Hey." He grinned. He was wearing a brand-new Michigan State sweatshirt. His parents had embraced school spirit in a big way and *all* of them had matching sweatshirts. "Want to go down to South Beach?" he asked in a loud stage whisper.

Surprised, I didn't hesitate. "Be there in a minute." I ducked back inside and hurriedly grabbed a hoodie. After the first time I'd taken Rory down to South Beach for the failed polar plunge, that spot had quickly become a special place we shared. We never talked about it, never brought other friends down with us. It was only for us. All through high school we hiked down the beach trail once or twice a month, even in winter. Sometimes we'd sit in companionable silence, nestled back against that same huge driftwood log, our log. Often we'd bring homework, but we seldom actually cracked a textbook. More often than not we'd end up talking for hours, arguing good-naturedly about books and movies, laughing and goofing around, talking about our hopes for the future. We'd share whatever snacks we had on hand and just enjoy the time together. There, in the salt-tinged air, with the majestic snowcapped mountains as a backdrop and the quiet lapping of the water, I was happiest and most at peace in the world. I always felt that way when I was with Rory, and the beach amplified it; for that space of time, all felt right with the universe. I was seen and known and accepted. We could sit together and simply be ourselves. It was the best feeling in the world.

But all that stopped soon after Rory started dating Jessica. He'd mentioned our beach trips to her once early on, and she'd insisted he not go without her. We never went again. Now I wondered what had changed to make him offer tonight.

He drove us down to the beach through the dark, quiet streets of Magnolia. We didn't see any other cars. It felt like we were the only living beings in a slumbering world. He parked illegally in the tiny parking lot. Technically we needed a permit to park there, but at this time of night, we were the only ones around. It was after ten but had just gotten dark. August twilight in Seattle was long and soft and slow.

We walked along the trail to the north part of South Beach, through the silence broken only by the gentle lapping of the waves. I'd thrown a hoodie over my tank top and thin cotton shorts but now wished I'd brought something warmer. It was always chilly down here, fresh and cool. The air smelled of wet sand and seaweed and salt. The moon was almost full, with wispy clouds scuttling across it, bathing the water in bright silver. The park lay wild and silent, and I shivered and pulled closer to Rory and the beam of his headlamp. Sometimes a bear or a cougar wandered down from the Cascades and found their way to the park. I could imagine eyes watching us in the near darkness.

We wound our way down a ribbon of sandy path to the beach, gravitating by unspoken agreement to our usual spot. We settled down in the sand, backs against the huge bleached driftwood log. There was a breeze blowing in off the water, and I shivered, scooting a little closer to Rory's warmth. We hadn't talked since we'd gotten in the car, and I wondered how to break the silence. It felt weighty. I could feel the heat of his body beside me, our thighs almost touching. I wanted him more than I'd ever wanted anything in my life. He was my first love. And I was pretty sure he didn't feel anything like that for me. I had no idea *how* he felt about me. I was a bundle of longing and nerves and anticipation and anxiety.

I leaned my head back against the log with a sigh and looked up, searching for constellations. The light pollution from the city was lessened here, and I found the Big Dipper, the rest of Ursa Major, Ursa

Minor, and at the tip of the Little Dipper, the bright North Star. The silence stretched long.

"Can I ask you something?" I asked at last. I'd been wondering about this since the night of the party at Jake Hollins's house.

"Sure. Shoot."

"That night of the party, Jake told me you'd warned all the guys on the sports teams that I was off-limits. Why did you tell them that?"

Rory shifted against the log. He was silent for a moment. "I guess I feel protective of you. I don't want anybody to mess with you or hurt you. When I saw Jake with his hands all over you at the party, not listening to you saying no . . ." He clenched his hands. "I've never punched a guy so hard in my life. I wanted to knock his teeth out. If he'd hurt you . . ."

I said nothing, just looked out at the water. What did it mean that he felt so protective of me? Like a little sister? Or something more?

Rory cleared his throat. "Can I ask *you* something?" he asked, turning to look at me in the moonlight.

I nodded. "Of course."

He paused. I could see him out of the corner of my eye, watching me. "What you said the night of the party, when I drove you home," he said slowly. "About how you thought I'd be your first kiss. What did you mean by that?"

I turned to him then, tracing the familiar lines of his face. Everything was bathed in silver tones, sharp and beautiful. I could shrug it off, pretend like I didn't remember, that it had been the vodka and adrenaline talking. But he was going away tomorrow. This might be my only chance to tell him the whole truth.

"I like you, Rory Shaw," I admitted. "A lot." I gazed at him, tucking my hands between my thighs to warm them. I was buzzing with giddy energy. Now that I had decided to be bold and tell him the truth, I found I wasn't nervous at all. "I've had a crush on you almost from the minute I first saw you," I told him. The confession felt good, freeing. He was staring at me, confusion etched across his face. I'd caught him by surprise.

"But what you said to Crystal . . . I heard you telling her once that you could never feel like that about me, that I was like a brother to you."

So he *had* overheard that conversation.

"That wasn't the truth." I shrugged. "I didn't want her to know how I felt. I was embarrassed because I didn't think you saw me that way."

He shook his head, bewildered. He seemed at a loss for words.

"It's okay," I said, calm now that I'd finally said the words. "You don't have to feel the same way."

He was quiet for a moment. "But what if I do?" he said softly. Something flashed between us, quick and strong as a jolt of electricity. His eyes were intent on my face, so close I could feel his breath against my skin. He was so beautiful in the silver light reflecting off the water. Without thought, I reached out and cupped his cheek, the skin warm, his stubble a little raspy against my palm. He felt so familiar.

"Do you?"

He laughed raggedly, the sound like tearing cotton, then turned his face into my hand and pressed a sudden, fervent kiss into my palm.

"Since the moment I first saw you," he confessed.

I drew back a little. "But I heard you, the night of the party. You told Jessica you thought of me like a little sister. You promised her, Scout's honor," I protested.

"Lolly, you know I've never been a Boy Scout," he said, his tone a little amused. And then suddenly he was reaching for me, his warm hand clasped firmly around my upper arm, tugging me down on top of him. I went willingly. For moment we stayed like that, pressed the length of each other in the sand, nose to nose, breathing the same air. Then he moved a scant inch and kissed me, one hand cupping the back of my skull, pulling me against him. He tasted like sweet tea and bourbon and Rainier beer, like falling in love, like coming home. It was not a brush of lips, not a chaste kiss. It felt like he was drowning and I was his sole source of air. I threw my arms around his neck, pressing hard against him with years of pent-up longing, kissing him right back, matching his ardor. It felt so right.

He was murmuring things against my mouth, but I could only concentrate on his lips on mine, on his hands tangled in my ponytail, the hard curve of his rib cage beneath me, his mouth full and hungry on mine. Finally. Finally we were where we belonged. He groaned and pulled me closer, my breasts pushed against his chest; we were locked together in an almost crushing embrace. I could feel his heart tripping fast against his ribs, his mouth trailing hot down the length of my neck. He said my name with a kind of desperation.

He was strong, but this was nothing like Jake Hollins. I felt safe with him. I knew he'd stop in an instant if I wanted him to. But good heavens, I didn't want him to. I wanted to kiss him forever. I wanted to melt into him till our bones fused together. We were burrowed in the sand, me half over him, kissing with a sort of desperation, like it was our last moment on Earth.

I came up for air with a gasp, dizzy with desire. Pulling back to look at him in the bright silver moonlight, memorizing this moment, the planes of his face. I was stunned and shaking and euphoric. "I love you, Rory Shaw," I said.

He went dead still in an instant, staring at me, the words sinking in, and then I saw a flash of panic cross his face. He pushed me back quickly, gently, raising his hands as though to ward me off, as though I were something dangerous to touch, as though I burned him. "Lolly, no. We can't do this."

I scrambled back against the log, hair and clothes disheveled, breathing hard. "What?" I asked, utterly confused.

"I'm sorry." He inched away, putting some distance between us. He ran his hands through his hair, a sure sign he was distraught. "I lost control. I'm sorry. It won't happen again."

"What?" I asked again. My voice sounded harsh in my own ears. I couldn't believe what was happening, that he was saying these words after he'd kissed me like that.

He deliberately looked away from me, out over the water, breathing hard and struggling to compose himself. "Lolly, I'm leaving tomorrow for college. I'll be on the other side of the country. And you're still here, still in high school. This isn't a good idea. The timing is all wrong. And there's Jessica. She and I are together. We care about each other. It's not fair to her, this—" He gestured between us, at the scooped-out hollow of sand between us where we'd just lain with our bodies pulsing for each other. "—this isn't who I want to be for you or for her. It's not honorable. I'm sorry."

I stared at him in disbelief. Fifteen seconds before his hands had been splayed across my back while he devoured me with his lips, and now he was apologizing? I'd just declared my love for him. I thought he'd do the same. "What are you talking about?" I cried.

He looked at me and his expression told me all I needed to know. Resigned, steeling himself for a hard task. He was staying with Jessica. He was not going to be with me. This had been a mistake. A mistake he was already regretting. My anger was instantaneous, a struck match, fueled by equal parts humiliation and disbelief.

"So that's it then? You're really going to kiss me like that and go back to her? You just told me you've liked me for five years!" I hated the protest in my voice. I knew I'd already lost.

He crossed his arms over his knees and stared out at the water. I knew that determined set of his jaw so well. Too well.

"I'm sorry, Lolly. If things were different . . . if I weren't going away for school, if you were done with high school. If I weren't with Jessica."

He gave a frustrated groan. "Lolly," His tone was pleading, his gaze on me earnest. "This can't happen. Not now. If we pursue this, if we try to be together right now, it's going to end badly, I know it. And I care about you too much to do that. You are worth more than this. Our friendship is worth more than this to me. Can't you see that? And I can't do this to Jessica either. It's not fair to her. We have to walk away. I have to walk away." He gave me one anguished glance, but I pointedly looked away. I would not acknowledge that this was costing him something. It was his choice. I was furious, spurned and rejected and horribly, deeply disappointed. I'd loved him for so long, but it wasn't enough. He was not choosing me. Tears stinging my eyes, I stood, and brushed sand off my shorts.

"I want to go home."

He drove me home in miserable silence. I was biting the inside of my lip, willing myself not to cry. I could still taste him, and the dissonance was torture.

He pulled up outside my house, the engine loud in the stillness of the night. "I'm sorry, Lolly," he said again. Nothing else.

"Don't call me. Don't text me. I don't want to hear from you ever again." I slammed the door hard and stalked up the sidewalk without a backward glance, vowing to do whatever I had to do to forget I'd ever given Rory Shaw my heart.

18

It was a dull gray late afternoon at the diner, in the lull between lunch and supper, and I was closeted in my office, slogging through a pile of paperwork and humming along to the country station turned down low on the radio. It had been two days since I'd confided in Eve about the lemon drops, and I was still waffling about what I would use my next lemon drop for.

I kept thinking of my mother, trying to imagine what it would be like to see her again. I felt giddy with the possibility, but nervous too. It was almost painful to think about. I wanted to be with her again so badly, but would I be able to enjoy just one day, knowing it would be the last day I would ever have with her? It felt like an emotional minefield. Was I brave enough to risk it? I wasn't sure.

For the next hour I filed papers, opened mail, and organized bills to pay, trying to get on top of my admin to-do list. Through the door I could hear Dad and Julio loudly rehashing the Seahawks' fall season as they prepped for dinner in the kitchen.

"Russell Wilson is a legend," Dad yelled across the kitchen admiringly. "And he runs like greased lightning." I could hear him vigorously chopping something.

"No argument here," Julio called back over the sound of running water in the sink. "But how about Tyler Lockett? I think he's about as good. He's underrated with the big dogs."

I tuned out as they started dissecting the Seahawks' strategy on offense. An unopened letter from the property tax office of King County caught my eye on top of the ever-present stack of mail on my desk. Probably the new annual property tax estimate for the diner. It only climbed higher year after year. Seattle had been booming in the last decade with the explosive growth of Amazon, Google, and Facebook headquarters in the city. Property was at a premium, and prices were eye-wateringly high. The new estimate was sure to pinch us financially even more.

Bracing myself for another thousand-dollar jump in taxes, the same as the last few years, I slid the single sheet of paper out of the envelope and glanced over the brief letter, then stopped and reread it more slowly with a growing feeling of dread. It was an announcement about a new tax policy for businesses that owned their own properties in our area of the city. Instead of taxing the business based on the actual estimated value of their property, the letter informed us that starting with the upcoming payment on April 30, businesses would be taxed based on the *potential* value of their property and land.

I studied the enclosed tax table in disbelief. Although the Eatery was sitting on a prime piece of real estate on the main street in Magnolia, the diner itself was a smallish, older building. Our normal property taxes, while still steep, were just barely manageable. But according to the new tax figures, we would owe almost twenty-five thousand dollars in property taxes for this year, an increase of almost fourfold. And the first half of the payment was due in just two months. I dropped the letter on the table like it was scorching my fingers. There was no way we could cover a tax increase of that amount. It was impossible. We were barely making ends meet as it was. I closed my eyes and tried to think, heart racing. Twenty-five thousand dollars. How in the world could we manage to come up with that amount of cash?

Picking up the letter, I stared at the number again in shock. I licked my lips and sank back in the chair. There was an acidic taste of fear on the tip of my tongue, caustic as lemon juice. I had to think of something. We simply couldn't close the diner. It was our livelihood, our legacy, the thing that held us all together. If we were forced to close, I feared it would kill my father, pure and simple. If we closed the diner, I would be breaking my deathbed promise to my mother. Yet deep down I had a terrible feeling that this letter might actually be what finally sank us.

I blew out a deep breath. Think, Lolly, think. We couldn't give up yet. I had to figure out a way to save us. I couldn't think of anything right now, but with a little time surely I could come up with something. I paused, considering. I didn't want Dad to know about this letter. He carried such stress constantly. I didn't want to add this burden to an already heavy load. Perhaps it was better to hide it away until I'd had a chance to come up with a solid rescue plan. Then I could present the problem and the solution together so it wasn't such a shock. Feeling a little guilty to be hiding the truth from him, but convincing myself it was the right thing to do, I tucked the letter in my top desk drawer, in the back next to the Sharpies, where no one ever looked. I'd concoct a foolproof way to save the Eatery. Then I'd talk to Dad.

Seven a.m. the next morning and I was already regretting saying yes to Daphne.

"Let's move into our first pose, the Half-Moon Pose," the tiny, Zen-like yoga instructor said, demonstrating the move. "Inhale with your arms up over your head and tilt sideways." Beside me, on her mat, Daphne inhaled happily and copied her. I focused on what the instructor was doing and clumsily tried to follow suit.

Daphne had cornered me at the diner yesterday afternoon, right after I'd hidden the horrible tax letter, and finagled me into coming to a yoga class at the studio where she worked. She'd cited all the health benefits, emphasized the stress relief angle, and finally just flat out pleaded with me to come.

"It's all the things you don't normally do. Stretch, breathe, and stop working," she'd coaxed, using puppy dog eyes and sticking out her lower lip. Still in shock over the enormous tax bill, I agreed in a moment of weakness, figuring anything was better than sitting around, fruitlessly stewing over how to save our diner. It was just an hour, after all. An hour where I could stop obsessing about the lemon drop dilemma or the tax bill problem. Now, however, I was rethinking my hasty decision. Turns out there *are* some things worse than worrying about property taxes.

Because what Daphne had neglected to mention was that this was a Bikram hot yoga class. The room felt like a sauna. I was already sweating and all I'd done was raise my arms. It didn't bode well for the rest of the time

"How hot is it in here?" I gasped as the instructor urged us to bend our bodies right and left, right and left, like graceful swaying reeds. The room was crowded, but we'd staked out a back corner for ourselves. The air smelled like sweat and natural deodorant—charcoal and lavender. We'd see how long that held up in this heat.

"About a hundred and five," Daphne said cheerfully. "It's good for circulation and flexibility."

"Yeah, if you can survive it," I muttered, barely swaying back and forth. For the next few minutes, we were silent, focusing on the moves.

"Hey, I wanted to talk to you about something," Daphne whispered at the tail end of the Eagle move, which involved standing on one leg with your other foot wrapped behind your ankle. I was wobbling so hard I had to give up and put both legs down and just squat that way, like a diver ready to spring into action at any moment.

"Oh yeah?" I was concentrating hard so I didn't topple over.

"I heard you and Dad talking about the Eatery's finances a week or so ago." Daphne kept her voice low. "I knew things weren't great, but I didn't realize it was so bad."

"It's always bad," I grunted, feeling sweat trickle down my temple. My thigh muscles were on fire. "It started slowly going downhill after Mom died, and it's just gotten worse year after year. Dining demographics have changed a lot. People don't want our kind of food anymore. Tastes evolve, and we haven't evolved enough to be competitive."

We moved on to a pose involving holding one foot straight out in front of us and bending over it. Daphne laid her entire lithe torso over the length of her thigh and held the sole of her foot in her interlaced hands. I bent my leg and managed to balance while holding on to my foot too. Sort of. *Good enough*, I thought. I was stretching. I was breathing. All while trying not to pass out in this heat. Had I really gotten up two hours early to make pies in the pitch-dark for this?

"Well, this might sound crazy, but hear me out," Daphne said, turning her head in my direction. For a moment I saw her again as a child, that motherless little tween with straggly hair and neon-rubber-banded braces. But I blinked and there she was, a grown young woman now, crackling with energy, exuberance, and confidence. Daphne had always flung herself out into the world, fearless and bold.

"Crazy how?" I grunted, holding on to my wavering foot.

"I want to quit school."

My mouth dropped open. "What?" I lost my balance and hopped to remain upright.

"Moving on to Standing Bow Pose," the instructor called, shooting us a censorious look. "Bend your leg back and pick up your foot from the inside of the ankle." Daphne followed the directions, and I copied her as best I could.

"What do you mean you're going to quit school?" My voice was too loud in the calm space, high-pitched in protest.

Daphne shrugged, holding her ankle and slowly easing forward, fingers pointed toward the far wall like Superman. "Cornish just costs so much money, and I don't know if I'll even use my degree. I want to do something more practical that won't be taking so much money from you and Dad for tuition. I want to help out."

"You can help out by staying in school and finishing your degree," I countered in a loud whisper. I wobbled forward and pointed my arm straight in front of me, not even trying to copy the move.

"But what if I don't want to finish it?" Daphne argued in a slightly softer whisper. "What if I want to travel and see the world? That can be more valuable than a college degree. Real life experience. I could get my yoga teacher certification somewhere really cool. Damien wants to go with me."

"You need to stay in school and get your degree. It will give you way more options for a good job in the future," I said firmly. When I glanced up, the instructor's gaze was on us, her brow furrowed. Oh great, she was heading our way.

The instructor glided up to me. "Let me help you with your form," she said in a low, soothing tone, a voice one would use for a petulant toddler. She was sweating but doing it in a calmly beatific way, glistening serenely. I caught a whiff of patchouli as she showed me the correct pose. I swiped a damp strand of hair back and adjusted the angle of my bent leg, not caring at all whether I was doing the pose correctly. Inside I was fuming.

Daphne had set this whole thing up. She wanted to have this conversation in a place where I wouldn't be able to openly respond to her bombshell. She was right, her tuition was a significant financial strain on our family. But I worked as hard as I could so that she could do the things I couldn't. We sacrificed as a family for her so she could have a brighter future than either Dad or I had. She was one of the main reasons I had given everything up ten years ago. If she gave up on school now, all that sacrifice would be worthless.

Apparently despairing of my form and lack of attention, the instructor returned to the front of the room.

"I just don't want to see you throwing away opportunities for your future," I said out of the corner of my mouth. "You've only got a year left anyway. Stick it out and get your degree, then go see the world, do your yoga training, whatever you want. Just finish school first."

"I don't want to waste any more time or money on school if I'm not going to use it," Daphne countered in a loud whisper. "I'd rather do what I want to do now. It doesn't make sense to wait. Damien agrees with me. We're going to go right after he graduates this spring."

"Step to the back of your yoga mat," the instructor called out, "as we move into Balancing Stick Pose. Just a reminder to keep the space quiet and full of positive energy." She looked straight at us and frowned reprovingly as she spoke.

I moved to the back of the mat and shot Daphne a warning look, the one I'd used since she became my responsibility, the one that conjured up as much maternal disapproval as possible. I telegraphed *This isn't finished* with my furrowed eyebrows. I was not about to let her waste her chance to get a college degree, not to mention throw away the years of study, tuition, and time she'd already invested.

She studiously avoided my eyes, keeping her own on the front of the room, but I could tell by the stubborn set of her jaw that she'd already decided. Well, we would just have to see about that. I wasn't backing down without a fight. Not where her future was concerned. I wanted more for her than I'd had—more chances, more fulfillment, more . . . life.

After the class I swung home for a shower before heading to the diner. I was sweaty, stinky, and grouchy. Daphne had stayed to teach another class as soon as our session had ended. As I drove, an old Tammy Wynette CD started playing on Florence's ancient CD player. It was stuck in there, so there were limited music options. It was basically Tammy or silence. "We're Gonna Hold On," Tammy warbled in a duet with George Jones. She had been my mother's favorite, the first lady of country music. My mother could sing all her songs by heart, belting out every word in her throaty alto.

Pulling into our driveway, I put the car in park but didn't get out. I was still reeling from Daphne's bombshell. She could be stubborn as a rock, but I could be stubborn too. There was absolutely no way I was letting her throw her future away now. I had sacrificed too much to let that happen. Her success meant my sacrifice was worth it. It was as simple as that. But how could I get through to her and convince her to stay in school?

I needed help, someone to talk to about all this. I was still in knots over the worrisome tax letter and now Daphne's crackpot scheme. I reached down and touched the lemon drops tucked safely in the pocket of my jacket, then took one out and considered it for a moment. There was only one person who would understand all this, who would offer sage advice. It was her death that had thrown us into this mess in the first place. Perhaps she could help get us out. All I wanted right now was the woman I had missed every minute of every day for the past ten years. I needed my mother.

19

I remember the call like it was yesterday. It was my senior year of college at Portland State University, finals week. I was almost done. Just one more test and I'd graduate the next week. Then a new life in Baltimore beckoned . . . and Rory. The future felt bright and full of promise.

My phone rang. Dad. I hesitated, almost letting it go to voice mail. I was studying after all. But Dad almost never called, he just chimed in from the background on Mom's calls to me. I picked up on the last ring.

"Lolly." His voice, strained and thin on the other end of the line. In an instant I knew something terrible had happened. "It's your mother. There's been an accident."

Mom had been struck by a car while crossing the street after mailing a letter at the post office. Dad had seen it happen through the front window of the Eatery. A distracted delivery driver from a local restaurant was going too fast and blew the stop sign, roared through the crosswalk, and flung her across the hood of his white Prius. The paramedics had transported her to the hospital in an ambulance. She was conscious but complaining of significant pain.

I drove the three and a half hours from Portland to Seattle on autopilot, a cold dread lying slick in the pit of my stomach.

"The doctors say she's got internal bleeding," Dad reported when he called me on the road with an update. "She's in surgery now."

"What's her prognosis?" I asked, feeling sick with apprehension as I stared ahead at the long stretch of highway, nothing but evergreens as far as the eye could see. I had to pee but was flying by every rest stop. Each minute seemed too precious to waste.

"I don't know. They're hoping the surgery will stop the bleeding. I guess it's pretty bad." His voice trembled. That scared me more than anything. I'd never, ever seen my dad so much as tear up except at the national anthem during baseball games.

"I'll be there as soon as I can." I pushed Florence's accelerator to the floor.

Mom was out of surgery when I arrived at the hospital. She'd survived, but her vitals were unstable. The doctors were not optimistic. It was touch and go as to whether she would pull through. She'd sustained significant internal damage. She was only fifty-four.

At her bedside at last, I found her alone, pale and worn-looking, her usually high color ashen. Dad had gone to pick up Daphne from school and break the news to her as gently as possible.

Mom lay on the single hospital bed like some Viking queen, her thick blond hair unpinned and spread out on the pillow, eyes closed. When she heard me approach, her eyes opened and her mouth curved into a small, satisfied smile.

"Lolly." She reached out a hand and cupped my cheek, and I clasped her palm to my skin. It was cool to the touch, almost clammy. Her voice was a low rumble. If I closed my eyes she almost sounded normal.

"How are you feeling?"

"Like a garbage truck ran over me at least twice." She grinned wryly. "But it was only a delivery driver with an order of Indian food."

"You'll be okay." I choked on the words, tears clogging my throat. She had to be okay.

"I don't think so, Lolly," she said matter-of-factly. "What a way to go. I always thought I'd die in my bed at a hundred like my grandmother. Longevity runs in our family. How's that for irony?"

Just then Dad arrived with Daphne, who launched herself toward the bed with a strangled cry as soon as she saw Mom. Dad grabbed her just in time and settled her in a chair, where she clung to Mom's hand, worriedly eyeing the monitors and wires crisscrossing Mom's chest. She glanced at each of our faces, trying to gauge how she should respond to the situation. She was so young, her eyes wide and lost beneath wispy bangs.

"Your mom's got good doctors," Dad assured her. "She'll be right as rain." I hoped to high heaven he was right. No one seemed convinced.

After a few minutes Daphne forgot to be afraid and chattered happily about the school play—*The Lion King*—and her role as Zazu the hornbill. For a moment, if we could ignore the antiseptic smell and the beeping and the fact that Mom was lying in a hospital bed in a thin cotton gown, bleeding beneath her skin, it could almost have passed for a normal family conversation.

"Okay, let's go, pumpkin. I'll take you to Charlotte's house," Dad said after about ten minutes. He had arranged for Daphne to spend the night at her best friend's house so he and I could stay the night at the hospital. We'd both agreed it was best. "We'll come see your mom tomorrow morning before school."

Daphne kissed Mom, then buried her small face in the shoulder of the hospital gown, holding on fiercely. Mom cradled her with one arm, stroking her hair with the other and murmuring things to her, too low for us to hear. When Daphne finally lifted her face, the shoulder of Mom's blue hospital gown was dappled with tears. Mom winced with pain but did not let go of Daphne's small frame. There was a resignation in her eyes that gave me a prickle of alarm. This looked an awful lot like a goodbye.

"Dad, I can take Daphne to Charlotte's so you can stay here with Mom."

"No." Mom's voice was surprisingly strong.

Dad looked torn. "Irene?" he said, but she waved him off.

"I need to talk to Lolly *alone*."

She waited until they left, until they were completely out of sight down the hall, then beckoned me over. She didn't look small in the bed. She looked too large, as though she had no business being there at all, as though it could not contain her force of will. She flicked a wire away in irritation.

"Lolly, I'm dying," she said bluntly.

"You don't know that," I protested, but she shushed me.

"I do. I can feel it. My body is giving in. I don't have much time."

I swallowed hard, trying to tamp down a rising panic. She couldn't be dying. It was impossible. She seemed so close to her old self that I'd been trying to convince myself she was fine. Her gaze on me was compassionate and resigned.

"I need you to promise me something." She grimaced in pain. She had demanded the lowest dose of painkillers the doctors would give her, wanting to be alert, Dad had told me. But it was costing her dearly. I looked down, trying to hold back my tears and disbelief. This couldn't be happening.

"Anything."

She took my hand in her own and pressed it gently, looking at me solemnly with her green eyes. The skin on the backs of her hands looked waxy, alarming—like something already dead, a lifeless thing stretched over her bones.

"Promise me you'll hold the family together no matter what. Daphne will need you, and your father too. They can't do it on their own. You'll need to help keep the Eatery running. It's our legacy and our lifeline. Promise me you'll take care of them and the diner."

"I promise." What else could I do? I didn't think about Baltimore and Rory, about my bright and shiny future hovering a few days away. I just promised. "But you're going to pull through," I insisted.

My mother smiled grimly. "To think that a Prius delivering an order of tikka masala will be the way I go. Well, everyone has to go somehow. I just thought I'd have more time." We locked eyes for a moment, and in hers I saw so much. Strength and sadness and a touch of resignation. I'd never seen my mother give up on anything in my life. That scared me more than anything.

"There's one more thing," she said, clearing her throat. "I need to tell you my lemon meringue pie recipe."

"Are you sure?" This was serious. More serious than her stating that her body was shutting down. The recipe had been passed down to Mom from her mother, who'd kept it a secret for decades. Only Mom knew the recipe now. She'd added a few tweaks of her own, perfected it even more, and kept the recipe a closely held secret all these years. I'd watched her make the pie dozens of times, but she'd never actually taught me how to do it.

"It's time," she said firmly. "Now listen closely. The first ingredient, the one that makes it so special, is Meyer lemons."

An hour later she was confident that I could recite the entire recipe from memory, knew all the little tips and tricks, and then she swore me to secrecy. Hand-on-my-heart secrecy.

"I promise I'll keep the recipe a secret and that I'll take care of Dad and Daphne if anything should happen to you," I recited the promises she'd asked me to give, adding, "although it won't because it can't. We need you too much."

She gestured me over and pressed a kiss to the top of my head. Later I understood it for what it was, a benediction, a final blessing. "I've always been so proud of you, Lolly. You're going to be just fine."

I closed my eyes and savored her embrace, the feel of her arms around me. Somehow, although most of me was still in shock and denial, a small true part suspected that this might be the last time she would hold me.

She managed to make it through the night. Both Dad and I were there at her side through the long dark hours, but somewhere in the early morning her vitals plummeted. I got the call from Dad just as I was picking Daphne up from her sleepover at Charlotte's house a little before seven in the morning. We'd decided to let her skip school and come say goodbye to Mom. We didn't think Mom had much time left.

"Lolly, she's gone," Dad choked out. "I was holding her hand and she just . . . stopped breathing."

I made a sound like the mewing of a kitten, a protest and a plea.

"What do we do now?" Dad sounded utterly bereft. My mother was a strong woman with a powerful orbit. She and my father had been, in certain ways, an unlikely pair, but they'd loved each other faithfully and worked hard side by side for more than twenty years. He would be lost without her.

"I'm coming," I choked out, already assuming the role I'd promised her I would take on. "Hold on. I'll be there soon."

I watched Daphne come out of Charlotte's house, a bounce in her step, waving goodbye, hair in a French braid and holding a Pop-Tart, unaware that her whole world had just shattered. Tears were rolling down my cheeks, falling on my hands and shirt, the steering wheel. I needed to call Rory and tell him Mom was gone. He was on his way, flying across the country as fast as he could. I was desperate to see him, to have him wrap his arms around me and tell me it would all some-how, someday be okay. I needed him here with me to face this un-imaginable loss.

Mom had been the glue that held everything together. Now she was gone, and there was only me to carry on her role. I clutched the phone and felt the weight of responsibility settle on my shoulders. I was the glue now.

"Five large egg yolks," I whispered, suddenly panicking. What if I couldn't remember the recipe? What if I couldn't keep my promises to her? What if I couldn't hold my family together? "One cup granulated sugar. The zest from one large Meyer lemon. One leaf of lemon balm . . ."

Mom's death had been ten years ago now, and still the memory made my heart crack open with sorrow. I sat in bed late at night after the disastrous hot yoga class with Daphne, wrapped in Mom's old pink terry cloth bathrobe, tears slipping down my cheeks as I thought back to that terrible day. I buried my face in the collar of the robe. It still smelled faintly of Pond's Cold Cream. I lay back in bed and held up the second lemon drop, the bright little candy wavering through the tears pooling in my eyes. Everything felt like it was coming apart at the seams all over again. All the things I'd worked so hard for, sacrificed for, were now in peril. Daphne's future. The Eatery.

I popped the lemon drop into my mouth, tucking it against my cheek, willing it to work. Tonight, I was so tired of trying to hold our family together. There was only one person I wanted to see. I needed desperately to hear her voice again, feel her ample arms press me close to her heart. I needed advice and motherly understanding. I needed her to fix everything like she'd done so many times before. I closed my eyes, overwhelmed with grief and longing. "Mom," I whispered, hoping against hope I could see her this one last time.

20

I *awoke to* the gentle rhythm of the surf and a subtle waft of plumeria on the warm breeze. Blinking in the bright sunlight filtering in through a set of jalousie windows, I sat up in the soft queen-sized bed and scooped up a pair of glasses with chunky petal-pink frames sitting on a side table next to the bed. Ooh, I wish I had these in real life! I slowly took in the room done entirely in a kitschy tiki theme with wicker furniture and a calligraphy wooden sign that read: ALOHA. Where was I? Hawaii? An iPhone sat on the wicker side table. I checked the time and date. Seven thirteen a.m. on Sunday, February 27. I had gone to bed last night in Seattle on Saturday, February 26. So far everything was proceeding true to form.

I rolled out of the queen-size bed and peered out the window. Palm trees, a strip of spiky grass, and a parking lot. It certainly looked like Hawaii. If I had to guess, I'd say I was on the Big Island, in Kona. Hmm, this was unexpected. Was Mom in Kona? In the mirror over the dresser I gave myself a quick once-over. To my relief, I just looked like me. Hair in a messy topknot and wearing a tiny pair of polka-dotted shorts and a tank top, but definitely my normal face and shape, the soft swell of my hips and little pooch of my tummy. I'd never loved that pooch, but after the too-skinny Lolly in Brighton, I was happy to see my own shape in the mirror.

"Lolly? Rise and shine, my girl. Coffee's ready." I froze, heart leaping in joyful recognition at the voice calling from down the hall. The lemon drop had worked!

"Coming!"

I practically skipped down the carpeted hallway and into a small, high-ceilinged living/dining room area decorated with more wicker and vintage Hawaiian travel posters and pillows that looked like quilted pineapples. Mom was in the kitchen, her back to me, standing at the open refrigerator. I stopped short, drinking in the sight of her. Irene Freya Blanchard. She was wearing a bright teal flower-print muumuu, which draped over her wide hips and flared into a flounce at the bottom. Her hair was threaded with silver, but still thick and straight, the rich golden hue of ripe wheat, pinned up the way she'd worn it ever since I could remember.

"Mom," I blurted out, hearing the disbelief and longing in my voice. She turned, her face softening into a smile.

"Good morning, my girl. Did you sleep well?"

She opened her arms, and I ran into her embrace, burying my face in her shoulder and holding her so tight she puffed a breath out in surprise. She smelled like herself, a mixture of lemons and Pond's Cold Cream.

"I missed you," I choked out, tears welling up. "Oh, I've missed you so much." I clutched her close.

"Oh goodness, I'm right here in paradise." She hugged me, swaying slightly, as though I were still a baby and she was rocking me to sleep.

I exhaled in a long sigh, not loosening my grip. How long had I been holding my breath just a little? A decade at least. Tears prickled hot behind my eyelids, and I blinked them back, not wanting to spoil the moment. Too soon, she pulled back, taking me by the shoulders and giving me a good once-over. Her eyes narrowed. "You look peaked. This calls for some vitamin D and a mai tai on the veranda."

"Isn't it a little early for a cocktail?" I asked with a choked little laugh. "It's barely seven in the morning."

She waved away my protest. "We're on Hawaiian time, sweetie. It's never too early for fruity drinks with umbrellas. Besides, mai tais don't count. They're just juice with a little extra kick."

This was patently untrue. Mom's mai tais were the stuff of legend. Mostly rum and curaçao with just a kiss of lime and fresh squeezed orange juice. They were delicious but potent. She bustled around the kitchen, cracking eggs and heating butter in a skillet while I watched.

"Go on out to the veranda." She shooed me back the way I'd just come. "I'll bring your breakfast out."

Obediently, I made my way through the condo living room and out a sliding-glass door to a small veranda with a glass dining table wedged amid a riot of tropical flowers and plants. Of course Mom had a veranda stuffed with growing things. I counted more than a dozen pots of gorgeous jewel-colored flowers spilling over the railing and trailing across the floor. Beyond the veranda the beautiful ocean view was picture-perfect. My parents had always intended to retire to Hawaii, but then when Mom passed, Dad had quietly laid those plans aside. I settled down in one of the chairs with a contented sigh. Seeing my mom was sheer perfection. Seeing her in Hawaii was the icing on the cake.

Hawaii had always been our family's favorite vacation spot. Every January we would close the diner for a week and head to "paradise" as my parents referred to it, escaping the rainy, gray Seattle winter days for the magical combination of sunshine, swimming, and family time. Those days were some of my happiest memories, watching the glorious sunsets from Hapuna Beach, Daphne toddling around in her sun hat and chunky thighs, with inflatable floaties jammed on her upper arms, slathered in Coppertone Water Babies SPF 50. Mom in a floral one-piece swimsuit with a skirt, wearing huge Audrey Hepburn–style sunglasses, sipping a double mai tai from a thermos. Dad, lean and brown, throwing himself over and over into the waves to bodysurf. And me, happy to just be with them, the people I loved most in the world, gobbling chunks of pineapple from a Tupperware container, my sunburned nose buried in one of the Baby-Sitters Club books. We'd soaked in the sunshine and the unhurried time together. Those had been halcyon days, the memory of them sweet and uncomplicated. I looked around, wondering where Dad was. Maybe he'd finally taken up sportfishing or kitesurfing, both hobbies he'd always said he'd like to try when he retired.

"Here we are." A few minutes later Mom appeared, bearing a tray with scrambled eggs and buttered English muffins, cubes of fresh papaya, and the promised mai tais. She settled down into the other chair with a big sigh and raised her glass. "To paradise." I joined her in the toast, then dug into the scrambled eggs. I was starving.

As I ate, I studied her across the table, soaking in her presence like sunshine. She looked older, but her color was pink and healthy, not the waxy hue of that terrible last day. She had always been plump and sturdy. A Danish workhorse, she called herself. She looked classically Scandinavian, with high, wide cheekbones, deep-set green eyes, and that thick wheaten hair. She was not beautiful in the traditional sense, but she was striking; people noticed her. She had a strong presence and radiated an air of capable optimism, a can-do attitude that energized every space she occupied. For as long as I could remember, she'd been the focal point of every room, the center of activity, the queen bee in the middle of every hive.

Now she had aged, with lines across her forehead and a certain shadow in her eyes, but her posture was relaxed, her face serene. Watching her, a feeling of pure elation bubbled up through my chest.

I couldn't believe I was actually here. My mother was sitting across from me amid a tumult of blooms and greenery, rocking a flashy teal muumuu and drinking cocktails for breakfast. It felt so marvelous, so deliciously improbable. It was a gift, pure and simple.

"It's so good to see you," I blurted out around a mouthful of eggs.

Her expression softened. "I've missed you, Lolly. It's been too long. I know you're busy running the Eatery, but don't forget to take time for yourself too. That's something I regret, that your dad and I didn't take enough time for ourselves. We worked too hard. Don't make our mistake."

"Speaking of Dad, where is he?" I took a sip of mai tai, savoring the cold, sweet punch of the rum.

Mom looked a little surprised, then a brief flash of sadness crossed her face. "In my bedroom, right by the window. He always loved the ocean. I wanted him to have a view." Her mouth twisted a little, and she cleared her throat and looked away. I froze, a forkful of eggs halfway to my mouth. *Loved.* She'd used the past tense. *He always loved the ocean.* I put my fork down. My appetite suddenly vanished.

"I'm just going to grab a glass of water. You need anything?" I stood hastily. There was an awful sinking feeling in the pit of my stomach.

Instead of going to the kitchen I slipped down the hall. I found her room next to the one I'd awakened in. It was simple—a queen bed with a birds of paradise coverlet, a dresser, and two small side tables flanking the bed. With a growing sense of dread, I stepped into the room. On the side table nearest the window that looked out at the water sat a small wooden box with a heart-shaped photo on one side. I bent down for a closer look.

The photo was of Dad in his navy uniform, his eyes upside-down crescents when he smiled, standing trim and straight in his jaunty white Dixie cup hat and neckerchief. The brief lines of cursive below the photo stated simply:

Martin Samuel Blanchard
Beloved husband, father, cook, and sailor
April 12, 1960–September 09, 2018.

Oh no. Oh no. This was a cremation urn. Dad was dead. I gave a muffled cry and jumped back so quickly I almost lost my footing. I gazed at the photo numbly. I couldn't quite catch my breath.

"Sweetie, are you okay?" Mom called from the veranda. "Are you finding everything you need?"

"I'm fine," I yelled back automatically, taking a deep breath and trying to steady myself. My hands were shaking and I couldn't take my eyes off the box. The meaning of it slowly sank in. In this version of my life, Mom was alive, but Dad was gone. I'd exchanged one parent for the other. I felt a sharp stab of disappointment. I had hoped I'd find my family complete and happy for one more day, not like this. Not fractured in a different way.

"It's just for one day," I whispered under my breath, trying to ease the icy knot of grief in my gut. In my real, normal life Dad was alive and well, presumably puttering around our kitchen, making coffee and catching up on the sports scores, swearing as he burned the bacon and slipping the tastiest bits to Bertha on the sly. In real life, my mom was lying under a patch of lawn at Evergreen Washelli Cemetery. Tomorrow, when I woke, it would be to that real, motherless reality, not this fatherless one. I had to remember that. Today was a gift, a single final day with my mom. I couldn't waste a minute of it.

Taking several deep, calming breaths through my nose (at least yoga had taught me something), I waited until my heart rate slowed, then headed back to the veranda. I kept my focus on the woman sitting there waiting for me. I was in Hawaii. With my mother. We had so little time, I resolved right then and there to make the most of every second.

21

Back at the table, I sank into my seat, trying to regain my equilibrium. I felt so off-kilter. I took a big swallow of mai tai, letting the cold, sweet, strong punch of the rum trickle down my throat. When I looked up, Mom was watching me. She leaned forward and studied my face, frowning a little.

"Lolly, my girl. Are you okay?"

I firmly put all thoughts of the wooden box out of my mind and focused solely on her.

"I'm great," I assured her hastily. "I'm here with you. We're in Hawaii. What's not to love?" It was an honest answer, though not a complete one.

She took a sip of her mai tai and made a little hmm sound of agreement. "Yes, it's paradise here. But that's not what I'm talking about. I'm talking about you. Are you happy? Are you sleeping well, eating enough? You're looking worn out and a little . . . on edge. What's weighing on you?" Her eyes never left my face, assessing. She had always had that motherly sixth sense about both Daphne and me, an instinct when something was amiss. It was hard to put anything past her. She had a nose for the truth.

Gazing across the condo's scrubby green lawn to the ribbon of white beach and the rolling ocean beyond, I pondered my answer. I had no idea what sort of life I was supposed to be living in this particular reality. She'd mentioned me running the diner. So apparently that was still happening.

"Just tired I guess. You know how it is running a restaurant." I shrugged. I went for generalities.

"It's a heavy load," she agreed. "It's hard to have any other life when you're tied to that place. I worry that it's too much for you." She took a bite of buttered English muffin and waited, watching me. I squinted out at the water, weighing my options. I'd come to see her partly for the sheer joy of being in her presence for one more day. I'd missed her every day for the last ten years. But I'd also come for advice, and I'd have to be honest and risk telling her at least the bare bones of my dilemma if I wanted her help. Not the specifics. But the gist of it, the parts where I was stuck. I glanced at her, waiting patiently in the sun for me to speak my mind.

"It's not the work hours that are wearing me down," I confessed finally, taking a deep breath. "I found my middle school journal recently. And it had a life goals list I'd written, all the things I had planned to accomplish before I turned thirty-three. I read the list, and you know what I realized?"

"What?" Mom took a sip of her mai tai, listening intently.

"I haven't accomplished a single thing on it. Not one thing. I've kept the legacy of our family going. I've kept the diner afloat against some pretty big odds. But I haven't actually achieved anything I wanted to when I was younger. And that feels . . . really sad. But I don't quite know what to do about it. Every choice means I sacrifice something else. I'm torn between what I want and what I think I should do." I picked up my mai tai and took a long swallow. The icy rum and curaçao and lime juice puckered my mouth but went down smooth.

Mom nodded, gazing out at the ocean. I watched her in profile, still dazzled by the reality of her, there in the flesh, sitting across from me in the hot tropical sun. She turned and smiled at me, showing the little gap in her teeth that made her self-conscious but that everyone else found disarmingly charming.

"Sometimes humpback whales breach out there," she said conversationally. "Keep an eye out. We may get lucky." She took a big bite of scrambled eggs and gazed at me with compassion. "What is it you want that you don't have right now? What was on the list?"

I hesitated. "I wanted to live abroad, open my own restaurant. I wanted a horse."

Mom chuckled. "I remember that phase. You were crazy for horses until you got old enough to discover boys. I think they were more interesting to you from then on. Well, one boy." She hesitated. "Do you still think about Rory? Some days I still can't believe it didn't work out between you." She sobered and shook her head, pressing her lips together. "He was like a son to me. I really thought you two . . . Well, it just goes to show you never know what life will throw at you." She sighed and put her fork down beside her plate.

I was surprised. Apparently, Rory and I were not together in this life either, although it sounded like we had been at one point. I'd always assumed that Mom's death was the reason he and I were not living happily ever after. The fact that we were not together here or in my life running Toast in Brighton was disappointing. I wondered what it was this time that had kept us apart.

"Yes, I still miss him. Every day. And I wish I didn't," I confessed. "If I'm honest, I feel like it wasn't supposed to turn out this way. My life wasn't supposed to be the way it is."

Mom blew out a breath. "Life often ends up different than we expect."

I thought of the little wooden box on her side table. "What do I do now?"

"My best advice?" Mom squinted at me appraisingly. "Let it fall apart," she said simply.

"What?" I stared at her in astonishment. This was not the answer I expected from my never-say-never, can-do-attitude mother.

She was quiet for a long moment, and when she spoke, her voice was soft and thoughtful. "You know what I've learned in these last few hard years since your dad died, Lolly? I learned that sometimes you have to let go. Sometimes it's the only way forward. For so many years I worked so hard, trying to make a good life and legacy for our family. I worked myself to a frazzle and did a disservice to your father and you girls by trying too hard to succeed with the diner. Failure wasn't a word I tolerated. I believed that if I did the right thing and worked as hard as I could, everything would turn out okay."

A look of profound sadness crossed her face. "But that was a lie. Four years ago, when your dad died, the safe, tidy, sensible world I'd worked so hard to build for us fell apart in one horrible instant. It was nothing I could control. I did everything right, and in the end his aneurysm blew out all my plans. And even then I couldn't let go of what I thought should have happened." She sighed and sat back in her chair.

"After your dad died I tried so hard to put our life back together as it was, to make it all work the same way again, but I couldn't get all the pieces to fit. It had broken so thoroughly that I could not glue it back together in the same way. I could not make it okay again. The moment I knew he was gone, I knew life could never be the same, but I didn't want to admit it. I couldn't. I was trying so desperately to make it come right."

She reached out and plucked the straw from her glass, stabbing a spear of pineapple with it and popping the fruit in her mouth. "It took me a while to finally understand the truth. Sometimes things don't work out the way we hoped, despite our best intentions. And when they go pear-shaped, you have to let them. You can't keep holding on, trying to redo the past and stop the bad things from happening. They happened, and you can't change that. You can't keep holding on to the vision of the future you imagined you'd have, the way you thought things would turn out. You have to let the present be what it is—broken, flawed, painful, but real."

I stared at her, ingesting her words slowly. "I don't know how to do that," I admitted. "If I let go, everything will fall to pieces. I can't let that happen."

"Honey, it sounds like whatever you're holding on to is probably already broken," she said kindly, "and you're just holding the pieces together and praying for some glue." She paused, considering. "Life doesn't work that way. If you cling so tight to something that's already broken, to a life and dream that can never come true, you don't have space in your life for anything else, for the good and real plan Bs." She looked me in the eye and said firmly, "Sometimes, Lolly, you just have to let go."

I waited, the ice melting in my glass, numbing my fingers almost painfully in the gathering morning heat. Was she saying what I thought she was saying? That it was futile to continue to hold tight to a course of action once life had changed unexpectedly? Was she releasing me, without even knowing it, from my deathbed promise to her? A promise I'd been holding myself to for ten years. A promise I'd given up my entire life and first love for. Was she saying it was okay for me to let go of her dream for our family's future and let life be what it was without her? As if sensing my internal question, she kept talking.

"When you told me you wanted to take over the diner, I let you," she said with a sigh. "Selfishly, I wanted you to make a go of it, make the dream I had for it real. And if that's your dream too, I'll support you till my last breath. But, honey, nothing is worth holding on to if it's holding you back. It's okay to let something go if it's time to move on."

And with her words something in me loosened, like the turn of a key, the click of a lock springing open. I'd been held under the burden of the promise I'd made to her for so long. It felt strange to think of being free of it now. Not free of Dad or Daphne or my responsibilities at the diner. Not free of the life I'd made in the ten years since her death, but released from the responsibility to keep everything as it was before her death, free from the burden of needing to stand in her shoes and carry out her vision for our lives. Free from the burden of her expectations, even from beyond the grave. I didn't know what to say.

"Life will give you plenty of lemons, Lolly," she said at last. "You know that as well as I do. I used to say when life gives you lemons you should make lemonade. I even had that sign up in the diner. Now I think you should take life's lemons and do whatever you want with them, whatever brings you joy. Maybe you make lemonade if that's your style. But maybe you get some gin and make yourself a strong double gin fizz. Choose what brings you life, my girl, and it will all come right in the end. Trust me on that."

I picked up my English muffin and took a bite, considering her words. They didn't fix everything. Didn't fix anything, really. There was still the sticky dilemma of my duty versus my desire. There was still the life goals list completely unmet. There was still the tiny issue that I was in love with a man I'd broken up with seven years ago. None of those were insubstantial. But looking at my mother, I wondered if perhaps she was right. What would happen if I just let go?

For a minute we both watched the curl of surf breaking against the white sand. In the swell of the waves, just before they crested, I could see dozens of brilliantly hued yellow fish swimming in the aqua-blue waves, backlit by sunlight. Yellow tangs, I remembered Dad telling me they were called.

"Thank you," I said softly.

"For what?" Mom asked.

"I can't even say."

She cocked her head and eyed me quizzically. "You're welcome," she said at last with a gentle smile. "A little hard-earned wisdom from your mother, who loves you dearly." We sat for a few minutes in silence, watching the water.

"What do you want to do today?" Mom asked, sucking on a cube of ice from her mai tai.

"I don't care. I just want to spend the day with you."

Today was my last chance. I wanted this day to be all about time with Mom, every second, every breath soaking up the last day I would ever spend with her. I took the final sip of my mai tai, swallowing down loss and unexpected second chances, the sour and the sweet.

22

We settled on a drive down the coast, Mom at the wheel of an older model aqua-colored convertible Ford Thunderbird with a scarf tied over her hair à la Grace Kelly. Our family had never owned anything but old Volvo station wagons, and to see her in something so peppy and cute was both surprising and endearing. She put a CD of classic female country singers, greatest hits on, turned it up loud, and we set off.

My hair whipped in my eyes as we took the curves of the Mamalahoa Highway a shade too fast for comfort, the sun shining on the crown of my head, the water far below us a sparkling blue, sharp and bright as cut glass. Over the speakers Tammy Wynette warbled about elusive dreams. With the wind whistling around us it was too loud to talk. That was okay. I was content just to be with her, in the warm sunshine, watching the tropical jungle of greenery slide by as we wound our way south. After twenty minutes or so of driving, Mom pulled off at the South Kona Fruit Stand.

"Let's grab some fruit for breakfast tomorrow. Do you still like those little apple bananas? I remember you and Daphne used to love them."

The small open-air stand was empty of customers but brimming with the tropical bounty of the island arranged in baskets on tiered wooden stands. I wandered around picking up various fruits, enjoying the laid-back island vibe.

"Speaking of Daphne, she called me a couple of days ago." Mom leaned over and gently squeezed an enormous avocado almost the size of a football. She frowned and put it back.

"Oh? What's she up to?" I paused, a bright, spiky fuchsia dragonfruit in hand. I'd almost forgotten that Daphne was part of the reason I wanted to see Mom. Maybe she would have some good advice about how to talk my sister into staying in school.

"She seems peachy. Says Bali is amazing. She's talking about staying on after her training ends and leading yoga retreats over there."

Bali. Daphne was in Indonesia? I thought back to Daphne's and my disastrous, heated argument yesterday in the Bikram yoga session. Maybe this yoga training was not just a passing fancy of hers. But I still wanted her to finish school.

"Bali, huh?" I set the dragonfruit down next to a basket of limes. Dragonfruit is wildly beautiful to look at but disappointingly bland. "What do you think of her being there?"

"I think it's exactly like Daphne." Mom chuckled. "She was always our wild card, the child who jumped first and looked later." Mom paused to gently press a large strawberry papaya, its yellow skin speckled with green, then tucked it in a reusable shopping bag she'd brought from the car. "Not like you. You were always . . . careful. Even as a child you'd calculate the risks and the odds of your success." She smiled at the memory. "I always knew Daphne would be the one who flew away from us. It was just a matter of time."

"Don't you worry about her long-term career goals? It could be hard to build a solid career with just a yoga certification," I argued.

Mom shrugged. "There are lots of ways to make a good life, Lolly.

Focusing on a career path is one, but there are many others. Daphne's making her own way. I think she'll be fine."

I frowned. "But wouldn't it be so much better if she got a degree in something, if she had some other job experience and education?"

"Maybe," Mom conceded. "But the thing you'll learn if you ever have children is that each one is their own person. You can't superimpose your own vision for their future on them. You have to let them find their own way."

I turned away, disgruntled. I wanted to protect Daphne, to make her see reason. I wanted her to make sensible choices and plan wisely for the future. Mom's advice was not helpful so far.

You want her to live your ideal version of her life, a little voice in my head whispered. *And hasn't there been enough of that in this family already?*

Humph. I set down a lilikoi harder than was strictly necessary. After paying for the papaya and a cluster of apple bananas, Mom suggested we head back north.

"Let's go into town. Gypsea Gelato still has that coconut flavor you love. My treat."

Back in the laid-back beach town of Kailua-Kona, we stood in the long line of sunburned tourists at Gypsea Gelato, then took our cups and strolled as we ate. We spent the afternoon happily poking around the shops, trying on oversize sunglasses and floppy hats, laughing about nothing, just enjoying each other's company. It was easy to forget that these moments were fleeting. They felt so normal. I fell under their spell and forgot all about the slow but steady passage of time.

Later, however, as we enjoyed a leisurely dinner at a local restaurant overlooking the water, the realization came rushing back to me. I picked at my grilled sand dabs and roasted vegetables. I had no appetite even though the food was fresh and delicious. I remembered what was coming, and the grief almost choked me. It was too soon. The day had gone too quickly. Already the sun was sinking low on the horizon.

"What do you want to do for the rest of the evening?" Mom blotted her mouth with a napkin and waved the server over for the bill. "Want to catch a movie or see if there's live music playing somewhere?"

"Can we go see the stars?"

We had such a little time left together. I wanted to stand with her in the darkness under the vast swath of the Milky Way and feel our tiny place in the universe. I wanted to remember how brief life was and how precious.

"Of course. Your father always loved to do that with you girls."

The mood was contemplative as we headed out of town. Mom pointed the car northeast on Mamalahoa Highway, then turned onto Saddle Road, climbing higher up Mauna Kea, the verdant volcanic mountain that makes up half of Hawaii's Big Island. It grew cooler as we drove, and Mom put the top up on the convertible. We saw few other cars. Behind us the mountain dropped away for miles in a long, slow slope down to the endless sea. It felt wild up here, remote and open.

Sunset was splashing the western horizon behind us in a tumult of orange and purple when we pulled off the side of the road. The visitor's center was still miles away up the mountain, but we had never made it that far, not even when I was a kid. Every vacation Dad took us up here on the last night of our trip. He knew all the constellations from his time in the navy, and he'd point them out to us. We'd shiver, teeth chattering, wearing too-thin nightgowns and warm jackets as the cold wind whipped our legs. It was surprisingly frigid this high up the mountain. The night sky was magnificent, but I was always a little bit relieved when we would wind back down the mountain into the tropical, warm darkness once more.

The temperature had dropped easily twenty degrees when Mom and I got out of the car, and I knew that as night fell it would get even colder. I was already shivering in my summer clothes. Maybe this had been a mistake. But Mom calmly pulled a fleece blanket and two jackets out of her trunk and handed me one. She also had a couple of folding camp chairs stashed back there, and we positioned them to catch the last of the sunset colors. Cocooned in warmth, we sat together as the light faded and night fell across the mountain. Soon we were swathed in a cold velvety darkness and a silence so complete I could hear my own breathing.

I sat wordlessly, my heart aching, wishing for more time, yet grateful for this taste, this brief, bittersweet moment with my mother. A shooting star arced across the sky, brilliant and fleeting. I closed my eyes and made a wish.

"Mom?"

"Hmm?"

"I'm scared to let things go," I confessed. "What if everything falls apart and I can't make anything good come from the broken pieces?"

A moment of silence. "You have to have faith, Lolly. It takes faith and courage to let things fall apart, not knowing what will happen after you do. But you are strong. You can do this. There is more for you, my girl. More life and love and good things, maybe babies if you want them." She chuckled. "This is not the end for you," she said simply. "There are good things ahead. Trust me. I'm your mother. I know this is true."

And then her hand, strong and warm, gripped mine. I leaned my head back against the camp chair and let myself cry silently, tears tracing warm and salty down my temples and into the shells of my ears. I'd made a promise to this woman and sacrificed everything to keep it. Now here she was giving me advice that felt like both absolution and an invitation. I didn't know how to do what she was suggesting. If I let things fall apart, I feared I would never find my way. In holding things together I was holding myself together too. If I let it all go, would I dissolve into nothing?

The drive home was quiet as we wound down the mountain, but when we reached the warmth and lights of the Mamalahoa Highway, Mom slipped the country singers CD out of the CD player and chose another artist.

"Figured we needed to lighten the mood." She smiled at me as the unmistakable opening bars of Elvis Presley's "Hound Dog" boomed through the speakers. She laughed at my startled expression and started to dance in her seat while she drove, bouncing and jiggling with abandon as she belted out the lyrics alongside Elvis's smooth Southern drawl. I gaped at her for a few seconds, then gave in and joined her. I'd forgotten how goofy my mother could be, how unabashedly she could let loose and cut a rug. I'd missed that about her without even realizing it was gone from my life. How long had it been since I'd sung along to the radio and danced with such carefree abandon? More than a decade, I guessed.

We laughed and gyrated our way through "All Shook Up" and "Jailhouse Rock," arriving back at the condo breathless and giggling a little after ten. Once inside, Mom checked her watch, then stifled a yawn and bid me good night.

"It's getting late for these old bones," she said. I hugged her tight, unable to let go. She pulled back with a little laugh. "Goodness, we'll see each other in the morning. Sleep tight, my dear girl." She kissed my forehead, then held my face in her hands and said firmly, "I love you, Lolly, no matter what. I want you to always know that."

I nodded. "I love you too, Mom." I choked up and blinked fast against the tears. Inside I was a welter of conflicting emotions. Gratitude and grief mixed. I was grateful for the absolution, for her words that freed me, but they felt like they came too late. I knew she'd only had these realizations because of Dad's death, but I wished I'd heard those words earlier, before she died, when Rory's ring was still on my finger, when my future was still bright and shiny with potential. I was glad to hear the words now, but I had already lost so much. And now I knew, with a sharp stab of sadness, that I was also about to lose her all over again. It was inevitable. There was nothing I could do to stop it this time either.

In the quiet of the condo I put on my pajamas and brushed my teeth out of habit, then crawled into bed, lying in the warm darkness, forcing myself to stay awake. If I slept, it would all be over. I would never see my mother again. After a few minutes I tiptoed to her door, hesitating outside. It was open a few inches and I could see her in bed, propped up against the headboard, her hair tied up in a silk handkerchief, reading a magazine. Dad's box of ashes was beside her on the table. She heard me at the door and waved me in.

"Can't sleep?"

I shook my head, though it wasn't quite the truth. I was trying desperately not to sleep.

"Come here," she patted the bed beside her, and I crept over like an obedient child and slipped between the sheets next to her, my head pillowed in her lap. She smelled so achingly familiar and I breathed her in, trying to remember her exact scent. She continued reading but began to gently rub my back with the tips of her fingers, just as she'd done when I was a child and had a nightmare and couldn't fall back asleep. Her touch was steady and warm. She didn't stop, just turned a page occasionally with one hand but never lost the slow, soothing rhythm on my back with the other. In the buttery pool of light from her bedside lamp, I tried to stay awake, but my eyelids drifted shut, and the last thing I felt was the gentle touch of my mother's fingertips tracing endless circles on my back.

23

When I woke alone in my own room in our house in Magnolia, once more in my normal life, I bolted out of bed, grabbed my glasses, threw my hair up in a messy bun, and dashed to Aunt Gert's cottage. It was early, barely dawn, the light still gray and the air chilly and smelling of rain and moss.

I found Aunt Gert in the middle of Mom's neglected edible-flower garden in the backyard near her cottage. Mom. I felt a pang when I thought of her and our day together. She had been so vibrant, so . . . alive. So close. It brought the grief of losing her swelling up again. I missed her practical wisdom, her zest for life, that wide-open laugh. Aunt Gert was crouched down in the garden, pulling weeds and shriveled dead flowers, wearing a paisley jumpsuit in a psychedelic print that looked like it was straight out of one of Andy Warhol's legendary parties.

"Can I go back again?" I blurted out, thinking of my mother and the utter impossibility of not seeing her once more. She had been there, real, solid, and alive as I drifted to sleep. I didn't want to say goodbye. I couldn't say goodbye. "Is it possible to have another day?"

"Good morning to you too." Aunt Gert looked up and waved me over. "I woke up with a compelling need to weed."

I knelt down beside her, ignoring the fact that the ground was damp and spongy from recent rain. The knees of my pajama pants were immediately soaked.

"Is there any way to go back to somewhere I've already been?"

"The pansies are overgrown with weeds and all dead now," Aunt Gert observed with a cluck of her tongue, ignoring my question. "And I think a snail has had his way with the impatiens. They didn't do much this year." She pointed to a few brown flowers. "The marigolds were still vigorous through November, however."

These few bedraggled flowers were all that remained of Mom's edible-flower garden. Every spring since her death I'd planted a handful of varieties in the hopes that it would foster more home cooking and a farm-to-table ethos in our house, but none of us had the time or energy to do much with it after long days at the diner. Now almost all of the plants were dormant or dead.

Gardening had been one of the only things Aunt Gert and I discovered we had in common. I liked it because Mom had loved it. It connected me with her. But despite the fact that we both enjoyed it, neither Aunt Gert nor I had found the time yet to restore the garden to its former glory. Now, in the last short days of winter, it was just a shadow of its past self. Perhaps someday I'd have time to garden again.

"Taste this." Aunt Gert offered me a bright green leaf. I took it and nibbled obediently. It always amazed me that some plants could grow year-round in the Pacific Northwest. With temperatures that rarely dipped below freezing, some hardier plants such as rosemary could stay green through the winter. This mint plant, sheltered against Aunt Gert's cottage wall, seemed likely to make it to spring.

"Persian mint," she explained. "I planted it last summer. The first time I ever had it was in Jordan, on a tour for educators. They serve a drink there called limonana, a frosty mint lemonade. It's divine in the scorching heat. Oh, that was the best trip. The food, the historic sights. Petra." She smiled, her eyes far away, and I caught a glimpse of what she would have looked like when she was young. Not pretty, exactly, but lively, with a quick smile, a wide expressive mouth that could curl up in amusement or turn down in distain, and a sharp wit to match those ice-blue eyes. She'd been strawberry blond, she'd told me once, prone to sunburn and freckling.

I shifted impatiently. I'd learned early in Aunt Gert's time with us that she was stubborn as a mule. You couldn't push her to do anything she wasn't good and ready to do. And obviously she wasn't ready to answer my question. However, I had no intention of leaving until I had an answer one way or the other.

"You used another lemon drop." She sat back on her heels and looked at me. The knees of her pantsuit were muddy brown circles. I nodded.

"And what did you choose?" she asked, and for a moment I contemplated not telling her, keeping the memory of my day with my mother precious and close. But this was Aunt Gert's niece we were discussing, my mother, the woman she'd loved almost like a daughter. Aunt Gert had never had children, and she'd picked my mom as her favorite from an early age. They exchanged letters back and forth, and Aunt Gert visited every few years. She even flew Mom to New York City as a surprise for her fifteenth birthday. Mom used to tell us about that trip, seeing a show on Broadway and tasting champagne for the first time.

"I went to see my mom." I reached down and plucked up a few dried stalks of cilantro. It had never really flourished in this spot and was now just shriveled and brown. "We spent the day together."

Aunt Gert nodded as though my words confirmed her suspicions, then picked up a pair of garden shears and cut back a dry and yellowed bunch of parsley. "How marvelous. And how was Irene?"

"She was amazing." My tone was wistful. "Happy. Opinionated. In Hawaii. Just . . . herself."

Aunt Gert sat back and sighed. "Dear Irene." She smiled sadly for a moment. "How wonderful to be able to see her again."

"Couldn't you go visit her if you wanted to? Just use one of the lemon drops?"

"Oh, I'm too old for all that now," she said dismissively. "I used a few of the lemon drops years ago, early on after I'd first been given them, but then after a while I felt they'd served their purpose in my life. Now I'm far past the days where I want to live any other reality than this one, hard as it sometimes is." She tossed the stems of parsley into her weed pile.

"I've been meaning to ask. Where did you get the lemon drops?" I'd been wondering since she gave them to me. If there was a way to get more of them . . . I caught my breath. I would give anything to spend more days with my mom.

Aunt Gert smiled, reaching down and pulling a few little clumps of weeds and tossing them over her shoulder into the yard. "Believe it or not, I got them from a fortune-teller at a county fair in rural Ohio."

"You're kidding."

"It's true." She paused. "It was 1962. I was twenty years old, and the carnival was in town. It was gaudy and a little tawdry, with a freak show and hawkers and tinny carousel music, but we all loved it and looked forward to it every year." Aunt Gert smiled at the memory. "And there was always a fortune-teller, Madam Esme. My mother disapproved. She was a devout Methodist and considered fortune-telling witchcraft. Well, I was a Unitarian Universalist and had always been curious about Madam Esme, and that night, for whatever reason, I went to see her."

"What did she tell you?"

Aunt Gert chuckled. "She was sitting in her tent smoking a cigarette. When I came in, she stubbed out the cigarette quick as a wink
and told me to sit down. She looked the part, tiny and wizened with
long silver hair and a red spangled headscarf. She took one look at my
plain face, pretended to consult her crystal ball, and predicted there
was a mysterious dark and handsome stranger in my future, then demanded I pay her fifty cents."

"And?"

"I laughed in her face and said I had no interest in a dark and handsome stranger in my future, that I'd already suffered a broken heart and
wanted nothing more to do with love."

Aunt Gert pulled up a dried clump of marigolds and tossed them
onto the growing weed pile.

"What did she say to that?"

"It got her attention." Aunt Gert smiled. "She wanted to know more.
I told her about being engaged, about how my fiancé left me for another girl in our senior class, Dorothy Allan. She was tall and blond
and had a laugh like a guinea hen. And I told her about my family and
our life—our struggling berry farm, my invalid mother and her frail
health. And about my father, who was bipolar, although we didn't use
that label back then. He was a brilliant, violent man, given to black
moods. We were so poor, always just scraping along, making ends almost meet somehow. My father didn't believe in women being edu-
cated. My mother had to fight hard just so he'd let me finish high
school. I was expected to run the house and the berry stand and take
care of Mother. That was going to be my lot in life."

"You told the fortune-teller all that?"

"Yes, and I told her I wanted so much more. A different life. I was
very bright and ambitious, I wanted to be a schoolteacher somewhere
far away from our poor little town. I dreamed of going to New York

City, but I was stuck in the gravity of my family and our little town with a whole lot of big dreams and little real hope for the future." She paused and rested for a moment, her tone of voice matter-of-fact.

"What did she say then?"

"Not a word. She got up, rummaged around behind a curtain, and when she came back, she gave me a handful of lemon drops. She told me her real name was Rena, that she was originally from Romania, and that everything she did for the carnival was a ruse. Reading people's fortunes was simply about reading people, she explained to me, about guessing their deep desires, their hidden longings. But the lemon drops were true magic, she assured me, the knowledge of them a secret passed down through the women in her family. The lemon drops, she said, had the power to show me a different future. And she warned me to use them well. Then she refused to take my money and dismissed me from the tent. I left with the lemon drops and a chance at a better future tucked safely in my pocket."

"Wow." I was impressed. "Was she right? Did they show you a better future?"

Aunt Gert paused and looked off into the middle distance, across the backyard to the tired gray paint and white shutters of our modest house. "To quote the Little Flower, dear Saint Thérèse of Lisieux, 'Only God can see what is in the bottom of our hearts; we are half-blind.' Did I make the right choice? I hope so. Some could look at my choice as selfish, an act of cowardice, of self-preservation. Others might see it as the ultimate bravery. I don't know anymore. I am content with the path of my life. My only sorrow is that it is almost over."

"What do you mean it's over? You've got more vim and vigor than people half your age," I protested.

She smiled enigmatically. "You're young, Lolly. All of life is before you. I'm old now. I've had my time. The world has very little use for an eccentric old woman." She sounded a little wistful. "It has been a marvelous journey, though. I just wish I had more time. There is still so much I want to do. I always planned to see the penguins in Antarctica . . ."

"It's not too late," I argued. "What about following your bliss? There's no expiration date on that, right?"

She glanced at me and sank her trowel deep into the soil. "Tell you what. Let's strike a bargain. You try hard to follow your bliss, and I'll strongly consider whether there's anything left for me to follow. I'm an old woman with most of my days behind me, but you, Lolly, have so many days ahead of you."

I stood, brushing at the muddy knees of my pajamas. "You sound like the fortune-teller," I said lightly.

Aunt Gert shrugged. "There's a kernel of truth in some of the most unlikely places." She picked up her trowel and gripped a large clump of dried daylily leaves firmly. "And to answer your question about whether you can go back more than once, let me say this: don't try to go back again, not yet. First use your last lemon drop. Use it wisely and well. Choose something you have not chosen before, some regret that lingers like a thorn in your heart, and when you have done that, come see me again."

24

After my early-morning conversation with Aunt Gert, the day dragged slowly. I was feeling restless and unsettled. I missed my mom. I missed Rory. Everything felt wrong. I glanced at the clock. Four p.m. Time enough to head out before the dinner hour started. Last I'd checked, the dining room was almost empty. Aunt Gert was sitting in a back booth reading Saint Thérèse of Lisieux's *Story of a Soul* and keeping an eye on the lone customer finishing his second slice of pie at a nearby table. No one would miss me for an hour.

"Dad, I'll be back before the dinner rush." I grabbed my rain jacket from my office and walked through the kitchen. Dad and Julio were done with dinner prep and were huddled together watching YouTube videos of the Seahawks' last season highlights. I was glad to see Dad sitting down. He'd been looking a little run-down lately, and I was concerned about him. He'd repeatedly brushed away my questions with gruff assertions that he was right as rain but I wasn't convinced.

I drove to Discovery Park and pulled into a spot in the small, al-most deserted parking lot at South Beach. No one monitored the parking lot in the off-season. I got out, wishing I'd worn tennis shoes instead of my cute little canvas shoes, and headed down the path toward the beach. I hadn't been down here in years, not since the day I'd broken up with Rory. As I walked, I replayed Aunt Gert's words. *Choose some regret that lingers like a thorn in your heart*, she'd instructed. What lingered like a thorn in my heart? One thing for sure. Rory Shaw.

The afternoon was waning toward dusk already. The late-winter days were startlingly short this far north. Just visible to the south, Mount Rainier was wreathed in clouds that were blushing in the beginnings of a spectacular sunset. Across the sound lay Bainbridge Island, and behind it soared the snowcapped majestic Olympic Mountains. Seagulls wheeled above me, and a pair of black scoters bobbed in the choppy gray water just offshore. A kayaker rounded the point by the lighthouse, his paddle dipping rhythmically. The beach was rocky and littered with seaweed, a chill breeze sweeping across the long, empty stretch of sand and black rock.

My feet took the familiar path toward the wilder, remoter north side of the beach, toward our special place. I found the driftwood log easily enough. Some kids had made a teepee of driftwood at the root end of it. There was no one on the beach other than a woman way down at the other end, throwing a stick into the surf for her Labrador. I sank down in the soft white sand, right where Rory and I always sat. So much had happened in this spot. I leaned my head back, fitting the rear of my skull to the smooth bleached-white curve of the giant driftwood log, thinking of all the things that had transpired in this little patch of sand. This was where Rory had first kissed me. It's where he first broke my heart. And it's where I broke his at the very end.

I usually tried my best to forget our past. I avoided this place because it brought everything up again. But today, raw and edgy and full of hope and regret, I closed my eyes and let myself remember—Oxford,

England, that fateful night at the pub, a padlock in the shape of a heart, and how, for one brief shining moment, I held in my hands everything I ever wanted.

TWELVE YEARS AGO
NOVEMBER

Don't call me. Don't text me. I don't want to hear from you ever again. That's what I'd told Rory after our disastrous night at the beach together, after our first passionate kiss followed by his rejection of me. I was hurt and humiliated and in that moment I meant everything I said.

He took me at my word. It was more than three years before Rory and I spoke again. I graduated high school and then finished my freshman and sophomore years at Portland State University. The fall of my junior year I signed up for a study abroad semester in London. It was the first stamp in my passport, the first time I'd set foot in another country.

I fell in love with the UK from the start. I was enthralled by London, with its crisp accents and famous landmarks—Trafalgar Square, Portobello Road, Big Ben, and the Tower of London. On weekends Eve and I and some of our fellow exchange students would take the train to other cities—Bath and Oxford and even once up to Edinburgh on a long weekend. But it was Brighton I loved best, with its salty air and jaunty holiday vibe, its windy cobblestone streets and pebble beach. I'd buy a takeaway fish and chips and eat it by the water, watching the gulls as they wheeled and cried over the ornate Victorian splendor of the Brighton pier. I dreamed big in England—of opening my own restaurant in Brighton, of making a life in this country that captivated me. My vision for Toast was refined as I browsed the gastronomic delights of London's iconic Borough Market. England ignited my imagination for my future.

After the debacle of that final night on the beach, I'd placed Rory firmly in the back of my head, labeling him an embarrassing first crush. The sting of his rejection was minimized if I told myself that I didn't still care for him or think of him. I tried to make it true. I unfriended him on social media and blocked his number on my phone. Then I posted gorgeous photos on my social media, me carefree with friends, eating and drinking and taking the railway around the country. Even though I'd unfriended him, a part of me hoped Rory saw each one. Occasionally I wondered what he was doing, if he thought of me, but I told myself I didn't care. I tried to live in a Rory-free world, but my defenses had one fatal flaw. My mother. She was still convinced we belonged together, and so she gave me regular updates on Rory, bits of information passed on to her from Nancy Shaw. I asked her to stop more than once but she blithely ignored the request.

"Rory broke up with that girl Jessica. Nancy is so relieved. She never did care for her," Mom told me only a week or two after Rory's and my disastrous night at the beach. I was surprised, and my heart leaped with a traitorous hope. Now that he was not with Jessica, would he contact me? Was he going to reconsider his words? But the days and weeks passed with no word from him, and I felt the sting of rejection all over again. I did not reach out to him, too humiliated and hurt to put my heart out there again. His silence spoke volumes.

Over the next few years I heard snippets of news about him from Mom.

"Rory is studying for the MCAT. Nancy says his professors think he'll do very well."

"Rory's planning to apply to med schools on the East Coast, all the best ones. Nancy thinks he might even get into one of the top schools in the country."

And then, a month into my semester abroad in England, "Nancy told me Rory's not coming home for Thanksgiving. He's going to backpack around Europe. You could meet up, you know, show him around London."

I ignored this last comment. I'd just started seeing someone, a young man I'd met the month before. Stephen was a student at Balliol College at Oxford and a member of the rowing club there. He had a deliciously plummy accent, some sort of minor title, and was studying economics. He was polite to a fault, keenly intelligent, and had a dry, understated sense of humor. I was intrigued by him, most notably how unlike Rory he was. Tall and blond and academic and self-effacing, he was enjoyable company. We'd spent every weekend together since we'd met. He'd take the train down to London, or I'd go up to Oxford, or we'd meet somewhere else and explore.

When I got the email from Rory, I was already planning to take the train up to Oxford to meet Stephen that weekend.

> Hey Lolly, I know this is out of the blue, but I'm heading through London on Saturday and wondered if we could meet up? I'd like to talk to you about something. If you're free just pick the time and place. Cheers. —Rory

I stared at the message, chewing over my options. Part of me wanted to refuse outright and then post some fabulous photos of Stephen and me having a marvelous time. But another part of me, the stronger part, was curious. Why did he want to see me after spurning me and then going silent for three years? Even though I wanted to claim I'd moved on, I couldn't help myself. I wasn't quite as over Rory Shaw as I wanted to believe. I'd give him a chance and see what he wanted to talk to me about.

Saturday 7 pm at the Turf Tavern in Oxford. I'll be in the
back garden. —Lolly

There. If he cared enough, he'd hop a train to Oxford and figure
out how to find the tavern, which was notoriously difficult to locate. It
was one of the oldest and most famous pubs in Oxford, accessed near
the Bridge of Sighs by the almost invisible Saint Helen's Passage, a
stone alley so narrow and claustrophobic you couldn't spread your
arms as you walked. I enjoyed having the upper hand and giving him
a bit of a challenge. After all, he'd rejected me and broken my heart. It
seemed only fair.

Saturday evening I arrived at the Turf with Stephen, telling him
that we were meeting an old friend. I wanted him there as a re-
inforcement, or maybe a morale boost, I wasn't sure which. I'd come
straight from the London train. Stephen had met me at the station. I'd
taken extra care with my appearance this evening, trying for chic and
nonchalant—a cherry-print blouse tucked into high-waisted blue sailor
pants, matching navy wool peacoat, my usual ponytail curled at the
ends, and a dash of cherry-red lipstick. I wore a favorite pair of
navy-blue-framed glasses to match. I thought the overall effect was
nautical, carefree, and confident, when what I actually felt was nervous
to the point of nausea.

The Turf's walled back garden, with its simple wooden tables and
slatted benches and chairs, had a casual vibe. When we walked in, it
was only a quarter full as it was early yet for the student crowd. That
late in November it was already dark, and the evening was a damp sort
of chilly with a low fog settling over the city. We chose a table close to
a large wire charcoal brazier that glowed orange and emitted enough
heat to take the nip from the air. Stephen went to get us drinks, and I
set my weekend bag down by the table and settled back onto the hard

bench against the pub wall, tugging my wool coat closer and shivering a little as I waited.

No sooner had Stephen stepped inside to order when Rory appeared at the entrance to the beer garden, wearing a fitted orange Patagonia puffer jacket with a small backpack slung over his shoulder. He'd managed to find the alley then, and he was only a few minutes late. Typical Rory to be a little tardy, but surprising he wasn't later given the difficulty of finding the place. Score a point for persistence. He looked around for me, scanning the tables, and I drank him in for a moment in the soft yellow light of the outdoor sconces, my heart jumping at the sight of him.

His hair was cropped short, perhaps a little too short, and he was leaner than I remembered, like a runner. His face was older too, no hint of adolescence left. He was a man now. He was handsome and all grown up but still undeniably Rory. He spied me and for an unguarded moment his eyes lit up, and he grinned, and we were young again, and it was as it always had been. He crossed the courtyard and dropped his backpack on a chair across from me. I stood. We both hesitated for an instant, but then I leaned in almost without thought, and he wrapped me in a tight hug. I inhaled him, reveling for a few seconds in the familiarity of his embrace. He smelled the same.

"Hey, it's great to see you," he whispered against my hair. I started to pull back but he didn't let go and I let myself sink into him for just a moment, a stolen, delicious moment, remembering the last time he'd held me, where we'd been doing much more than chaste hugging.

"Hello." Stephen's voice sounded a touch taken aback. I pulled away instantly, feeling my face flush. Stephen placed our drinks on the table—an ale for himself and a cider for me—and greeted Rory with a polite "Stephen Coventry" and a firm handshake. Rory looked him up and down in frank surprise. I could see him trying to work out who Stephen was and why he was here. Stephen slid in next to me on the bench and looped his arm across my shoulders. Rory's eyes met mine, his expression turning hooded in an instant.

"I'll just go grab a beer," he said, but Stephen sprang to his feet.

"Allow me," he insisted, ever the gentleman. When he disappeared Rory watched him go, then turned to me.

"I didn't know anyone was joining us," he said flatly. The levity from our initial moment of greeting was completely gone.

"Stephen and I already had plans this weekend." I met his eyes coolly. I thought of how we'd left things on the beach that night. More than three years ago and it still stung. I'd declared my love for him and he'd rejected me. *See,* I wanted to point out. *See how well I've done without you? Here I am in England, thriving in this amazing place, with a boyfriend who's got a manor house somewhere in the countryside. I'm completely fine without you.*

But my heart, my traitorous heart, still ached at the sight of him. I wouldn't admit it, but I had the uncomfortable suspicion that I was still in love with Rory Shaw. I wondered if it would ever go away or if part of me would love him until the day I died. I buried a resigned sigh in a sip of cider.

25

Stephen returned from the bar with a local pale ale for Rory and a few packets of crisps. We settled in for some polite, stilted conversation about school and London and Rory's trip. Rory was in his senior year at Michigan State and was hoping to be accepted to Johns Hopkins in Baltimore for medical school. I told him all about my study abroad program and my London adventure so far. Rory kept his warm brown gaze on me the entire time I was talking, ignoring both Stephen and the ale. It flustered me, his singular attention, and I tripped over my own words, my cheeks growing hot under the intensity of his focus. He didn't ask Stephen a single question, which seemed rude. I tried to cover it up by offering a few facts about Stephen, but Rory ignored my comments. When Stephen got up to fetch us all a second round, I waited until he was out of earshot, then swallowed the last of my cider and asked the burning question I'd wondered about since he emailed me. "Rory, why are you here?"

Rory shifted uncomfortably. "It can wait," he said.

"No, go ahead. You came all the way up here. It must be pretty important if you were dedicated enough to find the Turf."

"Yeah, thanks for that." He gave me a wry smile. "I wandered around for half an hour before somebody took pity on me and showed me the entrance." He spun his empty glass in a circle. "It's nothing. I didn't know you were . . . with someone." He nodded in the direction Stephen had gone and frowned.

I rested my arms on the table and leaned forward, fixing him with a pointed look. "Stephen and I are just getting to know each other. It's not serious, just . . . fun." I shrugged. "You sure you don't want to tell me now? What if this is your only chance?" I was enjoying the vague sensation of having the upper hand somehow. I'd declared my feelings for him and been rebuffed. He could be in the hot seat now and say whatever he had come to say. I was curious.

He let out a frustrated exhalation and leaned back, meeting my eyes. "Fine. You want to know why I came tonight?"

My heart skipped a beat. "Yes." Out of the corner of my eye I caught sight of Stephen, his hands full of pint glasses, maneuvering through the door of the pub and coming our way. *No, no. Not yet. Go back, go back*, I tried to telepathically signal Stephen, who did not get the message.

Rory ran his hands through his hair in agitation, then leaned toward me, taking a deep breath and looking me firmly in the eye. His face, almost as familiar as my own, was close enough I could see his individual freckles. I had the sudden crazy urge to kiss each one.

"Because I'm in love with you, Lolly Blanchard," he said bluntly. "I've loved you since the first moment I laid eyes on you, thirteen and so serious with your ponytail and your braces and that ridiculous frilly apron. I've loved you ever since, and it's driving me crazy."

A brief smile flickered across his mouth, but then he sobered, his eyes locked on me. I had a vague sense of Stephen approaching us, but my gaze was trained on Rory in pure astonishment.

"I've wanted to tell you every day for three years," he confessed. "I told myself I walked away from you that night at the beach because I was loyal to Jessica, that I was trying to be honorable, and that was definitely part of it. I was trying to be a man of integrity. But the other reason was that I was scared. I was terrified that if we tried to be together we might not work out and I'd lose you, the person I care most about in this world." He cleared his throat and took a swallow from his pint glass, glancing down at the table for a moment, seeming to gather his thoughts. He looked up at me again.

"The timing just felt so wrong. You were still in high school. I was going to college across the country. I was afraid that if we tried to make it work that we'd fail and I'd lose you for good. And I couldn't bear the thought of that. I couldn't bear to lose you." His eyes were pleading with me for understanding. I was too astonished to even know how to react. Rory paused and took another swallow of ale, his gaze never leaving mine. "So I chickened out. I didn't let you know how I felt, but I broke up with Jessica the week after that night on the beach. I knew that I loved you and I couldn't give her what she wanted. And then I waited and promised myself that someday I would tell you the truth. I told myself I was waiting for you to graduate from high school before I told you how I felt, but then so much time had passed I was scared to try to explain myself to you. You were already so furious with me I didn't know how to make it right again. You'd told me never to contact you. I was afraid that if I told you how I really felt, that you'd reject me, that you would smash my heart flat. I thought I was being patient, but I think I was just being a coward. And you know what?" He paused, waiting for my response.

I shook my head, managing to say, "What?"

"I'm done being a coward. I've been stuck for three years. In love with you but not courageous enough to tell you. That's no way to live, it's a shell of a life, a half life. So I made up my mind. I don't want to live with just the hope of you, Lolly. I've tried and I can't do it anymore. Holding on to the hope of you isn't enough. I want you." He took a deep breath and reached across the table, grasping my arm firmly. I glanced down at his lean, strong fingers gripping the sleeve of my coat, then up at him again, trying to comprehend his confession. His tone was ragged with pent-up emotion.

"Lolly, you are my whole heart. I've always been yours whether you knew it or not. I'm absolutely, completely, hopelessly in love with you. And I'm not asking for anything. But I had to tell you face-to-face. I love you, Lolly Freya Blanchard. I always have and I think I always will."

The moment of silence stretched long as I gaped at him, as his glorious declaration burst over the table like fireworks, raining down on me in a shower of dazzling golden words. Rory loved me. He'd always loved me.

"Ah, sorry. Shall I come back then?" Stephen cleared his throat from behind Rory's shoulder. He met my eyes and I saw hurt and surprise in his expression. Oh, Stephen. Good, polite, pleasant Stephen. He'd stepped into the middle of something so much stronger than he and I could ever be. He was a thoroughly decent man, but when I glanced between him and Rory, I saw the truth plainly. My heart had never really been free.

I walked Stephen to the street, where we both labored through my awkward explanation and apology. Ever the gentleman, he took it stiffly but didn't protest. We were both embarrassed, wanting the entire situation to be over.

"I'm so sorry, Stephen. It isn't you," I said again, wincing as I spoke the trite phrase. I felt terrible for putting him in such an awkward position. He wished me luck and without a backward glance, walked off down the passageway as fast as his long legs could carry him.

Back in the beer garden I slid into the bench seat opposite Rory and crossed my arms, my discomfort melting away at the sight of him. He was sitting back in the chair, arms crossed too, looking a little nervous. He raised an eyebrow.

"I have some things to say," I said calmly, although my heart was racing. "First, I forgive you for being a coward."

He gave a surprised laugh. "I don't remember apologizing."

"You didn't but you should have." I raised my chin and looked him in the eye. "You can do it later. You put me through hell. I deserve an apology. Now, there are some ground rules."

He waited, a faintly bemused expression on his face. "Okay, ground rules for what?"

I ignored his question. "If we are going to do this, I want us both to be in it completely. No trying this out and seeing what happens. My heart can't take that. If you want me, I'm yours, but that's it. We're each other's person from here on out. No cold feet or games, no giving in to fear. We will be honest and strong and together."

"Wait, are you saying . . . ?" he asked, sitting up straight, suddenly on the alert, his expression eager and hopeful. "Are you saying you still . . . care for me?"

I leaned forward across the small table until I was close enough to press a kiss on his lips, then I paused a scant few inches away from him. "Rory Shaw, I'm absolutely head over heels in love with you," I confessed for the second time in my life. And this time I knew I wasn't alone. He loved me back. The knowledge was momentous. It changed everything.

He broke into a grin, incandescent with relief. "Can I ask you a question?" he said almost shyly.

I nodded.

"Can I come sit next to you on your bench? It's freezing and I'm starving and I really, really want to kiss you. And after I kiss you for a very long time, I plan to order everything on their menu, even the weird stuff like haggis."

Laughing, I sat back and scooted over invitingly. "I don't think they serve haggis here. That's Scottish."

We cuddled close on the bench next to each other and talked and talked and kissed and talked some more.

"Do you remember the first time we touched? When I cut myself on New Year's Eve?" I smiled at the memory and nestled against his shoulder.

In the dim golden light of the beer garden, Rory pulled back and looked at me. "I'd been wanting to touch you for months," he confessed with a bashful grin. "I'd lie awake and imagine what it felt like to hold you, to slip my arms around your waist, to have you lay your head on my shoulder. You cutting part of your thumb off was a convenient excuse."

"And was it all you hoped and dreamed?" I murmured teasingly, rubbing my cold nose against his neck. My heart was inflating with joy, pressing against my rib cage. I felt like I could float.

"Better," he murmured against my temple. "With you it's always better."

Before the kitchen closed for the night, Rory made good on his promise. He ordered a wide selection of British pub delicacies—steak and ale pie, fish and chips, Cumberland Scotch egg, and something called a sticky pickle sausage roll.

"We can't possibly eat all this in one sitting," I protested, laughing and surveying the plates of food covering the table.

He pressed a firm kiss against my mouth and took a swig of beer. "Doesn't matter. I'm starving. Just got off the plane, remember, and came straight here. I want all the food and then I want you." His gaze was intense.

I took the pint out of his hand and set it down, then clambered onto his lap and kissed him until I was dizzy. He tasted of ale and prawn crisps and Rory. I couldn't get enough of him. "I don't think I ever need to eat again." I sighed dreamily, settling back against him while he held me with one arm and tucked into the steak and ale pie with the other hand. "I can just live on love. I'm the happiest girl in the world."

"We finally got it right," he said around a mouthful of pie, giving me a lopsided, entirely Rory smile. I nestled against his shoulder, warmed by the brazier and a feeling of contentment I hadn't experienced in so long. I knew we faced a few bumps in the road ahead. Navigating a long-distance relationship on opposite coasts until I could graduate and we could be together would be a challenge. Rory had years of medical school and residency ahead of him to achieve his dream of being a physician for a professional sports team. And I had already drawn up plans for Toast.

Tomorrow I would tell him about my desire to open Toast in the UK. I knew that might present an insurmountable obstacle if his medical license wouldn't transfer to the UK or if he didn't want to move abroad. But we would figure it out. Really I could open a restaurant in any cool city. Maybe I could reimagine Toast in San Francisco or New York. We'd figure it all out together later. Because, at the moment, nothing else mattered except that I loved Rory and he loved me. We were finally together. From here on out nothing would come between us. It was the next right chapter of our own beautiful, imperfectly perfect love story.

I snapped out of the memory of that long-ago night in Oxford and back into the present day, finding myself huddled cold and stiff against the driftwood log on the beach. My cheeks were wet, and when I licked my lips, I tasted salt. I scrambled to my feet, brushing sand from my pants. This had not been the catharsis I was looking for. It was agony to remember, pure and simple.

I headed back toward the parking lot, walking along the beach this time, rocks and shells crunching under my flimsy shoes. Halfway there I passed the abandoned lighthouse, jutting out from the shore on a spit of black rock. When the tide was low, as it was now, you could walk around it on the sand. The lighthouse was empty and shabby, with peeling white paint and an air of neglect. I stopped in front of it, then hesitated. I shouldn't have come. It still hurt too much, seven years on.

Turning to go, I drew in a quick breath when I spotted it. It was still there. Impossible. Rusty now with salt spray, a heart-shaped padlock was attached low on one of the metal sections of the fence surrounding the lighthouse. I'd thought it was a little cheesy at the time when Rory gave me the padlock and the key. It was August, the summer after our reunion in Oxford nine months before. He was twenty-two, just about to head to medical school at Johns Hopkins. I was entering my senior year at Portland State University. We'd been long-distance dating ever since that night at the Turf. My mother was still alive and well, with the accident and all that happened after it still to come. We thought all the hard times were behind us. Little did we know.

Rory asked me to come down to the beach with him one last time before he left for Baltimore. He had planned a farewell picnic, he said. He promised me triple crème Brie from France. Instead he surprised me by stopping at the lighthouse.

"You're the one for me, Lolly." He turned to me, his eyes warm and clear and so sure. "You've always had the key to my heart." I rolled my eyes at the combination of sweetness and theatrics. It was so Rory. Then I realized he was down on one knee in the sand and pebbles.

"What are you doing?" I gasped. He took my hand.

"I love you, Lolly Freya Blanchard. Will you do me the great honor of spending the rest of your life with me?" I looked into that beloved face, the lively light brown eyes, the square planes of his cheekbones, his freckles and ruddy auburn hair tousled by the wind. I had never loved anyone so much in all my life. I thought my heart would burst with joy.

After I nodded a tearful yes, he slipped a vintage square-cut emerald engagement ring on my finger, then pressed a kiss into the palm of my hand and folded my fingers around a key.

"Until we can be together, you hold on to this," he murmured, pulling me against his chest in a warm hug. "Nothing can keep us apart. It's you and me together forever now." I buried my face in his old fleece, inhaled his scent, bourbon and sweet tea, and nestled against him. The moment was absolutely perfect.

Together we fastened the padlock that matched the key he'd given me onto the fence. The day was cool and overcast, spitting rain, but it didn't matter. My fingers were cold as we pressed down on the padlock and heard it click. It was a promise to each other. A promise I had not kept.

I blinked hard, staring at the padlock, now crusted with salt. It pained me still to look at it there on the fence, weathered and forlorn. I closed my eyes and saw Rory kneeling before another woman, a willowy blonde in a strapless A-line dress. Her eyes welled with pretty tears as he gazed up at her in adoration. Emily. The woman he'd married six years ago. There was a lump in my throat that was threatening to choke me. I'd never told anyone about the padlock. I still had the key.

"I'll love you forever no matter what," he'd promised me as he held me against his heart. I guess some forevers are longer than others.

And yet, it wasn't really his fault.

He'd protected me, stood up for me, cared for me. Until I forced him to leave me. And even then he'd fought me, fought for me, for us.

A single tear slid down the side of my nose, hot with regret. Our love story had been pockmarked by missed opportunities, by hesitations and bad timing, and by a cruel twist of fate that we had no control over. Our friendship had been beautiful, easy, sweet. It was our love that was complicated, star-crossed, and finally impossible.

I opened my eyes and looked down, surprised to find I was holding the last lemon drop tight in one clenched fist. I rolled it between my fingers, for one brief second imagining a different ending—me in a tea-length vintage white lace dress holding a bouquet of apple blossoms, their fragrant, fragile beauty signifying "I prefer you before all." Rory gazing at me with the same expression of love and adoration I'd seen in his wedding day photo with Emily. The beautiful continuation of our love story, a story that was supposed to have played out over a lifetime.

The last time I'd looked Rory up on social media, almost five years ago now, he and Emily had been living in Tampa. Their family photo was taken on a pristine white-sand beach. Emily was radiantly pregnant, glowing and cradling her baby bump, wearing a gauzy white sundress. Rory was kneeling in the sand gazing up at her, one hand cupping the gentle swell of their baby.

I'd sobbed so hard looking at that photo that I'd burst a blood vessel below my eye. I never looked him up again. I couldn't. It hurt too much. It felt like self-harm, like flaying little strips of flesh from my heart just to see his face, the yearning for him its own torment. So I stopped. Deleted my social media accounts, distanced myself from Nancy, who had been like an aunt to me my entire life. It was self-preservation and the right decision, but in the absence of knowing, I did still wonder. What did he look like now? Was he happy? Did he ever wake in the early light of morning with the taste of me on his lips, yearning for the feel of us melded together like wax gone soft around the edges from the heat and light of a flame? Did he ever think wistfully of our innocent young love? Did he ever long for me like I still longed for him?

I stared hard at the lemon drop in my palm. I bit my lip and tasted salt and tears. I could do it. I could take the lemon drop and see what our life would have been like together. I had the power, but could I survive losing him all over again?

26

"What are you going to do with the last lemon drop?" Eve sat across from me in a booth at the Eatery, pale late-morning sun streaming in through the big windows. It was the quiet hour before the lunch rush and we were alone in the dining room. I'd asked her to stop by after she'd finished a delivery to a local boutique. I needed advice.

I hesitated. Three days had gone by since my visit to the beach, and I still hadn't used my last lemon drop. It wasn't because I didn't know which regret was lingering like a thorn in my heart. It was because I was just plain chicken.

As if conjured up by magic, Aunt Gert materialized in front of us, an order pad in her hand. "Ladies." She gave us a nod.

"Cool hat," Eve commented, surveying Gert's ensemble. Today she was wearing a red polyester shift dress and matching pillbox hat. I couldn't decide if it reminded me more of Jackie Kennedy or a Pan Am airline stewardess.

"Nice hair," Aunt Gert replied tartly. "They say pink is the new black. Now what can I get you today?" It didn't quite feel like she was taking our order, more like she was grilling a witness during a cross-examination.

"Um." I was embarrassed to be waited on by my octogenarian aunt. "I was just going to have a black cherry soda. But I can get it."

Aunt Gert frowned. She disapproved of sweetened beverages. "Your teeth are one of your best assets, Lolly." She clicked her tongue in reprimand. "You really should take care of them."

Eve snorted but covered it well by turning it into a fake cough.

"I'll take whatever the pescatarian option is for today," Eve said.

Aunt Gert nodded and scribbled on her pad. "One passable cod sandwich coming up."

She finished writing down our order and started toward the kitchen.

Eve shook her head in grudging admiration. "I want to be her when I'm eighty. Geriatric goals." She turned back to me, elbows on the table, leaning forward. "Okay, spill. What are you thinking?"

"I'm still not sure," I waffled. That was not true. I knew what I would choose. If I had the guts.

Eve tilted her head and surveyed me, sudden comprehension flashing across her face. She knew me too well. "You're going to see Rory." It was not a question.

I nodded. "I think I have to see him," I said quietly. "I'm afraid I can't move forward if I don't. I'm stuck holding on to the past because I don't want a future without him. Maybe if I see him I can finally let him go . . ."

Eve whistled. "Risky move. It could backfire."

"I know, but avoiding him for seven years hasn't seemed to work. I think I need to face this thing head-on. Who knows, maybe our life together will be horrible."

"And if it isn't?" Eve argued. "Will you spend the rest of your life agonizing because it really was amazing and you can never be with him again?"

"At least I'll know. I won't have to wonder anymore." I sounded surer than I felt. "I think the not knowing is the most painful of all." I wasn't convinced that was true, but it sounded good.

Eve shook her head. "That boy has always been your kryptonite."

It wasn't that Eve didn't like Rory. Quite the opposite. They'd grown very close in the years Rory and I had been together. She'd loved Rory like a brother and had been gutted when he left. But she resented what seven years of pining for him had done to me. If I couldn't have Rory, she wanted me to at least have a life. She twirled a saltshaker on its edge on the Formica tabletop, scattering grains of salt across the table, then frowned, considering. "I guess it's worth a shot. Maybe it will be awful. Maybe he's disgusting now." She visibly brightened at the thought. "What if he just sits around the house in his tighty-whities with a can of Rainier balanced on his beer gut?"

I looked down, a smile tugging at the corners of my mouth. "That would be, um . . . unexpected." Rory was passionate about sports and physical exercise. He was a physician for a professional sports team for heaven's sake. I couldn't imagine him with a beer gut. "I guess I'll find out," I said evenly, though my heart fluttered at the thought of seeing him again.

"Order up." Aunt Gert marched through the kitchen door and slid a fish sandwich with potato salad in front of Eve. She plunked my soda down. "Anything else?"

"Gert, I'm trying to convince Lolly here not to get her heart broken a second time," Eve said, taking a bite of fish sandwich. "You got any words of advice?"

"Eve knows all about the lemon drops," I assured Aunt Gert. "I told her everything."

Aunt Gert tipped her head, considering Eve for a moment. Her pillbox hat gave her a jaunty air. She turned her gaze on me. "You're going to see the boy you love." It was a statement. I hadn't told her about Rory, but she didn't miss much. No flies on her.

"I think I have to. He's my greatest regret."

She pursed her lips. "Be careful. That can be the hardest thing, I think." She gazed across the dining room, her voice growing soft and faraway. "To see someone who still holds your heart, but get to see them for only a moment. It's a taste, almost worse than nothing. Almost. The only thing worse than that single last day is not having it at all."

I stared hard at her. She spoke as if from experience. "How do you know?"

She brushed off my question briskly. "When you're in your eighties, you'll know a great many things too." She shot Eve an arch glance. "Geriatric goals," she said tartly.

Eve choked a little on a piece of potato salad.

Aunt Gert looked from Eve to me. "Use your last lemon drop to settle the final question in your heart," she said firmly. "And whatever happens, let it lead you toward your bliss."

The bell over the door jangled as two new customers came in. Gert called a greeting to them and hurried over, order pad at the ready.

Eve took a sip of water and met my eyes across the table. "Are you sure you want to do this?" she asked.

I nodded, feeling shaky but resolved. "I'm sure."

That night I took the last lemon drop. I lay stiffly in bed sucking the lemon candy to nothingness, heart pounding with anticipation and anxiety, waiting for sleep. Wearing my best pair of silk pajamas, I was freshly showered, legs shaved, and hair brushed to a chestnut gleam. I knew all my preparations probably wouldn't matter, but I wanted to feel ready. Could I ever really be ready for something like this? I felt tremulous and eager and terrified all at once. I had no idea where I would be when I opened my eyes. I had no idea the shape of my life there. I only knew, somehow, in a way I could not describe, that I had to do this last thing. If I wanted to move on and lay these blighted dreams to rest, I had to see him once more. In the dark, silent hours of the night, as I finally drifted off to sleep, there was only one name on my lips, bittersweet as lemon candy. "Rory Shaw."

27

Something soft yet firm was poking insistently into the small of my back. I blinked blearily, struggling to orient myself. Where was I? Just then a strong male arm curled around my middle and pulled me back against a lean, warm body.

"Oh!" I squeaked, scrambling to a sitting position, cheeks flaming as I realized what exactly had been poking me. The man lying next to me rolled onto his back, stretched, and smiled lazily. My heart leaped. Rory. I was in bed with Rory Shaw.

For a moment all I could do was sit and drink him in. He looked older—crow's-feet at the corners of his eyes and a few lines bracketing his mouth. His russet hair was adorably mussed, threaded with a hint of silver, and he was shirtless. Or naked. I couldn't tell which. My eyes darted to the edge of the sheet bunched around his hips, then rose to the bare upper half of his body. No beer gut. He'd kept remarkably fit. Oh but he looked good. Finally, I settled on his face. He was watching me, eyes crinkled with laughter.

"Morning, gorgeous." He pillowed his head on one freckled arm and reached for me with the other. He was still so appealing, with coppery stubble on his square jaw and the same shade of curly chest hair, just a dusting. I wanted to rub my face against his chest and curl up like a kitten. I struggled to remember how to breathe normally. I felt like I was hyperventilating and took a few gulps of air. It was all so . . . real. So beautifully, amazingly real.

"Quick, before they wake up." Rory wiggled his eyebrows with exaggerated suggestiveness and opened the sheet invitingly. Keeping my eyes firmly on his upper half, I stifled a high-pitched giggle, both at his expression and the glorious improbability of the situation. I was in bed with Rory Shaw. Who might not be wearing any pants. I was really tempted to peek.

I looked around for a moment, trying to get my bearings. On the side table by the bed lay a pair of glasses with square honey-colored frames. I grabbed them with relief, then surveyed my surroundings. We were in a huge and slightly messy bedroom, in a nest of luxurious gray sheets in a king-size bed. Strong sunlight streamed in through the windows. I could just barely catch a glimpse of what looked like palm trees outside. Where were we? Certainly not the Pacific Northwest. The light was wrong, too direct and bright. There wasn't much of a decorating scheme going on, and the room was untidy, jeans thrown over a chair, a pile of laundry spilling from a basket on the floor. I looked around for a cell phone on the bedside table to check the time and date but didn't see one. Hmm, I'd have to search for it later.

"You know what they say, you should seize the . . . um . . . carp," Rory interrupted my assessment of my new surroundings, his hand circling my wrist, tugging me back down into bed. His smile was all invitation. I laughed, torn between scooting back farther on the bed to put a little distance between me and his tempting invitation and leaning forward to kiss him on the mouth. It wasn't wrong if we were in an alternate universe type of situation, right? Here he wasn't married to blond, picture-perfect Emily. He was apparently, right now, happily married to me.

I glanced down, discovering to my horror that I was wearing a ratty oversize Mickey Mouse T-shirt and stretched-out cotton panties. *What* in the world had happened to my personal sense of style? In the gap between T-shirt and panties I caught a glimpse of a soft tummy streaked with silvery stretch marks. Well, that was new. Before I could fully digest these changes, there was a thundering of little feet and the door flew open. Two small bodies hurled themselves onto the bed in a shower of giggles and squeals, burrowing into the covers like tiny rodents.

Rory shot me an amused, resigned look. "Damn, missed our chance."

One of the children, a darling little girl who looked about six years old with long dark curls and freckles on her snub nose, sat up. "Daddy, we don't say bad words. You have to put a quarter in the bad words jar," she reprimanded, then looked at me pleadingly. "Can we have sprinkle pancakes for breakfast, Mommy? You promised."

I froze, my mind going a complete blank. *Mommy.* She had just called me Mommy. These were my children.

The littler one, also a girl, I guessed to be about three. She had messy copper-colored hair the exact shade of Rory's. She popped her head out from where she'd burrowed under his armpit. "Spwinkles!" she shouted at full volume, like she was commanding military troops. "I want gween spwinkles, Mommy."

I stared at my daughters for a moment, trying to comprehend the contours of my new life and suddenly feeling a bit panicky and overwhelmed. I was in bed with Rory Shaw, in what was presumably our home located in some tropical-looking location. I had two children, neither of whose names I knew. And I had to pee like a racehorse.

"Just going potty," I blurted out, scrambling off the bed. Dodging tiny splayed arms and legs, I escaped into the hallway. The bathroom was right next door. I locked the door and sank onto the toilet, mind whirring, taking deep gulps of air and trying not to hyperventilate. I stared at a bottle of Strawberry Shortcake bubble bath in the tub opposite me.

"I'm married to Rory. I'm a mom to two little girls. This is my life. This is my life," I repeated to myself, still stunned. It had worked. It had really worked. I was really here. This was what I had asked for, to see what my life with Rory would have been like if I had not chosen a different path. Granted, I'd somehow never considered that our life together might involve kids.

I had always dreamed of having a family. I loved kids, and I was good with them. I could connect with kids, listening and engaging in an aunty-like way. But there was a big difference between briefly interacting with children for a fun few minutes and being some child's mother, especially being a mother to two girls I'd just laid eyes on for the first time. It was a little unnerving. How was I going to be a good mother for an entire day when these children were strangers to me? I didn't even know their names!

"Mommy, Mommy, Mommy, Mommy," a chorus of high-pitched voices chanted from outside in the hallway. Someone was rattling the knob back and forth. Thank goodness I'd locked the door. Then a little hand slid *under* the door, the fingers searching for who knows what. I briefly panicked. Just then I noticed a My Little Pony creepily bobbing in a clear container of water next to the bubble bath, wide-eyed and upside down. Its blank, wide stare seemed to echo my own deer-in-the-headlights feeling. "I can sympathize, pal," I whispered to the pony. I was thrilled to be with Rory. I was terrified to spend a day navigating our domestic bliss.

"Let Mommy have a minute alone, guys. Come on, let's go get the pancakes started. Last one down's a stinky rotten egg." Rory's voice floated through the door from the hall, followed by cheers and pounding feet moving away from me. I flushed and washed hurriedly, then surveyed myself for a brief second in the mirror over the sink, trying to take stock of the situation. It wasn't good. I certainly looked the worse for wear. My hair was long, and I still had bangs, although they were desperately in need of a trim. I noticed a few strands of gray showing at the roots. Motherhood must really be taking it out of me. I had yet to find my first gray hair in real life. I did have slightly grown out but still pretty auburn highlights that accented my eyes. My very tired eyes. Since when did I look so . . . old and worn out? I squinted in the mirror. Was that grape jelly in my left eyebrow?

Hastily digging through the drawers, I found a toothbrush I prayed was mine, a few scattered cosmetics (the lipstick had the cap off and had been used to draw squiggles on the inside of the drawer), and a Tom's of Maine deodorant. I applied everything I could get my hands on, then tiptoed to the door and listened. No sound. I slipped into the bedroom and, finding my clothes in the walk-in closet, riffled through seemingly endless pairs of yoga pants. How many yoga pants did I own? Did I actually do yoga now? Daphne would cackle with glee if that were true.

I finally located a few sundresses in the back corner and shimmied into a cute yellow cotton one with pockets. A jewelry tree on the dresser opposite the bed held a dozen or so necklaces. A pretty one caught my eye—a delicate silver chain with a glass circle banded in silver hanging from it. Inside the glass circle lay a pressed white five-petaled flower with a yellow center. It was unique, striking in its simplicity. I'd never seen one quite like it. I admired it for a minute, then undid the clasp and quickly slipped it on. It would go perfectly with the sundress. A quick glance in the mirror. Much better. Now I just had to figure out where I was and what my life was like and then develop a strategy for navigating this beautiful, amazing, potential train wreck of a day.

I was trembling with a mixture of nerves and anticipation, eager for more of Rory and not sure how to act competently with the children I'd just acquired five minutes ago. If nothing else I really, really had to figure out what their names were. It seemed like a low bar, but I had to start somewhere.

On my way out of the bedroom, I peered out one of the windows. I was upstairs in a two-story house in a subdivision of large, almost identical houses. The yards were all being watered by sprinklers at the same time. There were palm trees and blooming vines and flowers in radiant hues. I could just make out a street sign: PALMETTO COURT. A Lexus SUV and a black BMW sat side by side in the driveway. If I had to guess I'd say I was somewhere far south. Florida maybe?

"Mommy, the pancakes are ready!" the older girl bellowed up the stairs.

"Mommy, the pancakes aw weady!" echoed the younger one.

"Coming!" I squared my shoulders, took a deep, bracing breath, and got ready to face my brand-new family.

28

Rory was standing at the stove in a spacious but nondescript tan-tiled kitchen wearing a low-slung pair of basketball shorts (ah, so perhaps he *hadn't* been naked in bed). The girls buzzed around him, giggling gleefully as he poured batter onto the hot griddle. "There, one Daniel Tiger pancake and one magical unicorn pancake coming right up," he announced.

The older girl ran up and hugged me, her arms encircling my leg and squeezing tight. She had my dad's and Daphne's build, slender but strong.

"You look pretty, Mommy. And you smell nice."

"Oh, thank you," I stammered. She smiled angelically up at me. "You smell like Starburst candies, the yellow ones."

The littler girl was running in circles around the kitchen island, yelling, "I zap you wif my magical unicorn power. Zap, zap, now *you* are a magical unicorn!"

"Sophia Scout, you get the syrup out. Freya, you help Mommy set the table." Rory pointed with his pancake turner. For a moment I was elated (yay, finally I knew their names) but then I froze. Freya, my mother's middle name. My middle name. And had he said Sophia *Scout*? As in Scout from *To Kill a Mockingbird*? The name I'd told him I wanted to use if I ever had a daughter all those years ago sitting at South Beach? All of a sudden this life seemed so much more real.

The older one, Sophia, unpeeled herself from my leg and got a bottle of maple syrup from the refrigerator, but Freya stopped short, looking confused.

"In the drawer with your *Paw Patrol* cup," Rory encouraged, and she raced over to a drawer and pulled out a stack of colorful plastic plates. He looked me up and down and whistled. "Hey, pretty lady, what's the occasion?"

Really? Was a sundress and some deodorant a high bar for me these days? What did I usually wear? This was just sad. "Just felt like enjoying the sunshine," I said cheerily.

Rory gave me a surprised look. "You don't usually celebrate Tampa weather," he commented, then added, "But I like it when you wear that necklace." He put the pancake turner down and came around the island, encircling me in a hug. I stiffened by instinct, then relaxed in his familiar embrace. He murmured in my ear, "Every time I see it on you it reminds me to never give up hope, to seek happiness, and to remember that life is full of second chances." He pressed a quick kiss to my temple and jogged back to the stove to flip a pancake that was starting to get too done.

"I love it," I said lightly. What was the significance of the necklace? Maybe an anniversary gift? I turned to help the girls set the table. Tampa. We were in Florida. A relief to at least narrow my location down to a city and state.

Through the sliding back doors I could see a fenced yard with a pool glittering in the sun, and outside the door the patio was a riot of blooms, pots holding dozens of edible flowers and herbs I recognized. Apparently, I was gardening in a big way in Florida. The sun was so bright already at eight in the morning. The light was sharp, piercing. It was true, I wasn't a big fan of sun. I was a Pacific Northwest girl through and through. Heat and sun felt foreign, almost a little hostile.

Rory slid pancakes from the griddle onto a plate. "Babe, can you grab milk for the girls and my cold brew coffee from the fridge?"

It took me a moment to realize he was talking to me. *Babe.* I paused for a moment, soaking it in. I was standing in our kitchen while a bare-chested Rory made pancakes for our children. My heart squeezed. How heartbreakingly, wonderfully improbable.

"Sure." I rummaged around the refrigerator and found the beverages. When I closed the door, a postcard caught my eye. It was a photo of Dad, his arms wrapped around a woman with dark red hair and kind brown eyes. She had her hand over Dad's hand, their fingers entwined. A small princess-cut diamond ring adorned her ring finger. I froze, staring at the ring, at the expression on Dad's face. My father was gazing down at her with a look of adoration. The text below the photo read:

> *You are invited to share in the wedding joy of Martin*
> *Blanchard and Ramona Flores.*

I caught my breath. My father was getting remarried? My father was in love with a woman named Ramona? I stared at the photo, dumbstruck. I had rarely seen him look so happy.

Glancing over at Rory, who was busy plating pancakes, I carefully removed the invitation from the fridge and flipped it over. It was crumpled at the corners and worn soft around the edges, as though it had been handled a lot. On the back were a few brief sentences.

> *Ramona came into Martin's life as his caregiver during his*
> *recovery.*

Recovery? Recovery from what? I wondered.

> *Martin was drawn to Ramona's caring spirit and her*
> *strength and energy. Ramona admired Martin's work ethic*
> *and his dedication to his family. They are so thankful to*
> *find love again and look forward to spending the rest of*
> *their lives making each other laugh. Please join them as*
> *they celebrate the start of their life together. For more*
> *information and all the details about the wedding and*
> *reception, please visit their wedding website.*

And then there was a website address for an online wedding-planning site.

I studied the photo again on the front of the card. Seeing my dad with another woman hit me like a punch in the gut. I was so not ready for this new twist. Although I had to admit that it beat finding Dad's ashes in a box, that was for sure.

"Pancakes are ready." Rory's voice snapped me from my daze. I hastily stuck the invitation back on the fridge and brought the beverages to the table. The girls helped me, so it took roughly three times as long. Doing tasks with children, I quickly realized, was sort of like performing every action while wrestling an octopus. You'd no sooner have one arm contained than the other seven were making mischief. Still, I couldn't stop looking at the girls, giving them sideways glances, these children who were such a mixture of Rory and me. Sophia had my pointed chin and wide brow, but her hair was dark, almost black like my dad's and curly like Rory's. Freya looked like a mini Rory—same lively brown eyes and high square cheekbones speckled with freckles, same gingery coloring, but her coppery locks were thick and straight like mine with adorable bangs. She was wearing only underpants, and her tummy stuck out like half a cantaloupe, her legs chubby with sturdy little knees. The girls were adorable. They were mine. Ours. I shook my head, dazzled at the thought.

We sat down and held hands for a quick blessing, and then, at Rory's prompting, each person said one thing they were thankful for. It seemed like a family tradition, and the girls jumped in immediately.

"I'm thankful for Olivia. She's my best friend," Sophia said solemnly.

"I'm fankful for Bunny. He's my best fwend," Freya echoed, clutching a very bedraggled neon-orange stuffed rabbit to her chest. Her mouth was ringed with syrup and half of her bangs looked suspiciously sticky.

"I'm thankful for my three girls and for our life together," Rory said. When it was my turn, I squeezed Sophia's and Rory's hands on either side. "I'm thankful to be here with you. I'm thankful for this day."

And it was true. As the girls kept up a constant stream of chatter, I picked at my pancakes and watched my new family around the table. Normal people got married, got used to being married, got pregnant and had a baby or two after a good long gestation, and then gradually adjusted to being parents. I'd awakened this morning to an instant family. It was all a bit overwhelming. Glorious and overwhelming.

After devouring a stack of pancakes, Rory pushed back his chair, gulped his coffee, and circled the table, kissing the girls' heads. When he got to me he leaned down and, instinctively, I raised my face to his. Like a thousand times before, his lips came down on mine, that delicious ridge of his upper lip, the taste of maple syrup and cold brew. I leaned in just as he pulled back.

"I'm going to head up to shower," he told me, obviously distracted, his mind already on something else. "One of the new recruits injured his knee training, and I've got to monitor the situation, see if he can still play. I'll get ready fast and get out of here."

He was so close I could feel the heat of his body next to mine. It was doing funny things to my insides. *Act normal*, I told myself. *It's just Rory.* But there was no "just" about it. It was Rory, here, in the flesh, so close I could touch him. For now he was mine once more.

"I'll be home in time for dinner," he continued, pulling back and heading for the stairs.

"Okay," I said with false cheer, attempting to cover the sinking feeling in my chest. He was leaving. Most of the day would be spent without him. How utterly disappointing. When I'd taken the lemon drop I'd imagined . . . what? Candlelight and wine on the veranda? Gazing at Rory for uninterrupted lengths of time? Not a day spent away from him while I navigated motherhood solo.

I glanced across the table to find two expectant little faces watching me. What did a day being a mommy entail? Did they go to school? What did a normal day look like for them? I stared at the girls across the table. They looked back at me.

"Do you know where my phone is?" I asked, feeling foolish asking the question.

Sophia squinted at me. "It's charging, silly." She took another bite of pancake.

Charging. Good. And where might it be charging? I jumped up and scanned the kitchen. Phone, phone. I knew it wasn't in the bedroom. I'd already looked. I found it in a small office/organizational area to one side of the kitchen counter, plugged in and charging as Sophia had said. I glanced at the girls, who were still eating their pancakes. They were arguing about which was actually real—unicorns or ponies. Sophia was trying to convince Freya that ponies existed but unicorns were made up. Freya seemed unconvinced.

I unplugged the phone and unlocked it with facial recognition. There were two new text messages. I couldn't resist opening them, curious to see if they were from anyone I knew. The first was from Eve.

Dotty had her kid, twins! I'm a goat grandma again!

Xo

My heart leaped at her name. We were still friends! She still had goats. At least something had stayed the same. I glanced at the second. It was from Daphne.

Hey Lolls! Yoga center is amazing and Ko Pha-ngan is AWESOME! Even better than Costa Rica. I can see the ocean from my hut. Also I'm totally not as flexible as the other instructors but I'm getting there. Haha. I think this was a good move. Hug the girls for me. D ☺

I stared at the message, vacillating between happiness and bewilderment. Happiness that Daphne and I were obviously on great terms. Bewilderment because where in the world was Ko Pha-ngan? I typed it quickly into Google. Up popped an advertisement for a yoga training course on a remote island in Thailand. Ah, that made sense. I stared at the photo of people in various physics-defying yoga poses in a picturesque bamboo hut on the beach. I guess any way I sliced it, Daphne was going to pursue yoga training. I texted back a heart emoji and couldn't resist adding a big-sisterly:

Be careful. Love you lots!

A calendar notification popped up on my screen. Sophia had kindergarten drop-off at eight fifteen. Freya had ballet at nine. A quick glance at the clock confirmed it was almost eight. We needed to get going. But where was I even taking them?

For a moment I considered playing hooky for the day, just letting them skip everything, but then Sophia tugged on the skirt of my sundress, her eyes worried. "Mommy, come on. I need my lunch, and we have to go. We're going to be late for school."

"Okay, um, just let me think." I looked at Sophia, realizing she was still wearing a nightgown emblazoned with some cartoon princesses I didn't recognize. Shoot, I needed to get them dressed. Freya. Where was Freya? In the time it took me to blink, Freya had stripped off her panties and was just disappearing up the carpeted stairs with a flash of little pink naked bottom.

"Freya? Come back here!" I raced after her. A high-pitched giggle was her only response followed by the sound of a slamming door.

I took the stairs two at a time and opened one of the closed doors on the second level. A home office of some sort, slightly messy. I heard hysterical giggling coming from behind the second door. Bingo. A bedroom done up in adorable girly style—bunk beds with cute forest animal duvets, a muslin teepee in the corner spilling stuffed animals from the doorway. Children's books splayed across the floor. A wooden dollhouse with white gingerbread lattice. And a very naked, sticky three-year-old running around the room shrieking. Sophia followed me in, and I barricaded the door and managed to corral both girls into the spacious walk-in closet. "Time to get dressed," I panted. I really needed to start doing more cardio.

29

Ten minutes of child wrangling later, the girls were dressed, sort of. Sophia was in a normal-looking outfit she'd chosen herself—a short-sleeved tunic and capris underneath. I'd finally given up and let Freya walk out of the closet wearing the outfit of her choice—fairy wings, glittery pink cowboy boots, and a full leotard with a raincoat even though it already looked hot outside with not a cloud in the sky. No one ever accused preschoolers of being rational. I herded them down the stairs and into the kitchen.

"Are we going to be late?" Sophia asked worriedly. I checked my phone, realizing I had no idea what school she attended or where it was.

"Do you know the name of your school?" I asked hopefully. She stared at me as though I'd grown two heads.

"Tampa Bay Montessori." She rolled her eyes. "Come on, Mommy."

"You got it!" I smiled enthusiastically as though I'd only been quizzing her knowledge. I wondered what other things I could glean from her. She could prove useful.

A moment later Rory rushed into the kitchen, glancing distractedly at his watch.

"Shoot, I'm running late again." He'd never been particularly timely, as I recalled. He seemed to run about five to ten minutes late no matter the occasion, ever the optimist about how much he could fit into his minutes and hours.

Freya giggled and Sophia shot him a censoring look. "Daddy, you have to put a quarter in the bad words jar. We don't say 'shoot' either."

Rory caught my eye over the girls' heads and grimaced jokingly. "Mommy can pay my fine," he said. "I'll pay her back later." He winked at me and chucked Sophia under the chin. She looked doubtful. He leaned down and hugged the girls, dropping a quick peck on my cheek as he hurried out the door. He was clean-shaven, in a pale gray polo shirt, and he left the barest hint of bergamot cologne wafting behind him as he left. I watched him go, the familiar set of his shoulders, that russet hair curling damply at the nape of his neck, and my heart broke just a little. I wanted more time with him. I wanted more of him.

"Mommy, we have to pack my lunch." Sophia tugged on my hand.

"Lunch. Right." I located Sophia's lunch bag, then tried to think what to fill it with. I stared at the shelves of the refrigerator, feeling the seconds tick away, then grabbed a Go-Gurt, a cheese stick, a handful of baby carrots, and an apple and shoved them in the lunch bag. Slapping peanut butter on a slice of bread, I was about to tuck that into a sandwich bag when Sophia stopped me.

"Mommy, we can't *have* peanut butter at school, remember? Because some kids are allergicked."

"Ah, okay, right. Yes." I stared at the offending sandwich in my hand, put it in the plastic bag, then shoved it in the fridge and stuck a little prepackaged container of hummus with crackers into the bag instead. Presumably, hummus was still allowed in schools. It had been a long time since my school days, and Daphne had always gotten hot lunches at school.

We were officially late by the time lunch was packed, but Freya had vanished. I found her in the downstairs half bath, pumping hand soap into the toilet and making bubbles with the plunger. Scooping a protesting Freya up around the middle, I herded Sophia through the kitchen and out the garage to the Lexus SUV. A few frantic minutes of fumbling with the buckles of unfamiliar car seats ensued. Had they always been so complicated? They felt secure enough to launch an astronaut into space. Sophia helpfully gave me instructions while Freya squirmed and giggled.

Sweaty and exasperated, I finally climbed in the driver's seat, cranked the air-conditioning, then opened my GPS and looked through favorites. Ah, there it was. Six minutes away. I turned on the car and drove as slowly and carefully as an octogenarian through a completely unfamiliar neighborhood as upbeat tunes from *The Little Mermaid* blasted from the sound system. When I glanced in the rearview mirror both girls were watching me silently.

"Under the sea," Sebastian sang. I smiled brightly at them, trying to pretend everything was under control. Freya was sucking on Bunny's paw, and Sophia looked on the verge of tears.

"It's okay," I said. "We're almost there."

The school had a drop-off zone, and one or two equally late SUVs were swerving slowly into the zone and disgorging a child or two before carefully inching away. We were the last car in line.

"I'll come pick you up after school?" I glanced at Sophia in the rearview mirror, hoping this was right.

She shot me a disappointed look. "No, Mommy. Olivia's mommy brings me home on Thursdays, remember? You're forgetting everything today."

"Of course! Olivia's mommy." I nodded in complete agreement, twisting in my seat and unbuckling her seat belt. "Great, well, have a good day ... sweetie." I handed her the backpack, which seemed ridiculously large and heavy for a child her size.

Sophia gave me an uncertain glance, then slid the backpack on and let herself out the back door. She slammed it and headed for the school, looking back once. I waved cheerily and she waved halfheartedly, then turned around and walked away. I wondered if she was onto me somehow. She seemed like she might suspect something was amiss.

I heaved a sigh of relief. One down. One to go. "You." I looked at Freya in the rearview mirror. She gazed back with round, innocent eyes. Her mouth was ringed by something brown and smudgy.

"What are you eating?" I twisted to get a better look, and she held up an empty orange wrapper. "How did you get ahold of a Reese's Peanut Butter Cup?"

She just blinked at me.

"Right." I sighed and turned around. "Okay, ballet."

At the ballet class I managed to squeeze Freya's little body into a pale pink leotard (thankfully already inside the bag marked "Freya Ballet" in the back of the car). The other moms smiled at me politely but were focused on their own children in the dressing room. Good, I didn't have to pretend I knew anyone. I led Freya into the brightly lit space with golden wood floors and a wall of mirrors. A graceful goldfinch of a woman with a tight bun greeted her and had her line up with the other children along the bar.

"We will see you in an hour, Mrs. Shaw," she told me. I nodded and left, rolling the moniker around on my tongue, marveling at the sweet feel of it. *Mrs. Shaw.*

Free for an hour while Freya had ballet, I debated what to do. My GPS showed a small park nearby and so I wandered over, enjoying the sunshine. I was a Seattle girl, born and raised with drizzle and cool salt breezes in my veins, but in early March the Florida warmth did feel delicious.

It was a pocket park, just a little square of tough grass with a gurgling fountain and a few benches nestled below blooming trees. No one else was around, so I found a spot near the fountain and settled down on a bench, swiping to my home screen and navigating to photos. I glanced around guiltily. Just like when I looked at the photos on my phone at Toast, it felt a little illicit, voyeuristic, but I couldn't resist this time either. I wanted to see all of it, experience it vicariously, this life I could have lived.

And there it was, my alternate life recorded in thousands of images. I cycled backward from the most recent photos. The girls' ballet recital, them in matching standard-issue pale pink tutus, hair scraped back in buns, grinning proudly as Rory handed them both little bouquets of roses. Christmas with Rory's parents, all of us gathered around the table as Nancy served her famous sweet potato casserole with candied bacon and pecans. A beach day, Rory squinting in the sun, laughing, half buried as the girls industriously poured shovelfuls of sand over him. There was an older boy with them in the photo, almost a teenager, helping the girls dig sand. He looked vaguely familiar, but I couldn't place him. He had a cute, kind face and curly coppery hair, the exact shade Rory's had been at that age. A cousin of Rory's, perhaps?

Next were a couple of dark selfies of Freya's blurry face, taken at night by our bedside. In the background I am a snoozing lump, unaware of my youngest child's nocturnal antics. Then a cluster of photos in what looked like an industrial kitchen, all gleaming metal surfaces and several people I didn't recognize in hair nets, facing the camera with me, all holding up jewel-colored popsicles and grinning. I paused, puzzled, wondering what that was all about, but moved on.

I scrolled ravenously, faster and faster, devouring the history of my life with Rory and the girls. Birthday parties. Family picnics. Start-of-school photos. A handful of photos with people I didn't recognize, including a few more with that boy from the beach. A photo of me with Daphne, who was gorgeous and tanned and laughing. A hundred more funny, imperfect moments captured on film—goofy faces and jammy fingers, a five-second video clip of a shirtless Rory standing at the stove using a pancake turner as a microphone, belting out "I Got You Babe" in an off-key baritone. Then Freya's birth, me in a hospital gown, big as a whale, red-faced and sweating. And her, equally red-faced, scrunched and mad, held in Rory's capable hands. The look on his face stopped me cold. Awe and adoration, vulnerability and joy. I felt like I was standing on holy ground, glimpsing these intimate moments of our life. I hesitated. Was it good for me to do this? Was it helpful? Maybe I should stop looking, concentrate on this day, this moment, and let it be enough. But I couldn't seem to stop my finger from swiping backward, ravenous for each photo, the documentation of a life I would never have.

A series of pregnancy belly shots, week by week in reverse, with me in yoga pants, turned sideways, with an ever-decreasing tummy. Wobbly videos of a younger Sophia learning to ride a trike, learning to walk. Us in front of our current house, pointing to the SOLD sign, wearing huge matching grins. Then I found a dozen or more photos of what looked like a wedding. There were round tables with gorgeous cream floral decorations, a couple dozen nattily dressed guests dancing to a live jazz band. I flipped backward a few more shots. Rory and me and baby Sophia in a tiny frilly dress, all solemn eyes and dimpled elbows. She looked like she was maybe a year old in the photos. Whose wedding was this? I kept scrolling then stopped. It was a photo of Dad in a white short-sleeved shirt with a lei around his neck, standing under a bower of flowers on a beach. And in front of him, holding his hands in hers, was the red-haired woman, Ramona. She was wearing a pale cream dress and matching crown of flowers over her long curls. I stared at the photo. She was smaller than I'd pictured, petite even next to Dad, who was not a tall man. Now I understood. This was their wedding.

The postcard on the fridge was not an invitation for an upcoming event. It must have already happened. Dad was not about to marry this woman. They'd already been married, for several years by the looks of it. Sophia had been a baby in the photos, which meant it was at least five years ago now. I stared at the photo hard, seeing the adoration in his eyes, how he leaned toward her as though pulled by a magnet. Her face tipped up in what looked like the moment before a kiss.

I stared at the photo for a long time, trying to grapple with the reality of what I was seeing. Dad was married to this woman. He had a new life here. I studied his face and hers, how they radiated joy. Then I clicked off the phone, leaning my head back. I couldn't take seeing any more. I had to stop. I knew there were probably thousands more photos, Sophia's birth, our own wedding, med school graduation for Rory, so many moments in our shared history. But my heart was breaking. I wasn't ready to see my dad marry another woman, but my feeling of grief was due to far more than that.

This could never be mine. All of it—the sticky pancake fingers and rumpled sheets on our bed, the pink ballet tutu and lunch box, the scratchy warmth of Rory's neck—all of this was ephemeral, for only a day. I would never live this life. In real life I would never hear Freya call me Mommy or Rory press a kiss on the top of my head. All of this was so beautiful and so fleeting. I had only a few more hours left. *Maybe it will be awful*, Eva had said hopefully. And it was. But not in a way that freed me. This was a glimpse of a life I deeply longed for, with the person I still loved. I had a feeling this life might just haunt me to the end of my days. It was horrible because it felt so deeply right.

Heart aching, I stood and put my phone away. I would not look at any of the rest of the pictures, I promised myself firmly. It would do me no good. I could not ever experience all of the moments they showed me. But what I could do, what I was determined to do, was enjoy the moments and hours I had left. Right then and there I vowed to make the most of every second of this day. I might have only one day, but at least I had something. Why waste even an instant lamenting what couldn't be changed? I would press into it, allow myself to live it fully. Tomorrow I would have only the memory of it, and it was going to hurt like hell, but at least I would have gotten the chance to taste this messy, wonderful, perfectly imperfect life. For now I had to let that be enough.

30

"I did big, *big* jumps," Freya told me grandly as I ushered her out the door after her ballet class. "As high as the sky." She demonstrated her grand jeté. In the dressing room I helped her out of her tutu, marveling at her round tummy, the impossible proportions of her little three-year-old body.

"Did you have fun in class?" I asked her.

She nodded, but her mouth turned down in a frown. "But I missed *you*, Mommy. I always miss you when you're gone."

I looked at her earnest little face, and my heart melted. "I missed you too, sweetie," I told her, brushing a piece of hair back into her pigtails. To my surprise, I realized it was true. I felt myself falling for this little person more and more.

I managed to get us back to the house, thankfully finding our home address stored under favorites in my GPS, and the remainder of the morning passed leisurely. After cleaning up the kitchen from breakfast, I fed Freya an early lunch of boxed mac and cheese I found in the pantry, taking several big bites for myself as I stirred in the powder, her chattering all the while. Afterward we walked to a playground I'd spied on the way home. There she played in the sandbox, and I pushed her on the swing until she started to droop, her eyelids growing heavy. Then I carried her home, the weight of her slowly going soft in my arms as she fell asleep. I maneuvered her through the garage and up the stairs while she lolled, boneless and limp as a jellyfish, against my shoulder. She was surprisingly sturdy for such a little person. I was huffing by the time I got to the top of the stairs. I tucked her into bed with her bedraggled stuffed bunny, then wandered around the house restlessly, exploring.

The last door upstairs was the home office I'd glimpsed earlier. I opened the door and poked my head in. A **GRAND OPENING** banner in candy-bright colors caught my eye. I went in and glanced around. There was a tall stack of pamphlets on the corner of a very messy desk. I picked one up. "Lolly's Pops," the pamphlet announced in the same bright letters as the banner. "New location opening soon!" I flipped it open in surprise. There I was in a little thumbnail photo, smiling brightly and holding a rainbow of popsicles up for the camera. Underneath, it said, "Lolly Blanchard Shaw, owner." Well, this was interesting. I had my own company?

I skimmed the pamphlet. Lolly's Pops was an organic popsicle company that specialized in handmade popsicles created with locally sourced fruits and edible flowers. It had two locations in Tampa and a mobile Lolly's Pops popsicle truck in Seattle. How unexpected to find I was the owner, that this cute small popsicle business was my own brainchild! It wasn't Toast, but it looked fun, and I'd always loved edible flowers and local produce. I studied the pamphlet for a moment longer, then set it down with a twinge of envy. How amazing that in this life I was both a mom and running my own small business, that I was accomplishing so much of what I'd always dreamed of. I lingered for a moment longer, enjoying the novel sensation of being a businesswoman.

Then I noticed a cell phone sitting on the desk. It was vibrating with an incoming call. "Watson's Organic Grocery" it said on the screen. I hesitated. Should I pick it up? I let it go to voice mail. When I glanced at the screen again I saw there were twenty-one unread text messages. I opened one or two and quickly surmised that this must be my work phone. Everything seemed to be entirely related to Lolly's Pops, and none of the questions and points of business were things I was familiar with. I thought briefly of trying to wade through the messages but decided to ignore them all for now. I knew from my day at Toast how complicated stepping into the running of a business was. And I wasn't here to run Lolly's Pops. I was here to spend time with Rory and now the girls. I set the phone back on the desk and closed the door to the office gently behind me.

While I waited for Freya to awaken, I tidied the house and did a load of laundry. Before I threw it in the washer I clasped Rory's ratty old T-shirt to my chest, allowing myself that small indulgence, burying my nose in it. Every moment seemed significant and yet so normal. It was all so fleeting, so precious and mundane. I made myself some lunch, did the dishes, and puttered around, waiting for Freya to awaken from her nap and Sophia to get home from school. A car horn honked in the drive at a little after three. Sophia came bounding up the driveway, her giant backpack bouncing on her shoulders.

"How was your day, sweetie?" I gave her a big squeeze, marveling at the fragile birdlike feel of her collarbone, the scent of her hair. Syrup and strawberry shampoo. I had missed her. In some way I felt I had been missing these two girls all my life. It was a thought that cut me to the bone.

"Good. We had spelling, and I got four right and one wrong," she told me gravely. "I forgot what makes the 'sh' sound, so I put 'sip' but it was supposed to be 'ship.'"

"Well, four out of five is still good," I assured her. "You're still learning, right? Do you want a snack? How about we feed that growing brain of yours?" I walked with her into the kitchen, relishing the simplicity of the moment. I cut apple slices and found some Annie's cheddar bunny crackers in the pantry. Since when did I allow so many processed snacks in the house? What had happened to my eco-friendly, less-is-more, farm-to-table ethics? Surveying my pantry stuffed with Costco-size snack boxes, I surmised that those ethics must have died a slow death somewhere along the road of parenthood.

As Sophia ate her snack, we chatted about her day. A boy named Atticus had pulled her hair on the swing set. The class was getting a hamster as a class pet, and she wanted to name it Butterscotch because her teacher, Mrs. Thatcher, told them it was going to be a golden color, but another girl, Isabelle, insisted they should name it Goldie, which Sophia felt lacked imagination.

"Butterscotch is a better name because it's poetic," she told me earnestly. "Gold is just a color."

Toward the end of snack time, Freya came trudging down the stairs, trailing Bunny, groggy from her nap and in a grouchy mood. I plied her with crackers and apple slices, which seemed to improve her outlook slightly, but she still glowered at me like a tiny gremlin from the table.

After snack they begged me to play with them. For the next couple of hours we made Play-Doh animals, drew pictures, galloped around the house with My Little Ponies, had a dance party, pretended to be going on a pirate treasure hunt, and played hide-and-seek. I was buzzing with energy and completely exhausted at the same time. Being a mommy was incredibly hard work.

The moments ticked by slowly as the afternoon wore on. It was all normal and slightly boring, and yet I was captivated by the girls. Every word, every second, I fell more in love with them. I couldn't get enough. Was this what motherhood felt like? I wondered, glancing at their heads bent low over a game of Chutes and Ladders as Sophia helped Freya move forward five spaces. Was it this sweet ache lodged in the center of your breastbone, a powerful feeling of protection and adoration of these little people in equal parts that eclipsed all exhaustion, all inconvenience? It was boredom and panic and satisfaction and heart-melting sweetness all rolled into one. It was its own kind of bliss.

I kept my eyes firmly off of the clock, choosing to ignore the fact that the hours were slowly slipping away, that my time with them would soon be over. It was not nearly enough. Maybe parenthood always felt a little like this, like there was so much love and never quite enough time. It all was going so fast.

Just as the sun was sinking low over the trees we heard the garage door open.

"Daddy's home!" Sophia jumped to her feet in excitement.

Dinner! I hadn't even thought about dinner. I panicked for a moment, but when the door opened, Rory was carrying a pizza box.

"Honey, I'm home!" he exclaimed in a very poor imitation of Ricky Ricardo from *I Love Lucy*, then dropped into his normal voice. "Sorry I'm late. Traffic was the pits."

I untangled the plastic diamond tiara from my hair and gave him a joyful, sloppy kiss, taking the pizza from him.

"Daddy, Daddy, pizza, pizza!" The girls were bobbing around him, bubbling with anticipation.

"It's my turn to choose the movie for family movie night!" Sophia shouted jubilantly.

"Yes, but first a bath for you two little rascals," Rory announced, planting a loud kiss on Freya's cheek. "Why are you so sticky?" He pulled back and looked at her skeptically. She giggled in response. He shot me a look over her head. "Want me to take them up and bathe them?"

"I'll do it," I offered quickly. "You get things set up down here."

Bath time was a twenty-minute affair involving lots of bubbles, bath crayons, tears over Freya having her hair washed, an argument between the girls about who got to sit near the tub faucet as that was the place with the most bubbles, and at least two tsunami waves of water over the side of the tub that drenched the front of my sundress.

At last the girls were moderately clean, toweled off, and in matching rainbow-unicorn nightgowns. We ate slices of cheese pizza and cut-up apples and all cuddled up together on the couch while we watched *Frozen*, Sophia's pick.

"Do you think we'll ever get to watch a different movie?" Rory whispered in my ear. "I literally had a dream that I was Elsa lost in the frozen woods last week. And I was singing all the songs, even the high notes. Are they too young for *Alien*?" He was holding the remote as he was the appointed fast-forwarder for any parts Freya found scary. The girls were transfixed, humming along to every song.

"If we're lucky, maybe we can swap it out for *Beauty and the Beast* or *Finding Nemo* next year," I murmured back, nestling against him on the comfy couch. He leaned his head against mine, and for one perfect moment, the world stood still. I let myself stay there in the moment, listening to his heartbeat, curled up against him, the two girls so close I could reach out and smooth their wet hair. I had never felt so utterly content. I wanted it to last forever.

31

Both girls drifted off before the film was over. I took Freya, and Rory picked up Sophia. Freya wrapped her arms and legs around me like a starfish, still asleep. I gently carried her upstairs, careful not to rouse her. We tucked them into bed in their room, standing over them for a silent moment. The night-light illuminated their sleeping little faces, angelic in stillness. I would not see them wake in the morning. The thought constricted my heart with grief. I would never again hear Sophia call me Mommy or turn around to find Freya streaking through the living room in her cowboy-bunny underpants.

"We sure made good ones, huh?" Rory whispered, gazing down at the girls with a look of pure adoration. I nodded wordlessly, unable to speak around the lump in my throat. I'd known them for only a day, it was true, but it felt unbearable to lose them now. Every day from now on I would know that they were what I could have had.

For the first time I wondered if it had been a mistake to take the lemon drop. It was agony to think of never seeing them again. It seemed impossible. I leaned over and pressed a kiss on Sophia's forehead, smoothing Freya's flyaway hair and burying my nose against her pillowy cheek that was still somehow slightly sticky, even after a good scrubbing. I looked back once more from the doorway, cementing the scene in my mind. For a day they'd called me Mommy. For a day they had been mine.

In the dimness of the landing, Rory came up behind me and wrapped his arms around me. I leaned back into him, resting my head against his chest. I needed him.

"Want a drink? We can sit by the pool." He sounded tired.

"Sure, that would be great."

"A margarita?" he asked, moving toward the kitchen. I reluctantly let him go.

"Sounds perfect," I answered honestly. Maybe tequila would dull the sharp edge of what I knew was coming too soon.

Outside the night air was a touch cool, a light breeze rustling the dry palm fronds with a raspy clatter. I lay back in one of the loungers by the pool, enjoying the mild night. I was bone-tired after a day of chasing the girls and trying to keep one step ahead in this new life. Parenting was unbelievably exhausting. Now I understood the moms who came into the diner with their messy buns and lightly stained shirts and weary eyes. Being a mother was far harder than running the diner, no question. My hat was off to all parents everywhere. Every parent deserved a medal just for sheer survival. How did they do it? I yawned as Rory appeared with a lowball and a wide-mouthed margarita glass in his hands. He was shirtless and wearing a pair of green board shorts.

"Here, babe."

I relieved him of the margarita and took a sip. It was so cold and puckeringly sweet and sour, and he'd even done a salty rim. "Mmmm. Thank you."

He sank back into the lounger next to mine, kicking off his shoes and taking a gulp of what looked like bourbon and Coke. His drink still hadn't changed, I noticed.

"Ah, there it is." He sighed, visibly relaxing. It was twilight, the evening sinking into shadows. The pool gleamed a brilliant blue, lights from the tiled walls illuminating it so it looked glamorous and inviting. The yard was large but a little scrubby, lined with palm trees and a tall fence. Everything we owned spoke of an upper-middle-class family, not of outrageous wealth but of comfort.

We talked for a few minutes about his day, the players, his differences of opinion with the coach. I shared a few funny things the girls had said and done. After a few minutes we lapsed into silence. I lay on the lounger, aware of the minutes ticking away, dreading what I knew was coming. So soon, this would all be gone. So soon, it would only be a memory. I desperately craved more—more time, more Rory, more to carry with me when I left.

"Do you think we're happy in our life here?" I asked, taking a sip of my margarita. It was a question I'd been wondering about all day.

Rory looked at me in surprise. "Are we happy? Sure. I mean, I think so. We've got our share of stuff. My dad's prostate cancer diagnosis was hard this year. I know you don't love Florida, and we miss being closer to our families, the usual stuff everyone deals with, I guess. I don't always see eye to eye with Coach, but we've got two beautiful, healthy girls. I love a lot of parts of my job. Your business is doing well and expanding locations, which is great. And we still can't keep our hands off each other. Yeah, I'd say we're happy. Why?" He peered at my face as though suddenly unsure.

"Just checking." I took another sip of the margarita.

"Are you happy?" He swirled his drink around in the glass, watching me curiously.

"Right here, right now? Absolutely. I just wish it weren't going so fast," I said wistfully.

"Tell me about it," he agreed. "How do we have a kid in school already? Next thing you know we'll be old and gray, living out our golden years in a retirement community in Palm Beach, where we drive a golf cart to shuffleboard."

"Sounds pretty perfect to me." I gave a little laugh, but I was serious. Growing old with Rory—nothing sounded better.

Rory stood, set his glass down, then came over to me. He sat down on the edge of my lounger, his expression serious as he gazed at me. "I don't take you for granted, Lolly, or our life together. I hope you know that. I'm grateful every day for you and the girls, for what we have. It's a gift, one I don't take lightly." He reached out and smoothed his hand over my hair, tracing the line of my jaw. "I love you, Lolly Blanchard Shaw. Since the moment I first saw you."

I looked away, blinking back sudden tears at the raw honesty in his voice.

"I love you too," I said thickly. "I always have and I always will."

He leaned forward and pressed a kiss against my forehead. "I'm going to take a quick dip and head for bed. I've got an early appointment tomorrow. That kid who messed up his knee probably needs surgery." He rose, then paused at the edge of the pool, the planes of his shoulder blades illuminated in the reflected pool lights. I drank him in, cementing the image of him in my mind. He dove into the water cleanly and swam to the other side of the pool, turning and coming back, swimming laps over and over, his motions smooth and focused. He'd always been a strong swimmer.

I watched the coil of muscles in his arms as he sliced through the water, the gleam of water droplets streaming from his hair as he raised his head for a quick gulp of air. I sat there as the minutes ticked by, as darkness crept fully over the sky, listening to the quiet splash of Rory in the pool, the cacophony of night insects around me. The margarita grew warm in my hand, and my head felt a little fuzzy and light from the tequila. I couldn't tear my eyes away from him. He was the most beautiful man I'd ever seen.

Almost on impulse I rose, set my glass by the lounger, slipped off my flip-flops and glasses, and jumped feetfirst into the deep end of the pool, still wearing my sundress. The water was shocking, cool and silvery against my skin as I came up for a breath of air. Rory was at the opposite end of the pool from me when I blinked the chlorine from my eyes, treading water in my sodden yellow sundress.

"What's a nice girl like you doing in a place like this?" he called, grinning.

I grinned back. "Looking for trouble," I answered cheekily.

He dove under the water, sleek and graceful as a seal. I lay back and splayed my arms and legs, resting gently under the velvet night sky. Time felt suspended, the night a little surreal although my every sense was heightened. I floated as though boneless, relaxing into the moment, the night, the spell of what might have been. I knew given half a chance I would stay here like this forever. Not a single speck of me wanted to leave. I turned my head as Rory popped up next to me.

"Looks like trouble just found you," he said with a wicked grin.

He slipped his arms around me and I bobbed upright in the water, facing him, wrapping my legs around his waist. He kissed me, a quick peck on the lips. I tightened my hold. He stilled, studying my face for a moment, then pulled me close, threading his fingers in my wet hair and kissing me deeper than before, with a hunger, an intensity. His tongue was in my mouth and he pulled me against him, clasping me with one strong arm. He took a few slow steps until my back bumped against the pool wall. All that was between us was a sodden sundress and a pair of swim trunks. I didn't think about tomorrow, about the desolation of waking up in a lonely twin bed. I didn't think about the fact that this would undoubtedly be the last time I ever in my life kissed Rory Shaw. Instead I splayed my hands across his bare back and pressed my mouth against his and stopped thinking about anything else at all. He felt so familiar, so familiar and so very right.

He slipped one strap from my shoulder, dipping his head and pressing a series of kisses down my shoulder blade. His other hand started working the buttons on the front of my sundress. His breath was hot against my collarbone, and he nipped at the nape of my neck with his teeth. I yipped and he chuckled low in his throat, pushing me firmly against the side of the pool and pressing against me. I wanted him, wanted him more than I'd ever wanted anything in my life. It would be so easy to simply give myself to him, this man I'd loved forever.

But suddenly I saw us, entwined in the muggy night, and I caught a glimpse of his other life, a different gold wedding band on his finger, sealing him to a woman who was not me, the glint of blond hair on the pillow next to him, his real wife. I stopped short at the image, the reality. Emily. Remembering her doused my ardor like a bucket of cold water.

I slipped sideways out of his embrace, giving him a quick peck on the lips, then slid my strap back up, hating every second of letting him go. But I couldn't be the other woman, not even in this alternate life. He was not mine for real, no matter what I might wish for.

He pulled back, eyes questioning. In the half-light his face was so familiar, the curve of his mouth, the stubble and freckles and clear brown eyes. I cupped his jaw with my hand for a moment. This man, my first and only love.

"Just feeling a little tired tonight," I hedged, backing away, putting a few inches of air between us. "That margarita was strong." I didn't meet his eyes. He slid his hand along the small of my back, drew me to him and pressed a quick kiss on my lips.

"Okay, you head up to bed then. I'm going to do a few more laps."

He sounded disappointed. So was I. I nodded, unable even to look at him. If I did, I would change my mind and throw caution to the wind, but I'd regret it tomorrow. I didn't want our last night together to be tarnished in any way. When I woke tomorrow, I would have only this memory for the rest of my life, and I wanted to be able to hold it close, a beautiful, treasured thing.

I turned away.

32

I woke early, alone in my own bed, as I knew I would, in a tangle of twin sheets with the taste of Rory still on my lips. Leadenly, I rose and sought out Aunt Gert, not even bothering to change out of my pajamas. The world felt leached of color. Her cottage was dark, but I found her posed on a patch of grass next to the herb bed, arms outstretched and hands floating through the air softly. It was Thursday. Her tai chi morning.

It was raining as I approached her, a fine mist that filtered down through the fog, soft as a sigh. She was wearing her tai chi outfit—a voluminous satin top, the deep yellow hue of egg yolks, with a mandarin collar and frog buttons, and matching satin pants. Beside her on the damp grass sat an ancient cassette player with the volume turned down low.

"And now the Cloud Hands Pose," the soothing voice from the cassette player intoned, accompanied by tinkly Eastern-sounding instrumental music

"Good morning." Aunt Gert continued her movements but took inventory of my disheveled appearance. I bit my lip, trying to taste

Rory, desperate for the last vestige of him on my skin. Already the memory of falling asleep last night chastely curled against him in our big bed in Florida seemed like a lifetime ago.

"You used your last lemon drop," she observed conversationally, stepping backward a few paces and almost treading on a bedraggled rosebush. She stuck one leg out and swept her arms in a wide arc.

I nodded, wrapping my hands around my bare arms and shivering a little in the wet chill.

"And how was it?" Her voice sounded oddly compassionate.

"It was . . ." I stopped, unable to categorize it.

I still loved Rory Shaw, had never stopped loving him, not even for a minute. But the girls. They were the unexpected treasure of the day. I closed my eyes, feeling the sticky warmth of a little hand in mine, pudgy arms around my neck, their sweet, sweaty smell after they'd been running around pretending to be unicorn princesses. I had not expected to fall for two headstrong, funny, ornery little people so fast and so hard.

"Yesterday I woke up with two beautiful little girls and a whole life with the man I've loved for twenty years," I said slowly. "And today I woke up and they're all gone. I don't know how to live with that. I mean, it was so real. It felt so real. I don't know how it all works, the lemon drops and waking up in a different life, but I know it wasn't a dream. I didn't dream them. They're real and they're out there somewhere, somehow. And I don't know how to think about never seeing them again. It feels impossible. I can't bear it."

"Now move to Hold the Ball Pose," the voice instructed. Aunt Gert bent her knees slightly and held her arms out in a circle, as though clasping a giant invisible beach ball.

"Would you go back to them if you could?" she asked calmly, conversationally.

I stilled instantly, my heart leaping with a sudden hope. "Can I?"

The thought of snuggling those two little wiggly warm bodies, reading stories, and smelling the strawberry bubble bath wafting from their skin. Drifting off to sleep curled against Rory even for one more night, so close I could feel the steady rhythm of his heartbeat. Ecstasy and agony. I wanted nothing in the world as much as I wanted one more day with them.

"Yes," I said without hesitation. "Yes. Absolutely. How can I do it?" I held my breath, as though afraid that even a tiny exhalation would shatter the fragile possibility.

"Now Snake Creeps through the Grass," the voice intoned. Aunt Gert extended her left leg and bent low, stretching her arms along her leg. She was surprisingly flexible for an octogenarian.

"There is a way, but there's a catch."

"What is it?"

Aunt Gert frowned, wiping a wisp of white hair from her forehead and pausing in a half crouch. "If you use a lemon drop to go back a second time to a place you've already been, you can't come back to your normal life again. You will stay there permanently. That will be your life for good." She looked up at me intently.

"Oh," I took an involuntary step back. I could go back, but I could not return to this life. I would stay there permanently. I thought of the places those lemon drops had taken me. Toast. Brighton. My mother. Hawaii. The box on her side table with my father's face on it. Rory and the girls in Florida. I could choose one of those, but it would be my only choice. I felt the weight of the decision, but the possibilities it opened up left me breathless.

"I can choose?" I hardly dared to hope.

Aunt Gert swooped her hands gracefully like swallows, following the movements from the tape, then dipped into the pocket of her satin pants.

"Here." She held out her hand. I obediently put out my palm and she placed a single lemon drop into it. "Take care. This is the last one."

My fingers wrapped involuntarily around it, holding it tight, safe. That one little candy held all my hopes and dreams now.

"It's up to you if you will use it," Aunt Gert said. "Only take it if you're certain you are following your bliss."

"I will," I promised. We looked at each other for a moment, the silence stretching long. She was still crouched in a low pose. Her core strength was admirable. I thought of the life she'd led, the prestige and accolades and adventures. Now it all made sense. She must have used a lemon drop and chosen to stay in the best version of her life for good. How astonishing to be able to choose in this way. No wonder she'd led an amazing existence.

"I offered the lemon drops to your mother once, you know," she said finally, casually, rising from her position. Her knees creaked.

"You did?"

She nodded, moving smoothly back into the next pose. Needle at the Bottom of the Sea. "It was just after her accident when her situation was . . . critical. I called her and offered to fly down that very night. I told her about the lemon drops. I told her I thought they could save her life. She could have taken two, chosen a version of her life where she was strong and healthy still. I thought it might work. It was worth a try."

"What did she say?" I was surprised, trying to picture what could have happened if she'd taken them.

Aunt Gert shrugged, pushing one hand firmly out in front of her as though stopping traffic. "Irene thanked me politely and then she declined. She said she'd lived the life she wanted with the people she loved most. She didn't want a different life, even if it meant living longer. She said she was sorry to leave the world so soon, but she wouldn't change her life, not one bit. She died the next morning."

I stepped back, stunned. How incredible for Mom to have been offered the chance of a different life and to turn it down. How amazing that she had a life so fulfilling that she could not imagine a better one. My mother had crafted a life for herself that was what she wanted. I longed to do the same.

"Be honest. Pay attention. Seek joy," I whispered. I clutched the lemon drop in my hand. I had the world spread before me all of a sudden. Everything seemed possible. I could choose.

33

"You're kidding, right?" Eve eyed me askance as she carefully poured caustic lye onto cubes of frozen goat's milk in the bottom of a big metal soup pot. "You're telling me you can go back again? Permanently?"

"That's what Aunt Gert said. I can go back once more, but then I would stay there. That would be my life." I tapped my fingers agitatedly on Eve's dining room table, late-morning sun streaming in the window, as Eve whipped up a batch of goat milk soap. I had been tasked with cutting and wrapping already-cured batches of soap but was neglecting my chore, too intent on the choice before me. In the background, with quiet ferocity, Pat Benatar was singing about how we belong.

I'd made it to Sunday, carrying the lemon drop around in my pocket like it was a grenade. I was by turns terrified and giddy, completely topsy-turvy. In short, I was a mess. This morning I woke early, made the pies as quickly as I could, and headed to Vashon on an early ferry. Sundays at the diner were always leisurely in the morning, so I could see Eve and be back in time to help out with the weekend lunchtime crowd. When I'd arrived at the farm, Eve fed me a giant bowl of oatmeal with cinnamon and sliced bananas to fortify me and then put me to work helping ready soap for the farmers market.

"Your life is absurd. You know that, right?" Eve was wearing bright blue latex gloves and carefully stirring the mixture with a silicone spatula. The smell of ammonia was eye-watering as the lye melted the frozen goat's milk. "I mean, it was weird when you were going back for a day, but choosing a different life? This is a whole new level." She shot me a skeptical glance. "Are you sure you're not having some sort of slow emotional breakdown? No judgment if you are. It was the best thing that ever happened to me."

"I know it sounds completely crazy." I ran a finger over the top of a bar of soap; the flecks of orange zest and cloves suspended in the soap were the color of dying embers. "It feels completely crazy. But it's real, I swear, Eve. A few days ago I held those little girls in my arms. Rory kissed me. It was him. He tasted like bourbon and Coke and smelled like sweet tea. And it's completely wrecking me."

"No beer belly and boring personality then?" Eve sighed with evident disappointment. "It would have made things so much easier."

"I'm afraid not," I said. "Sorry to disappoint. I'm still completely head over heels for him, and now I'm total smitten with the girls too."

"Are you going to do it then?"

I hesitated. "I want to. My heart is saying yes, but it's a . . . huge decision. I want to think it through carefully before I leap."

"Well, what are the options?" Eve asked sensibly. "You already know you don't want to choose Toast."

"Right." I lined up a long rectangle of cured activated-charcoal soap on Eve's soap cutter and sliced the blade through it with satisfying ease, making uniform slices over and over. "I could always stay here and just keep living my life, doing the same thing I've been doing for ten years." The thought curdled my stomach.

Eve cast me a skeptical look as she poured almond fragrance oil into a mixture of other moisturizing oils. The smell was heavenly, like marzipan. "Come on, Lolly. Are you really telling me that you could be happy doing that? After you've seen all the other options?"

I thought of Aunt Gert's admonition for me to follow my bliss. *Be honest. Pay attention. Seek joy.* I had been paying attention. I was trying to be honest. And I was desperate to find my joy, to find more of what I'd felt in flickers during those days with my mom and with Rory.

My mother's words came back to me, what she'd said in Hawaii that night on the mountain under the stars. *There is more for you, my girl. More life and love and good things, maybe babies if you want them.* I wanted the more my mother promised me with everything in my heart.

"I can't live this life anymore," I said bluntly. "Something has to change." I put my head in my hands and pressed my palms into my eye sockets.

"Preach!" Eve whooped. "Okay, keep going."

I blew out a long sigh. This was hard. I admired Eve for having the guts to just up and change her life to something she found satisfying. And for her it was not about having a romantic partner or making a lot of money. She'd had both those things, but it turned out she didn't want them. What she wanted was to live on a little plot of land on a remote and beautiful island with her goats, single and happy, making soap at her kitchen table.

"What about your mom? Have you considered going back to her?" Eve poured the lye–goat milk mixture into the oils.

"If I choose her, I lose Dad." I grabbed a square of parchment paper from the neat stack I'd made, and wrapped a bar of charcoal soap, affixing a label to the front. "And I'm not with Rory there either. I couldn't quite figure out what happened, but we weren't together. Mom alluded to it."

Eve stuck a hand blender into the soap mixture and turned it on low, churning the creamy yellow substance. She wisely said nothing. This wasn't a choice anyone could make for me.

"You know, Aunt Gert told me she offered the drops to Mom when they knew she was dying. And she said Mom refused them." I set down the soap and looked at Eve. "Mom said she wouldn't change a thing about her life. She could have taken the lemon drops and lived longer, but she wanted to keep her life this way. As much as I miss her and wish I could have more time with her, I think I have to respect her decision and not change what she chose to do. I have to let her stay gone."

"So that leaves Rory," Eve said quietly over the hum of the mixer.

"That leaves Rory."

We were silent for a minute. I tried to envision myself in that life—with Rory, in the Florida house, with the girls, running my own business. There was a tug on my heart every time I thought of the girls. Could I do it? Could I choose that life for good? The thought was both thrilling and terrifying. It felt so surreal to even be talking about all this. It felt like I was being handed the biggest gift in the world, the ability to choose. I knew what I'd experienced. I didn't understand the mechanics of it, but I understood how I felt in my heart. I would do anything, risk anything, for a chance of a life with Rory and the girls. They were my joy, pure and simple.

"Pros and cons?" Eve asked. She carefully poured the blended liquid into a long rectangular wooden soap mold lined with waxed paper.

I ticked off the reasons in its favor. "My dad would be happily married." I pictured Ramona Flores, the quiet adoration in Dad's eyes in the wedding invitation photo. Even though it had been shocking to see him gazing at another woman that way, I wanted to see him that happy again. "And Daphne would be doing what she seems bent on doing anyway." I'd already filled Eve in on the whole Bikram yoga argument that Daphne and I'd had. Since that conversation, Daphne had not budged in her determination to quit school and pursue her yoga instructor certification. She and Damien were "exploring options," she told me.

"What about the Eatery?" Eve called as she carried the empty soap pot to the kitchen sink.

"I don't know about the Eatery. I forgot to check when I was with Rory. But I guess if Dad is happy and Daphne is doing what she wants to do . . . maybe it doesn't matter?" It was a weird thought.

Eve reappeared, two bottles of home-brewed kombucha in her hands. She sat down across from me and handed me one. "Earl Grey and grapefruit. A new batch."

"Ooh, fancy."

She shrugged. "That's how I roll. Cheers." She clinked bottles with me, and we both took a sip.

"What are the cons?" she asked.

I hesitated. "I think that's the wrong question. I'm sure there are some cons, probably more that I'll discover along the way. But I'm not looking for the perfect life. I'm just trying to do what Aunt Gert keeps urging me to do—follow my bliss."

"And is this life with Rory and those girls following your bliss?" Eve was watching me over the top of her kombucha bottle.

I nodded. "Yes, I think it is."

In the background Pat Benatar wailed about love being a battlefield. It was so like Eve to choose eighties rock-chick power ballads as an ironic soundtrack for the most crucial decision of my life. I slipped my hand into my pocket and ran my fingers over the gritty little surface of the last lemon drop. "I can't live the rest of my life without him, Eve, without Rory and the girls. Not when I have a chance to be with them." I looked at her, pleading for understanding, for her support.

Eve sighed as though she'd expected this outcome all along. "Okay then," she said, and took a long pull of kombucha. She set her bottle down. "I just have one question for you."

"Yes?"

"Are we still friends in this new life of yours?"

"Absolutely," I said firmly. "You texted me photos of the goats. Dotty had twins."

"Good. Then you have my blessing. Use that lemon drop and go follow your bliss."

We sat in silence for a few minutes.

"You know, my mom loved lemons," I said thoughtfully. "She believed they have special powers. She always told me that lemons clarify things; they symbolize happiness and hope. But when she died I stopped believing lemons were anything more than a chore, something sour to squeeze every morning for pie. How ironic that it's a lemon drop that's changing everything for me."

Eve gave me a sideways look. "This is so weird," she said, shaking her head. "And the only reason I'm not completely worried about you is that I actually think this is somehow good for you. I can't explain any of it, but I have this gut intuition that it's all leading in the right direction."

"Me too," I said, looking up and meeting her gaze.

"You're really going to do this, aren't you?" Eve eyed me with a touch of amused disbelief.

I didn't answer, just drained my kombucha in a few gulps, trying to tamp down the fluttering of nerves in my chest. I closed my hand around the lemon drop, holding it like it was my last chance on Earth. It was. It was my chance to right the wrong turn my life had taken so long ago. I was finally going to get Rory Shaw, and with him the life and love I'd purposely shattered so many years ago and longed for ever since.

34

One cool Saturday morning in spring, three years after my mother died, Nancy Shaw came to see me. It was early, before the Eatery opened, and I was baking the day's pies. She tapped on the back door and stepped inside.

"Nancy." I was surprised to see her, the surprise instantly melting to concern. "Is everything okay? Is it Rory?" I'd been trying to get ahold of him since yesterday and was growing increasingly worried by his uncharacteristic silence.

"Everything's fine." She gave a little laugh. "I didn't mean to startle you. I just wanted to have a chat, a little girl talk."

I exhaled in relief. "I've been calling and texting Rory since yesterday. Has he contacted you? He was supposed to find out which residency program he matched with, but I haven't heard from him yet." Which was baffling, as the location of his residency would determine our next several years of life.

Nancy hesitated. "I'm sure he'll call today, Lolly. You know how busy he is right now."

I nodded, unconvinced. He'd learned Monday that he'd been successfully matched for residency somewhere, but we were on pins and needles to find out where, desperately hoping he'd been matched with the University of Washington program so he could be close to me in Seattle. His residency match was a life-altering slip of paper, a slip of paper he and every other fourth-year medical school student had received yesterday. And yet he had not called.

"I wanted to talk to you about Rory, actually," Nancy said a little hesitantly. Her tone put me on instant high alert. Something was up. "He doesn't know I'm here." She looked nervous, although perfectly appointed as always in her crisply elegant linen pants and tailored blouse. I suddenly wished I wasn't wearing a butter-smudged kitchen apron, my hair tossed up in a loose bun. Although she'd been my mother's best friend and had been unfailingly kind to me, Nancy's understated elegance always made me feel frumpy, like I was never quite polished enough.

"Talk to me about what?" I grabbed a sponge and wiped down the stainless-steel table, sweeping up the raw piecrust trimmings into a little pile. Even though I was curious to hear the reason for her visit, I had to keep moving. Time and kitchen duty waited for no man.

The timer buzzed. "Here, I just have to get these pies." I motioned her to sit down on a metal stool on the other side of the prep table. She perched gingerly on the stool as I slid on giant oven mitts and opened the industrial-size oven. My six lemon meringue pies sat golden and perfect in neat rows. It had taken me about six months of trying before I'd really gotten the hang of my mom's recipe. Now the pies turned out exactly right every time. I slid the first one out and carried it carefully to the table. They had to cool for an hour before they could be refrigerated for four hours and then be ready for the lunch seating. I took the rest of the pies out one by one.

"What did you want to talk about?" I prompted, gripping the last pie in my mitts.

"I'm here to ask you to end your engagement to Rory," Nancy said bluntly.

I dropped the pie. It landed meringue-side down on the tile floor with a splat. "What?" I couldn't believe my ears.

She clasped her hands in front of her, steeling herself, and repeated her request in the same calm, even tone of voice.

I stared first at her, then down at the smashed pie. Sunny yellow filling was oozing slowly across the tiles. "Why would you ask me to do that?" I was completely stunned. I left the ruined pie on the floor and turned to face her, still wearing the oven mitts.

She twisted the gold wedding ring on her finger over and over nervously. "Now, just hear me out, Lolly, please. We both love Rory. We both want what's best for him. I know you love him and that he loves you. And I know it's been so hard for you since Irene . . . died." Her eyes glistened with sudden tears, and she blinked and ducked her head, regaining her composure.

I nodded warily. It had been terribly difficult since my mother died, and I was still struggling to manage her responsibilities at the diner. Some days I felt like it would take three of me to replace her. I finished each night far after midnight and drove home with a pounding head and an aching heart. My father was faring worse than I was, however. He was still heartbroken. Daphne, at thirteen, was moody and volatile. It had been a grueling three years, and there was really no end in sight. We were doing the best we could.

"It has been so hard," I agreed. I took off the oven mitts and waited for Nancy to explain.

"Your mother's death changed all our lives, none more so than yours. It's a tragedy in so many ways." Her voice was compassionate, grieved. "Rory tells me you plan to stay here and keep running the diner?"

"I can't leave now. Not with Dad needing so much help, and Daphne's still so young. She needs me too." I looked down at the smashed pie on the floor. "I'm holding everything together right now. Perhaps in a couple of years . . ." But I had a strong feeling that it was wishful thinking. My plans for moving to Baltimore and for Toast had been put on hold after my mother's death. Our wedding was postponed indefinitely. Rory and I still talked about a wedding, but sometime last year we'd stopped discussing the date. The cold hard logistics seemed impossible unless he got a residency spot in Seattle. We'd refused to talk about the alternatives if he didn't.

Nancy took a deep breath. "Lolly, Rory wasn't matched with UW for residency. He was matched with Duke."

"Oh." A flood of dismay and disappointment in that one tiny exhalation. He would not be in Seattle. And then a flicker of anger. He'd found out about his residency and hadn't told me? He'd told Nancy, obviously.

Nancy saw my expression. "He hasn't contacted you because he doesn't know what to say. UW was his top choice because you're here, but Duke . . ."

"Duke is the best fit for him," I murmured numbly.

Nancy nodded. "Rory has such a bright future ahead of him. He's excelling at one of the top medical schools in the country. Duke is a brilliant opportunity. It will make his career. You know he's dreamed of being a physician for a major league sports team since he was twelve years old. It's all within his reach now." Her tone was pleading.

"I've always supported Rory in whatever he wanted to do," I stammered, feeling like a trap was about to spring shut. I just couldn't quite see it yet.

"Yes, I know." She nodded vigorously, her hairdo still perfect. It was the color of Rory's, a rich auburn, which she highlighted and styled like Nancy Reagan.

"But, Lolly, how will it ever work?" Nancy gently voiced a conundrum Rory and I had both been too nervous to acknowledge. I'd asked Rory once about what would happen if he didn't get a residency in Seattle, and he'd refused to discuss the topic, saying only, "I want to be with you, Lolly, for the rest of my life. End of story."

"Rory will have three years of residency at Duke," Nancy said. "Then a fellowship in sports medicine somewhere else in the country. You wouldn't be together for at least four more years."

"Three," I corrected her. "UW has a great sports medicine fellowship. He could do that."

Nancy nodded, her expression sympathetic but firm. "Maybe, if he's very lucky, he'll get a one-year fellowship in Seattle. But what then? He'll need to go wherever he's offered a job. Seattle has a few major league sports teams, but the odds of him getting a job here are quite slim." Nancy hesitated. "I'm only telling you what Rory already knows. It's tearing him apart, the reality of his predicament. He told me . . . he told me last night that he's thinking of refusing the residency at Duke. And you know what that means. He doesn't get another chance for a residency. All his hard work in medical school will be for nothing. He's strongly considering coming back home and getting whatever job he can find, just so he can be with you, Lolly." There were tears glinting in her brown eyes, those eyes that looked so like Rory's. "Don't let him do that. I'm begging you. He loves you so much he'll destroy his own future for you. I'm asking you to love him enough to not let him do that."

I stared at her in horror. "He's thinking of giving up his residency?"

Nancy nodded, once more composed now that she'd made her plea. "I know you love him, Lolly. I know you're a good, strong girl. And that's why I'm asking you to do the right thing and let him go. I know right now you think you can figure it all out, that your love will triumph despite the circumstances, but it doesn't always work out that way. Someone will have to give up what they love, either you or Rory, to make this work. Are you prepared to walk away from this diner and your father and Daphne?"

I couldn't answer for a moment. I knew only two things right now. I loved Rory Shaw more than anyone on Earth. And I simply could not leave my family or the diner, not for the foreseeable future, not for a long, long while. I shook my head. "No." A whisper, an admission. It was impossible.

"Don't make Rory give up everything he's been working toward since he was a boy," Nancy warned me, her eyes flashing with a fervor I had never seen in her. "Because if he chooses you, he'll regret not following his dreams, all that he could have been, for the rest of his life. You don't want to be the girl he gave up everything for. That's a heavy burden for any woman to carry. He'll end up resenting you and this diner and the choice he made. If you make him choose, it will end up destroying both his life and your love."

I couldn't think straight. On the one hand, her logic made perfect, awful sense. Rory had wanted to practice sports medicine since middle school. He was passionate about it; he lived and breathed his dream to be part of a team. And to do that he had to take every opportunity—the best programs and fellowships, contacts and options—no matter where they were in the country. We knew the odds of him getting a good residency in Seattle were long. And Duke was a golden opportunity. He simply had to take it.

But it was Rory we were talking about, Rory and me. How could we not be together? Even the thought of it was like a punch to the heart. Impossible. We were destined for each other. Yes, the last three years had been increasingly tough. Med school and running the diner and parenting a teenager left us both exhausted and often on opposite schedules. Gradually I'd noticed we had less and less to talk about. Our lives were completely removed from each other, and what held us together still were the engagement ring on my finger and our long history together.

Our relationship was feeling strained right now, worn thin by circumstances and distance and the stress of our other responsibilities, our separate lives. I'd convinced myself that all we needed was time together, to be in the same space once more, and that was undoubtedly true. If he had gotten the residency at UW, chances were good that everything would have worked itself out somehow. But he hadn't gotten a residency here. He'd gotten a fabulous residency all the way across the country. Three more years, maybe longer. I bit my lip. Could we make it work long-distance for three more years? I felt despair welling up at the idea of it.

One thing I knew, he couldn't give up his residency. It would be the death of his dream and, I feared Nancy was right, eventually the death of us. If he did come back, what sort of life would he be coming back to? Trapped with me running the diner, working long hours, handling the drama of a headstrong teenage girl. He would be miserable and restless. He could easily grow to resent me and my family, the diner, our constricted life. But the thought of living without him was impossible. We were meant to be together. Somehow we would figure it out. We had to.

"How can you ask me to do this?" I whispered, stricken. Nancy saw my expression and her face softened.

"I love you like a daughter, Lolly. Your mother was my best friend. But Rory is my only child, and I would move heaven and earth to keep him safe and give him all he deserves. I'm sure Rory would be furious if he knew I was talking to you about this. It's your choice if you tell him about our conversation or not. The thought of you together always made me so happy." She stopped, too choked up to continue. After a moment she composed herself again. "But now, I fear for you both if you try to make this work. I know you may not believe me. When you're young you believe love can conquer all, but the truth is that sometimes you can love someone, and yet it's impossible to make a life together. Sometimes the strength of your love for each other just isn't enough. Sometimes you love someone so much you have to let them go."

She stood and paused, then rounded the table and embraced me. She smelled like honeysuckle and starch.

"You're a good girl, Lolly. I know you'll do the right thing," she whispered in my ear as she pressed her cheek to mine for the briefest instant. Her skin was firm and soft as a rose petal.

After she left, I sat staring into space for a minute, trying to catch my breath. Then, numbly, I cleaned up the pie mess on the floor, wiping up the bright filling and dumping the crumbled crust into the compost. One less pie was inconsequential. Nothing mattered except Nancy's words ringing in my ears and the hollow, terrible feeling in my gut that she could possibly be right.

35

SEVEN YEARS AGO
MARCH
Later that day

After Nancy Left, the rest of the morning passed in an awful haze, the knot of anxiety in my stomach growing with each passing hour of silence. I texted Rory. He didn't reply. I waited on customers, made endless pots of coffee, helped Dad jerry-rig the broken oven door with a metal coat hanger, served pie. Over and over, Nancy's words ran through my head, each time the stark, horrible truth of them echoing louder in my mind. I wanted to fire back a perfect response, defend our love, convince her that we could find a way, that our love could find a way. But I didn't have the words. I desperately needed to talk to Rory.

Just as the modest dinner rush was waning, the bell over the front door jingled. I looked up as I was taking orders from a family celebrating their grandmother's birthday and froze. Rory was standing in the doorway. He looked travel-tousled and a little uncertain, his face drawn with concern. When he saw me his eyes lit up, the corners of his mouth curving up in a sweet smile. He raised his hand, and I felt a wave of relief. Rory was here.

I hastily handed my tables off to Beth, the other waitress we had at the time, and gestured for Rory to meet me out back. He was waiting by the dumpsters when I came out, and for a second we just looked at each other. He was wearing jeans and a mustard-yellow Patagonia fleece. He looked exhausted. I was furious at him for not contacting me and relieved that he was really here, but beneath those surface emotions was a queasy sort of anticipation heavily laced with dread. Everything had changed in the past few hours. Something was coming; I just didn't quite know what yet.

We stood awkwardly a few feet apart.

"Hey." I could see the question in his eyes. He didn't know how to begin. I made it easy. I was frustrated and scared and worried, but I was also still desperately in love with this man. I walked into Rory's embrace, colliding with his chest, wrapping my arms around him and holding on as tight as I could. He was solid and warm. He smelled like stale airport air and Rory. We clung to each other, his cheek pressed against my hair, my face buried in his neck. I could feel the tension in him, humming through his muscles like a live wire. Neither of us said anything. I didn't want to be the one to break the seal. He was pressing little kisses on the top of my head, the shell of my ear, holding me so tight I couldn't breathe. I think he felt it too, that something momentous was coming, some reckoning. Nothing would ever be the same after tonight, whatever the outcome.

I pulled back, scrubbing my hands down his cheeks, the stubble rasping like crusted sand on a shell. He looked older than even a month ago when I'd seen him last. There were worry lines pinching the corners of his mouth.

"Why didn't you call me?" I asked finally. "I had to hear it from your mother."

Rory pulled back and stared at me. He had not realized I knew about the residency. He must have flown all the way here from Baltimore to break the news to me himself. "What about Mom?" He looked puzzled.

"She came to see me this morning. She told me about Duke."

Rory dropped his head. "Can we go to the beach?" He sighed. "I think we need to talk."

I drove us in silence down to the beach parking lot. It was a raw March day, the light fading toward evening, and no one else was there. Rory spoke as I pulled Florence into a parking space.

"I didn't know how to tell you," he said finally. "I'm sorry. I wanted to wait and tell you in person. I really wanted it to be UW." His tone was flat, discouraged.

We headed toward the north end of the beach, past the lighthouse. We skirted the fence with the heart-shaped lock, taking the other way around. I didn't want to look at that optimistic little token of our love, not when my heart was roiling with such turmoil. We scrambled through the blackberry brambles and madrone trees, clambering over driftwood logs and down a sandy little trail to the water.

The air was calm, but I could smell the rain coming. Huge dark clouds piled up against the Olympic Mountains to the west. The color was leaching slowly from them, the oranges and pinks of a spectacular sunset fading to purple and indigo. We settled against our usual drift-wood log, fitting next to each other like two peas in a sandy little pod. I shivered and zipped my jacket, scooting closer to Rory. How many years had we sat side by side like this? I looked around, seeing us standing there in our swimsuits as young teens, pale and shivering. In the very spot where we sat, I pictured us in a tangle of limbs and fe-vered kisses that night before Rory went off to college. The night I declared my love for him. Had things come full circle? Would this be the place where we began and ended?

I settled back against the log, my arm pressed against Rory's, and we watched dusk fall gently over the water.

"So, Duke," I said finally.

Rory nodded. "Yeah." He darted a look at me.

"Do you want to go to Duke?"

Rory didn't say anything for a while. "Duke is a great program, one of the best," he said at last, a hint of wistfulness and excitement in his voice. "I'd get a world-class residency. It would have been my top choice if not for . . ." He didn't finish his sentence.

"Me being stuck here in Seattle," I supplied.

He nodded. "Would I like to go to Duke? Yeah, in another life. But this is *our* life, our story, so it doesn't really matter."

"Why doesn't it matter?"

He turned to me, lacing his fingers through my cold ones. "Because I'll move heaven and earth not to lose you again, Lolly." He sounded so sincere. He was so sincere.

"If you say no to Duke, what will you do?"

He shrugged. "Get a job at a hospital or maybe as a high school coach. I'll figure something out." He sounded resigned, no spark of joy as he discussed his options.

I listened to his lackluster ideas and thought of Nancy's prediction and felt cold to the marrow. *If he chooses you, he'll regret not following his dreams*, she'd warned me. *All that he could have been, for the rest of his life.*

I wanted her to be wrong, willed her to be wrong. But if I was honest, I suspected she was right. He was planning to give it all up for me. I couldn't let him do that. I could see it now, playing out so clearly. He would give it up for the love of me—his dreams, this golden opportunity, the life he'd been planning since he was twelve years old. He'd do it because the alternative was unthinkable. He was loving and loyal. He'd never choose his own interests over me.

But I knew him, I knew what he was made for, his passion for medicine and athletics, his deep commitment to every team he'd ever been a part of. I knew that he'd give his dream up for me, but he'd suffer greatly for it. In some part of him he'd carry regret for the rest of his life, and it would be because of me.

"You can't say no to Duke," I said firmly. "Rory, you have to go."

He shot me an incredulous, hopeful glance. "Are you saying you'll come with me?" I heard the lift in his voice.

And for a minute I hesitated. The temptation was almost unbearable, to leave it all, to walk away. No more trying to mother a teenager who didn't want me meddling in her life, no more accounts and inventory and ever-diminishing profit margins, no more coming home smelling like Danish meat loaf and red cabbage. No more rising early every morning to make those endless lemon meringue pies. I could just walk away. I could be free.

For a brief tantalizing moment I pictured it. Rory and I could rent a shabby little apartment near the campus. He'd work crazy hours. I'd get a cat for company. I could see the comfy brown couch, a table set for two, a row of potted herbs and flowers on a windowsill. Simple. The life we could have together. But to walk away was . . . impossible.

If I left, what would become of the diner, my father and my sister, and my family's legacy? How would my father cope? The diner was what got him up in the morning. It was his way of carrying on without Mom, of holding us all together. I think it was what held him together too. He would be flattened if I left, and we couldn't afford to hire someone to do all that I did anyway. The diner was our livelihood too. Without it I didn't know how we would survive financially. And besides, leaving Dad and Daphne to fend for themselves was unthinkable. Daphne hated me trying to mother her, but she needed me more than she even knew. Dad was still mired deep in grief, and he had no idea what to do with a high-spirited teenage girl. Daphne pushed me away at times, but at others she clung to me like the scared child she still was inside. I was the glue holding my fractured little family together. If I left, everything would fall apart. My father and Daphne, our home and family and finances. It would be selfish and callous of me to leave. I couldn't do it. It was impossible.

"No." Just the one word but it shut the door to a world of possibilities, a life I ached to have as my own. "I can't leave them. You know that," I whispered, the words sticking in my throat like a crust of dry bread.

"I know." He sighed. "So we just keep doing long-distance for, what, another three or four years?" His tone was flat and resigned.

The past three years had been hard enough on us. We'd talked about it often. We couldn't rely on just a commitment to each other regardless of time and distance. No matter how much we cared for each other, we couldn't keep living separate lives. It was unraveling us. We both knew it. We couldn't make it another three or four years, I was positive. There would be nothing between us by then except memories and regrets.

I shook my head, tears prickling hot behind my eye lids. "We'll never survive that." I blinked them back and looked at him, the planes of his cheekbones stark in the gathering darkness, the fresh breeze ruffling his copper hair, his eyes on mine, searching, anxious. I loved him too much to let him destroy his life this way. And for the first time, I let myself acknowledge what that meant. I could not leave to go with him. And I couldn't let him give up everything to stay with me. It would be the end of us one way or the other. I saw it clearly now.

"I think, no matter how much we love each other, our lives are pulling us in separate directions." I said the words aloud, the truth starkly clear.

Rory pulled back, his expression stricken. "Lolly, what are you saying?"

I started to cry then, hard, ugly sobs. The truth was agonizing. It felt like the same pain as the day my mother died, a grief so huge it swelled up in my chest like an atomic mushroom cloud. My heart was imploding. I had loved Rory since I was thirteen. I felt like I would love him till the day I died.

"I love you more than anyone in this world, but we're not going in the same direction. I don't think we're meant to live the same life." I choked on the words. "If my mom hadn't died. If I didn't have to run the diner and take care of my dad and Daphne . . ." I couldn't finish the thought. I doubled over, hugging myself to keep from disintegrating altogether. In another world, Rory and I would have lived happily ever after. In another lifetime, we would have been each other's forever. But this was not that world. And there was no way to change it.

"No, Lolly. Listen. We can work it out somehow. I'll figure something out here in Seattle. Not residency, but something." He sounded desperate.

I shook my head. "If I let you say no to Duke, you'll regret it for the rest of your life. You know it's true. You'll always wonder 'What if?' You were made for athletics and medicine. You live and breathe it. If you give it all up, you'll be living a smaller life. It will be the wrong shape for you. Don't you see that? And it will be because of me. And, yes, we'd be together, but in a life neither of us wants. I don't want you to resent me. You have to go, and I can't come with you."

I saw the flicker of understanding cross his face, the truth of my words resonating with him, even as he fought them. He knew I was right. I could see that he did, but he couldn't acknowledge it to be true.

"Lolly, listen to me." Rory put his hands on my shoulders, turning me to face him, his eyes searching my own. I looked at him long and hard, etching him in my mind. All those years of loving Rory culminating in this moment. Root beer and shiny pennies, Daphne's baby belly laughs when he'd toss her above his head, the length of his lean body against mine, the smell of him, bourbon and oak and sweet tea. The feel of his mouth, so tender and strong it broke my heart.

"I can't let you go," he said, and the words were broken, a plea. "We can try long-distance. We'll figure it out, make it work."

"Maybe. Maybe we could limp along for another few years long-distance, but what then?" I asked gently, looking him in the eye. "What happens after you're all done? What if you can't get a job in Seattle? You know how slim those odds are. Are you willing to do all those years of school and possibly never get to do the thing you love? Rory, this isn't going to work."

He opened his mouth to protest, but the words shriveled on his tongue. I saw the light go from his eyes. He was glimpsing that future; he was glimpsing the truth.

"I don't want to live without you," he said again simply. He was crying. I watched him, feeling a strange detachment. Inside I was hollow and cavernous, just echoes where my heart had been beating seconds before.

"I know," I said gently. "But I can't let you ruin your entire life trying to keep me." I wrestled off my engagement ring, holding it out to him, insistent. Tears made silver tracks down his cheeks and mine. The emerald solitaire caught the light of a rising full moon. It flashed dark and brilliant, a fleeting spark swallowed by the darkness.

"Don't do this, Lolly," he pleaded. "I can't let you go." He held out his hands, palms up, refusing to take the ring, refusing to do what needed to be done.

I looked out over the water, away from him, steeling myself for the rest of my life. Almost without thinking I drew back my arm and in one smooth motion tossed the ring as far out as I could into the water. It glinted for an instant in the light of the moon, arcing down toward the waves, and then it was gone.

"The truth is, we're already done."

36

"Julio, where's Dad?" I walked back into the Eatery from making soap at Eve's just in time for lunch to find Julio manning the grill alone. Dad was nowhere to be seen. That was unusual.

Julio didn't hear me as he flipped a half dozen Danish meatballs in a skillet while some sort of terrible screaming heavy metal music pulsated faintly from his headphones. I poked my head into the dining room. There were a few customers seated in booths, and Aunt Gert, wearing a sixties block-print shift and giant bug-eyed white glasses, appeared to be coercing a group of bird-watchers into dessert. The birdwatchers all wore khaki vests and had binoculars around their necks and were nodding halfheartedly as Aunt Gert extolled the virtues of our pie. I returned to the kitchen and tapped Julio on the shoulder.

"Where's Dad?" I yelled, trying to be heard over the music he was listening to. Julio pulled off his headphones and jerked his head toward my office as he plated the meatballs and added a heaping scoop of potato salad.

"I saw him go in there."

The office door was closed. I was sure I'd left it ajar when I left.

"Dad?" I opened the door and poked my head inside.

He was sitting in my office chair, his head bowed, his entire posture one of defeat. My desk drawer was open and in his hand was the devastating amended tax bill for King County.

He looked up. "Hey, girly." His face was haggard, voice a little hoarse. It looked like he'd aged ten years in the few hours I'd been gone. "I was looking for a pen. Found this." He cleared his throat. "That's a pretty big number. Sort of a shock to the system."

My heart sank. "I was going to tell you," I said quietly, slipping inside and latching the door behind me. "I just hadn't found the right time. I wanted to have some sort of plan in place before I told you about the tax increase." I pinched the bridge of my nose, trying to figure out what I could say that would sound reassuring.

He laced his fingers and rested his arms on his knees. His hands were shaking. "Yeah, it's pretty bad. I don't know how we're going to get through this one."

"I don't either," I admitted, perching on the edge of the desk. I still had absolutely nothing concrete to offer. "Maybe we can do a crowdfunding campaign. Like GoFundMe. People like those. We'll figure it out. We always do."

He sighed. "You're right. But there comes a time when a man has to face facts, no matter how hard he tries. This might be that time." The resignation in his voice alarmed me. He looked lost.

"Hey, don't give up yet," I urged. "We'll think of something."

He sat back and winced, rolling his shoulders and massaging his left bicep.

"You okay?" I asked.

He nodded. "Just getting old. I was cleaning a bird's nest out of the sign in front this morning, and I think I pulled a muscle in my shoulder. It's feeling a little numb and tingly. Nothing a little Advil won't set right."

"Be careful. You're not a spring chicken," I chided, feeling like a mother hen. I took the tax letter from him and tucked it back in the drawer, out of sight. "Let Julio get up on the ladder next time, okay?"

"Speaking of Julio, I'd better get back to the grill." He got to his feet slowly and cast another worried look at the drawer. There was something alarming in the slump of his shoulders. Was it only fatigue or did it spell defeat?

"Dad, why don't you take the rest of the afternoon off? Julio and I can manage for a few hours." I paused, eyeing him. "Are you sure you're okay?"

He waved off my concern. "I've been carrying the weight of this place on my shoulders for a lot of years. I'm not about to stop now. Just feeling a little tired is all, can't seem to clear my head today. I'll just pop an Advil and have another cup of coffee and be right as rain."

I watched him as he returned to the kitchen, not entirely reassured but knowing I couldn't stop him if I tried. We'd always put the Eatery first, the whole family. It was our highest priority. The sense of responsibility had come down from my grandparents, who had put their whole hopes and dreams into making it a success. My parents had taken up that mantle when they took over. It was the life we knew, it was legacy, and we were raised to put the Eatery before anything else. Our family's success was its success. It was an unspoken but ever-present belief. But now I wondered why we clung so hard to this place. Was it really the best way to spend our lives? I cast a look at the drawer with the tax statement. My mother's voice came back to me. *Sometimes you just have to let go.* What would happen if we didn't save the Eatery this time? Would the world stop turning on its axis? Or would we figure out a new way of living? When I took the lemon drop and returned to a life with Rory, I supposed I'd find out.

In the kitchen I could hear my dad arguing sports with Julio. Unlike other days, he sounded halfhearted about it. I dropped into the chair and opened the drawer, taking out the vile letter. So many zeros. Seemingly impossible. My hand drifted to the pocket of my jeans, fingers closing around the lemon drop once more. I thought of the wedding invitation I'd seen on Rory's fridge, the joy on Dad's lined face as he gazed down at Ramona. Taking the lemon drop would solve so many things. I closed my eyes and imagined the smell of strawberry shampoo and a squishy little person nestled in my arms. The intent look in Rory's eyes as he'd slipped the sundress strap off my shoulder and kissed the tender skin in the hollow of my clavicle. I swallowed hard, almost dizzy with desire for him, for our life together. I couldn't wait. Deep down I knew that my future lay with Rory and the girls. Now I just needed to take the last lemon drop and restart my life the way it was supposed to go. Tonight I would do it. Tonight everything would be set right again.

"We've got an order of klar suppe and a kid's meal with Danish hotdog," I called a few hours later, pushing through the kitchen door. It was the height of the dinner rush, and Daphne had been delayed across town—a bus breakdown. I was covering for her and helping Aunt Gert get through the surprisingly busy dinner hour. Once a waitress, you never forgot the skills. "And the family at table five is requesting another order of french fries. Their toddler dumped a glass of ice water into hers."

At the grill Dad was standing bowlegged and intent, a metal turner in his hand, hovering over rows of grilling fiskefrikadeller. At the counter next to him, Julio prepped plates with sides of boiled potatoes and red cabbage.

I grabbed ramekins of chocolate mousse from the fridge for the corner booth by the window. A ladies' book club reserved that booth for dinner once a month to eat dessert and discuss the latest celebrity memoir, which, to the best of my knowledge, none of them actually ever read. Two had ordered the mousse, the rest wanted pie.

"Is table four's order ready?" Aunt Gert charged into the kitchen. "What's the holdup? They've eaten through two baskets of bread so far, and I'm afraid they're going to start on the napkins next."

Looking harried, Julio picked up his pace. "Sorry, we're running slow tonight," he said. "Marty, are those cod cakes ready yet?"

No response. I glanced up, holding the mousse in my hands. Dad was standing at the grill, one arm raised, the other hanging limply at his side. Something wasn't right.

"Dad?"

He turned slightly. The left side of his face looked strangely slack. "I don't feel so good, Lolly girl," he slurred, and then, as if in slow motion, he collapsed on the floor.

"Call 911!" I screamed, the dishes of mousse slipping from my fingers and shattering on the tile.

The next few minutes were a blur. Aunt Gert dialing 911 and requesting help, giving the dispatcher the information in a loud, commanding voice while I knelt over Dad, hyperventilating and trying to rouse him. A smoky pall of burned grease hanging over the kitchen. Julio scraping blackened cod cakes into the trash and turning off the grill. My own high-pitched singsong voice, over and over, urging, "Dad, can you hear me? Dad, stay with us." And my father, who woke every morning already in motion, who was the epitome of scrappy endurance, lying slumped over on the sticky tiles, his skin gray and clammy to the touch. Then the back door burst open, and the paramedics filled the space in a flurry of efficiency. I was pushed to the periphery as they took his vitals and hoisted him onto the stretcher.

"Is someone coming with Mr. Blanchard in the ambulance?" one of the paramedics asked. I froze, suddenly remembering the full tables out front.

"You go with Marty." Julio laid a hand on my arm, his young face looking suddenly far more mature. "Gert and I will handle things here."

37

Thirty minutes later Dad and I were sequestered in a private bay in the emergency room of Swedish Hospital while a team of doctors, nurses, and technicians swarmed around us like busy worker bees. I sat numbly in a chair in the corner, watching the commotion with a cold sense of dread.

I remembered the last time I'd been in this hospital. My mother pale and resigned in the bed. My father's shock. Daphne's incomprehension. My life and our family had shattered that day. I couldn't lose my other parent. We couldn't handle another loss.

"Please be okay, please be okay." I whispered, the panic coming in waves like nausea. Over the next frantic hour, as the medical staff tested and measured and scanned Dad, I exchanged staccato texts with Daphne and Eve, keeping them abreast of the situation. When an orderly wheeled him back in from his CT scan, Dad opened his eyes and saw me.

"Lol." He slurred my name, reaching his good hand out.

"I'm here, Dad. It's okay. Everything's going to be okay." I rushed to his side and gripped his hand, repeating words intended to soothe us both. A few minutes later the emergency room doctor, a slight, bespectacled woman named Dr. Cho, came into the room and delivered the diagnosis.

"Your father has suffered an ischemic stroke," she said, her expression both weary and sympathetic. "This is the most common type of stroke. It occurred on the right side of his brain. He is experiencing many common effects associated with a stroke—loss of movement in his left side, slurred speech, confusion. This is all to be expected. We have started him on an IV of powerful medication called tPA to break up the blood clot that caused the stroke. We will be admitting him as a patient to the stroke center and monitoring him closely for the next few days."

"Is he going to be okay?" I asked, dreading and anticipating the answer.

Dr. Cho hesitated. "Your father is stable for now, and the medication he is receiving should stop the blood clot from causing further damage. He was very fortunate that he got treatment as quickly as he did."

I nodded, lowering my voice and darting a look at Dad in the bed. His eyes were closed. He appeared to be dozing. "Is there any way to know how much . . . damage the stroke did to his brain?" My voice shook. Actually, I realized that my entire body was shaking with fear and shock. I wrapped my arms around myself and held tight. I couldn't fall apart right now.

Dr. Cho shook her head. "It's too soon to give a prognosis of recovery, but because we caught it early, you can be assured that the damage will be far less severe than if it had gone untreated. Your father may recover fully after physical therapy and rehabilitation. However, many times stroke victims do not return to all of their previous functionality. They often experience some cognitive and physical challenges as a result of the stroke. Memory loss, personality changes. The brain is so complex that every stroke event and recovery is different. We simply cannot predict what will happen. However, you need to be aware that recovery from a stroke is often a very slow and lengthy process. You will need to prepare yourselves for that." She delivered the news as gently as she could.

After Dr. Cho left, I sat silently, trying to process her words. A slow and lengthy recovery. Cognitive and physical challenges. My phone buzzed. Daphne.

We're in the lobby

Daphne, Aunt Gert, and Julio were waiting in the lobby when I arrived. Aunt Gert was pacing. Julio sat on the edge of a chair, still wearing his kitchen whites, turning his Seahawks baseball cap nervously in his hands. When I appeared, Daphne launched herself at me, hugging me hard around the neck. She was crying.

"Is Dad going to be okay?" she asked tearfully. I hugged her back, instantly slipping into the role of the capable, maternal one.

"He's in great hands. Swedish has one of the best stroke centers in Washington State." I had no reassurance that Dad would be okay, but I wanted to take every scrap of hope and comfort I had and offer it to Daphne. I knew Dad's prognosis was still unclear, but I wanted to be optimistic. Daphne hugged me tighter. I could feel her trembling. She was scared. So was I.

I met Aunt Gert's eyes over Daphne's shoulder. She raised her eyebrows, and I shook my head slightly and shrugged in an *I don't know* gesture.

"What did the doctor say?" Aunt Gert asked, and I repeated Dr. Cho's diagnosis, trying to soften the parts about uncertain long-term prognosis.

"They're going to transfer him to a private room soon, so I'd better get back there. I'll text you as soon as he's settled, and you can come up and see him." I patted Daphne, who was still clinging to me like a baby koala. This must be triggering so many painful emotions for her, bringing up what had happened with Mom. I was feeling them too.

"We closed up the diner," Julio said, clearing his throat. He shifted from foot to foot, looking ill at ease.

"We served anyone already seated and then closed up early," Aunt Gert clarified. "We gave each customer a free dessert for their trouble."

I nodded. "Good thinking. Thank you." I couldn't think about the diner, only Dad, alone in that bed, his left side immobile. I couldn't begin to process what this would mean for our lives. That realization would gradually come later, I knew. For now I could only concentrate on the present, the next step.

"You're a mess." Daphne sniffled. "You've got chocolate mousse all down your front." She pulled back a little and surveyed me. I glanced down at my checkered blouse and cuffed jeans. There was a long brown smear down the left side of both. I had been too distraught to notice.

"Here, I've got an extra set of clothes." Daphne rummaged around in her backpack and handed me a pile of yoga gear. It wasn't my usual vibe, but it was comfortable and clean.

"Thanks." I slipped into the ladies' room down the hall from the lobby and changed clothes hurriedly. If Dad woke, I wanted to be right there with him. I splashed water on my face. In the mirror my reflection was drawn and pallid, worry tightening the corners of my mouth. I had chocolate mousse splattered on my arms and scrubbed it away with a wet paper towel from the dispenser. I wasn't thinking clearly, my thoughts ping-ponging around in my head like crazy. I was on high alert but felt helpless. How could this be happening? What should we do now?

Back in the lobby Daphne took my soiled clothes and stuffed them in her backpack. "I'll take care of these," she offered.

"Thank you." I squeezed her arm. "I should get back to Dad. Do you want to come see him?" I wanted to be next to him if he awoke.

Daphne tearfully nodded.

Julio cleared his throat. "Um, so what are we going to do about the diner? We're closed tomorrow like usual, but what about Tuesday?"

I paused. In its over sixty years of operation, the Eatery had been closed unexpectedly only three times. Once when Magnolia sustained an unheard-of amount of rain in October of 1977 and the entirety of McGraw Street flooded, and once when the power went out completely for three days in 1988. And the third time on the day of Mom's funeral. That was it. To close it now felt ominous, like waving a white flag, but what could we do? Aunt Gert and Julio couldn't run it by themselves, even if Daphne helped out. And I couldn't leave Dad alone until I knew more about his condition. I doubted we'd be ready to open on Tuesday.

"Put a sign on the door: 'Closed until further notice,'" I said heavily, finally. "Hopefully we can be back up and running before the weekend." They all nodded, looking sober.

Thirty minutes later, I sat next to Dad in a dim hospital room. After they'd peeked in and seen Dad, who was still asleep, Daphne and Aunt Gert headed home to feed Bertha and get some sleep. We agreed that Daphne would take over from me in the morning. Dad did not awaken, which the nurse had told me was to be expected. He looked so small, almost frail, lying there. The lines of his face were slack, his sleep unnaturally still. I was exhausted but strangely wired, hyped up on a potent cocktail of anxiety and relief. What was going to happen now? He was still with us, but he was not himself. The left side of his face drooped, a snail track of drool tracing its way down his chin.

I put my head in my hands, rocking slightly back and forth. This was all too much. I felt like a drowning woman, flailing to keep her head above water, and someone had just handed me a thousand-pound weight. I simply couldn't keep afloat. I had thought it was the tax bill that would be our undoing, but I was wrong. This stroke was going to sink us. There was no way around it. We couldn't keep the diner open without Dad as head cook. Julio was a good sous-chef, but he couldn't manage a kitchen and handle all the cooking alone. He just wasn't ready, and we had absolutely no finances to hire a new chef. And even if we did manage to squeak by, who was going to care for Dad if his recovery took a while? And there was still the matter of the looming tax bill. Any way you sliced it there was no way out. We were going down.

And then I stopped, a thought dawning on me, simple and obvious. The lemon drop. It could fix all of this. It was a solution to this entire mess. Neat. Tidy. Perfect. In the panic around Dad's collapse I'd forgotten about it momentarily. I had planned to take it tonight. I still could. The thought brought a sweet rush of relief. I glanced at Dad.

Suddenly he went rigid in the bed, his eyes rolling back in his head, and he started jerking uncontrollably. I lunged for the call button and pressed it frantically, then bolted into the hall, crying out for help. Within a few seconds there was a flurry of lights and beeping and people in uniform rushing in and surrounding him.

"What's happening to him?" I cried. He'd been sleeping peacefully a minute ago. What had gone wrong?

A nurse who was hurrying out of the room turned as she passed. "It's a seizure, sweetie. Common in stroke victims." And then she was gone. A minute later they wheeled Dad away too.

Alone, I sank into a hard vinyl chair, mind racing. Was he okay? Was he dying and no one was telling me? The minutes ticked by with agonizing slowness. Forty minutes later Dad was still not back. I asked at the nurses' station, but received no helpful information—only that he was stabilized and they were running tests. *Stabilized*. That was a relief. The immediate danger was over, but what had happened to him?

After what seemed like forever, an exhausted-looking Dr. Cho entered the room.

"Your father is stable now," she told me. "It is not uncommon to have a seizure after a stroke. The good news is that with anti-seizure medication this should not occur again. Unfortunately, after running further tests, I'm afraid that the extent of damage to your father's brain is more than we'd initially hoped." She frowned.

"Damage?" I stumbled over the word. "What does that mean for his recovery?"

Dr. Cho stuck her hands in the pockets of her lab coat. "Again, there is no way to know at this point, but the extent and severity of the stroke are more than we first thought. I want to prepare you. His recovery will be slower than you might be expecting, and the extent to which he regains his verbal and motor functions may be considerably less as well."

"Oh." I sank back in the chair, her pronouncement a sucker punch in my stomach. "Is there . . . is there anything we can do?"

Dr. Cho shook her head. "There is nothing we can do at this point except monitor his condition and wait. When the time comes for him to be released, we can recommend some excellent rehabilitation facilities. Again, we don't know exactly how much rehabilitation he will need, but it is best to be prepared. I'm sorry, but only time will tell."

I was hardly aware of her exit from the room. *There's nothing we can do*, she'd said. But she was wrong. I could do one thing to fix all of this. I could erase this terrible night. I could restore my father to health. Give Daphne the life she was longing for. Bring Dad a new love. And finally have the chance to live the life I had pined for all these years. I took a deep breath, sure this was the answer to everything. There was no time to lose. I was going home to take the last lemon drop.

38

In the back of an Uber, I pressed my forehead to the window and watched my childhood slide quietly by as we headed through the darkened village center of Magnolia in the direction of our house. It was almost midnight, and I was going home to save my father and reclaim the life I'd always wanted. It was as simple as that. And yet not simple at all. I had not anticipated the wave of nostalgia that swept over me as I watched the shops and bakeries and cafés of Magnolia pass in a rainy blur of dark windows and lit signs. Magnolia's Bookstore. Petit Pierre. The Eatery. When I awoke, what would be different? I could only guess. If all went well, I would never again walk home after closing up, never wake in my single twin bed in the little garret bedroom that had been mine all my life, never bake those six lemon meringue pies every morning like clockwork. I shivered at the thought—delicious and a little terrifying.

When I woke, I hoped, it would be to a new life—better, but strange—Daphne would be on an exotic island. My dad would be healthy and happily in love, married to Ramona. The Eatery would be . . . I didn't know. And I would be wife to the man of my dreams and mother to two energetic, hilarious, sweet little girls. I could hardly breathe I was so eager to start this new life.

By force of habit, I slipped my hand in my pocket, reaching for the hard, gritty reassurance of the lemon drop. But my fingers found no pocket at all. Only a smooth fabric waistband. I glanced down, panic spiking through my chest. And then in a flash I remembered. Daphne. The change of clothes. I was wearing her yoga pants. In the whirlwind after Dad's stroke, I had changed out of my chocolate-smeared jeans. Daphne had taken them with her when she left.

I drew a quick sigh of relief. It would be all right then. Daphne was famous in our family for her procrastination about doing any sort of housework. It was almost a sure bet that she'd simply dropped the clothes in my room or left them by the front door. The lemon drop was almost assuredly nestled safely in my jeans pocket. Still, I leaned forward in the back seat of the Uber, eager to get home and have the lemon drop once more in my hand. It held all our futures now.

Bertha greeted me at the door with a happy tail wag. The house was dark and silent. Daphne had texted me earlier to say that she was going to stop by the house to grab some things for overnight and then head to Damien's apartment. Tonight she didn't want to be alone.

Inside I poked hurriedly around the most likely spots, looking for my clothes, checking all the usual areas with a growing sense of concern. Bertha trailed me, standing in the doorways and snuffling. I checked the shoe area by the front door. My room. Laundry room. Bathroom hamper. Even the trash under the sink. Nothing. Where was it? Maybe she hadn't dropped my soiled clothes off at home like I predicted. Feeling a little panicked, I texted Daphne.

Hey, looking for the dirty clothes you brought home for me. Any idea where they are?

It was late, but she was naturally a night owl, so chances were good she and Damien were still up.

Ping! A text. I fumbled with my phone.

> Threw them in the wash with my yoga stuff when I got home. Should be dry by now. I know. I'm amazing.

And a smiley face emoji with hearts for eyes.

Oh no. Oh no oh no oh no. I tore into the laundry room, ripping open the dryer, pawing through the hot pile of staticky clothes inside, stifling a scream. There they were, the blue jeans I'd worn, smelling faintly of fabric softener. I pulled them out and frantically searched the pocket, willing the lemon drop to still be there. It had to be. It *had* to be.

Empty. The pocket was empty. Just a tiny sticky circle and the faintest whiff of lemon candy.

"No." I sank back on my heels on the tile floor with a strangled cry, numb with disbelief. It was gone. My last chance was gone, disintegrated with hot water and Tide. Everything I was going to fix, to change, to make okay again. No healthy Dad. No Rory. No Sophia and Freya.

"No! *No!*" I screamed, slamming my hand against the dryer, bruising my palm. "It doesn't end like this. It's got to be here somewhere." It had to be. Everything depended on that little yellow oval.

With a blind determination, I searched every crevice of the laundry room, even sticking my hand down the dryer hose and turning the trash cans upside down in a shower of dryer lint and gum wrappers, hyperventilating, desperate for the impossible. But there was no little spot of yellow sunshine amid the detritus of our lives. It was truly gone.

Slowly, so slowly, I sank to my knees, then curled up in a fetal position on the cold tile floor, lying so still and quiet I wasn't even sure I was still breathing. I felt completely numb. Bertha watched me uneasily from the doorway, whining and shifting from foot to foot. Slowly, starting from my chest and radiating out to my limbs, I began to shake, from the cold floor or the shock, maybe both. I couldn't stop. And then the tears came, silent at first, and then great wracking sobs. I was choking on the tears and grief, sobbing at the memory of my dad splayed out on the kitchen floor—his worn face a slack, pallid gray—sobbing for the loss of my one last chance to have so many good things.

I had lost my mother, now perhaps my father, very likely our family's diner—our heritage and livelihood. And now I had also lost Rory and the girls for good. The thought was unbearable. Loss upon loss. I'd had to give Rory up before, and this was my second chance. But now I would never be his wife, never be a mother to those two sweet little girls. There was no way to turn back the clock, reverse time, make a different choice. My future had just imploded all over again.

Early the next morning I blinked groggily, my head pillowed on a pile of clean towels, coming to consciousness stiff and sore and freezing on the hard tile, with Bertha's wet nose pushing into my ear.

"Ugh." Scrambling to a sitting position, I struggled to remember where I was and why I was there. In the cool gray light of early morning, the events of the night before all came rushing back in a terrible moment of recollection.

"Oh no." A whisper, sheer despair. I wrapped my arms around my legs and hugged myself, trying to get warm, trying to grapple with the truth. There would be no fixing this, no second chances. Bertha snuffled my face worriedly and grumbled, and I rubbed her ears, not able to offer my usual words of reassurance. I was not all right. Nothing was all right. I feared nothing would ever be all right again.

My phone buzzed with a text and I searched the laundry piles, locating it under some towels. Daphne.

> I'm at the hospital. Where are you? Couldn't sleep
> so I came over early. Nurse says Dad's stable. He's
> asking for you.

I swallowed hard.

> Be right there.

I typed the words woodenly. There was only a dull ache in my chest.

Staggering to my feet, I tried to think. I needed a shower. Coffee. To feed Bertha and let her out. To reverse time about twelve hours so I didn't change out of my jeans. To reverse time about a decade, before all the worst things of my life happened one after another.

Fifteen minutes later I was passably clean, dressed, and gulping down a cup of coffee standing at the sink. I saw Aunt Gert's light blink on in the cottage and in a split second made a decision. I set the cup down, half-full, and slipped out the door, heading for her little house.

She opened the door at my knock, improbably dressed in a pair of red woolen long underwear, the kind prospectors and miners wore in the 1800s.

"How's Marty?" she asked immediately, brow furrowing in concern. With her thin white curls and tubby belly she looked like a dour elf.

"He had a seizure last night after you left, but he's stable now. I lost it," I blurted out. "I lost the last lemon drop. It was going to fix everything."

She eyed me for a moment, then tilted her head. "Come inside."

She was steeping a jasmine tea ball in a porcelain tea bowl at her tiny table for two. I dropped into the chair opposite hers, and she took her seat calmly. Before her, the tea ball began to unfurl in the hot water, the petals fanning out like a delicate sea creature as it bloomed.

"Tea?" she asked. "Full of antioxidants. Boosts brain function."

I shook my head.

"Tell me everything," she said. "Start at the beginning."

I took a deep breath and burst out with the whole story, from the day I first washed windows with Rory to last night and the disintegrating lemon drop.

"It was my only hope to make everything all right," I said in despair. "And it's gone. Unless . . . do you have another one, one last lemon drop?" I caught my breath at the thought. *Please say yes, please say yes, please say yes.*

"Sadly no." Aunt Gert shook her head. She gave me a sympathetic frown. "That was truly the last one, I'm afraid."

"Oh." My shoulders slumped in defeat. It was done. The sense of loss was instantaneous, so strong I felt it squeeze the breath from my lungs. I choked, coughed. She watched me impassively.

"I can't believe this is how it ends," I whispered.

"Who said anything about ending?" Aunt Gert snapped. "One door has closed, with great pain and disappointment, I'm sure. This is a setback, it's true, but not the end of everything for you. And while you don't see it yet, to paraphrase the great English poet John Milton and only slightly less famous American chanteuse Judy Garland, every cloud has a silver lining. You just have to find it." She sounded bracingly unsympathetic.

"There's no silver lining." I shook my head in despair. "Everything's ruined now." I had never felt so hopeless.

Aunt Gert took a sip of the tea, considering. Her tone softened. "You must follow your bliss, even in this, Lolly. Things feel dark, it's true, but there will always be a spark of light. Follow that. It will show you where you need to go."

"I can't. This is too big, too broken." I put my head in my hands in despair. "I don't see the spark of light. Everything has fallen apart."

Aunt Gert sat in silence for a long moment, then cleared her throat. "Some things aren't meant to be mended," she said finally, gently. "Sometimes it's in the breaking that the light can finally shine through."

39

Two days after Dad's stroke Daphne found me in the dim, empty dining room of the Eatery at three in the afternoon.

"Hey, Lols," She came through the door from the kitchen and saw me standing at the empty pie case, staring blankly inside. The diner was still closed, an unprecedented occurrence. "What are you doing?" She set her messenger bag and bike helmet on a nearby table and lightly touched my shoulder.

"Trying to figure out how we can possibly reopen without Dad," I admitted. "I don't know how we're going to manage it."

Dad continued to stabilize, to our great relief. His speech was still pretty garbled, and there were moments of confusion when he'd look at me with a lost, bewildered expression that broke my heart. He also still had no sensation on his left side. The physical therapist who assessed him at the hospital told me that he would most likely make slow but steady progress to regain some of what he lost, but no one could tell us how complete his recovery would be. It was a waiting game.

In a few days he would be discharged to a utilitarian rehabilitation facility about ten minutes from our house. The arrangements had been made just this morning. He was going to hate it, I could tell. The place smelled like a gym crossed with a hospital, and I could already see that he was humiliated by the necessity of having someone help him urinate and dress himself. He was not going to be an easy patient. Still, we were incredibly relieved that he was alive and recovering after such a major stroke.

Daphne looked around and frowned. "Yeah, kind of difficult to run a restaurant without a cook."

I nodded. "Julio can't handle running the kitchen by himself, and we can't afford to hire a chef. I don't know what to do." I sighed in exhaustion. It all felt like too much.

"Want a soda?" Daphne asked, heading for the kitchen.

"Sure." Maybe the sugar would be a much-needed pick-me-up. I wasn't doing well. I wasn't eating, wasn't sleeping. The bags under my eyes were dark smudges of exhaustion. Every time I thought of Rory and the girls my heart crumpled with sorrow. To come so close only to have it all taken from me once more was absolutely crushing. I ached for Rory, for the girls, for the might-have-beens and almost-weres. I couldn't reconcile what I had finally allowed myself to hope for and believe could happen with the horrible reality of how it had turned out. I was plodding through each waking hour numbly, making decisions to try to keep us afloat while secretly I was drowning inside.

"Here. Come sit." Daphne returned and slid into a booth near the front window, gesturing for me to join her. I sank down opposite her with a weary sigh. Everything felt like such a mess.

"Hey, I need to talk to you about something." Daphne twisted off the tops of both sodas, handing me the black cherry and keeping the vanilla cream for herself. She and Dad both liked the vanilla cream flavor. Rory had always liked the orange cream best. He was the only one. After he left our lives there was always a disproportionate number of orange cream sodas left in the fridge.

"Oh, is this a soda conversation?" I asked, suddenly feeling a touch uneasy. "I'm not sure I can handle one of those right now."

For as long as I could remember Thomas Kemper sodas had signaled some change in our family. My parents had sat me down with a black cherry soda to tell me that Mom was pregnant with Daphne. I'd given Dad a vanilla cream soda to gently break the news that I had called off my engagement to Rory. A soda conversation meant something big was up in our family.

She didn't answer directly. Instead she clinked glass bottles with me and took a long pull, then looked around and said, "This old place. It's had a good run."

I took a sip gingerly. The soda was sticky-sweet and dark and so fizzy it made me want to sneeze. "A good run?" I said mildly. Her words sounded ominous.

"I got some news today." Daphne spun her bottle between her fingers.

"Oh?"

"I've been accepted to a yoga instructor training course in Costa Rica."

I stared at her. "What?"

She didn't meet my eyes. "It's one of the best yoga training courses in the world. I'll be certified at the end of it. Damien's going to come with me and get his scuba diving instructor certification. We're talking about staying on afterward for a while if we like it."

I was gobsmacked. "You're joking. Tell me you're joking."

She shook her head. "It starts in May, so I've still got a few months before I go."

"You're springing this on me now?" My voice was rising with every word. "Now? We're drowning here and you're just going to go away? That's so . . . that's so . . . what about Dad? He's still in the *hospital*. He's had a major stroke. And what about the diner? You can't leave. We need you here helping out."

Daphne was young and could be self-centered, but this took my breath away. She leveled a calm stare across the table at me. "Come on, Lolly. Be realistic. We can't keep the diner running, not without Dad."

"It would be a challenge," I admitted, massaging the back of my neck where there always seemed to be a permanent knot now. *Challenge* would be an understatement. It felt impossible. And that wasn't even taking into consideration the enormous tax bill looming closer every day. My mind was racing, trying to fit all the pieces back together. "Maybe if Dad recuperates really quickly?"

"Really? That's your grand plan?" Daphne looked skeptical. "Lolly." She spoke gently, as though she were the parent and I were the delusional child. "Dad's not recuperating quickly. He's not coming back. Not to cook at the restaurant. Even if he recovers, he can't handle the stress. Didn't Dr. Cho say his stroke was probably a result of all the stress he'd been under and that to recover fully he's got to not be under pressure?"

I nodded. "Well, stress and the Camels he was smoking on his breaks every chance he got." But I knew she was right. He couldn't handle the stress of coming back, even if he physically recovered. "But we have to make it work somehow . . ." I blew a breath out, and it caught on the sob stuck in my throat. "Please don't go."

Daphne kept her eyes down, fidgeting with her bottle, peeling away the corner of the paper label with her fingernail. "Lolly, I love you and Dad so much. I'm not trying to abandon you. I'll help as much as I can before I go. It's not for two months. But I can't live someone else's dream anymore. You're sinking, this place is sinking, and I can't sink with you. I have to let go. It's time. You should let go too."

Anger flared in my chest, white-hot and instantaneous. "That's so incredibly selfish, Daphne. To abandon us when we need you the most. After all we've sacrificed for you? All the hours and years I've set my own life aside so you could have a good life, a stable life? This is what you do?" My tone was harsh with disbelief and outrage.

A mutinous look crossed Daphne's face, and she slammed her bottle down on the Formica tabletop, meeting my irate gaze with a steely one of her own. "I didn't ask for you to do any of that. You *chose* that, Lolly. You *chose* to put your own life on hold for Dad and me. Am I grateful? Yeah, I am. It was horrible when Mom died, and you were always there, always available. I know you sacrificed so much for me, and I'll always be grateful for that. You were like my big sister and my mom all rolled into one. But I've watched what you've become, this shriveled, beat-down version of who you used to be. All the stress of keeping the diner going, all those unmet life goals written in your diary. I don't want to live life the way you do. I want to be my own person, live my own life. I love this family. I love you. But I won't let it swallow me like it has . . . consumed you." She faced me, eyes flashing, so young and confident and sure of herself. "What are you holding on to here, Lolly? Why are we working so hard to keep this place running? It's done. Can't you see that? This is over."

I gaped at her, trying to absorb her words. "I'm trying to keep our family together," I ground out through gritted teeth. "I'm trying to keep everything together."

Daphne shook her head, her expression sad. "Lolly, look around. You're not holding anything together; it's already fallen apart. You're just holding everything back, most of all yourself." She pressed her lips together and looked me in the eye. "It's time to let it go," she said finally, and then she slid from the booth, grabbed her messenger bag and bike helmet, and walked out the door without a backward glance.

I sat motionless, fuming, gripping my soda bottle so hard my knuckles ached. "She doesn't understand," I said aloud, teeth gritted. "She doesn't know how hard we've worked to make it all okay for her."

I was furious with Daphne, furious at her casual disregard for our family's history, and deeply hurt that she would abandon us in this way. But at the same time, if I was perfectly honest, I had an uncomfortable, niggling suspicion that she might possibly be speaking the truth. Her words seemed familiar somehow. I paused and thought back. There it was. What Daphne had said was an eerie echo of what my mother had told me during our brief, beautiful day together. I closed my eyes, trying to remember, and heard Mom's voice again, felt the Hawaiian sun hot on the crown of my head.

Honey, it sounds like whatever you're holding on to is perhaps already broken and you're just holding the pieces together and praying for some glue.

I blinked in surprise. Both Daphne and Mom had said the same thing. Was it true? Was I just trying to hold together the shattered pieces of our life and legacy? Was I holding on to something that was already broken? I spun my soda bottle in a lazy circle on the tabletop, trying to sort through the welter of thoughts and emotions churning inside me. I thought of Aunt Gert's instructions. *Be honest. Pay attention. Seek joy.* How did I do that at a time like this?

I took a deep breath. Be honest. Okay. What did I know to be true? What was I not admitting to myself? I stilled myself and thought about it. I took a breath and closed my eyes and let everything slip away. And there it was, the truth, rising up in that moment of silence, breaking through my fear and frenzy.

If I was honest with myself, I knew this was broken. I knew it had been broken for a long time now. Our family. The diner. My heart.

"Mom," I whispered. "I don't know what to do. Everything feels smashed to bits. I don't know how to fix it."

And then I heard her voice again, repeating the wisdom she'd given me that sunny morning on her veranda. I felt her presence so strongly with me, radiating warmth and love. *Sometimes things don't work out the way we hoped, despite our best intentions. And when they go pear-shaped, you have to let them. Sometimes you just have to let go.*

Tears sprang to my eyes at the gentle sound of her voice, speaking a hard and freeing truth.

What would it mean to let go?

I looked around, trying to pay attention as Aunt Gert had instructed. As I did so, I saw things in a new light. The diner looked tired, a little shabby as always, but now it seemed empty. So empty. Not just of customers, but empty of our family. There was no one left here now. Dad could not continue his work here. Daphne had her own dreams. And me . . . well, I was trying hard to follow my bliss, whatever that meant.

With a sudden clarity, I saw the truth at last. The Eatery had outlived its purpose. It had been the central point of gravity for our family for three generations, but the shape of our family had changed so drastically that it was no longer the case. Mom was gone, Dad was disabled, and Daphne was jetting off on an adventure of her own. I was trying to keep something going that was already long past. It was time to move on. The revelation took my breath away. I stared down at the bottle of soda in my hand.

But move on to what? Dad would be moving on to rehab and trying to rebuild his health. Daphne would be moving on to her dream in Costa Rica. I wasn't sure what Aunt Gert was going to move on to. Maybe Antarctica. And that left me. How could I seek joy? Where was my bliss? What did I really want?

"I don't know," I said aloud, knowing as I spoke the words that they were not true.

I did know. I wanted so many things I couldn't have now. My mother back with us, she and Dad running the diner, the pillars of the community and our family as they'd always been. Rory's hand in mine, fingers laced together, his heart my home. Those two little tousled heads on the pillow in the morning, dark and copper, sleek and curly. My girls. I wanted to have a sense of the freedom I'd barely tasted in Brighton with Toast, the sensation of endless possibility, a heady mix of purpose and potential.

Sitting there in the dim, empty dining room, thinking of all my heart longed for and all I had lost, I became aware of the rest of the picture. I was not just holding on to the broken pieces of our family dream for the diner. I was holding on to so many other things in my life that were already gone, so many wonderful things I had tasted and then lost. All the dreams I'd had that were now shattered. I was holding on to the pieces and trying to put together things that were irreparably broken.

If you cling so tight to something that's already broken, to a life and dream that can never come true, you don't have space in your life for anything else, for the good and real plan Bs. My mother's words to me that day in Hawaii came back to me now. True but hard. I knew she was right, but . . .

"How in the world can I let them go?" I whispered, thinking of Rory, of the girls, of all that I could never have now.

You have to have faith, Lolly, she'd told me as we stood together in the cold darkness on the side of Mauna Kea, tiny human dots under the vast swath of the universe. *It takes faith and courage to let things fall apart, not knowing what will happen after you do. But you are strong. You can do this. There is more for you, my girl. More life and love and good things . . .*

I closed my eyes, choking back a sob. Did I believe my mother's words? Was I strong enough, brave enough? Could there possibly still be good ahead for me? I wasn't sure, but I knew one thing. I was tired of holding the broken pieces together with my bare hands. I was tired of trying to fit them all back into a shape that could never be whole again. I was tired of working my fingers to the bone for a dream that was dead. And I was so damn tired of waking up six days a week at the crack of dawn to make those six lemon meringue pies. I couldn't do it anymore, any of it. Whatever came next, my mom was right. Daphne was right. It was time to let go.

I laid my cheek against the cold Formica tabletop, breathing in decades of stale fried potato grease, cold coffee, lemon pie. My history. Our history. Our family the way I wished it still was. All was dim and silent, the only sound the hum of the refrigerated pie case and the ticking of the wall clock. On impulse I got up and crossed the room, soda in hand. There was a quarter lying on the lip of the jukebox, and I slipped it into the slot, punching a number I knew by heart. F4. "I Will Always Love You." The song that always reminded me of Rory, of the first day I'd laid eyes on him, of the star-crossed arc of our young love. The jukebox clicked and whirred to life, and a moment later Dolly Parton's signature warble filled the empty dining room, singing about lost love and endings. I stood in the center of the room and closed my eyes.

Hey, Marty, two of the pork roast specials with a side of roasted po-tatoes for table six. It was the echo of my mother's voice. I could see her bustling through the swinging kitchen door with a push of one wide hip, dessert plates of lemon meringue pie marching up her arm, the warmth of the kitchen wafting behind her, redolent of crispy roasted potatoes and the sharp, sweet tang of red cabbage sauerkraut. I'd do my homework at the back table while the dining room filled with customers for dinner. Later, in high school, Rory was often waiting at the back door for me when our shifts ended. We'd take off our aprons and head down to the beach together. I remembered the giddy feeling of untying those strings and slipping out the back door into the wide, waiting world. My mother frowning at us and flicking a dish towel at

Rory, admonishing us to be good. My dad humming along to the Eagles as he flipped cod cakes on the grill. Everything was light and laughter and warmth.

"Lolly, Lolly, look at me. I can do the splits!" A six-year-old Daphne in a bright leotard and pigtails entertaining the patrons by doing her entire gymnastics routine in the aisle between the booths and tables. Later, after my mom's death, she'd been the one doing her homework at the back table while I tried desperately to fill Mom's shoes.

I swallowed hard, thinking of all the hours I'd spent in this room. The diner had nurtured me, coddled and challenged me. It had been my home since before I was born. I trailed my fingers over the slightly sticky Formica of the counter, over the cold chrome of the pie case. Dolly trilling softly in the background. Outside, in the pale afternoon light, the rain whispered down. The jukebox clicked off. All was silent. I let out a long, slow breath. It was time.

Time to pull myself up and stop living in the past. I couldn't change what had happened. Wishing and waiting would not bring any of it back. There had been a chance with that little lemon candy, but that chance was gone. All the chances were gone. The only option I had now was to move forward, look ahead. *Be honest. Pay attention. Seek joy.*

How could I do that now? I had paid attention. I had been honest. And I had tried to seek joy. And all it had gotten me were crushed hopes and a broken heart all over again. And yet . . . and yet . . . I couldn't fool myself; I couldn't unsee what I'd already seen and knew to be true. I had no idea if I could ever find joy again, but I couldn't go backward to that quiet misery again. All I could do was follow any tiny glimmer of light and keep moving forward, come what may.

I blew out a deep breath and took a long pull of my cherry soda. It tasted like my first crush on Rory, the day I got my period, the day I held my red-faced, squirming baby sister for the first time—my childhood and adolescence, so many memories in that bottle. I glanced at the clock. It was growing late. Grabbing my soda bottle and Daphne's barely touched one by their long glass necks, I started for the kitchen.

"It's over." I said to the empty space, feeling a lightness and a sorrow both. Tomorrow I would break the news to Dad. It was time to move on.

40

"Bertha, I'm home." I unlocked the front door and carried my Safeway grocery bags into the front hall. Rifling through them, I pulled out the box of dog treats and the pint of Ben & Jerry's Cherry Garcia. Bertha waddled into the hall, saw the pint of ice cream in my hand, and came over to me, tail wagging, completely ignoring the box of dog treats in my other hand. She followed me into the kitchen. No one was home. Aunt Gert's cottage was dark, and Daphne was out somewhere with Damien.

Grabbing a spoon, I collapsed on the couch, still wearing my rain boots. Bertha nudged my hand with her cold nose and gazed at me dolefully, waiting patiently in the hopes that I would cave. I opened the box and tossed her a dog treat, which she ignored.

"They're bacon flavor," I told her. She wagged her tail and kept her gaze trained on the ice cream. "Not going to happen," I warned her. "This is all mine."

I pulled off my rubber boots, scratched her head for a moment, and then cracked open the pint of ice cream. I had a laundry list of things to do but needed to take a pause. Time for an ice cream break.

It had been one week since my momentous decision to close the
Eatery. I'd gone to the hospital the following morning to talk things
through with Dad. He cried when I told him how I felt, but in the end
he agreed with me. It was time to let it go.

The following two weeks had been a whirlwind of activity. I'd
found a local real estate agent who'd met me at the diner and given me
the good news. Even though the building was old and in need of re-
pairs, the real estate market in Seattle was hot, and she quoted an asking price that made me almost cry with relief. If we got even close to
that amount, it would be enough to set Dad up nicely with a modest
retirement and even cover the cost of a caregiver during his recovery.

Since that point, I'd spent every waking minute getting ready to put
the diner on the market. Aunt Gert had been helping me and had
proved surprisingly handy with a paintbrush. She insisted on working
in a high-necked white painter's smock that looked like a nightgown a
Puritan might have worn. This amused Daphne to no end, and she'd
taken to dropping by the diner at odd hours just for the joy of watching
Aunt Gert paint in her smock. Every time I found her loitering, I put
her to work. We had a lot to do.

For her part, Daphne was still planning to go to Costa Rica, but had
been good about helping as much as she could before and after school.
She had assisted me in getting Dad settled in the rehab facility after
he'd been discharged from the hospital. He was, as expected, not a
good patient. He was stubborn to a fault. The staff had found him collapsed halfway up a flight of service stairs a few days before. He'd been
determined to prove he could go up all three flights, but his leg had
buckled halfway up the first set of steps. Two aides had gotten him back
to his room. He was uninjured, but they told me he cursed all the way
down the hall, a barely intelligible string of very colorful navy swears.
However, all that stubbornness was paying off. He was making good
enough progress that he was being sent home in a few days. Which

was both gratifying and terrifying because I had no idea how to care for a stroke victim.

I glanced at the handful of pamphlets splayed out on the coffee table with titles like "Life After a Stroke" and "Living with Limits" and dug a maraschino cherry out of the ice cream.

"Bertha, where do we even start?"

She wagged her tail and looked hopeful. I sighed and dropped a small dollop of ice cream, sans cherries or dark chocolate flakes, on the carpet near Bertha's feet. Although I was thrilled that Dad was well enough to come home, I didn't feel prepared to care for him after his return. Damien was coming over later to install a rail in the shower, and we were making a bedroom in the den for Dad until he could navigate the stairs on his own. I needed to buy a walker too, and make sure all the rugs had anti-skid pads beneath them. But the most pressing item was to find a caregiver for him, someone who could help him at least part-time while I was handling prepping and selling the diner.

"Okay, we need to find an awesome caregiver, Bertha. Got any good recommendations?"

Bertha huffed and licked her jowls. I tossed a bacon-flavored dog treat onto her paws. Which she ignored.

"Okay, have it your way." I scooped some ice cream into my mouth and stared at my laptop screen. Where to start? My fingers hovered over the keyboard, and on impulse I typed in "home health care Seattle." Instantly a long list of results sprang onto the screen. I scrolled through a few agencies, checking Google reviews, getting a feel for services and prices. It was far more expensive than I had anticipated, and my heart sank. How were we ever going to make this work? And who should I choose? I stared at the list of options, something niggling in the back of my mind. Where had I heard about home health care recently? I shut my eyes and tried to think back. And then I remembered. Rory's fridge. My father's wedding invitation. Ramona. Wasn't she a caregiver of some sort?

No. It was an impossible long shot. But on impulse I googled Ramona Flores. The top search hit caught my eye. "Helping Hands: Kind and Caring Personal Home Health," the tagline read. It had dozens of five-star reviews. Was this agency somehow related to Ramona? I clicked on it, scanning the "about" page. The agency had been in business for twenty-two years providing skilled nursing and home health care. Its goal was to provide individual care for patients in their own homes. It had a staff of five care providers. I clicked on the staff page and four pictures popped up. The first one stopped me in my tracks. There she was. Her wavy red hair and warm dark eyes were so familiar.

"Ramona Flores, Owner," the caption below the photo read. It was her, the woman from Rory's fridge. The woman my father had been gazing down at as though she'd hung the sun and the moon and maybe the stars to boot. I'd found my father's second wife. She was a registered nurse with twenty-five years of experience, and she specialized in rehabilitation from surgery and strokes.

"It's you," I murmured, staring at Ramona, dumbfounded. What were the odds I'd actually find her? Her hair was shorter, a little brighter red than in her wedding invitation, but her eyes were just as kind. She was wearing pale pink scrubs. I swallowed hard and clicked on the contact tab.

There was an address listed in Burien, Washington. Just a few miles south of Seattle. She was here, within reach. Heart pounding, I didn't stop to think. I just picked up the phone and dialed her number. A click and then a woman's voice answered. "Hello, this is Ramona at Helping Hands. How can I help you today?" She sounded both compassionate and competent.

I took a deep breath, heart pounding in my ears. What was I thinking, meddling this way? But it had been too many years since Dad had lost the love of his life. He was lonely. He deserved to be loved. I couldn't do anything about my own broken heart, but I could try to help mend his. And this might be the best chance I could give him. I didn't know if it would work. He was, after all, now so physically diminished, but I had to at least try. I crossed my fingers and said a little silent prayer.

"Hi, Ramona. My name is Lolly Blanchard. I'm calling on behalf of my father, Marty."

41

"Okay, folks, who wants another slice of pie?" From the open pie case I held aloft one of the fifteen lemon meringue pies Daphne and Eve had helped me bake that morning. A cheer went up from the gathered crowd. It was six p.m. on a Saturday night, and the diner was crammed with people, every booth brimming, every seat full. People were standing along the walls and leaning against the counter. We were probably violating every fire code in the book, but tonight it didn't matter. This was the Eatery's last night, and we were celebrating its closing in style. It was also my thirty-third birthday, but I wasn't telling anyone that. A farewell to the Eatery made a far bigger reason for a party.

Eve and Daphne wove their way through the crowds, doling out complimentary slices of pie to everyone. Damien stood at the door, taking coats and directing folks to open spaces, only a few inches of his high-top fade visible above the crowd of patrons. Aunt Gert was trundling through the aisles, double fisting coffeepots and visiting every table and booth for top-ups.

From the jukebox June Carter Cash twanged out "Keep on the

Sunny Side." I smiled at the irony. Someone had a sense of humor and a quarter to spare. I picked up a copy of my mom's famous lemon meringue pie recipe, printed on nice card stock. There was a stack on every table. At the top I'd dubbed it "Irene's Best Lemon Meringue Pie." It was a secret no longer. Time to share it with the world.

The door opened with a gust of cool, wet air, the bell's faint jingle audible just above the din. I glanced up. It was Dad, navigating the doorway with his shiny metal walker. Beside him, holding the door with one hand and gripping his arm with the other, stood Ramona. I'd had to beg, plead, and finally drive down to Burien to convince her in person before she finally agreed to care for Dad herself, but from the first day she'd been a godsend. She was quick, efficient, and compassionate. And best of all, she cheerfully made Dad toe the line. Somehow she got him to do what she wanted with a mixture of good-humored cajoling and an iron will. I'd never seen him so agreeable. And she assured me he was making good progress in his recovery.

We cleared a place for Dad and Ramona at a small table near the center of the room, and Daphne got them each a slice of pie. I banged a clean pie tin with a spoon, and the chatter slowly died away until every eye was trained on me.

"Thank you for coming tonight to celebrate the Eatery with us." I cleared my throat. I'd had a stiff little thank-you speech planned out for days, but now, in the warmth of the room with the fug of wet outerwear, bitter coffee, and live bodies packed in like sardines, those preplanned words escaped me. I glanced around. Helen, who had given my mom her quarterly cut and color for over twenty years, was sitting by the jukebox. Aunt Gert was pouring Norman a second cup of coffee at his usual table, which he was sharing with a few other regulars tonight. Aunt Gert was even smiling at him, albeit a little grudgingly. Over in the corner the entire celebrity memoir book club was squeezed into their regular booth. I scanned the rest of the room. Julio and An-

gel and their family stood in the back near the kitchen. The staff of
Magnolia's Bookstore was there, as was our mail carrier and the folks
from many of the businesses up and down the street. So many familiar
faces. So many I had grown up with. I swallowed hard, then said the
words that rose in my throat without thinking about them.

"This restaurant was founded by my grandparents because they
wanted to provide a warm, welcoming gathering place in Magnolia.
Their dream was to bring people together in the community over a
good Danish meal and a slice of homemade pie. And for more than
sixty years our family has been doing just that." A few people around
the room gave solemn nods.

"I look out at so many of you tonight and realize you have years of
history at the Eatery. This place has seen so many celebrations—birthdays,
anniversaries, a few proposals, even a funeral luncheon or two." A polite titter of laughter ran through the room. There had been thousands
of smaller celebrations too. Family dinners, book clubs, old friends
meeting for coffee and a chat. So many years. So many memories.

"My parents raised two strong girls in this diner." I met Daphne's
eyes and smiled. She smiled back. Since I'd decided to close the diner,
we'd been working on making peace with each other. "This place was
a gathering spot for the people of Magnolia. It helped build our community. It helped make us who we all are today. And that legacy will
last long after the Eatery sign is taken down and this restaurant is
gone."

"Hear, hear!" someone shouted from the back. A few people banged
their tabletops in agreement. I continued.

"Tonight we are saying goodbye not just to this much-loved space
but to an era, a shared experience. And I know that can be hard and
sad. There is grief in the goodbye. But we are saying goodbye so we can
embrace better things for all of us. It is time to move on now. As we
close, we want to say thank you. Thank you for being our loving com-

munity. Thank you for walking through those doors for birthdays and anniversaries and ordinary mornings too. We are so appreciative. And while the Eatery's doors are closing, you are still our larger family, and we continue to value the friendships and community we've helped build here in Magnolia." I raised my bottle high. "To the Eatery. To Magnolia. To us."

There was loud cheering and thunderous applause and then the clinking of cups and glasses, and that was it. After more than sixty years, all of my life and my mother's life and most of her parents' lives, it was over.

Someone put another quarter in the jukebox, and the decibel level of chatter elevated quickly over Hank Williams. I stood by the counter, sticking my fork into a piece of lemon meringue pie over and over but not taking a bite. Now that my speech was over, I felt removed from the party, weary and a little sad, but also very, very relieved.

Aunt Gert swung by, empty coffeepots in both hands. Tonight she was wearing an elegant three-piece suit in powdery blue brocade. She even had a matching pocket square in the breast pocket. She looked like a cross between the French Sun King Louis XIV and David Bowie. She leaned close to me and yelled over the din, "I've come to a decision."

"Oh?" I raised my eyebrows.

"You were right. There's still time for me to live the grand adventure. I am going to continue to follow my bliss." She nodded firmly, decisively. "I thought you should know."

"That's great," I said, genuinely pleased to see her so lively and determined. "I'm glad to hear it."

"Happy birthday, by the way."

"Thank you." I still felt a twinge of disappointment about my birthday, about the list and my failure to accomplish anything on it. I'd stashed the unicorn diary in a drawer at home and tried not to think about it. Instead I was moving forward, determined not to dwell on all I didn't have. I'd spent enough time stuck in regret.

"Come with me. I have something for you." Aunt Gert gestured with the coffeepots. I followed her back into the kitchen, which was brightly lit but quiet and empty, a relief from the loud crowd. She slid the coffeepots back in the coffee makers and punched the buttons to make fresh coffee.

"Here." She withdrew a hard rectangular package wrapped in a brilliantly colored silk scarf from the pocket of her brocade pants. For a wild moment I wondered if she was giving me a box with another lemon drop inside, if she had found one somehow. My heart thudded against my chest as I unwrapped it. But it was an old book with a cracked spine and an embossed silver flower on the cover.

"The Art of the Edible Flower Garden," I read the title. "Thank you." It was kind of her to think of me, although I wasn't sure what I'd do with the book. Gardening was the last thing on my mind right now.

"That was my mother's book. It belonged to your great-grandmother," Aunt Gert explained. "She loved to have a little edible-flower garden too, right outside the kitchen door when we were growing up. She made the best lemon cake at Eastertime, covered in whipped cream and edible spring flowers. Now it's time to pass the book along to you. I have a feeling it will come in handy for you soon."

"I love it." I was touched. I had no other keepsakes from my great-grandmother.

Aunt Gert pursed her lips. "You may not see it now, Lolly, but one day you will be able to look back and catch a glimpse of the silver lining in every difficulty. Keep your chin up and keep moving forward."

I nodded. "I'm trying as best I can."

She arched a brow at me. "I know you were disappointed to lose the last lemon drop, Lolly, but take it from me, you can still build a wonderful life without the help of those lemon drops. My own life is a testament to that."

I gave her a puzzled look. "What do you mean? Didn't you use a lemon drop to choose the life you wanted to live?"

Aunt Gert looked astonished. "My dear girl. You think I've lived the life I have because of a lemon drop?"

"Didn't you take a lemon drop and choose to stay in a different life?" I was getting confused. "I thought you said that you got to see the lives you could have, and you chose one that got you out of rural Ohio, out of the life you didn't want."

Aunt Gert shook her head. "Oh, Lolly. You misunderstood me. I did use the lemon drops. And they showed me the lives I could have had. But I didn't choose any of them. Instead I chose to make my own way in the world, full steam ahead, under my own power, nothing more."

"Really?" I stared at her, mind whirring, thinking of the vibrant, exciting life she'd had—international travel, academia, New York City. Shanghai. Moscow. Rio. "You didn't use a lemon drop and go back permanently? But the life you've led . . ." I trailed away in surprise.

"Was entirely of my own making." Aunt Gert nodded. "It wasn't easy. I succeeded because of my own stubborn courage and hard work. I made my own way in the world, and I have never regretted my choices."

"But how did you manage to do everything you've done?" I leaned back against the prep table, still trying to comprehend this unexpected twist.

Aunt Gert gazed past my shoulder, a faraway look in her eyes. "I followed my bliss," she said simply. "Mind you, it often wasn't easy. I left home on my twentieth birthday, took a bus to New York City. I was young and poor, working dead-end jobs while trying to get into college, living in a fifth-floor walk-up in Queens with four other girls and working in a greasy spoon diner. For several years I was pinched and threadbare and lonely. I was ostracized from my family for much longer than that. But I didn't give up. I followed every little glimmer of light, every little spark of joy, and eventually, through a lot of perseverance and hard work and frankly luck, I got a full ride to Columbia." She shrugged. "The rest is history. But it is a history I made with my own grit and determination and more than a few tears."

I stared at her in shock. In the background the coffee was percolating, a happy bubbling sound. From the dining room I could hear raucous laughter and a George Jones song on the jukebox.

"You did it all on your own," I clarified.

"Yes." Aunt Gert nodded firmly. "And I've never regretted it, not for a second."

"I don't know what to say." I looked down at my feet in their bright red leather Mary Janes. I felt even more in awe of my aunt.

Aunt Gert reached out and gripped my hand, her fingers strong and leathery against mine. I glanced up, surprised, and met her eyes.

"Take it from me, Lolly," she said, her tone surprisingly soft. "There are better things that lie ahead for you. You're a smart girl, a hard worker with a good head on your shoulders and a kind heart. You've got grit, and that will serve you well wherever you go. Follow your bliss, every glimmer of light, and it will guide you on your true path."

The coffee makers beeped and the moment was broken. She dropped her hand. "And now back into the fray," she announced. She grabbed the two coffeepots and went through the swinging doors. After a moment I followed her, slipping the little old book into my pocket, head spinning with all I'd just learned.

42

"Great party." Eve sidled up to me in the packed, raucous dining room and leaned back with her elbows against the counter. She had to yell in my direction to be heard. She bumped my shoulder with her own in solidarity and twisted the top off her bottle of ginger ale.

I nodded and surveyed the crowd. It was a strangely freeing feeling, this goodbye party. We were closing the Eatery. The world hadn't stopped turning.

"What are you going to do now that this place is officially closed?" Eve asked loudly.

"I have no idea," I admitted. I was still trying to comprehend what Aunt Gert had just told me. She had not taken a lemon drop. She had made her own way. I knew it was important somehow. If she could do it, surely I could too . . .

"You should come live with me. Get away from the city for a while. Take a break till you figure out what comes next." Eve tipped her head back and took a long pull of her ginger ale. "You can make some soap. Milk goats. Roam the woods."

I leaned in closer to her to be heard. "That sounds tempting, but what about Dad?" I nodded to him across the room. Ramona was leaning toward him, laughing at something he said. He had a mischievous twinkle in his eye as he looked at her.

Eve observed them for a moment. "He looks like he's doing just fine to me." I'd told her about my secret plan to bring Dad and Ramona together. So far it was going in a good direction. Ramona was having a remarkably positive effect on him. She was tough and pushed him to expand his comfort zone daily. They took walks, rain or shine, at a snail's pace that was excruciating to watch, but I was proud of him. He was determined to get better as quickly as possible. When he grew frustrated by the limitations of his own body, Ramona normalized it and then urged him to keep trying. They made a good pair.

"If Dad's recovered enough, I could come once I've got all the details of closing this place ironed out." We had accepted a good offer on the building, but it would take a few more weeks at least to finalize the sale, and by that point Dad might be self-sufficient enough for me to leave him for a bit. The idea of being at the farm on Vashon for part of the late spring and summer was appealing.

I took a drink of the black cherry soda, enjoying the sharp fizz of the bubbles and the syrupy cherry flavor coating my tongue. Daphne was weaving her way toward us through the crowd, clutching a little cardboard box protectively.

"Happy birthday, Sis," Daphne said loudly, setting the little box on the counter next to me.

"What's this?" I asked, surprised.

"A slice of birthday pie. Cherry streusel. Your favorite. There's even a candle in there so you can make a wish." She leaned forward and gave me a quick squeeze.

"You remembered." I was touched.

"And there's an envelope waiting for you at home," she added. "It's a round-trip ticket to Costa Rica from Damien and me, if you want to come visit?" Her sentence ended on a question.

I understood the gift for what it was. A peace offering and an invitation to come see her new life, to be a part of it. "Can I come in January when I'm desperate for some vitamin D?" I asked with a smile. "And can I drink fruity cocktails out of halves of coconuts?"

Her face broke into a grin. "Come whenever. You can have all the coconuts and vitamin D you want."

Across the room Damien gestured for her, calling her name over the happy din. His hands were full of dirty pie plates

"I better go," she said. "Damien and I are on cleanup duty."

I blew her a kiss. "Love you much," I said.

She caught the kiss and pressed it against her cheek, grinning. "Love you more."

I watched her go, feeling proud and grateful. I was sad she was going far away, but glad she was following her own bliss.

"Are you going to make a wish?" Eve asked, gesturing with her ginger ale to the box with the slice of pie in it.

I opened the top of the cardboard box and looked at the candle stuck in the latticed top of the pie. I'd honestly never liked lemon meringue. Mom had made a cherry streusel pie like this one every year on my birthday, just for me. It was my favorite. I pulled out the candle and sucked the jammy filling off the waxy end. What did I want to wish for? I closed my eyes and thought of Aunt Gert and what she'd told me about finding her own way. I wanted that too, more than anything.

"Help me follow my bliss," I whispered, the words equal parts hope and prayer. "Show me how to seek joy and give joy to others. Show me what comes next."

43

What came next was shoveling goat poop.

The day after I handed over the keys of the Eatery to the new owners, I moved part-time to Vashon, taking Eve up on her offer to stay. It
was early May, a perfect time to enjoy the rural respite of the island.
Daphne had just left with Damien to start her yoga certification in
Costa Rica. Dad had improved significantly and could now manage on
his own with a little help from Ramona, and Aunt Gert was around to
keep an eye on Dad if he needed something when Ramona wasn't
there. It was time for me to move on. The problem was, I had no idea
what exactly I was moving on to. While I waited for inspiration to
strike, I helped Eve with the goats. I'd been here a few weeks, and it
was proving to be a therapeutic effort.

"When in doubt, shovel shit!" Eve said cheerily, coming out of the
house with two Mason jars of clear green liquid. "It clears the mind."

"And the sinuses. Phew! This stinks." I brushed a wisp of hair back
from my eyes and dug my shovel into another pile of dirty straw. The
goats bleated and tried to nibble the tops of my rain boots and generally made nuisances of themselves as I cleaned their pen. It was hard,

smelly work, but I was glad for the manual labor. It got me out of my own head and let me focus on something tangible, a welcome break from the existential wrangling going on in my mind.

Eve leaned over the girls' pen and handed me one of the Mason jars. I took the jar and set down my shovel. Time for a breather. I let myself out of the pen, and we stepped out of the barn into the bright sunshine. Spring on Vashon was glorious. Most days were in the seventies with a light breeze. Everything was green and blooming. It felt like heaven on Earth.

"I'm getting ripped biceps." I grinned. I sniffed the contents of the Mason jar. "What's this?"

"Mint-grapefruit kombucha," Eve said. "My newest concoction." She liked to experiment with brewing kombucha and kept a huge glass jar of it in the pantry with a floating black fungus thing on it that looked like a jellyfish. I took a sip.

"Pretty good. It needs a low note, though. Ginger maybe?"

Eve tasted her kombucha. "You're right." She took another sip. "You've got a good palate, Lolly. You have a knack for combining flavors that really work together."

I nodded and took a long swallow. "I've been having a thought about that."

"Oh?"

"I told you about the business I had created when I was with Rory, right? Lolly's Pops?"

Eve squinted in the sunlight. "Organic popsicles, was it?"

"Botanical popsicles with flowers and herbs. I saw a pamphlet in the home office advertising them the day I spent in Florida. The pictures were beautiful, and the flavor combinations were really unique. You can see the petals suspended in the popsicles. It was a creative idea." I took another sip of kombucha.

Eve nodded thoughtfully. "Sounds intriguing. I've never seen anything like them. You should make some for the farmers market. You could sell them at my stand. I bet they'd sell well."

I paused, turning my Mason jar in my hands. "Actually, I think I might want to do more than that."

"Really?" Eve gave me her full attention. "What are you thinking?"

"What if I made Lolly's Pops real?"

Eve cocked her head. "Real how?"

"I mean what if I took the concept I already had in Florida and actually start the business here for real?" I was warming to the topic. "I've been reading that edible-flower gardening book of my great-grandmother's that Aunt Gert gave me for my birthday. It's giving me lots of inspiration. I love growing edible flowers and herbs, and I could partner with local farmers to supply the fruit. It encourages people to eat local food, and I could have eco-friendly packaging. What do you think?" I'd been mulling the idea over for the past few days but was just now voicing it aloud for the first time.

Eve tapped her finger on her lips, considering. "I think that could really work," she said.

I nodded eagerly. "I think so too." It already had a great name and a unique and appealing concept. Eve could help me figure out how to get the business license and paperwork done and get space at the farmers market. She'd had to do it all for Gritty Girl Soap Co. This could actually happen, I realized with a dart of excitement.

"You've always said you wanted to use food to help connect people and bring them joy," Eve said slowly.

"And what's happier than a popsicle?" I agreed. I pictured a cute little food truck, brightly painted, me in red lipstick, handing popsicles out the sliding side window to small, perfectly pressed children in pinafores. It was an appealing image. It made me smile just thinking about it.

"I love the concept, but is this something you really want to do?" Eve said. "You just got out from under the Eatery. Do you want to start another business so soon? Don't get me wrong. I think it's a great concept, and I think you could make it successful. I just want you to be positive it's what you really want to do."

It was a fair question. I considered it for a moment. The idea of opening Lolly's Pops was enticing, but was it something I wanted to do day in and day out? I'd made myself a promise that I'd try to pursue only what gave me joy from here on out. Would opening Lolly's Pops bring me joy? Was it following my bliss?

I closed my eyes and thought about it for a minute. There was something that felt so enticing about the idea. I'd lost Rory and the girls, but I could still take something good from that life. It felt redemptive somehow. It just felt . . . right. I opened my eyes, took a deep breath, and went with my gut.

"Yes. I want to open Lolly's Pops for real." I tested the words as I said them. They felt good, not scary. Well, a little bit scary, but a good kind of scary. "Botanical popsicles are the new Toast."

"Okay then, to Lolly's Pops!" Eve raised her Mason jar, and we clinked in celebration. I felt giddy and a little nervous but also happier than I'd felt since I lost the last lemon drop. When I thought of that popsicle truck, of starting Lolly's Pops for real, I felt a flicker of hope and excitement. And that was a great place to start.

"First things first, I want to rescue your garden," I announced to Eve as we munched sandwiches for lunch later that day.

I'd been eyeing the neglected patch of ground outside Eve's guest room window for the past week. It looked like it had been a good-size garden at some point before Eve bought the place. Well located on the sunny side of the property and not too overgrown.

"Can I bring it back to life and use it to grow the botanicals for Lolly's Pops?"

"Be my guest." Eve crunched a pickle and waved her hand in the general direction of the garden. "Garden away."

The next morning I took the ferry into Seattle and headed directly for Swansons Nursery, a Seattle institution for gardening since 1924. Grabbing a flatbed cart, I wheeled through the aisles, feeling a little like a kid in a candy store. Persian mint. Cilantro. Tuscan blue rosemary. Lemon thyme. Thai basil. They all went into my cart. In the section with edible flowers I stopped short, a bright yellow-and-purple pansy in my hands, hearing my mother's voice from long ago.

Pansies are the showgirls of the flower world, but they taste a little grassy, she'd confided to me once as we pulled weeds in her herb and flower garden. I put a dozen pansies in my cart and moved on to carnations. *Carnations are the candy of the flower world, but only the petals. The white base is bitter,* she'd instructed, handing me one to try. In my young mind carnations had been in the same category as jelly beans and gumdrops. Treats to enjoy.

"Impatiens." I browsed the aisles of Swansons, reading signs aloud. "Marigolds."

Marigolds taste a little like citrus, and you can substitute them for saffron. My mother's face swam before my eyes, imparting her kitchen wisdom to little Lolly. *It's a poor woman's saffron. Also insects hate them; they're a natural bug deterrent.*

I placed a dozen yellow-and-orange marigolds into my cart along with a couple different varieties of lavender and some particularly gorgeous begonias I couldn't resist. I had a sudden flash of memory: my mother's hand in her floral gardening glove plucking a tuberous begonia blossom and popping it in her mouth before offering me one. I was four or five years old. It tasted crunchy and sour, a little like a lemon Sour Patch Kid. I liked the flavor and sneaked a begonia flower every time I was in the garden for the rest of the summer.

I smiled at the memory. I'd loved those times in the garden with my mom. They were my favorite few hours of the week. Monday, our day off, I would get my little hands dirty alongside my mom, listening to her share tidbits about soil acidity and what each type of flower needed to be happy. It felt like a miracle to grow something we could eat, especially something as lovely as a flower. It was pure magic. I still missed those hours all these years later. How I wished I could turn back the clock and sit in the dirt with my mom again. How I wished she were here to see me starting this new venture. I was taking life's lemons and turning them into a lemonade popsicle. I knew she would be so proud.

At the end of the morning I loaded Florence with a several hundred dollars' worth of herbs and edible flowers and drove out of Swansons with my bank account and my heart both significantly lighter.

"I'm really doing this!" I told Eve excitedly as I pulled into line at the ferry dock to return to Vashon, calling her to let her know I was on my way home. "I bought the whole nursery. Be home in an hour." I glanced in the rearview mirror at the riot of blooms and stems filling the back seat and trunk space. The whole car was a cacophony of delicious floral and herby smells all jumbled together. I inhaled deeply, breathing in a feeling of anticipation, breathing out a sigh of contentment. In the plan to make Lolly's Pops a reality, step one was complete.

44

"smart of you to have your grand opening in the middle of a heat wave." Eve stood back from my truck window, squinting in the blazing sun of midsummer. Today was the day. Two months after my trip to Swansons Nursery, Lolly's Pops was finally ready to open to the public. I was set up in the middle of the Magnolia Farmers Market, in a choice spot where anyone walking through the market would see me. It felt good to be back in the happy bustle of downtown Magnolia again. I'd missed it.

"How does it look?" I leaned out the sliding-glass window and adjusted the brightly colored GRAND OPENING banner that hung below the little Formica service counter under the window.

"Good enough to eat." Eve grinned and gave me a thumbs-up.

My business idea had blossomed in the two months since I'd first decided to make Lolly's Pops a reality. I'd purchased an old ice cream truck from a woman in Portland and repurposed it for popsicles. I'd had the truck repainted, white and mint green, a nod to the Eatery, and set up the inside with two small chest freezers. The sign on the outside read: LOLLY'S POPS—UNIQUE, ORGANIC, BOTANICAL. Eve had helped me get the permits and do the paperwork. I'd sunk all the money I had into the venture, plus $5,000 of our profits from the sale of the Eatery. Dad had insisted on being a silent partner, and truthfully, his support meant a lot financially and emotionally.

I was still living at Eve's during the weekdays and staying with Dad on weekends, though thankfully Dad was doing so well in his recovery that he needed little help anymore. It was probably more for my peace of mind than his that I continued to visit every weekend. He still insisted he needed Ramona to come every weekday, though. They spent a lot of time taking slow walks and playing gin rummy. Seeing their friendship deepen was immensely satisfying and a little bittersweet at the same time. Mostly sweet, though.

"You feeling ready to go?" Eve asked.

I took a deep breath and nodded. I'd spent all of last week hand-crafting batches of popsicles for my grand opening. Today was the day. I'd been nervous that no one would give my little truck a second glance, even though it was adorable with its cute vintage vibe and hand-lettered signs. But luckily summer had obliged me by giving the Pacific Northwest a streak of over-ninety-degree weather, almost unheard of in Seattle. Local news issued heat advisory warnings for the elderly and pets. Stores sold out of fans, sun hats, and sunscreen. Drivers were overcome with heat rage and honked and cursed in rush hour. And I was opening my popsicle stand on the hottest day of the year. I took it as a favorable sign.

The farmers market was due to begin any minute, and I was a bundle of nerves. If today went well, I'd spend the rest of the summer and early fall trailing Eve around the farmers market circuit in Seattle, setting up shop in the neighborhoods of the city, each with its own distinct flavor and vibe—Wednesdays in Wallingford, Thursdays in Queen Anne, Fridays in Phinney Ridge, Saturdays in my old stomping ground of Magnolia, and Sundays at the big Ballard Farmers Market. And if Lolly's Pops was a hit, I had even grander plans in mind.

"Opening time," Eve called. She gave me a big grin. "I'll be your first customer. One of the usual, please." She pulled a wad of bills out of the pocket of her overalls and held out a five-dollar bill.

I took a popsicle out of one of the freezers. It was her favorite—sugared violets, mint, and lime zest. The flowers were frozen in the translucent green popsicle, their gorgeous deep purple petals suspended amid tiny flecks of lime zest and a few sprigs of mint.

"The first popsicle is complimentary for my landlady and best friend." I handed her the popsicle and waved away the cash, pulling out a compact mirror to check that my red lipstick was not melting off my lips. I smoothed the skirt of my mint-green-and-white-checked sundress that I'd bought specifically to complement the Lolly's Pops color scheme. I'd even splashed out on a new pair of glasses to coordinate with the dress, darling white-rimmed frames that made me feel a little like a young Brigitte Bardot.

Eve sucked her popsicle happily, eyes closed. "Mmmm. I predict you're going to sell out today. Good luck! I'll check in with you later." She gave me a jaunty two-finger salute and then sauntered off, back to her tent, a block down on the other side of the street.

I leaned out and adjusted the GRAND OPENING banner again, printed in the candy-bright letters I'd mimicked from the GRAND OPENING sign I'd seen in my house with Rory. I wasn't trying to re-create something that was clearly gone. I was just taking the inspiration where I found it and making it my own.

Eve's words were prophetic. As soon as the farmers market opened, I had a steady stream of customers. I counted change and doled out popsicles, handed out recycled-paper napkins and chatted with friends and neighbors, eyeing the growing line snaking away from my truck with a mixture of glee and nerves. It was working. It was actually working. Lolly's Pops was open and doing well.

An hour and a half later I was just handing a customer their popsicles when I heard a familiar voice.

"Lolly? Is that you?" Standing next in line, wearing a look of pure astonishment, was Nancy Shaw. She approached the window.

"Nancy." I stood up straighter, wishing I had a moment to smooth my hair and refresh my lipstick. Nothing like unexpectedly seeing your almost-mother-in-law while sweating in ninety-degree heat.

"Oh my goodness, is this your business? I saw the name, but I just thought it was a pun on *lollipops*." She peered at the menu.

"This is my business." I smiled, feeling a touch awkward. "Handmade bespoke popsicles using local ingredients. I grow all the flowers myself."

The Shaws had relocated from our street to a beautiful condo on Lake Washington a couple of years after Mom passed away, and I hadn't seen Nancy since they moved. Truthfully, I'd been grateful. When I cut myself off from Rory, it hurt too much to see his mother.

"Well, it's a very charming idea, and you look wonderful." She looked me up and down.

"As do you," I told her truthfully. Nancy had always been an attractive woman, and she was aging well, silvery-streaked brunette hair perfectly styled. Rory had her forehead and chin.

"You know, Rory's back in town right now," she said, looking as proud as if she'd announced that Gandhi himself had taken up residence in Seattle.

"Rory's in Seattle?" I stumbled over the words, caught off guard, darting a glance around as if he might appear suddenly. I definitely needed a warning if I was going to see him again. The very notion made me feel flushed and queasy.

"Oh yes." She nodded vigorously. "They're living near us in Madison Park, renting a lovely little cottage just a few blocks away. We're loving having them so close now, especially after . . . Well, it's been a difficult year for them." She pressed her lips together and looked grave.

"I'm sorry to hear that," I said. There was a line forming behind her, people beginning to fidget and grumble in the heat. I needed to end this conversation and soon. I had customers to serve, and I didn't want to hear another word about Rory's perfect family or wife or life or the charming cottage they were living in together. And I could not, could *not* see him. It would break me.

"Nancy, please enjoy a Lolly's Pop on the house." I reached back and grabbed the first popsicle I found in the freezer. Lime and begonia blossoms with a touch of elderflower simple syrup. I held it out to her. "It's so good to see you." I looked past her at the line of customers.

She glanced backward. "Oh, I see you're very popular today." She took the hint and the popsicle. "Thank you, dear. Take care, Lolly. So good to see you."

As she turned and walked away I sighed with relief. I wanted as much distance as possible between myself and Nancy Shaw.

"So Rory's back in town." Eve propped her Doc Martens up on a stump and leaned back in her Adirondack chair with a sigh. It was the evening of the grand opening. We'd just finished a celebratory dinner, a light grilled salmon salad with baby greens and pansies from my garden, eaten al fresco at the old red-painted picnic table I'd dragged over, and a bottle of champagne.

"That's what she said." I handed Eve her dessert, a new organic popsicle flavor I'd created, this one dandelion buds and lemonade. Since deciding to open Lolly's Pops I'd been experimenting with the flowers and herbs from my garden, mixing them with local fruit from the farmers markets to create bespoke flavor combinations. There had been a few failures. Too late I learned that some people have a strong allergic reaction to tulip petals. Just touching that popsicle to her tongue made Eve's mouth go numb. But recently I'd been crafting some truly surprising and yummy combinations—elderflower limeade with clover blossoms, coconut water with rose syrup and candied rose petals, a strawberry-basil concoction sprinkled with marigold petals. I loved dreaming up unique combinations and then creating them. A few ingredients and a wooden stick. It was simple, local, and environmentally friendly. Not to mention delicious. I'd had a full roster of yummy flavors for the opening of Lolly's Pops earlier that day, but I was still experimenting with new flavors.

"In theory this one's good"—Eve grimaced—"but it needs more simple syrup. It's puckering the inside of my mouth. Whew."

I took a lick of mine. "Oh yes, way too sour. But I like the flavor combination." I whipped out my little idea notebook and jotted down a reminder to increase the simple syrup in the recipe. "Here, try this one. Blueberry lavender." I handed her another, gone slightly slushy at the edges.

"Gorgeous color." Eve eyed her popsicle appraisingly. She took a bite. "So, are you going to see him?"

"No way. Not if I can help it," I said firmly. I nibbled the top of my popsicle. I could taste the lavender, but it didn't overpower the blueberries. And the brilliant purple color was eye-catching. "I think this one is a winner." I made a note in my book to add this one to the rotation. "I have no desire to see his perfect family and perfect wife and perfect life, especially when I feel like I'm just getting back on my feet again. It would be excruciating and completely unhelpful. I'm doing my best to follow my bliss now, and Rory Shaw needs to stay where he belongs. In the past."

45

"Thank you so much. Enjoy your Lolly's Pops and be sure to visit again next week!" I smiled cheerfully at the two teenage girls and slid their order—blackberry-and-violet popsicles—through the delivery window. One week since the grand opening and the summer heat wave was still going strong. While Seattle wilted in the blazing sun, business was brisk for Lolly's Pops. I'd enjoyed the rounds of the farmers markets all week, and now we were back in Magnolia again. It was a sunny Saturday afternoon, and the thermometer was hovering around ninety. It was almost the end of the market, and I was tired and sweaty but happy.

I tucked a wisp of damp hair back into my ponytail and slicked on some tinted lip balm. Thank goodness the mint-green dotted Swiss sundress I was wearing was relatively lightweight. It was sweltering in the back of the truck. Almost time to close up. I glanced out the window. No one waiting in line. Taking advantage of the brief lull in customers to catch my breath, I opened the freezer nearest me and stuck my head inside, just for a second. Ahhh . . . deliciously cool and quiet.

So far Lolly's Pops was a smash success, better than I could have imagined. The business was, as Eve had predicted, turning a good albeit fairly modest profit, and I was thoroughly enjoying myself every step of the way. I loved crafting the popsicles, and I loved interacting with customers and the happy buzz of the farmers markets. I felt a little giddy when I considered how well it was going. Maybe it was too early to tell, but I had the most delightful feeling that this was actually going to work. And the best part was that Lolly's Pops was something I had chosen by myself, on my own initiative, with my own creative expression. It wasn't Toast; it was better.

The realization was powerful, euphoric. I thought briefly of my seventh-grade journal, sitting in the back of my dresser drawer, and of those optimistic unicorns and the life goals list I'd spectacularly failed to accomplish. Well, not quite. I mouthed the points of the list into the coolness of the freezer, considering them in a different light.

1. Live in another country

I had spent a semester abroad in London, and while I'd planned on it being longer, I'd done it nonetheless. Those had been some of the happiest months of my life.

2. Own my own restaurant somewhere amazing

If you could consider a popsicle truck a restaurant, then yes, I was accomplishing that one right now. Plus, I had big plans for Lolly's Pops if all went well. A fleet of Lolly's Pops trucks for weddings and birthday parties and bat mitzvahs. Maybe a brick-and-mortar store with the same cute vintage vibe.

3. Fall in love

The list had not stipulated that there had to be a happy ending to that love story. I had fallen in love with Rory. For a time, I had been the happiest girl the in the world, adored by a good, strong, sweet man. Despite the pain and heartache and regret at how it ended, I would not trade loving him for anything. Maybe I would get the chance to love someone that way again someday. But if not, I was glad I'd loved Rory. I'd also fallen in love with our two little girls. I thought of Sophia and Freya, their dark and copper hair, Rory's eyes and my chin. My heart still ached for them.

4. Have my family be happy together 4 ever

In a strange way this was coming true too. We could not control Mom's early passing, but Dad had made great strides in therapy with Ramona coaxing him on. He seemed more relaxed than I'd ever seen him before, like he was truly starting to enjoy life again. He had just this week switched to a new home health aide, a kind woman from Ethiopia, so that he and Ramona could start seeing each other in a personal capacity. Last night he'd taken her to dinner and a movie in a theater. A real date!

And Daphne. Daphne was enjoying her course in Costa Rica and was starting a new life with Damien there. They were renting a tiny beach house painted bright orange and planned to stay, teaching yoga and scuba diving. In the photos she texted me she looked tanned and blissfully happy with her new hippie beach life.

For her part, Aunt Gert had been true to her word and decided that at the ripe old age of eighty she was too young to quit living. As soon as the Eatery closed and Dad's health improved, she signed up to take a tour with a group of retired academics. The first trip was to the Smithsonian and United States Botanical Garden in Washington, DC, but she had more exotic destinations in her sights.

5. Get my own horse

I snorted at that one. Eve had been right. This would have been the easiest thing to accomplish on the list. I should have just bought a horse.

In a strange way, sitting there in the quiet coldness, I realized I had accomplished everything on that list (except for the horse, that is). Not a single goal had happened in the way I'd imagined, but I'd achieved them nonetheless. It was a surprising realization. Perhaps even more so was the revelation that came on the heels of that discovery.

At thirteen, when I'd penned them, those goals had been fresh and full of possibility. Now, at thirty-three, with my head stuck in a freezer, surrounded by the pretty frozen fruits of my labors, I realized I was done with lists. No more striving and feeling like a failure. No more trying to twist my life into the shape I thought it should be. No more items to tick off one by one. There was just this—my life as it was now. *Be honest. Pay attention. Seek joy.* These were my true goals now. I vowed then and there to be grateful for all I had been given. To try to bring joy to others and seek joy in my own life. And to try my best to follow my bliss every moment of every day for the rest of my life.

46

"*Lolly?*"

Still bent over the freezer, I stilled with my head right next to the coconut milk, ginger, and fresh pansy popsicles. I knew that voice. I recognized it in the marrow of my bones. Shivering from more than the chilly air, I lifted my head slowly and gazed straight into the warm, surprised brown eyes of Rory Shaw.

"Hi." I cleared my throat, trying for lighthearted but landing more on stunned.

"Hi." He gave me a quizzical look. "My mom told me she saw you here last week. She said something about flowers you can eat?" He glanced at my sign.

"Popsicles," I clarified. "Bespoke, organic popsicles made with herbs and edible flowers. I grow them myself." I sounded like an advertisement. *Be cool, Lolly*, I admonished internally. *You can do this.* I stood up and leaned slightly out the serving window, getting a good look at him.

My heart was pounding so hard I was sure he could hear it. He looked almost the same as he had that day in Florida—the same laugh lines and cinnamon stubble—a little younger even. His hair was a bit longer, curling at the collar of his T-shirt. It suited him. He eyes looked sad, though. He seemed a little worn around the edges. Nancy had hinted it had been a hard year for Rory and his family. I wondered what had happened. Job loss perhaps? That would explain the move back to Seattle.

I gazed at him, and for a moment I was back in Florida, curled up in bed next to him, falling asleep to the steady rhythm of his breathing. We were kissing in the pool, the length of his body pressed against mine. I blinked, heat flaming in my cheeks. Whatever had happened, it was not in this life. In this life he was not mine. In this life I had lost him for good.

My heart squeezed so sharply I gave a little silent gasp. I clenched my hands, digging my fingernails into my palms, using the pain to center me. *Be strong, Lolly. You can get through this.* I couldn't help it, though. I glanced around involuntarily, looking for two little heads— one dark and one coppery. I knew it was impossible, that the girls were not here with him, but I desperately, desperately wanted it to be true.

"You were always so good at growing things." He smiled up at me, meeting my eyes, and there was something in his look I couldn't decipher; it almost seemed wistful. I shook off the thought. *Stop dreaming, girl. Get back to reality.*

"Your mom told me you're back in Seattle," I said brightly, managing to keep my voice steady and normal-sounding. *Yes, good, that's it.* A warm and friendly tone but distant.

I felt so awkward. What should I do with my hands? I tucked them in the pockets of my sundress and bit my lip. I had to remember that our life in Florida was not reality. He had a real wife now. They had a child together. In this life, we had gone our separate ways years ago.

"Yeah, we're here for a few months at least." He was looking over the flavor board. "Hey, can I have . . ." His brow wrinkled. "You choose. Whatever you think I'd like. You know me." He smiled, that sweet,

slightly mischievous smile, lips curving up at the edges. It was so familiar I sucked in a breath. He looked up at me, and for a moment I was
thirteen again, standing in the diner, a bottle of glass cleaner in my
hand. *Oh, Rory, I loved you from the start. How did we get here? How
did I ever let you go?*

I swallowed hard and turned to the freezers, blindly grabbing the
first popsicles I could find. Raspberry mint with marigolds. "You like
raspberries, right?" I said stiffly. "Here, on the house. Welcome back."
I handed him two through the window opening. "Does your wife like
mint?"

He looked surprised for a moment, then hesitated, his smile falling
away. "Ah, ex-wife, actually." He reached out for one of the popsicles.
Our fingers brushed as he took the stick from me. "The divorce was
finalized a few months ago. Emily's still back in Florida. It's been . . . a
really rough year."

"Oh." I was speechless. Stunned. Emily. Ex-wife. Those straight
teeth and fall of silvery-blond hair, the kind of figure that made mom
jeans look ironic and actually good. "I didn't know." I stammered finally.

He nodded, then said, sounding resigned, "That's why I'm back here
for the summer. Just needed to get away for a while, gain some perspec-
tive. I brought our son, Noah, with me to visit my folks. He and I are
here for the summer."

"Oh." I couldn't quite get my bearings. I felt like the floor of the
truck was tilting under my feet.

"I got a six-month leave of absence," Rory explained. "Figured we'd
live here this summer, let Noah spend a lot of time with his grandparents, and then we'll head back to Florida before school starts. Here, this
is Noah. He's at the children's museum with my mom right now." He
pulled his phone from his pocket and swiped it on, holding it up so I
could see it. A cute freckled kid with berries smeared across his face

was mugging for the camera. He had Rory's coppery curls, but looked more like Emily in the eyes. He seemed vaguely familiar. Perhaps echoes of Rory as a child.

"He's adorable." I felt my throat close around the words, imagining for a moment another little face on that screen, smudgy face and copper hair and a neon-orange bunny.

"He's a great kid." Rory put his phone in his pocket, smiling the proud smile of parenthood. He took a bite of the popsicle. His eyes widened. "Okay, I admit I was skeptical about eating flowers, but the flavor is amazing. Lolly, this is really good."

"Thanks." I looked down at the popsicle I'd fished out as a goodwill gesture for his wife. Now ex-wife. I placed it back in the freezer. Rory was newly single, with a son and a job in Florida. But no Emily. No wife. And no girls either. I didn't know what I felt more strongly, relief or grief.

A trio of white-haired ladies in hiking outfits wandered over and stood in line behind Rory. He quickly moved to the side but lingered, watching me as he ate his popsicle. I served the women, patiently answering questions and accepting their suggestions for new flavors. I could feel his eyes on me the entire time, and it made me so nervous I fumbled and dropped one of the popsicles and had to get a new one. I was so aware of him, standing there licking his popsicle, so relaxed in his cool burnt-orange-colored shorts and vintage national parks T-shirt, looking like he had all the time in the world.

Finally, after what seemed like an interminable amount of time, the ladies moved on to the handmade cheese stand next door. I took a quick peek around. The farmers market was winding down. Just a few minutes to go and the crowd was thinning out. Making a split-second decision, I flipped my sign over to CLOSED.

"Stay right there," I told Rory. Not exactly sure what I was doing or why I was doing it, I slid the window closed and grabbed two popsicles from the freezer. I locked the door of the truck behind me and mo-tioned Rory to follow. "Come on."

We passed Eve's stand on the way. She saw Rory and raised her eyebrows in consternation. I gave her a thumbs-up behind his back, and she gave me a slow nod as we went by. Rory didn't see her, and she didn't call out to us.

When we reached the front window of the Eatery, I stopped. It had a shiny new sign, RIND AND VINE, but wasn't open till later in the day. The new owners were a sweet couple from Northern California who had opened a wine and cheese shop and tasting room in the space. Frankly, I wasn't sure how well it was doing. I'd driven by a couple of times on my way to see Dad, and there never seemed to be a crowd inside. Rory stepped back into the street and surveyed the building.

"Wow, this brings back a lot of memories." He shook his head rue-fully. "Time marches on, huh? We spent a lot of good hours here."

I stood next to him, melting popsicle running from the seams of the wrapper down my hand. "Yes, we did."

We stood for a minute side by side. I could see our reflection in the glass. So many years ago we'd been on the other side of this glass, side by side then too. It had been the start of something tragic and wonder-ful. I wondered briefly what today would turn out to be. I had no idea what to think or feel, still flummoxed that he was standing next to me.

"Here, let's sit. I've been on my feet for hours." I motioned him over and we perched on the lip of the low windowsill. It was too narrow for comfort, but we sat together, so close my skirt brushed his thigh. I handed him a popsicle, my new favorite flavor, rose petals and Rainier cherries. As we licked our treats, I stole a glance at Rory. How astonish-ing that we would find ourselves back here all these years later.

"I'm sorry about Emily," I said, finding that, in a way, I was. He looked like he'd been through the wringer. I could tell it had cost him greatly.

He nodded, looking down at his hands, turning the melting popsicle as it dripped onto the pavement by his Rainbow flip-flops. "I didn't see it coming. Sometimes life just upends your plans, you know? You think the future holds one thing, and it actually turns out to be something totally different."

"I know how that goes," I said softly.

He glanced at me. "Yeah, I know you do."

We licked our popsicles in silence for a minute. There was so much history between us. It didn't feel like sitting with someone I hadn't seen or spoken with in seven years. It felt like, in some way, we could take up our friendship right where we'd left off. After so many years together there was a deep sense of familiarity I found comforting.

"You know, I thought about you a lot since we parted ways," Rory said conversationally, quietly.

My heart sped up. "Oh?"

"Wondering where you were and what you were doing."

"It wasn't all that interesting," I said, trying to lighten the moment. "There's a good chance I was either making pies or unclogging a toilet."

He chuckled. I didn't know where this was headed, but my hands were shaking slightly with nerves. I had a feeling my life was about to take another unexpected turn. I had a choice. Protect my heart or be honest and see what happened.

"I wondered the same thing about you," I said truthfully, not meeting his eyes. "More than was good for me probably."

When I glanced up, Rory was looking at me intently. "Lolly." His voice was low. It had been years since I'd heard that tone. The tenderness in it sent a tingle down my spine. His expression was raw, unguarded. In it I saw pain and uncertainty, regret, a touch of longing.

He shifted on the narrow ledge beside me. "I loved Emily. I think I was a good husband to her. I tried to make the best life I could with her after you broke up with me. I was hurting so much, and she was right there for me. We married fast, way too fast, and if I'm honest, I think there was always a question in my heart, even before she left me."

"What question?" I swallowed hard, nervous to ask.

"What if?" he said quietly. "What if your mom hadn't died? What if we'd moved to Baltimore together? What if I'd stayed here instead of leaving for med school?" He was watching me, searching my face. I didn't know what he was hoping to see.

"I've learned that every 'What if' can have its own complications," I said gently. "It was a long time ago. We've lived a lot of life since then."

He blew out a breath, gave me a quick nod. "Yeah, that's for sure. I guess there's no going back, right?"

"Nope." I swung my legs slightly, smiling ruefully to myself. I'd gone back, and it had just put me right back here, facing forward instead of looking behind me. "If I've learned anything in life so far, it's this," I told Rory. "Trying to change the past is pointless. We can only change our future by the choices we make today."

"That sounds like it belongs in a fortune cookie," he teased.

"Doesn't mean it isn't true," I insisted with grin. I took a last big bite of my slushy popsicle. I was feeling strangely happy.

We looked at each other then, the seconds stretching long. "I just have one more question," Rory said, his face serious.

My heart skipped a beat. "Yes?"

"Can we please move and sit somewhere else? This windowsill is so narrow my legs are going numb."

I burst out laughing and stood. He joined me, shaking his legs to restore circulation. He still had sexy soccer-player legs, I noticed, all lean muscle and toned calves. I licked the last few drops of the sugary syrup from my popsicle stick.

"Lolly, can I see you again? Please?" His gaze was so hopeful.

I paused for half a second. "I'd like that very much."

He broke into a huge, delighted smile, the kind that made his eyes crinkle at the corners. I'd forgotten what that smile did to me. It was like the sun breaking through the clouds. Everything felt warmer all of a sudden. "Can I buy you breakfast tomorrow morning?"

"You're not wasting any time." I laughed.

He leaned toward me, his warm mouth brushing my hair, grazing the shell of my ear. "I think we've wasted enough time, don't you?"

A shiver went down my spine, pure anticipation. I pulled back and looked at him, really looked at him. Whatever was happening felt too good to be true.

"Tomorrow morning I've got to be at the Ballard Farmers Market," I said.

His face fell.

"But we could have breakfast beforehand," I offered.

He met my eyes and grinned. "I'll be there."

47

The next morning we met at a restaurant in Ballard, a trendy spot known for hearty Americana brunches just a few blocks from the farmers market. Eve had volunteered to get the Lolly's Pops truck all ready to go so I could spend as much time with Rory as possible before I had to open for business.

It was a beautiful day, sunny and promising to be hot again. We sat at a tiny table in the window of the restaurant, our knees bumping beneath it. He ordered the sweet-potato-and-salmon hash, and I ordered chicken and waffles drenched in maple syrup. We shared our meals and talked and talked and laughed like fools. We got refills of coffee and let them grow cold.

He told me all about Noah and the work he dearly loved with the team. I told him about Aunt Gert, whom he was eager to meet, and filled him in on Daphne's adventures and on Dad's stroke and recovery and his budding romance with Ramona. I remembered as we talked why we'd become such good friends and why I'd fallen so hard for him. He was kind and funny and smart and it felt easy between us, like no time had passed. Yet, as I looked at us in the reflection from the window, I saw how we had both grown. We were adults now, older and wiser, with wounds and scars and places that were barely healing over.

Over the last crumbs of our meal, Rory sat back and gave me a rueful smile. "Lolly Blanchard. All those years ago when I first saw you, I never could have predicted we'd end up here," he mused.

I nodded. "I didn't think I'd see you again," I said honestly.

He looked a little bashful. "Lolly, I'd love to see you again."

I took a deep breath. *Be honest. Pay Attention. Seek joy.* I took a risk. "I'd love that too," I told him.

He grinned, then reached out and took my hand, gently rubbing his thumb across the back. "I don't want to waste any more time, Lolly," he said simply, frankly.

I nodded, trying to swallow the lump in my throat. "Me neither."

My heart felt like it was beating out of my chest. I looked at our hands clasped on the table amid the waffle crumbs and sticky spots of syrup. I didn't know what this all meant. It was happening so fast. Could this really be another chance for us? It felt too good to be true. It felt absolutely right.

A firm knock on the plate-glass window near my head made me jump. It was Eve, standing outside and pointing to her watch, reminding me that the market was opening in ten minutes. Rory saw her and lifted his hand in greeting. She crossed her arms and gave him the stink eye, then relented and flashed him a broad smile and a thumbs-up before going back to her booth. We hastily paid the bill, and Rory walked me to Lolly's Pops. All around us people were unpacking their wares.

"Ooh, look!" On impulse I stopped at a booth I'd seen before, a local jewelry maker. I'd noticed her at a previous market but hadn't had a chance to see her wares yet. I needed to open Lolly's Pops but couldn't resist pausing for a moment to look. Rory stopped beside me. The woman crafted jewelry from pressed flowers, preserving their delicate blooms in glass. They reminded me of my mom.

"These are lovely," I told the artist, perusing the rows of necklaces and earrings. One in particular caught my eye. A simple chain with a hammered silver band encasing a glass circle. Inside the glass was a perfectly preserved delicate flower with five creamy white petals around a starburst of yellow center. It looked strangely familiar, but I couldn't quite place it.

"This one is pretty. What is it?" I pointed. The artist studied it.

"Let me see. That's a flower from a lemon tree. Very unique, isn't it?"

I picked up the necklace, the weight of it oddly comfortable in my hand. Where had I seen it before? I knew I recognized this necklace from somewhere. I closed my eyes and tried to picture it. And suddenly I remembered. Nestled against my clavicle, in the mirror of our house in Florida. I had worn this necklace to complement the yellow sundress I'd chosen on that single beautiful day with Rory and the girls.

I stared at the necklace, frowning in bewilderment. How was it possible that it was here, in my hand, if I had already worn it in a previous day in an alternate life? It was a distinctive piece. I'd never seen anything else like it. What were the odds? What was going on?

"That's pretty," Rory said over my shoulder.

"A lemon flower stands for clarity, happiness, and hope," I told him, still feeling confused. "That's what my mom always said."

Rory studied the necklace and then me. "Clarity, happiness, and hope, huh?" His gaze was warm on my face. "Can I buy it for you?" He turned to the artist and pulled out his wallet.

"You don't have to—" I protested, but he was already handing over the cash.

"Please? I want to. Every time you wear it, you can be reminded to never give up hope, to seek happiness, and to remember that life is full of second chances." He gave me a crooked smile, so genuine and filled with eagerness that it almost broke my heart. But his words echoed in my head with uncanny clarity. *To never give up hope, to seek happiness, and to remember that life is full of second chances.*

I stared at him, dumbstruck. Rory had said those exact words to me before, standing in the kitchen of the Florida house, surrounded by sticky chaos and the smell of pancakes. I remembered them clearly. He'd said the same words like they held significance, like they meant something special to us, like we had a history tied to them. I'd had no idea at the time what they meant. But now. What did it mean that he had just said them to me here, in exactly the same way?

I stared at the necklace in my hand, my mind racing, trying to catch hold of something, a niggling premonition, a spark of hope. I glanced from Rory to the necklace. Yesterday morning I'd awakened with the sure knowledge that Rory was lost to me forever, yet here we stood, and I was holding a symbol of hope and happiness. A symbol I'd been wearing on our one beautiful day in Florida together. What did it all mean? I couldn't quite put the pieces together.

Something Aunt Gert had said to me came back to me then. *Often we say "impossible" when what we really mean is "unknown." So many things are possible; far fewer are known to us. You will discover this soon enough.*

And then it came to me, a flash of possibility, a wild, glorious improbability that made me gasp out loud. What if . . . What if . . . Could it be that I'd gotten it all wrong? What if that day in Florida, our life together there, those sweet few hours with the girls . . . What if that day was not an alternate life at all? What if it was not a vision of a different life I could have had, a life that was lost to me forever with that last, melted lemon drop? What if I had instead seen a vision of our potential future together, a life that could still come true?

I clutched the necklace in my hand, fingers closing around it as tight as I'd held that last lemon drop just a few months ago. Astounded, barely daring to hope, I tried to make sense of it all. That day in Florida I hadn't paid any attention to the year in the calendar app on my phone. I'd been so focused on playing Mommy I hadn't checked anything except the activities for the day. I had assumed that I had awakened the morning after I'd taken the lemon drop, in the same year, just like in Brighton and Kona. But what if I hadn't? What if something different had happened that time? What if I had actually glimpsed my possible future instead?

All of it came back to me in a rush. A thousand snapshots of our life together—the photos I'd scrolled through on my phone, sitting in the park during Freya's ballet lesson—birthdays and ballet recitals, family vacations and Christmas dinners. Our first house, nine months of pregnancy, blurry selfies, normal everyday moments, and Dad's wedding to Ramona. The gangly redheaded adolescent who kept popping up in the photos. The one who bore a remarkable resemblance to Rory's son. Could that boy be Noah a few years in the future? He certainly looked like Rory. And the photo of me holding popsicles in that industrial kitchen, was it proof of the success of Lolly's Pops? I'd named my new little business in honor of the one I thought I would never have, the successful business I'd glimpsed in my home office in Florida. But perhaps my little vintage ice cream truck from today came first and Lolly's Pops would one day be large enough to include that industrial kitchen in the photo.

I thought of the two little girls with dark and copper hair, Sophia and Freya, and my heart squeezed with a desperate hope. What if it wasn't too late after all? What if I could still have the girls, Rory, a life together as a family?

What if all of it could still be my life?

The idea left me light-headed with a longing so intense I couldn't breathe. Could it be? I'd never wanted anything more.

"Lolly? Are you okay?" Rory touched my elbow. His concerned eyes were focused on mine, his mouth so close I could have kissed him in an instant. Between us lay a hundred unspoken things, affirmation and desire and tantalizing possibilities for the future. I was dizzy with it, intoxicated. I clasped the necklace close to my heart and nodded, so elated and giddy I thought my heart might burst with joy. Could this truly be just the beginning?

"I need a minute to catch my breath," I murmured.

"Here, I've got you," Rory said. He took my hand, and I laced my fingers through his. I couldn't be sure I was right, of course. Perhaps I was wrong, perhaps our future would look very different indeed. But I knew one thing for sure, no matter what it looked like, I was eager to embrace whatever lay ahead.

EPILOGUE

EIGHT YEARS LATER

"Lolly? Where are you, girly?" Dad bellowed from the kitchen.

"Here. In the dining room," I called back, putting the finishing touches on the new chalkboard menu. I glanced around in satisfaction. The vinyl booths were freshly updated. The chrome edges on the tables gleamed. Even the warm old pine floors seemed to have a satisfied sheen. The old Eatery—or, should I say, the very first brick-and-mortar Lolly's Pops location in Seattle—had never looked so good. Last year Rind and Vine had closed down, just in time for me to buy the building back from them. We were almost ready for the grand opening of Lolly's Pops in Magnolia in just a few days.

"I got the new freezer all set up." Dad came through the swinging door, wiping his hands on a dish towel. He was older now, almost completely bald, but there was a twinkle in his eye that warmed my heart. He still had a slight limp and a little droop on the left side of his mouth, a reminder of how close we'd come to losing him. Since his stroke, Ramona had kept him on his toes, cheerfully insisting he stay active and eat "rabbit food" instead of his morning bacon. He complained, but secretly I knew he liked to be cared for.

"That machine's so fancy you could practically fly it to Mars. Who's going to help me stock it with popsicles now, though? Where are my helpers?"

"Here we are." A small dark curly head popped up from behind the counter, closely followed by a coppery one with a suspiciously purple-smudged mouth. "I can be your helper." Sophia scrambled around the counter in whirl of long limbs and missing front teeth.

"Me too, me too!" Freya was practically hopping with suppressed excitement.

"What have you been doing, you rascal?" I ruffled Freya's tousled hair. At four she was just beginning to lose her tummy and lengthen out into little girlhood, but her mischievous grin was the same. She kept us all on our toes.

"Sampling the pwoduct," she said slyly. I peered over the counter at a wrapper from one of our new flavors, violets and local grape juice. That explained the purple ring around her mouth.

"Okay, smarty-pants, no more samples for you. Go help Pop Pop with the new freezer." She raced off after her sister, legs and bangs flying. I watched them go, heart swelling with joy. Sometimes when I looked at them, I still couldn't believe it was true, that when I kissed them good night I would wake with them piling on top of us in the morning, laughing and pleading for pancakes with unicorn sprinkles. It was a miracle. It was divine.

I looked around, amazed to be back in this space. It was an unexpected twist, but the right move. In the eight years since I'd opened Lolly's Pops, we'd expanded from my little green-and-white truck to two popular locations in Tampa and a small fleet of vintage trucks and vans, each one unique. Now we were opening the very first Seattle brick-and-mortar store. How fitting that it would be here, in this space. I was back, but doing what I loved, something that gave me joy.

From the kitchen I could hear squeals and giggles as Dad tried to corral his helpers' silliness into productivity. "Mission control to astronauts Sophia and Freya, come in. I repeat, this is mission control," Dad said in his best 1980s Dan Rather TV-anchor voice. "We have liftoff. I repeat. We have liftoff."

I smiled. He had his hands full with them, but he loved every second he got to spend with the girls. Tampa was too far away. Rory and I agreed on that. We missed Seattle, but Tampa was home for the next few years at least. Noah was fourteen now, and we both felt we needed to stay in the same city as Noah and Emily until he graduated high school and started making a life of his own. We saw him weekly, and the girls adored him. But in a few years, when he was in college, we were planning to move back to Seattle.

For now, though, we managed as best we could. Rory was still with the team, and I was heading up a small but growing company bicoastally. Dad had agreed to help at this store once we opened, and I'd hired a great manager to handle the day-to-day operations on the West Coast. It was a bit complicated to run a business on both coasts, but I had a good feeling about it. It was going in the right direction.

"Coming in for a landing," Sophia yelled from the kitchen, making a rocket engine sound.

"You're coming in hot," Dad replied. "We have a situation. I repeat, we have a popsicle emergency."

Freya shrieked with laughter. "Mayday, mayday," she sputtered.

In the momentary lull, I whipped out my phone and checked my messages. Daphne had sent a photo of herself reclining in a hammock slung between two palm trees as Damien wrapped his arms around her from behind. We'd visited them last Christmas and couldn't wait to return to enjoy their relaxed, beachy life in Costa Rica. I sent a photo of myself, slightly disheveled hair and popsicle-stained apron, in front of the counter with a **Look familiar?** xoxoxo.

There was also a new email from Aunt Gert, titled "WE HAVE CROSSED THE DRAKE PASSAGE . . . AND NOW THE PENGUINS!!!" Every email from her was composed mostly of exclamation points and sentences in all caps. They made me smile. She and Eve ended up getting along so well that after Rory and I married and moved down to Tampa and Dad and Ramona had their wedding in Hawaii, Aunt Gert decided to move to Vashon Island. She now lived in a whimsical tiny-home caravan tucked beneath the trees at the back of Eve's property. As full of salt and vinegar as ever, she had taken over and expanded my edible-flower and botanical garden and would now supply our Seattle Lolly's Pops location with most of the botanicals for our popsicles. A couple times a year, however, she would leave the garden in Eve's capable hands and disappear for a few weeks at a time with her retired academic pals. We'd receive emails with photos and updates from her latest fabulous adventures—a Danube River cruise past Prague and Budapest, a blurry photo of herself standing stoically in front of the Taj Mahal at sunrise. And now this. I grinned, imagining her in a full bright yellow waterproof suit, climbing into the helm of a Zodiac boat (she was still surprisingly nimble at eighty-eight) to finally see the penguins. She was following her bliss, wherever it led her. And apparently it had led her all the way to Antarctica.

The doorbell jingled and I glanced up. He still made my heart skip a beat, even now, after all these years.

"Hey, handsome."

"Sorry, my flight was delayed." Rory dropped his overnight bag with a thump and wrapped his arms around me, planting a firm kiss on my mouth. He was in town only a few days for the opening. I'd fly back to Tampa next week with the girls. I leaned into his kiss.

"You taste like . . . goat cheese?" I pulled back, puzzled.

"Oh yeah, I saw Eve on the way in. She sent you this." He pulled a little packet from his pocket.

"Ooh, Brie. That's new." I examined the package. Eve had expanded her goat empire in recent years to include a line of handcrafted goat cheeses. The first few batches had been hit-or-miss, but she'd been improving as of late. Her black pepper and chive feta was spot-on. "She said she'd stop by after the farmers market." Rory glanced around. "Place is looking great, by the way. How's my favorite popsicle magnate?"

"Ready to put my feet up." I stepped back, cupping my rounded belly and laughing. I was seven months pregnant. Already my ankles were swollen at the end of a long day. Maybe it was the result of this being number three.

"And how is Junior?" Rory bent down and pressed a kiss on my belly. We'd chosen not to find out the gender of this child. We wanted it to be a surprise.

"Junior is making Mama tired and ready to sit down."

"Here, you sit. Doctor's orders." Rory led me to a seat by the freezer case and pulled over another chair so I could prop up my aching feet.

"Did you save me a piece?" he asked hopefully as he pushed the chair in at just the right angle to support my legs.

I nodded. "In the back, safely hidden behind the tray of pansies in the fridge."

He disappeared into the kitchen, and I could hear the girls' squeals of joy when they saw him. A few minutes later he came out holding a pie plate and fork. On the plate was a tall, glistening slice of lemon meringue pie, vivid yellow and fluffy white. He pulled up a chair opposite me and straddled it backward, eagerly digging his fork into the tremulous tower of meringue. "You know I dream about this slice of pie all week long, right?" he said, taking a big bite.

"And me. You also dream about me," I teased him.

He raised an eyebrow. "Of course I dream about you . . . giving me this pie."

I rolled my eyes at him, and he grinned, mouth full of pie.

Every Saturday I made two lemon meringue pies and served them to the first lucky handful of customers through the doors of our flagship Tampa location. The last piece of pie I always saved for Rory. I'd modified my mom's now-not-so-secret recipe, adding an element all my own—a lemon drop melted into the lemon-sugar mixture. I wasn't convinced it changed the taste that much, but Rory said it was the best pie he'd ever had. He swore the lemon drop added a touch of kitchen magic, but I knew better. It wasn't magic at all. It was revelation.

Every Saturday morning I rose early while Rory and the girls still slept, put on some classic country music, and started rolling out crusts. I did it partly for fun but mostly to remember. I never wanted to forget where I'd been and what I'd learned along the way. I used Meyer lemons and good French butter. I zested and stirred and thought of my mom as I worked. And to every hot, bubbling pan of lemon pie filling, I added a single lemon drop. As I watched it melt into the sugar and lemon juice mixture, I reminded myself of the truth I now knew. That you don't need magic to change your life. You just need to follow your bliss as best you can. If you follow the light, no matter how dark the circumstances, things will come out right in the end. That's the true recipe for joy in this life. That's the true magic of lemon drop pie.

"We'd better get the girls and go feed them some dinner." I leaned forward with a groan.

"In a minute, but first . . ." Rory licked his fork clean, sprang from his chair, and sauntered over to the old juke box sitting in its place by the door. Dad had stashed it in our garage when the Eatery sold, and we'd dug it out and had it rehabbed after I bought this place. Rory fished a quarter out of the bowl sitting on the lip of the jukebox and pressed a button. I knew what he'd chosen before I heard the first chords. F4. "I Will Always Love You." A moment later Dolly Parton's unmistakable quaver filled the room. "I will always love you," she sang. I smiled, closing my eyes, transported back over twenty years—same room, same song, now a brand-new chapter of our lives.

Rory came toward me and held out his hand in invitation. I hoisted myself up, and he slipped his arms around my waist, pulling me as close as he could. It was awkward, like dancing while balancing a basketball or a water balloon between us, and I giggled. From the kitchen I could hear the sound of the girls chattering to my dad. I glanced out the window at the LOLLY'S POPS COMING SOON banner and thought about the strange and wonderful path that had brought us here, to this moment.

Somehow, miraculously, everything had fallen into place as it was supposed to all along. Through heartbreak and sorrow, sacrifice and drudgery, through hope lost and hope regained, I'd learned little by little to be honest. To pay attention. To seek joy. And through all the ups and downs, the tears and bittersweet lessons, my lemon of a life had gradually been transformed into this—the most deliciously sweet, perfectly imperfect second chance I could ever imagine.

"Happy?" Rory asked, swinging me very carefully away and then twirling me back slowly.

"Blissfully," I answered instantly, leaning precariously forward so I could nestle my head against his shoulder, right where I belonged.

LOLLY'S LEMON DROP PIE

*Lolly's Lemon Drop Pie is silky smooth, surprisingly
rich, and deliciously sweet and tart! A fresh twist
on lemon meringue pie to brighten your day.*

CRUST

1 piecrust (store bought or homemade, as you prefer)

FILLING

2 Meyer lemons (larger is better than smaller if you want a rich
lemony flavor)

2 eggs

4 egg yolks

7 tablespoons granulated sugar

7 tablespoons good quality European butter (if unsalted, add $1/8$ teaspoon
salt with the butter)

1 lemon drop hard candy

MERINGUE

4 egg whites

$1/2$ teaspoon cream of tartar

$1/3$ cup granulated sugar

A dash of salt

PIE CRUST PREPARATION

Blind bake the piecrust for about 15-20 minutes at 375°F, or if you are using a store-bought crust, simply follow instructions on package. Prick shell bottom with a fork before baking. If you are using beans or pie weights to keep your piecrust bottom from bubbling up, remove them halfway through blind baking so the bottom can bake some. Set piecrust aside and turn down oven to 350°F.

TO MAKE THE FILLING

1. Grate the zest from both lemons into a small bowl. Squeeze the juice from both lemons into the bowl and stir.

2. In a heavy saucepan beat the eggs, egg yolks, and sugar until mixed. Add lemon juice and butter. Add the lemon drop candy.

3. Cook the mixture over medium-low heat, stirring constantly, until it thickens enough to coat your stirring utensil. It will look almost like pudding. Remove from heat and let stand for 5–10 minutes. Stir a few times until it is fairly smooth again.

4. Fill prepared piecrust with the mixture. Bake at 350°F for 12–15 minutes. Remove from oven. Turn oven up to 375°F.

5. While the filling is baking, prepare the meringue. Using a completely clean bowl, beat the egg whites and cream of tartar until soft peaks form, roughly 3–5 minutes. Make sure your egg whites have no yolk in them, just

whites. Add sugar and salt and beat on high until glossy stiff peaks form, about 2 more minutes. Spread the meringue around evenly on the filling, making sure the edge of the meringue touches the edge of the crust all the way around the pie. This helps the meringue not weep.

6. Bake the pie at 375°F for about 10 minutes, until meringue is nicely browned.

7. Remove from oven and cool at room temperature for 1–2 hours, until pie is no longer warm. Enjoy Lolly's Lemon Drop Pie!

ACKNOWLEDGMENTS

A book is born from the efforts of so many wonderful and talented folks, and this story is better and stronger because of them. So much gratitude to the following:

My stellar agent, Kevan Lyon, who is a dream combination of remarkably experienced, meticulous, insightful, calm, and kind.

My amazing editor at Berkley, Kate Seaver, who is both delightfully positive and tremendously skilled at knowing how to make a story shine. Her keen insights strengthened and deepened Lolly and Rory's story in a marvelous way. I'm so grateful!

The top-notch publishing team at Berkley. I'm thankful for their excellent efforts to bring *The Magic of Lemon Drop Pie* to the world and fortunate to have them all on my side.

My test readers, Sarah Smith and Sarah Wolfe, who are that rare combination of both very supportive and very honest. They're such insightful readers that I'm always on pins and needles to see if they like whatever new story I send their way!

Mallory MacDonald at Maxwell Creative, who is truly the brand goddess extraordinaire. She spotted the elements that make up my brand and brought them to life so beautifully.

Rachel McMillan, insightful author/agent/avid reader, who encouraged me to come up with "another good idea" for my next book. On an airplane paper napkin the next day I scribbled down the question that would later become the basis of *The Magic of Lemon Drop Pie*: "What happens if a woman gets the chance to redo her three biggest regrets in life?"

The fabulous Maggie Ritchie, who helped me create and refine the real Lemon Drop Pie recipe in my kitchen. The process was so fun, and the results were delicious!

Dr. Marisa Smith for providing medical school information and being the consulting doctor in our family. All errors regarding medical terms or facts are strictly my own.

The supportive and wonderful authors of Tea & Empathy for sharing advice, commiserating, and always encouraging each other! Every writer should be lucky enough to have a tribe as consistently kind and generous as these ladies are.

My fabulous 10-Minute Book Talk bestselling author friends Marie Bostwick and Katherine Reay. I'm so glad we get to share our love of books with readers every week for those ten short and sweet minutes online.

Author Susan Meissner for being such a calm and wise resource and a genuinely lovely person. Author Melissa Ferguson for being such an encouragement and a great sounding board and talking me down off the ledge if I have an author crisis!

Independent bookstores across the United States that share their love of books with readers and help us authors keep writing our stories. Of particular note, a giant thank-you to Watermark Book Company in Anacortes, Washington, and in Seattle, Island Books on Mercer Island, Magnolia's Bookstore in Magnolia (yes, the same one I mentioned in the book; it's real and it's lovely!), and Queen Anne Book Company. Their love of books and support of authors mean the world to me and many others.

Kristy Barrett for championing authors by her efforts through A Novel Bee. Thanks, Kristy!

My sweet A and B. You have my heart. I love being your mommy.

My generous and supportive husband, Yohanan, who sacrifices so I can do what I love. I love you, Big Bacon.

I'd also like to thank Tillamook ice cream for helping me through writing *The Magic of Lemon Drop Pie* during the pandemic lockdowns of 2020. Good thing we were all wearing yoga pants that year. My waistline does not thank you, but my sanity is so grateful.

The Magic of Lemon Drop Pie

of

RACHEL LINDEN